D0912591

The DRAGON SONGS Saga · BOOK 1 ·

SONGS OF INSURRECTION

A LEGENDS OF TIVARA STORY

JC KANG

Cover Layout and Maps by Laura Kang

Logos by Emily Jose Burlingame

Cover Art by Binh Hai

Second Edition: March 2021

To my uncle, Professor David Jones, for inspiring me with stories of true women warriors, and theorizing that sometimes, dragons aren't always what we think.

Map of Tivaralan

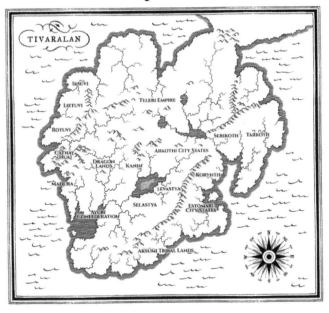

Map of Cathay

Who's Who in Songs of Insurrection

Imperial Family:

Wang, Zhishen:	*Tianzi* (Emperor)
Wang, Kai-Guo:	Crown Prince
Zhao, Xiulan:	Crown Princess, of Ximen Province
Wang, Kai-Wu:	Second Prince
Wu, Yanli:	Second Prince's fiancée, Zhenjing Province
Wang, Kaiya:	Princess

Hereditary Lords and Families

Chen, Qing:	*Yu-Ming* heir to a Jiangzhou county
Lord Liang:	*Tai-Ming* heir to Yutou Province
Lord Liu:	*Tai-Ming* heir to Jiangzhou Province
Lin, Ziqiu:	Kaiya's cousin, daughter of the Lord of Linshan
Peng, Kai-Long:	Second son of *Tai-Ming* Lord of Nanling Province
Peng, Kai-Zhi:	*Tai-Ming* heir to Nanling Province
Peng, Xian:	*Tai-Ming* Lord of Nanling Province
Tong, Baxian:	*Yu-Ming* Lord of Wailian County
Wang, Kai-Hua:	Kaiya's cousin, daughter of the Lord of Jiangzhou
Lord Wu:	*Tai-Ming* Lord of Zhenjing Province, father of Yanli
Lord Zhao:	*Tai-Ming* Lord of Ximen Province, father of Xiulan
Xu:	Elf counselor
Zheng, Han:	*Tai-Ming* Lord of Dongmen Province, father of Tian

Ministers, Secretaries and other Officials

Geng:	Minster of the Treasury
Hu:	Minister of Appointments
Hong, Jianbin:	Secretary of Appointments
General Shan:	Minister of War
Song:	Foreign Minister
Tan:	Chief Minister
Yan:	Deputy of Information, Black Lotus Clan Master
Chu:	Harbormaster official

Military:

General Lu:	Commander, Army of the North
General Shan:	Minister of War
General Tang:	Commander of the Huajing Division
General Zheng:	Commander of the Imperial Guard
Chen, Xin:	Imperial Guard Captain
Zhao, Yue:	Imperial guard
Xu, Zhan:	Imperial guard
Ma, Jun:	Imperial guard
Li, Wei:	Imperial guard

The Black Lotus Clan

Yan, Jie:	Half-elf Black Lotus Fist, adopted daughter of Master Yan
Zheng, Tian:	Planner, fourth son of the Lord of Dongmen Province
Master Yan:	Master of the Clan
Feng, Mi:	Black Lotus initiate
Huang, Zhen:	Black Lotus initiate
Chong, Xiang:	Black Lotus Fist
Wen:	Female Black Lotus Fist
Bu:	Black Lotus Fist
Li:	Black Lotus Fist
Qu:	Black Lotus Fist

Others

Ding, Meihui:	Princess Kaiya's *pipa* teacher
Fang, Weiyong:	Imperial Physician
Fu, Jinxian:	Owner of Golden Fu Trading
Gu:	Agent for unknown conspirator
Han, Mei-Ling:	Handmaiden to Princess Kaiya
Jiang:	Victorious Trading Company manager
Little Ju:	Tian's messenger
Song, Xingyuan:	Son of Minister Song
Doctor Wu:	Head Imperial Physician, master of the *Dao*
Yong, Shu:	Princess Kaiya's *erhu* teacher

Foreigners:

Aryn Corivar:	Second Prince of Tarkoth
Captain Damaryn:	Koryn's aide
Peris:	Aryn's aide
Koryn Vardamcar:	Crown Prince of Serikoth
Hardeep Vaswani:	Prince of Ankira

Legendary Figures:

Aralas:	The elf-angel
Avarax:	The Last Dragon
Yanyan:	Slave, founder of Dragon Songs

8

Kaiya's Relationships

The Imperial Family

Wang, Kai-Hua
Cousin
16

Peng, Kai-long
Cousin
Nanling P.
22

Lin, Ziqiu
Cousin
Linshan P.
12

Wang, Zhishen
Tianzi, Father
52

Wang, Kaiya
16

Wu, Yanli
SIL to be
Zhengjing P
21

Wang, Kai-Wu
Second Prince
Second Brother
22

= = =

Hardeep Vaswani
Love Interest
Prince of Ankira
23

Zhao, Xiulan
Crown Princess
Sister-In-Law
20

Han, Mei-Ling
Handmaiden
17

**Imperial
Guards**
Chen, Xin
Li, Wei
Ma, Jun
Xu, Zhan
Zhao, Yue

Wang, Kai-Guo
Crown Prince
Eldest Brother
23

Black Lotus Clan

Yan, Jie
Half-Elf
Black Lotus Clan
29

Zheng, Tian
Childhood
Friend
Dongmen P.
18

PROLOGUE:
The Dragon Scale Lute

With the echo of the Dragon Scale Lute fading around him, Avarax coiled his hind legs and vaulted skyward. He stretched out his wings to catch an updraft. Cool wind caressed his scales as he climbed higher. After three hundred years imprisoned in the pathetic body of a human, it felt good to be a dragon again.

Down below, in the sparkling city of domes and spires and canals, thousands of bronze-skinned humans pointed at him and screamed. The world thought he had slumbered for a millennium, telling stories about how a honey-toned slave girl sang him to sleep with a Dragon Song. He had let them believe that tale, to prevent enemies from tracking him down.

He belched sparks with his laugh. Now, it was time to announce his return with a blast of his fiery breath. It would immolate a million people, and the city. More importantly, it would destroy the artifact that could again force his unwilling transformation. He filled his lungs with a deep breath and exhaled in an ear-splitting roar.

Nothing.

Not even sparks. Avarax's breath remained locked away. He wrapped his consciousness around the gemstone in his gullet, a dragon's source of almost infinite energy. Its pulsations pounded like an angry river against a dam.

Below, the Dragon Scale Lute's strings moaned again, vibrating in answer to his roar. Its wail swelled, scattering the pitiful humans like a disturbed rats' nest. Then, with a disjointed pop, the sound ceased.

CHAPTER 1
Not-So-Chance Meetings

If marriage were a woman's grave, as the proverb claimed, sixteen-year-old Kaiya suspected the emperor was arranging her funeral. Entourage in tow, she shuffled through the castle halls toward the garden where General Lu waited. Given his notorious dislike of the arts, the self-proclaimed *Guardian Dragon of Cathay* had undoubtedly envisioned a different kind of audition when he requested to hear her sing.

After all, she was dressed like a potential bride.

She buried a snort. The Guardian Dragon—such a pretentious nickname. The only real dragon, Avarax, who lorded over some faraway land, might make for a more appealing audience. A quick trip down his gullet would spare her a slow death in a marriage with neither love nor music.

And she wouldn't have to wear this gaudy dress. It compensated for her numerous physical imperfections, but stifled the only thing that made her special. How was she supposed to sing with the inner robe and gold sash squeezing her chest, in a futile attempt to misrepresent her woefully underdeveloped curves? The tight fold of the skirts concealed her lanky legs, but forced a deliberate pace. At least the short stride delayed the inevitable, while preventing her unsightly feet from tripping on the hanging sleeves of the vermilion outer gown.

At her side, Crown Princess Xiulan glided across the chirping floorboards. Kaiya suppressed a sigh. If only she could move with the nonchalant grace of her sister-in-law, or even the six handmaidens trailing them. She dug her nails into clammy palms. Through this choreographed farce, appearances had to be maintained, lest she embarrass her father, the *Tianzi*.

Chin up, back straight. A racing heart threatened to ruin her already meager semblance of imperial grace. Eyes forward. Servants knelt on either side of the looming double doors, ready to slide them open. She forced a smile, with her best approximation of feminine charm. If only she'd lived before Dragon Songs had faded into legend, she could've sent the realm's victorious hero fleeing with the song he supposedly wanted to hear.

An aging palace official stepped into her line of sight.

Singular focus on the doors broken, she blinked. Her fluttering pulse lurched to a stop as she blew out a breath.

His blue robes ruffled as he tottered forward with averted eyes and a bobbing head. He creaked down into a bow. "Emergency, *Dian-xia*," he said, using the formal address for her rank. "The *Tianzi* commands you to greet a foreign delegation in the Hall of Bountiful Harvests."

Her heart remembered to beat again, and she looked first toward the doors and then down at the man, whose insignias marked him as a secretary for the Ministry of Appointments. Outlandish excuses had mercifully cut short each of her previous meetings with eligible young lords: six times in all.

But a foreign delegation? Before even meeting the suitor? *That* was a first. Her expression slipped as much as it could beneath the layers of pearl powder caked to her face. Mouth dry, her voice came out hoarse. "There must be a mistake. Surely the honor would fall to the Crown Prince."

He bowed his head again. "No, *Dian-xia*. With your linguistic talents, the *Tianzi* thought you better suited to meet with them."

Apparently, small talk with some foreign lord's wife constituted an emergency these days. Still, the unspoken message needed little interpretation: the foreigners were beneath a prince.

At least it meant delaying the matchmaking. Kaiya cast a glance at Xiulan. "Then shall the Crown Prince take my place and sing to General Lu?"

Her supposed chaperone covered a giggle with slender fingers. The wide sleeves of her aquamarine gown slid and bunched in her elbow, revealing the porcelain-like skin of her arm. It was as perfect as her complexion.

The man's eyes darted back and forth, his lips quivering. "I...I..."

Xiulan stepped forward and brushed a gentle hand across Kaiya's arm. "Go on, meet with the foreigners. I will explain things to the general."

Kaiya bowed her head. "As you command, Eldest Sister." She turned to the official, gesturing with an open hand for him to take the lead.

As she wobbled after him, two of her handmaidens fell in behind. They were more beautiful than her, even after her hours of preening to smother meddlesome acne and subdue unruly hair.

Which now meant she'd look ridiculous receiving dignitaries. Like an opera singer, maybe. "Who are our guests?"

The official coughed. "Prince Hardeep Vaswani of Ankira."

A man? Kaiya's stomach leapt into her throat. With limited court training, she *might* be able to entertain a lady. But a prince... Without any experience in diplomacy, that was an international incident waiting to happen. Given the choice between greeting foreign royalty and the prospect of marriage, that trip into Avarax's jaws sounded tempting. "What does he want?" she asked.

"He has been in the capital for a week now, incessantly requesting an audience."

And now they were sending her, an awkward sixteen-year-old, undoubtedly as a message. Prince Hardeep wouldn't see the *Tianzi* until her complexion

16

cleared or the orc gods returned on their flaming chariots, whichever came first. A betting princess would wager her money on the orc gods.

She sighed. After preparing to play the role of demure and dainty maiden before a potential husband, this new situation required a confident demeanor...and neither came easily.

There was no time to tone down the make-up or change the extravagant gown. Unpinning the outer robe's constraining fold, she squared her shoulders and lengthened her gait.

No, this wasn't bad. A reprieve from meeting a dour general. She could do this. How hard could it be? With each step, she concentrated on composing a dignified expression. By the time they arrived at the moat separating the castle from the rest of the sprawling palace grounds, she'd mentally transformed herself from prospective bride into imperial representative.

Right. She still looked like the former, and felt like neither.

At the head of the bridge waited eight imperial guards dressed in blue court robes. The magic etched into their breastplates' five-clawed dragon evoked awe, though she'd grown used to it over the years.

"*Dian-xia,*" the guards shouted in unison. They each dropped to one knee, fist to the ground. The most talented swordsmen in the realm submitted to a pimply girl, for nothing more than the circumstances of her birth.

If only she could live up to the accompanying expectations. Kaiya acknowledged them with a nod.

17

Bowing, the handmaidens shuffled back. The imperial guards deployed behind her. She crossed the stone bridge, leaving behind the relative comfort of private life to enter the formal world of the imperial court.

They wound through stone-paved alleys. White buildings with blue-tiled eaves rose up beyond spotless courtyard walls with circular windows. At the Hall of Bountiful Harvests, Kaiya walked up the veranda and stepped over the ghost-tripping threshold.

Inside, three chattering men gestured at the green ceiling panels and gold latticework. Their burgundy *kurta* shirts hung to their knees, collars riding high on their necks. On their left breasts sparkled an embroidered nine-pointed lotus, the crest of the embattled nation of Ankira.

The visitors' discussion came to an abrupt halt as they turned to greet her, heads bowed, and palms pressed together. Dark bronze skin and rounded features marked them as ethnic Ayuri. Meticulously coifed black hair fell to their shoulders. The centermost man looked no older than twenty. Taller and more handsome than his companions, he met her gaze.

With blue irises. Luminous like the Blue Moon, Guanyin's Eye. They captured her image in their liquid depths and reflected it back, more beautiful than make-up could ever accomplish. Maybe even as beautiful as Xiulan.

He tilted his head and flashed...a smoldering smile.

Kaiya cast her eyes down, only to peek up through her lashes. Her lips twitched, struggling against all discipline in their urge to return the smile.

Ridiculous! Where had the carefully crafted mask of an imperial diplomat fled to? She tightened her mouth, squared her chin, and looked up.

When he spoke, his deep, baritone voice flowed out of his mouth like honeysuckle vines, entangling her. "I am Prince Hardeep. You must be the Princess of Cathay. The stories of your beauty do you no justice."

What? Nobody could say her plain looks warranted praise, at least not sincerely. Yet his earnest words sounded nothing like the hollow compliments of court sycophants and suitors.

Heat rose to her cheeks, threatening to melt away her make-up, and her nominally dignified expression with it. His language tumbled off her tongue, accent lilting in her ears. "Welcome to Sun-Moon Palace, Prince Hardeep. I act as the ears of my father, the emperor."

Cringe-worthy. She could speak Ayuri better than that. Almost perfectly, but—

"And your voice! Saraswati, our people's Goddess of the Arts, would be jealous. Perhaps you would sing for me?"

Kaiya's head swam. Her mouth opened to beg off the unexpected request, but no words came out.

He waved a hand, and his manner stiffened. "I forget myself. Your song would certainly invigorate me, and I confess I hoped to catch a glimpse of you during

19

my visit. However, my country's needs are more pressing. I have a request of your emperor."

Whatever spell his previous tone had woven through her mind loosened enough for her to find her voice. "I am afraid you misinterpret his intentions. By sending me, he has already denied you."

No. Did she just say that out loud? Kaiya covered her mouth. If only Avarax would swoop in and devour her now.

The Ankiran prince's lips melted into a frown and his attention shifted to her slippers. "Please hear our entreaty. The Kingdom of Madura occupies almost all of Ankira, in part because of their twice-renewed trade agreement with your glorious nation. For almost thirty years, Cathay has sold them firepowder. Now, our soldiers are weary, and our coffers depleted. The agreement expires soon. We ask—no, beg—that you not renew it."

Released from his gaze, her mind began to clear. "How were you able to make it through the Maduran lines?"

Prince Hardeep raised his head. Kaiya avoided those mesmerizing eyes, and instead focused on his chin as he spoke. "One of your lords, Peng Kai-Long, has long supported us. I came with him on a Cathayi trade ship."

It made sense. Cousin Kai-Long served as a trade negotiator in Ayuri lands and knew many influential people in Tivaralan's South. He had recently returned to the capital to attend the upcoming wedding of Second Brother.

"He is my father's favorite nephew," she said. "I am sure he could present a more convincing argument to the Son of Heaven than I."

Prince Hardeep shook his head. "Search inside yourself and speak with your heart. A father cannot deny the compassionate voice of his beloved daughter. Please. Our riches have been plundered; our people enslaved." His voice beckoned her head up. "Widows must sell their bodies, while orphans starve in the streets."

His dejected gaze twisted into her. Her heart, suddenly hot, sank into her belly. All those unfortunate people, suffering because of Cathay's firepowder, while she enjoyed the comfort of the palace. Father must not have known the consequences of the trade agreement, since he ruled with the moral authority of Heaven. Someone had to speak for these downtrodden people.

"I will convey your message. Please make yourself comfortable until my return." She paused for a moment to search his expression. All signs of his earlier frivolity were gone. He'd just been toying with her to get what he wanted.

It didn't matter. It was the right thing to do. All the heroes from her favorite songs would've rushed to his aid. He was only asking her to speak to Father. With an inward sigh, she turned and swept out of the hall, her guards marching behind her.

Outside, Kaiya took a deep breath of cool spring air to calm her thoughts and ease the hot constriction in

21

her chest. Never before had a man made her pulse race like that. Then again, she had nothing but six fawning suitors with which to compare him.

No, this had nothing to do with Prince Hardeep's charm. An entire nation suffered, with Cathay's complicity. Father had always preached morality, demanded her to always do the right thing.

In her mind, she hummed a ballad recounting heroic Dragon Singers and the perils they willingly faced. Her heart swelled, and she turned to the official. "Where is the *Tianzi* now?"

The old man gawked. "I do not think—"

She cast a silencing glare.

He bowed his head. "In the Hall of Supreme Harmony."

As the palace's central audience chamber, the Hall of Supreme Harmony was just a few minutes away, up one hundred sixty-eight arduous steps. Father rode an ornate golden palanquin to the top, but Kaiya, like anyone else who wasn't the *Tianzi*, had to climb.

Each step planted a seed of doubt in her head. A princess had no business in politics, besides solidifying loyalties through marriage. Remonstrating the *Tianzi* in front of all the lords and ministers would embarrass Father, so much that he would have no choice but to punish her.

CHAPTER 2
Treacherous Intents

Eighteen-year-old Zheng Tian knelt by the blockwood door, cursing under his breath. In his former life as Princess Kaiya's childhood confidante, he would've never broken into a warehouse. Now a *Black Fist*, whose clan served the *Tianzi*, he was picking a warehouse lock.

And failing.

"Hurry up." Cell leader Yan Jie's whisper tickled his ear. "The guards are halfway to the corner."

Tian glanced up to the south, where the alley between the warehouses provided a view of the smallest of the three moons.

Swirling with colors like a soap bubble, it waned to its fourth gibbous—two hours before dawn. The guards were running ahead of schedule. He hadn't heard them coming, but Jie's half-elf blood gave her adorable pointed ears with exceptional hearing.

He motioned to the lock. "Shine the light there."

The roll of her eyes carried in her hushed tone. "A blindfolded orc with three fingers missing would have broken in by now."

Now, even his ears picked up the guards' laughter. He twisted the pick in the narrow hole for the third time. With a soft click, the lock yielded. A little pressure on the door confirmed the hinges were well-oiled, and he pushed it open. Without a sound, he pulled Jie in and closed the door behind them.

In the silent darkness, Jie tapped her fingers on his forearm in clan code. *Two guards, now turning corner... Now passing door... All clear.*

He blew out a breath. As risky as the work was, he fit in better among spies and assassins than with the realm's ruling elite. Not like he could ever go back to that life. Not after what he'd done to Princess Kaiya.

A dim light from Jie's magic bauble spilled from between her fingers, casting her childlike features in a shadowed hue. Though ten years, three months and two days his senior, she looked no older than fourteen, thanks to her elf heritage.

He rotated the lock back into place with another quiet *snick*. "It's a new device. Dwarf-made. Very expensive. I noticed it during the last harbormaster inspection."

Jie's large almond eyes narrowed to normal Cathayi size as she squinted at the door. That look...she was more interested than she let on, if only about the dwarven lock. "A nice lock doesn't mean they are hiding anything."

How could he even begin to explain the incremental increase in value on deliveries using specific ships in specific months, to this specific warehouse, when specific customs officials were on duty? The patterns, so clear to him, never made sense to anyone else. "Their manifests were suspicious. Come on." He beckoned her toward the dozens of wooden crates.

Yawning, she padded after him. It was doubtless feigned boredom—if anyone ever supported him, it was Jie, the clan master's adopted daughter.

He stopped at a crate with the word *fragile* painted around the lid. Its markings listed an origin of Wailian County in the unsettled North, with a destination of Yutou Province in the South.

He slid a finger over the rough edge of a crate and held it up. "Ground rice powder."

"So, they want to keep something dry. That could be just about anything. Beef jerky and pearl powder aren't going to lead to the realm's downfall." Shrugging, she produced a nail extractor from one of the twenty-seven hidden pockets in her utility suit.

"Wait." Tian stayed her hand. If only he could explain things as quickly as the thoughts came to him. Customs forms declared the box's contents to be sesame seeds, whose oils would be ruined by rice powder. Not to mention that Yutou Province was the largest supplier of sesame seeds in the realm. So unless Yutou's *Tai-Ming* Lord Liang planned on cornering a low-margin market by buying up every seed in the nation and

25

labelling them fragile, it wasn't sesame seeds in that crate.

He picked up a nearby crowbar and gingerly wedged it under the lid, far from any of the nails. Wailian County's chief resource was saltpeter, shipments of which were restricted to the capital. It wouldn't do to send any sparks flying. Opening the lid sent a cloud of rice dust into the air.

Jie waved a hand in front of her eyes and peeled open the cloth lining inside, revealing… "Imagine that, a box marked *sesame seeds* having…sesame seeds."

With a frown, Tian knifed his hand into the seeds. Half a foot in, his fingers, rough from ironpalm training, thunked against wood.

Her ears twitched. "How deep?"

"Seven inches." He indicated a handlength, then eased a large box out with a rustling of sesame. This was why he was meant for spying. Even if it meant never seeing Princess Kaiya again.

He cast a triumphant glance at Jie. "There's more in there. Several."

"I could've told you that." She blinked innocently as she ran a hand across the lid.

Of course. He swatted her hands away. Opening the box revealed a fine black powder. Tian had expected coarse white saltpeter. He exchanged glances with Jie. "What is it?"

She sucked on the right side of her bottom lip. "I don't know."

"Take a sample—"

Jie's ears perked up and her head jerked toward the door. She stashed the light bauble, drowning the room in darkness.

The door whispered open with a breeze, and light crept in from a light bauble lamp. Three cloaked men pushed their way in and closed the door behind them. None of them looked familiar; they were certainly none of the sixteen guards who rotated shifts around this building. Their clothes bore no identifying sigils.

Pulse racing, Tian eased the lid back on top of the incriminating crate as quietly as he could. His fingers worked the nails back into their holes. If the conspirators discovered the tampering, they would cover their tracks.

"There are twenty crates marked fragile," said the smallest of the men, his enunciation thick with the North. He held up the lamp and opened its shutters. It illuminated the front third of the building, leaving Tian and Jie in the dark. "I'll show you where they are spread throughout the warehouse."

The largest man crossed his arms. "You could have put them all together, close to the front. The porters' guild would charge you an extra ten percent."

"Then it's a good thing you aren't with the guild." Lamp Man's lips drew into a tight frown.

The porter crossed his arms. "I'm sure the porters' guild, harbormaster, and other authorities might take issue with, how shall I say…"

The third man, a fellow with a fat nose and the telltale bump of a short sword concealed beneath his cloak, exchanged glances with Lamp Man, then waved a hand. "My lord is more than willing to pay five percent."

Tian's ears perked up. Fat Nose's lord was someone from the South, if he shared the same rough features and accent.

The porter grinned. "Plus a silver *jiao* for dragging me over here at this hour."

"Two silver *jiao* for the inconvenience and discretion," Fat Nose said.

The porter licked his lips. "The porter guild is scheduled to unload the *Wild Orchid* at first light. My other men will come to collect your shipment tonight."

Tian tapped his chin. The *Wild Orchid*, belonging to *Tai-Ming* Lord Peng in Nanling Province, had been sighted at sea late this night. *Yu-Ming* Lord Tong of Wailian County had never before used it to transport the questionable shipments.

"Then we are agreed." Fat Nose gestured toward the crates, inviting the men to follow him.

Tian's muscles tensed. If the conspirators discovered them, someone would likely die. He backed deeper into the warehouse, with Jie pressing her back into his stomach as if he needed the prompting. Her fingers tapped on his forearm. *Left two mine. If necessary. On my signal.*

Of course she would leave the one with the sword to him. Hopefully, it wouldn't come to that. What was the old proverb Princess Kaiya had first told him, four thousand, twenty-one days ago? *Hold the dragonfly with care, for even their fleeting lives have value.*

What was the value of a man's life? Tian looked from face to face. As long as these new arrivals didn't find evidence of tampering, they would live to see the morning.

There had to be a way to ensure that, if only because the porter had a family to go home to. At least, the carp marriage charm around his neck implied as much. He tapped on Jie's forearm. *I distract, you seal crate.*

"That one." Lamp Man led the way, pointing to several of the boxes marked fragile.

Treading quietly just outside the edge of the lamp's light, Tian worked his way toward the entrance. If they moved the light over too much, they'd see him.

As the three men continued, the light shifted deeper into the warehouse. Once the darkness enveloped the front door, he eased it open and slipped out. On the other side, he closed the door and looked past the setting full Blue Moon to the Iridescent Moon. Never moving from its seat in the heavens, it now waned halfway between its fourth and fifth crescents. An hour and a half to dawn.

He rapped on the door. "Harbormaster's office here," he yelled.

A brief commotion broke out, followed by silence. A set of footsteps approached the door. It opened, and Lamp Man peered out and scrutinized Tian up and down.

"Harbormaster's office." Tian flashed an apologetic grin. With a black utility suit instead of the blue robes marking him as a government official... "Two ships coming in. Before dawn. Anything to declare?"

Lamp Man's forehead crinkled. "Who are you?"

"I'm from the Harbormaster's office. On my way to work. I saw you three enter." Tian memorized Lamp Man's fine features and light complexion as he stalled...with the light at the door, Jie could work those nails back into place with her iron palms.

Lamp Man looked Tian over again. "You don't look like an official."

"Just a scribe, sir." Tian wiped his hands over his clothes. Almost all people in Cathay believed the Black Fists to be nothing more than boogeymen who kidnapped unruly children. At least, that's what mothers told children to keep them in line. "My robes are at work."

Lamp Man reached into his cloak, sending Tian's hand for his hidden knife. Then, Lamp Man proffered a copper *fen*. "What's your name, boy?"

"Zheng." Tian peered at the coin for a few seconds, then plucked it up and bobbed his head. Let Lamp Man believe a bribe went a long way, as it certainly did with many government officials, and it might be a means of finding out more information.

"Well, Little Zheng, I may need you in the future."

Tian bobbed his head a few more times. "Happy to help. But soon. I will be transferred in a few weeks."

Lamp Man nodded. "I will be visiting the harbormaster's office this afternoon. I will need some help filing some documents." A silver *jiao* appeared in his hand.

Filing, or perhaps forging. Tian feigned an avaricious grin and swiped it. There was a conspiracy brewing, and his curiosity would nag at him until he put all the pieces together.

CHAPTER 3
Incendiary Rumors

As a half-elf raised among humans, Jie hated being treated like someone half her age. Especially by Tian. She'd been in charge of him since he'd joined the clan as a sheltered, clueless kid eight years ago.

Now that they were safe in a nearby alley, she swatted his hand away as he tousled her hair. He was just as impertinent as he'd been as a child; but whereas he'd been pudgy and smelled of sweet red bean paste back then then, everything about adult Tian was honed, tempered steel.

"You left me!" she said. And not for the first time in their lives as partners.

"My improvisation worked, right?" Tian's grin begged to be slapped.

Jie snorted. When he improvised, it usually led to disaster. His plans, on the other hand, had a high rate of success, as long as she was the one executing them.

He tapped his chin. "Did you push the nails back in place?"

Jie made a show of examining her fingernails. "Yes, but with such calloused fingers, I won't be sent to the Floating World to trawl for information anytime soon."

"You wouldn't belong there, anyway. The Night Blossoms of Floating World are beautiful beyond compare." Tian reached for her hair again.

As if he didn't remember she'd once trained to be a courtesan there! It's where they'd met. And he remembered everything. With a swipe of her hand, she seized his and pushed up on his elbow to put him in a chicken-wing lock. Before she could finish the motion, he grasped her wrist and twisted. Not to be outdone, she snaked her arm out of his grasp.

"Are you quite done?" she asked.

"Yes." Tian pointed to the warehouse entrance, a block away. "I'll keep an eye on Fat Nose until I report to work. You check out the *Wild Orchid*'s cargo."

Jie sucked on her lower lip. Not only did he treat her like a little girl, he also gave orders–even though she was his senior, the clan master's adopted daughter, and the cell leader. The things she tolerated, if only from Tian. "Fine."

He didn't even notice, so intent was he on crouching by a stack of kegs and peering at the warehouse. Harrumphing, Jie turned toward the docks.

Night still hung over Jiangkou's harbor. Even if her no-good father had abandoned her as a baby, at least he had left her with exceptional elven senses. Now that the crescent White Moon and the Blue Moon Guanyin's Eye had set, human eyes would strain in the darkness.

33

However, the world appeared clearly in shades of green to her elven vision.

Pausing in an alley between warehouses, she uncovered the plain breeches and shirt she'd stashed just for this purpose. After slipping into them, Jie adjusted a thick headband to cover her ears. When the clan needed a seasoned Fist disguised as a kid, she was the one who invariably got stuck playing the part.

She peered out onto the long stretch of wharfs along the harbor front. An enormous sablewood vessel towered over the local trading ships. A handful of non-guild longshoremen milled about, scrounging for a piece of Cathay's wealth.

With its ships and trade routes dominating the western seas, the nation was like a golden pig, fattened to the point that the lords swam in riches and even the poor wanted for little. If only the citizens knew what the Black Lotus Clan did: that yet another rebellion brewed in the North. Fueled by greed, it was kept in check only by the delicate systems of interdependence set up by the dynasty's founder.

Out in the water, the *Wild Orchid* made its way toward a pier. Sails lowered; its oarsmen rowed to the beat of a drum. Jie headed in the same direction, slipping between the growing crowds of workers. With dawn stretching tendrils of red and pink through the morning clouds, her vision shifted to color. Her attention was drawn from the *Wild Orchid* to the huge black ship, already docked. Its green flag, emblazoned with a silver sun with nine points, marked it as Tarkothi. With treaties demarcating trade spheres between the world's great naval powers, it was strange to see one this far west.

By the time she reached the *Wild Orchid*, dockworkers were already tying down the moorings. Jie sighed as she mixed in with the queue of garlicky-smelling child laborers.

With the possibility of insurrection, there were a dozen more interesting and less malodorous places to be than here. All on Tian's hunch. The sailors' banter, laced with language that could make a Night Blossom fake a blush, provided the only entertainment during the wait.

At last, the gangplank lowered. Twenty-one black-haired, bronze-skinned people wobbled down. The men wore threadbare *kurta* shirts, while faded *saris* hung from the women's shoulders. Ayuri folk, but from which nation, and why would they come to Cathay? "Finally!" Speaking in the Ayuri language, a middle-aged man with a scar on his cheek dropped to his knees on the dock.

A woman patted him on his shoulder. She had a large birthmark on her neck, and a toe ring marked her as married, per Ayuri custom. "We can start a new life here."

A younger woman, face partially obscured by a scarf, found Jie's gaze. Unlike her comrades, this one had a lighter, cinnamon complexion and more slanted eyes. Half-Cathayi, perhaps, and beautiful in an exotic way. She ducked her head and hid her face beneath the scarf. In that flash of her hand, a black birthmark, or perhaps a tattoo, peeked out from the brown henna patterns on her wrist.

As curious as she was about these people, Jie couldn't ask in their language lest she reveal herself as anything other than a boy looking for a job. Still, it wasn't hard to deduce their story: refugees from Ankira, which was steadily losing a thirty-year war to Madura.

At the head of the dock, a group of Cathayi men dressed in the red-and-black livery of Nanling Province approached. Their leader pressed his palms together and bowed his head in Ayuri fashion to the refugees. In perfect Ayuri he said, "On behalf of Young Lord Peng Kai-Long, I welcome you to Cathay."

All the refugees returned his salute.

"You must be tired after your long journey. Young Lord Peng has made arrangements for you to join your countrymen. Please come with me."

"I need ten boys," yelled a voice in Cathayi from the gangplank. "Two copper *fen* for a day's work."

Just what she had been waiting for. Forgetting the Ankirans, Jie deftly slipped between the reaching, shouting boys.

At the front, a man with a leathery complexion chewed on what appeared to be salted meat, pointing at recruits. Jie hip-butted a kid and placed herself in the line of his finger.

He started to shake his head, but paused. His focus locked on her. "No, you'll do. It takes small, nimble hands for the job I have in mind." He beckoned the boys up the gangplank, but smacked an unchosen one who tried to board. He led the group across the deck, pointing out work.

When they passed the hatch to the lower decks, Jie waited for him to turn his back, then dashed through and took the steps down two at a time. Dimly lit by banks of oar holes, the open space was full of benches and oars, small chests and hammocks. It reeked of sweat and seawater. Crew berths, in all likelihood, with plenty of places to hide. With their backs to her, six men worked winches, bringing a platform of crates up from yet another hatch near the middle of the ship.

Using the creaking of pulleys and yawning of ropes to mask her footsteps, Jie crept closer, and then dropped behind a nearby bench. They unloaded the crates and lowered the platform.

"Load up!" a man shouted down.

When they carried the crates to the upper deck, Jie slunk forward and inspected the hatch. Ropes attached to pulleys and winches led down into the very bowels of the ship; below the waterline, by her best estimate. Below, a man set a keg on the platform and spun around.

She leapt down, catching one winch line and swinging to another before landing in a forward roll. It stank of sweat and curry powder. Even her elven vision wouldn't penetrate the darkness here; luckily light bauble lamps provided illumination as well as shadows in which to hide. If any of the porters had seen her before she ducked behind a crate, they were hopefully too concerned with their own work to care about a trespasser.

Jie picked her way among the cargo, glancing back at every voice and footstep. Red paint marked contents and destinations. The bulk of the crates were labelled as Ayuri gooseweed and Levanthi spices, imported by Golden Fu Trading Company, bound for Nanling Province's villa in the capital. Tian's suspicions, though rarely wrong, were wrong now. Hardly worth the risk of mingling among boisterous sailors. If they discovered her, found out she was a girl…

The smell of rotten eggs, unmistakable but likely undetectable to a human nose, caught her attention. She sniffed, following the scent to several kegs. The writing marked the contents as turmeric, a ubiquitous ingredient of Ayuri cooking, originating from Pelastya and bound for Wailian County.

Jie examined one of the kegs. Well-sealed, no residue. There was no way of telling the contents without opening it. However, turmeric didn't smell like rotting eggs, and Pelastya didn't grow turmeric. It *did* have volcanoes and sulfur mines.

Sulfur, bound for Wailian County, the world's only major source of saltpeter. As clan master's daughter, she was privy to the closely guarded recipe for firepowder. The only major ingredient left would be charcoal.

Against the laws of interdependence that kept the nation at peace, someone was making firepowder in the rebellious North. If that was the mysterious substance they'd found in the warehouse, it was being sent south to Yutou Province. An alliance of North and South, ready to fall on the capital.

Jie needed to alert the clan. She started back toward the hatch.

"You!" a male voice called.

CHAPTER 4
Intents and Purposes

The shuffling of court robes and the cloying scent of incense greeted Kaiya as she stepped over the high threshold and into the cavernous hall. Dozens of golden columns vaulted toward the ceiling, where a tiled mosaic depicted a dragon and phoenix circling each other. Chest so tight that each breath hurt, she considered their symbolic significance. The male dragon and female phoenix represented balance, even though men and women's roles were far from equal.

All the more reason not to be here, presenting a case Father had no intention of hearing. Palms clammy, Kaiya ventured down an aisle formed by dozens of kneeling ministers and hereditary lords. Save for Eldest Brother Kai-Guo, all pressed their heads to the marble floor as she made her way toward the white marble dais. Carved into its sides were dozens of bat and lotus symbols, which she counted to calm her nerves.

Father slouched on the Jade Throne, which was chiseled in the form of a coiled dragon. Yellow robes embroidered with auspicious symbols on the chest and elbows hung over his gaunt frame. Gone was the robust optimism she remembered from her childhood. Mother's recent passing had left the gold phoenix throne at his side as empty as his heart. As always, General Zheng, bearing the Broken Sword, stood a step behind him.

A lump formed in Kaiya's throat. She sank to both knees. Stretching her arms out to straighten her sleeves, she placed her hands in front of her as she pressed her forehead to the floor.

The *Tianzi*'s voice wobbled. "Rise, my daughter."

Kaiya straightened and met his piercing regard, one that warned not to mention the foreign prince. Her clenching chest squeezed out all her resolve.

No, Father would never condone the suffering of Prince Hardeep and his people for mere profit. The assembled lords must be hiding the truth. Someone had to tell him, lest Heaven punish the realm for its immorality. She lifted her chin. "Please hear the request of Prince Hardeep Vaswani of Ankira."

Behind her, the lords and ministers stifled gasps.

Yet Father's expression softened. "What does Prince Hardeep ask of Cathay?"

"*Huang-Shang*," she said, using the formal address for the *Tianzi*. "He asks that we cease sales of firepowder to the Madurans."

The ministers broke into a low murmur until Chief Minister Tan rose to one knee, head bowed. "*Huang-Shang*, I negotiated our original agreement with Madura. It has been mutually beneficial."

Beneficial. Riches for Cathay, conquest for Madura. Misery for Hardeep's Ankira. The Dragon Singers from the old songs would've never tolerated

41

such injustice. Breaking all decorum, Kaiya spun and scowled at Chief Minister Tan. Fine lines of age framed his triangular face, giving him a foxlike appearance. When she released him from her glare, he averted his eyes as protocol demanded.

Knees beginning to ache, she turned back to Father. "*Huang-Shang*, do the Five Classics not say that a ruler must act morally? Our actions have led to an unenviable situation in Ankira that we should seek to rectify."

Cousin Kai-Long rose up to one knee. "*Huang-Shang*, I agree with the princess. Not only that, but once the Madurans pacify Ankira, and the trade agreement *does* expire, they will turn their ambitions toward us."

Chief Minister Tan shook his head. "We are their source of firepowder. They will make war with someone else."

And spread despair, with Cathay's complicity. Kaiya formulated a dignified response in her head. What kind of country put profit over people? Not only should they not renew the trade agreement… "A moral nation would terminate the treaty now."

More murmurs, undoubtedly from greedy lords and officials who cared more about gold than morality.

"Unfortunately, that is not an option," the Chief Minister said. "In the original negotiations, I bore an imperial plaque. To go against our word, sealed with a plaque, is tantamount to the *Tianzi* forsaking the Mandate of Heaven. It would invite another Hellstorm."

Kaiya sucked in her breath at the implication. Three centuries before, the last emperor of the Yu Dynasty had reneged on his plaque-bound obligations. The gods rained divine fire from the sky as punishment, blasting open a new sea in the fertile plains of the Ayuri South and plunging the world into the Long Winter.

It was unusual for an imperial plaque to be used in simple trade negotiations, since it represented the honor of the *Tianzi*. However, as a girl—even as a princess—she couldn't challenge the Chief Minister's word directly. She raised an eyebrow at him. "How much longer does the agreement last?"

Tan's brows furrowed as he looked to the ceiling. "A year, maybe? I do not recall."

Prince Hardeep didn't have a year. Kaiya turned back to Father. "Should we delay a decision until we find the original contract in the Trade Ministry's archives?"

The *Tianzi* straightened on the throne. He waved toward the lords and officials. "Everyone but Crown Prince Kai-Guo, Young Lord Peng, and Princess Kaiya will withdraw for tea."

All present bowed their foreheads to the floor before rising. Whether they drank tea or not, the *Tianzi's* suggestion left no doubt, they would drink something, somewhere else. They filed out in precise order.

Pulse skittering, Kaiya folded her hands into her lap. Father's stare might as well have been a dwarven anvil on her shoulders.

Once the room cleared, servants closed the doors. The hall seemed more cavernous with only Eldest Brother, Cousin Kai-Long, and a dozen imperial guards remaining, and was made even more so by the *Tianzi's* echoing voice.

"Kai-Long," he said. "It seems the foreign prince ignored the unspoken denial and deigned to pressure the princess into acting as his mouthpiece."

Cousin Kai-Long pressed his head to the floor. "*Huang-Shang*, forgive me for suggesting it."

Kaiya found him in the corner of her eye. Her stomach felt hollow. She'd failed all their expectations, even when doing the right thing by helping Ankira.

"I warned you, Cousin." Eldest Brother Kai-Guo's lips drew into a tight line. "Kaiya isn't trained. She should have just occupied him with idle banter. She is more musician than diplomat."

Heat pulsated in Kaiya's cheeks. Apparently, they'd forgotten she was kneeling right there beside them. Then Eldest Brother's attention fell on her hand, which was subconsciously twirling a lock of her hair, proving his point. She jerked the hand back to her lap.

Kai-Guo looked to the throne. "Father, may I speak freely?"

"I would not have sequestered the family if not to allow you the latitude."

Kai-Guo bowed his head. "Then if I may, you dote on Kaiya to the detriment of the realm. She wastes her time on music when she should be learning how to be a proper princess. You could have ordered her to marry any six of the previous young lords she met. Instead, you not only allowed her to choose, you pulled her out of matchmaking meetings."

Father's brows clashed together for a split second. "She is not ready to be married, not to one of those men."

Kaiya's head spun. So the interruptions had been Father's doing, but why? What was wrong with those suitors, besides their lack of wit and self-absorbed attitudes?

"She *needs* to marry one of *those* men," Kai-Guo said. "A princess' duty—"

The *Tianzi*'s lip quirked just a fraction into a frown. Kai-Guo fell silent and bowed.

Father's expression softened as he turned to her. "My daughter, it was unfair of me to assign you this task after shielding you from court intrigue all this time. I indulged your love of music when I should have prepared you to become my eyes and ears in your future husband's fief."

Suppressing a sigh, Kaiya bowed her head. To the realm, her worth as a musician would never surpass her value as a bride. "Why one of those six men?"

Father's eyes searched hers. "What do they have in common?"

Besides having less personality than a rock and egos larger than the three moons combined? Kaiya cocked her head. "They are all sons of *Yu-Ming* lords."

"Yes. Second-rank prefectural and county nobles." Father's stare bored into her. "From where?"

Why was it important? Especially compared to Ankira's plight? She caught herself before twirling the stubborn lock of hair again. "The North. Regions near the Wall."

"What can you tell me about the area?"

Had she known a geography test would follow matchmaking and greeting foreign dignitaries, maybe she would have stolen a few minutes out of her rigid schedule to study a map. Her brows furrowed. On her last trip, she'd seen… "Rolling hills rise into mountains. Bloodwood and Yue trees dot the mountainsides. The land is poor for farming, but the counties thrive from mining."

He looked to Eldest Brother and Cousin Kai-Long. "See? She understands more than it appears." He turned back to her. "My daughter, while the realm may seem prosperous and stable, not all under Heaven is well. My spies say several of the lords of the North harbor rebellious intent. They are as hard as the mountains they defend. To keep them content and docile, we buy saltpeter from their mines and process it in the capital to make firepowder."

Kaiya stifled a gasp. For Prince Hardeep and his Ankira, that meant… "We need foreign markets to sell the firepowder to."

The *Tianzi* tilted his head a fraction. "We reserve the freshest for ourselves and sell older stocks."

She sucked in a breath. "What about Ankira? We profit from their misery."

"Sometimes, practicality shades moral precepts."

At her side, Brother nodded. Cousin Kai-Long's lips pursed.

Kaiya lowered her hand from where she was again twisting that lock of hair. Her own father was rationalizing actions which caused another people's suffering. Wasn't this the paragon of nobility who had taught her songs of past heroes and ingrained a sense of morality in her? "But—"

His eyes narrowed, their warmth replaced by authority. "Convey my regret to Prince Hardeep."

Cowed by his stern tone, she bowed. Kai-Guo and Kai-Long followed suit.

When she raised her head, Father's regard softened. "You are so beautiful, my daughter. I will announce your betrothal at the reception tonight. After you send the foreign prince away, go meet with General Lu."

The bottom dropped out of her belly. Betrothal! To the commander of the armies in the North. Their planned meeting had been more than a choreographed farce, and with a possible rebellion brewing, perhaps the self-proclaimed Guardian Dragon of Cathay had not been the one to request it after all.

She started to speak, but Father's genuine smile stifled her protest. Her heart sank into her stomach. Betrothal appeared as immutable as Cathay's agreement with Madura. She'd be married, probably as soon as she flowered with Heaven's Dew, perhaps even forbidden by

47

a dour new husband from singing. Forget her stomach; her heart lay shattered on the marble tiles.

Rising, she trudged out of the hall, back into bright sunlight. This had to be a dream. Marriage. Like Xiulan, night after night of trying to make babies with Eldest Brother Kai-Guo. Monotonous routines all day. But at least Xiulan could practice the magic of her Dragon Script with friends and family.

Not Kaiya. She'd be shipped away to barren hills. Devoid of music. Alone. No, it couldn't be real. She took a deep breath to slow her stuttering pulse. A smooth river pebble found its way from her sash into her hand.

Cool and soothing, it was a token from her childhood friend Zheng Tian, the boy she'd once laughingly promised to marry. How simple and carefree those days were! When there was no grey area between Right and Wrong, just like in the songs. If only she could marry him instead of some pompous soldier. But no; even though he might be the son of a first-rank *Tai-Ming* lord, he'd been banished years ago for a stupid mistake.

She glanced back at her senior-most imperial guard, Chen Xin. He was looking at her pebble, frowning. Even on the worst day of her life, it would not do to let anyone see weakness. With a wistful sigh, she straightened her spine and squirrelled the keepsake back into its place in her sash. Before meeting her future husband, there was first the equally onerous task of walking back and denying a desperate plea. Thoughts of her own dismal future would have to wait.

Outside the Hall of Bountiful Harvests, she paused and composed herself. Prince Hardeep was just a man. A handsome one, for sure, but she'd met many other good-looking men without wilting into a starry-eyed fool. Steeling herself against whatever magic Prince Hardeep had used to beguile her, she stepped over the threshold.

The prince pressed his hands together and bent his head as she entered. He looked up expectantly.

His irises. They again entranced her.

Her straight posture softened as her insides somersaulted. She bowed low. It broke formal court etiquette, and indeed, the ministry secretary clucked his disapproval. At least it would conceal her spine melting to jelly. She held the position and focused on the prince's red-and-gold-threaded shoes. "I am afraid that Cathay must honor its agreements, lest the *Tianzi* lose the Mandate of Heaven and the realm descend into chaos."

"Do not apologize." His voice was sweet again, with a touch of melancholy. General Lu would probably never speak to her with such affection. "Please, raise your head."

His last words filled her like a warm breath into a soap bubble. She straightened.

Shoulders slumping, the prince tilted his eyes downward. He was handsome, even in sadness. "Will you sing for me? As a memory of our meeting?"

A song. Kaiya's heart flitted. She would do this for him, appropriate or not. At least someone today would appreciate her voice. She looked over her shoulder toward the official, who scowled and shook his head. No? Who was he to defy her wishes?

The prince's lips trembled into a brittle smile.

Her first foray into diplomacy might have ended in disaster, but with music, very few in Cathay could rival her. Perhaps if the fabled magic of Dragon Songs still existed, she could sing the rebellious lords into submission. Then, Father would value her ability over her marriage prospects. She lifted her voice in song, her soul soaring with each breath. The *Broken Sword* recounted how the Founder had transformed weakness into strength. Perhaps it would give Hardeep hope.

Exultation surged through her spine, into her limbs. All uncertainties and self-doubts melted away. With each note, she shed her poor imitation of imperial grace, replacing it with the sincerity of her soul. Not even the tight dress could contain her. Verse upon verse rose to a crescendo, her spirit floating with it.

Prince Hardeep's blue eyes sparkled. "Even Yanyan would envy your voice."

Heat rose to her cheeks. How could he compare her to the girl from a thousand years before, who had summoned storms with her music and sung the dragon Avarax to sleep? "Yanyan charmed an orc army into surrender with her song. I could not even convince my father to change his mind."

"You spoke from your heart, and the emperor listened." His forlorn smile sent a chill up her spine. "With an indomitable spirit, you can move your people to do the right thing."

Could she? Besides Cousin Kai-Long, none of the men in the Hall of Supreme Harmony had shown any concern for morality. She sighed. "If I had the voice of Yanyan, he would have listened."

Those blue eyes searched hers. "Channeling magic through artistic endeavor is the gift of your people, just as the fighting arts are ours. Come with me, and scatter the Maduran armies with the power of your music."

Was he suggesting running away? With him? Escaping marriage with General Lu? She glanced back at the official. If he told anyone, the prince might lose his head. And if only shirking duty were so easy. They wouldn't make it to the front gates, even if she could bring herself to take up his offer.

And who knew? Maybe he was trying to kidnap her, and hold her hostage to get what he really wanted: an end to Cathay's trade agreement with Madura.

Tearing her gaze away, she shook her head. "Even though master performers from our past could accomplish amazing feats with Dragon Songs, those skills have since faded into legend. You would need an elf." Like Father's councilor, Lord Xu. Too bad nobody could predict when the enigmatic elf would make an appearance.

51

Prince Hardeep took her hands in his. Excitement rose in his tone. "With your voice and musical talent, you have the potential. We will research. I can help you scour your records. Together, we could learn how the masters of old did it."

His touch sent heat up her arms and into her core. Behind her, the official sucked in a sharp breath and the imperial guards stepped forward. Kaiya withdrew, for his safety, and raised an open hand to assuage the guards. Was Hardeep's idea even possible? "How can I learn from books what the elf angel taught Yanyan?"

"I would hazard to guess that singing a dragon to sleep is just a little more difficult than convincing a doting father to do the right thing." He put a finger to his chin. "And if—no, *when*—you succeed, you will save my nation."

Yes! No. Even if it were possible to learn from dusty old books, using magic to change a *Tianzi's* mind flirted with treason even more than running away. She met his gaze again. Those eyes implored her, making her belly flutter. No, helping Ankira was the moral thing to do. Here was a chance to show that music was still worth something. That she was worth something, beyond her value as a bride to some lord. "I will try."

A grin bloomed on his face. "Ankira owes you a debt of gratitude. *I* owe you."

Kaiya twirled an errant lock of hair. "We will need to retrace Yanyan's steps. To find out exactly where she met the elf angel." Which meant a trip to the imperial archives.

After the mandated matchmaking with General Lu.

She looked into the prince's eyes. No. He was here, close, and marriage to the general seemed so far away. Hardeep's people needed her help, because everyone else would just let them suffer. Again, her hand found Tian's pebble, firm and resolute beneath her sash. He'd support her decision.

They'd go now, even though it meant disobeying Father.

CHAPTER 5
Crooked Detours

Clothes swished and footsteps shuffled across the marble floors as Kaiya gawked at the rows and rows of books bound in silk cords. When Father ordered her to send Prince Hardeep away, he likely didn't expect the route out of the palace to include a stop at the imperial archives.

Maybe it was a bad idea. *Her* bad idea, on the preposterous assumption she could learn the dead art of Dragon Songs.

A battalion of grey-robed scholars hovered nearby, their annoyance at the unannounced visit clear in their tight frowns. Though they hadn't dared oppose an imperial princess, they'd dispatched an apprentice clerk to lodge a complaint with the Ministry of Appointments.

All trouble waiting to happen, if the old secretary's wringing hands were any indication. She'd abused her position and strong-armed him into delaying the matchmaking meeting with General Lu. No doubt both the Ministries of Appointments and Household Affairs scoured the grounds for her.

Her imperial guards Chen Xin and Zhao Yue stood nearby, their usually stoic expressions now shadowed by uncertainty. Nothing good would come of this visit, no matter how noble the intentions. She'd tarnished her already-poor façade of Perfect Princess, and disobeyed the *Tianzi's* command to meet General Lu.

Was it worth it? She looked over at Prince Hardeep, a book in each hand, his face brightly illuminated by the magic baubles suspended from the ceiling. So handsome in his need! And unlike everyone else, he believed she could become more than an awkward political bride. Her stomach fluttered like a swarm of butterflies. She didn't need to be beautiful or graceful to revive Dragon Songs and save a downtrodden people.

If she could do it.

If they even had enough time. The scholars were being intentionally unhelpful, stalling.

She scanned the labels. "According to legend, Yanyan's magic awoke in the place where the elf angel Aralas revealed himself. Before the War of Ancient Gods."

Shrugging, Hardeep held up one book, entitled *The Fall of the Yu Dynasty*. "It's in your language, not mine, but the illustrations tell me we are in the wrong era." His sheepish smile was too adorable.

She covered a laugh with her hand. "That is about seven hundred years too late."

One scholar's face flushed red, while others glared at Hardeep's hands on their precious books.

His perfect lips formed a perfect circle. "The Hellstorm and Long Winter, then."

She stifled her giggle. There was nothing amusing about fire raining from the heavens, nor the three years of starvation in its aftermath.

Prince Hardeep returned the *Fall of the Yu Dynasty* to the shelf. With the other book cradled in his hand, he tapped his chin, just like her childhood playmate Tian. So cute, even more so with the pointed beard. "Where do we find the right era?"

Not like she knew where those historical accounts might be stored. She'd only visited the archives a few times in the past, always on a tightly regulated schedule. Kaiya turned to the irritated scholars. "Take us to the documents on the War of Ancient Gods."

A bearded middle-aged man bowed low and extended an open hand. "This way, *Dian-xia*." His begrudging tone left no doubt as to his opinion of an unauthorized visit by a girl, princess or not, and a foreign prince who might be trying to smuggle out a book.

She followed as he shuffled down the rows, Prince Hardeep at her side and the two imperial guards a sword's reach away. The Foreign Ministry secretary and the gaggle of scholars trailed an almost-respectful distance behind, though most kept staring at the book the prince swung about in his hand. If the archives had windows, they would have been eyeing the Iridescent Moon with a dwarven timepiece, counting the minutes until some bureaucrat, and maybe a few imperial guards, arrived to usher her out. The low-level archive clerk they'd sent must've reported to the Ministry of Appointments by now.

Which gave them ten, maybe fifteen minutes at best to find out where Aralas had met Yanyan a millennia ago. Over the next several twists and turns, the air became more stale and musty, the books more dusty and faded. They also dwindled in number, replaced by sheaves of unbound scrolls: Historical accounts. Interpretations of those histories. Financial implications of the interpretations. Somewhere in the mass of information, they could probably uncover how many demon hearts the Sun God Yang-Di paid the dwarf Da-Jin to forge the world for the Goddess of Mercy, Guanyin.

The head scholar came to a stop and bowed again. "Here, *Dian-xia*." His tone carried an unspoken warning to be extremely careful with the brittle-looking scrolls. As if she wasn't in enough trouble already, without damaging a priceless book or three.

Kaiya scanned the shelves. Labels protruded from each roll, inviting a browser to learn the title of the work without actually having to touch it. A few steps ahead, Prince Hardeep had all but forgotten her, his attention locked on some scroll. She shrugged the outer gown off her shoulders to expose her collarbones, the most feminine of her otherwise uninspiring features.

No response. He seemed fixated on that scroll. Maybe he saw her as a mere tool, a means of getting into the archives. She dug her nails into her clammy palms.

He apparently didn't care about the risk she was taking for him.

No, not for him. He was just a man she'd just met, and good looks and charm had never swayed her before. Like the Dragon Singers of old, she took these risks for Ankira and the people suffering for Cathay's profit.

And, of course, for the chance to learn Dragon Songs. Fists loosening, she turned back to the rows of shelves. A newer-looking book, bound in leather like those of the fair-skinned people in the East, stood out among the scrolls. Gold Arkothi lettering emblazoned on the spine screamed for her to read it.

She tilted her head to decipher the foreign words. *The Nine Loves of Aralas*. Countless Cathayi accounts told how the elf angel Aralas taught different types of magic to his human lovers so that they could help overthrow the orcs who enslaved them during the War of Ancient Gods. Invariably these stories emphasized Yanyan's role as the most important. Perhaps a foreign version might have a different opinion. Gesturing toward it with an open hand, she beckoned the head scholar. "What is an Arkothi book doing here?"

Without even looking at it, the scholar harrumphed. "The imperial archives have the largest collection of information in the world. Works come from all over the continent. If you wish to know this particular book's provenance, I would be happy to delve through piles of records to find out." His pursed lips and flippant tone suggested otherwise.

Curiously, two of his underlings stared at the book with narrowed eyes and leaned toward each other. Her sensitive ears made out their furtive whispers.

"Where did that come from?"

"I've never seen it before."

Exchanging a glance with Prince Hardeep, she thumbed through the pages to Yanyan's story. The handwritten foreign words came slowly.

He reached in and turned the page. The heat from his closeness sent her arms tingling. She looked up at him to find his eyes darting back and forth.

"Here," he said, pointing to a paragraph. "Yanyan labored in the rice paddies near Sun-Moon Lake. She stumbled upon the elf angel Aralas when he was investigating the remains of the dragon Pyarax."

Sun-Moon Lake! It was here in the capital. But... "I've never heard of dragon remains here."

He flipped another page, revealing a map.

Kaiya stared at the confusing lines. She might be talented at music and nominally good at pretending to be perfect; maps and directions were another story. "Dragon remains could be anywhere."

The head scholar's scoff transformed into a cough. Accentless Ayuri slid off his tongue. "If I may, *Dian-xia*, the book the prince holds might be of use." He extended an impertinent finger at the tome Hardeep had carried from the previous section.

Prince Hardeep gawped at the book as if it had magically appeared in his hand. With a sheepish grin, he offered *Geomancy Studies of Huajing* to the scholar.

The scholar blew out a sigh that managed to mix exasperation with relief, and gingerly plucked the volume from the prince's hands. "As Queen Regent, the Founder's consort commissioned several *Feng Shui* masters to lay out Huajing's precisely gridded network of roads to ensure national prosperity."

With fanatical reverence, he turned one page. Then another. In the time it took him to flip a page, empires could rise and fall. Maybe he was just biding time until a high official came to remove them from the archives.

And drag her to meet General Lu. Studying Hardeep's jawline, she twirled a lock of hair. They couldn't have much more than five minutes now.

At last, he held it open, beyond anyone's reach, revealing an illustration. The fearsome dragon looked nothing like the graceful, serpentine spirit dragons that controlled the weather and acted as Heaven's messengers. Not like any of the latter had appeared in three hundred years.

"Such a horrible beast." Hardeep recoiled. "Thank the gods that only Avarax remains."

She nodded. "And that he is content with controlling the Dragonlands."

"Content..." He looked up at her. "What do the words say?"

Kaiya read the passage aloud. "When the orcs thought they had finally exterminated the elves, they turned on their dragon allies in the Dragonpurge. Their gods descended in flaming chariots and slew the great wyrms until only Avarax remained."

Hardeep sucked in a sharp breath. "Avarax was too powerful, even for the Tivari gods."

With a nod, she skimmed into the next paragraph. "With the establishment of the Wang Dynasty, the Queen Regent ordered the construction of the Temple of Heaven over Pyarax's bones, and placed the chunk of a fallen star from the Founder's homeland there."

Reaching past her toward the book in the scholar's grasp, Hardeep's trembling hand flipped the page. He pointed. "Look."

A diagram showed the dragon bones as columns, protruding from the ground and forming the outline of the temple's elliptical walls. She shook her head. "Even the Emperor himself requires a special blessing from the temple priests to enter the tower, and he only goes on New Year's Day."

"Which is in four days." He held up four fingers.

She fiddled with a lock of hair. There was little hope of convincing Father to break three hundred years of tradition by allowing a foreigner to join in a trip to a set of dragon bones. And in four days' time, she'd already be betrothed to a different kind of reptile.

Muffled by distance and the labyrinth of bookshelves, boots clopped and slippered feet shuffled somewhere near the entrance. It was the Ministry of Appointments coming for her, no doubt, along with imperial guards to help Hardeep find the palace exit.

The head scholar cleared his throat and closed the book. "I am pleased to have been of service to the princess."

Though his tone implied otherwise, Kaiya nodded. "Thank you."

The scholar's shoulders relaxed as he returned the leather-bound book to the shelf. From somewhere closer to the entrance, voices spoke and footsteps approached.

"One more thing," she said.

The head scholar tensed up again, and his colleagues all muttered. "How may we serve the princess?"

"Would you happen to have any books of Yanyan's songs?"

"No." A tentative smile formed on the scholar's face. "If any survived, they would be in the Hall of Pure Melody."

Hardeep turned to her. "Where is that?"

"The music hall. Just across the central plaza." Kaiya pointed, toward what she hoped was the right area.

Tapping his chin, Hardeep looked the other way. He didn't seem to notice her poor sense of direction. No, he was in deep thought, perhaps thinking…

The same thing as her. She said, "Maybe if we saw what Yanyan sang, we could figure out how she did it."

"Yes," the head scholar said. "I think that is a wonderful idea."

62

Or was it? Kaiya fiddled with the long sleeves of her formal gown. She couldn't traipse all around the palace grounds while General Lu waited. Especially into the Hall of Pure Melody, which housed priceless musical instruments from antiquity.

As the old proverb said, there was opportunity in danger. Here was a chance to revive the lost magic of Dragon Songs and save a conquered nation. General Lu could wait.

Now if only they could get there before the Ministry of Appointments came and dragged her off to the self-proclaimed Guardian Dragon of Cathay. It would be much more interesting to charm a real dragon.

Dozens of footsteps and voices grew louder. They had to get out. She might know a path, since she'd once made Tian play hide-and-seek in the archives when they should've been studying... but that was over a decade ago...

CHAPTER 6:
Misdirection

In the three thousand, one hundred and forty-seven days since his banishment from the capital, Tian rarely had time to ponder how he, the fourth son of a *Tai-Ming* lord, had ended up as a *Black Fist* adept. All he knew was that the clan was the only place he fit in, the only place where his talents outweighed his lack of social graces.

None of his colleagues in the harbormaster's office knew of either his noble birth, his childhood friendship with Princess Kaiya, or his identity as a spy; only that he could scribble notes quickly and accurately.

Nobody seemed to notice how often he visited the records room today, nor that he lingered there an extra twenty-six seconds longer than average as he surreptitiously reviewed copies of the *Wild Orchid's* manifests and logs. Owned by Nanling Province, it had followed an unspectacular trade route over the last two years.

From here in Jiangkou, it would sail south to Yutou, then to its homeport in Nanling Province, then into the foreign waters of Ankiras and Ayudra Island. In addition to transporting Ankirans out of Ayuri lands, it leased cargo space to several trading companies. The only company that had ever stood out to Tian before was Golden Fu Trading, a newer corporation that imported addicting but legal gooseweed from the Ayuri South. So why had Yutou Province decided to use the ship for smuggling?

"Little Tian," his supervisor yelled from the main office.

Tian poked his head out of the records room. "Yes sir?"

"A trading company representative wants your help with a shipping declaration."

Lamp Man, no doubt, perhaps with unspoken answers. Tian walked out into the rows of knee-high desks, making a show of bumping into one of them. His twenty-seven kneeling colleagues all startled and shook their heads.

Old Chu, an honest licensing official, snorted. "You've been here a year and you still careen into desks. Once the Ministry of Trade ships you off to the barbarian lands, I can't say I will miss the shock to my old heart every time you crash into mine. I will miss your thoroughness, though."

A compliment, perhaps? They were rare. Tian bobbed his head, all the while keeping a surreptitious eye on his own desk.

Lamp Man stood there, his gaze roving over the clutter of brushes, inkstones, and papers. He bowed his head as Tian approached. "Scribe Zheng, thank you."

"How may I help you?" Tian dropped into a cross-legged sit on the floor.

Lamp Man sat down across the table, then withdrew two sheets of folded rice paper. "My company is new, and I want to make sure this customs declaration is correct." He proffered the sheets.

New, of course—likely a shell company creating another layer to protect whoever was behind the smuggling. Tian examined the neat handwriting. *Victorious Trading Corporation. Bloodwood furniture out of Wailian County.*

Victorious...the written character was rarely used, usually only in names like Princess Kaiya's. As for furniture, it provided an easy way to smuggle, as long as the right customs officials were bribed to ignore secret or not so secret compartments. Tian looked sidelong at a few of the most egregious offenders at their desks. "Everything seems to be in order on the first page." He started to flip the page.

Lamp Man's hand shot out and he shook his head. *Not now*, he mouthed. "Thank you for your help, Scribe Zheng." Bowing his head, he stood up and left.

Waiting for all eyes to return to their own work, Tian peeled away the top page, revealing a paper treasury note worth ten gold *yuan*. That was a substantial bribe, three and a third times more than the largest bribe he'd ever seen taken in this office. Lamp Man wanted something big, and the second page...

Beautiful script meandered over the sheet, seemingly moving of its own accord. He blinked several times and shook his head. Victorious Trading Company apparently employed a Dragon Scribe, someone who had hoped to put the reader under some sort of charm. Thankfully, Black Lotus training involved exposure to many forms of Artistic Magic, conferring a mild resistance.

His head might be spinning now, but the uninitiated would likely feel drunk, and open to the command written in the words: *Bring all original manifests for the* Steadfast Mariner *to the warehouse at the third waxing gibbous.*

Stuffing the page and cash into the fold of his robes, Tian glanced at the dwarf-made water clock. The third waxing gibbous was just past sunset, six hours and ten minutes from now. The *Steadfast Mariner,* registered to Yutou Province, was the suspicious ship that had first led him to the warehouse that morning. If Lamp Man wanted the originals, it was probably to destroy the evidence and tie up loose ends.

Did he see Tian as a loose end? Or as a resource for future smuggling?

Tian scribbled two coded messages, one for Jie and the other for clan superiors. Waiting for the instant all heads focused on their work, he slipped out of the building.

In the mid-morning sun, longshoremen, dockworkers, and sailors all bustled about, too busy with their own affairs to care about him. After scanning the docks and ships for any sign of Jie, he beckoned his usual runner out of a crowd of boys looking for odd jobs.

Up to now, Little Ju had proven reliable and discreet. The tween grinned and hustled up. "What do you need, Mister Zheng?"

With a street performer's sleight of hand, Tian retrieved the missive for his Black Lotus superiors from his sleeve. Creased into a twenty-fold shape that would tear apart if opened by untrained hands, it instructed them to track down Victorious Trading's incorporation papers. He pressed it, and the silver coin Lamp Man had given him that morning, into Little Ju's hand. "Run this to Sweet Lotus Shrine. Drop it in the donation box."

The boy dipped his head and dashed off. Making sure no one was looking, Tian stashed his note for Jie into the light bauble lamp sconce on the right side of the door. It might be out of her short reach, but she'd never failed to retrieve his messages before. Hopefully, she would do so before he reached the warehouse, just in case Lamp Man saw him as a loose end in need of tying up…at the neck.

CHAPTER 7
Resonance

Pages ruffled as Kaiya flipped through ancient musical texts with Prince Hardeep under the bright illumination of unshuttered light bauble lamps. She'd performed in the Hall of Pure Melody's acoustically perfect main chamber for large audiences of hereditary lords several times before, but it had been years since she visited its library.

Her two imperial guards stood at the doorway, expressions marked by tight-drawn lips and narrowed eyes. The Ministry of Appointments secretary clasped and unclasped his hands, turning his head out into the hall over and over again. He resembled a dwarf-made mechanical doll. Unlike those silent automatons, he had reminded her several times on the jaunt across the central plaza that General Lu awaited her, and that perhaps she should preen a little first. When it came time for him to file a daily log with his ministry, there was no telling what he would say about her.

Perhaps he would mention how she'd dallied with a foreign prince instead of meeting her future husband. The rumors would swirl through the palace for days, humiliating her—and worse, embarrassing Father.

Shifting her gaze from Prince Hardeep, she stifled a sigh. Helping him had sounded just and righteous earlier. Now though, rummaging through the music library, without permission no less, for the sake of a foreign country… Father might very well order her married immediately, before she even flowered with Heaven's Dew.

And for what? The possibility of unearthing lost Dragon Songs seemed bleak so far. None of the hundred song transcriptions looked out of the ordinary, beyond the beautiful sound they each sang in her head. Gritting her teeth, she replaced yet another bundle of brittle rice-paper scrolls.

With the enthusiasm of a puppy, Prince Hardeep pointed to a wall of books bound in faded silk cord. "Perhaps we should search the oldest ones."

A smile came unbidden to her lips. General Lu would never look at her like that, never think of her as more than a stepping stone. Never care about what was important to her. Yes, this was the right thing to do. Her hand left Tian's pebble and reached for one of the books—

"What are you doing?" a male voice barked from the door.

Kaiya's heart leapt into her throat. She swung around.

The Hall of Pure Melody's steward marched in, his blue robes swishing. His glower fell on her, widened, and then shifted downward as protocol demanded. "*Dian-xia*, I was not informed you would visit today."

She nodded. "I am…" She looked to Prince Hardeep, then back. "I am looking for a song to play for my brother's wedding." A cringe-worthy lie.

The steward shuffled on his feet. "It is uh, highly irregular for people to visit the musical archives, particularly the rare, and uh, especially delicate volumes. Perhaps I can help?"

"Yanyan," she said. "Do you have any of her music here?"

Frown returning to his face, the steward favored the prince with a furrowed brow. "Who is this?"

Kaiya straightened and channeled her most authoritative voice. "A guest of honor."

"And a fellow lover of music." Prince Hardeep pressed his palms together. "I have researched your peoples' music for years." He hummed a familiar tune.

Da-Xiong's Lullaby? The famous flautist Da-Xiong, one of the last to master Dragon Songs, had calmed a furious Yu Dynasty emperor with that song, sparing hundreds of innocents from his wrath. Prince Hardeep knew the song, while the only songs General Lu probably knew of were war chants.

He wasn't even using a flute to achieve the deep notes. His hum hung in the air, each note heavier than the next. Kaiya's shoulders relaxed as the melody settled her skittering pulse.

The steward's ridiculous grin spread from the edge of each eye, while he blinked as if he had dwarven

71

anvils for eyelids. His Ayuri came out with a halting accent. "Simply amazing! Few have heard of that song, let alone can hum it. I am duly impressed."

"You are too kind." Nodding at the steward, Prince Hardeep winked at her. "I would love to see Yanyan's songs. Even if none of my people could invoke the magic in her tunes, legend has it the melodies are beautiful."

"Alas." The steward sighed. "Her songs were transcribed in one single book, lost in the chaos after the Hellstorm."

Prince Hardeep's lips quirked upward. "A shame. In any case, though I appreciate the offer, we do not need your help. You may all leave us."

"Let me know if you do." The steward bowed. He turned and left, the secretary and imperial guards escorting him out.

Leaving her alone. With Hardeep. Whose command both the steward *and* the secretary *and* guards had obeyed. Kaiya's heart buzzed like a dragonfly's wings. Maybe the secretary would report back to Father that she was alone with a man.

Hardeep brushed a finger across her thumb, and then clasped her hand. Excitement jolted from her palm to her chest. Smiling conspiratorially, he tilted his head toward the older books. "Come."

She cast her gaze down. Heat flared from her toes to her head. To think that an hour before, marriage seemed so onerous. With him, however... He

72

understood her. Maybe he even liked her. She let him guide her toward the books.

He pulled a few off the shelves, handing her some while flipping through the pages of others. She peeked up through her lashes a few times to catch his singular focus on the task. From the bounce of his head, he could clearly read the musical transcription.

He passed another book to her. "What does the script say?"

The song itself was innocuous enough, a piece for the four-stringed, fretted *pipa* from the preceding Yu Dynasty. In that era, when the *Tianzi* had kept a large harem, a court musician had cheered a depressed concubine with it. "*Once you have seized the song's emotion and made it your own,*" she read, "*you must project it. Rooted to the ground, your spine aligned, let your heart impel your voice.*" Rooted to the ground, spine aligned…it sounded like her doctor's breathing exercises.

"As if people were trees." He laughed, clear and jubilant. Still, his eyes darted over the page before searching hers. "I wonder what it sounds like."

Her lips quirked upward as she contemplated his hand. Her own shot out to take his and she gave him a tug toward the exit. "Come."

"Where are we going?"

"The main hall," she said before she could change her mind. It was one thing to go to the library, but the main hall was off-limits except on rare occasions.

If the *Tianzi* found out, he might never let her perform here again. Maybe it wasn't worth the risk.

Yes, it was. Here was a chance to evoke a Dragon Song, something no Cathayi artist had accomplished in centuries. She could be special, something more than just a chess piece in the game of national politics. And Prince Hardeep wanted—no, needed—her to succeed. She squared her shoulders and shuffled ahead of him.

Though steeply pitched eaves of blue tile capped the Hall of Pure Melody on the outside, the main hall vaulted in an elliptical dome. Prince Hardeep looked upward, his irises tracing the coffering that partitioned the porcelain tiles.

"We need an instrument." Kaiya beckoned him toward the front of the chamber, where she knelt and slid aside a wall panel to reveal a storage room. If he loved music as much as she, wait until he went inside. She invited him in with an open hand.

His hands barely brushed over her shoulder as he passed, sending a shiver through her. She stood and followed him in, almost running into his back when he skidded to a halt.

Arms outstretched, blue eyes round with wonder, he spun in a circle, pausing on some of the finest instruments: An antique *guzheng* zither, said to be worth more than a ship. An array of knobbed bronze bells, played only on New Year's Day.

And finally, a pipa, believed to have been given to Yanyan by her lover, the elf angel Aralas, resting on a cloth-covered pedestal. Its sound plate glittered in gold, while the strings caught the light like a spider web at dawn. The smooth resonator, supposedly made of a dragon's eggshell, swirled with color.

"What a beautiful lute!" Hardeep strode over and reverently picked Yanyan's pipa up in two hands. If only her potential suitors had even a fraction of his interest in music! No, they were more interested in talking about themselves. He presented the instrument with an encouraging nod.

She hesitated. Only designated people were allowed to touch any of the artifacts. Then again, she hadn't stopped him, either. Bowing her head, she received the pipa in two hands.

And almost dropped it. It seemed alive in her palms, pulsing ever so subtly, as if it had a heart, beating in harmony with hers. As if it belonged to her. She started to return it to its stand.

It felt like leaving behind a long-lost friend. She looked up to see Hardeep disappearing into the performance hall. Breaths rapid and shallow, she cradled the pipa against her chest and followed.

When she reached the door, he was scooting a bloodwood chair, carved with nightingale patterns, to the most ideal spot in the chamber for playing. He set the music book on it and gestured for her to sit, then walked across the chamber. Though the location wasn't marked on the white marble floors, he stopped where her father might relax—the most ideal spot for listening. Pressing his hands together, he bowed his head. "Please play."

Kaiya looked at the instrument in her hands, then up at him. Of all the pipas, he had chosen this one. "Do you know the significance of this lute?"

He shrugged. "It drew my eye. It was the most beautiful in the storeroom."

"Yanyan used it during the War of Ancient Gods."

His mouth formed a perfect circle. "Then you *must* play it."

She studied the pipa. She might be a talented musician, but... "No human in living memory has coaxed a sound out of it." Hushed rumors spoke of the elf lord Xu performing for Father twenty-nine years ago; other than that, the last masters to play it lived almost three centuries before, and had all died under bizarre circumstances.

Tapping his chin, he regarded her. "You won't know unless you try."

Kaiya's head spun. If she succeeded where even the best musicians in the realm had failed, it would prove the worth of music. *Her* worth.

Then again, if the pipa didn't respond, it would only confirm what Eldest Brother Kai-Guo and the other lords believed: her only value was that as a bride to General Lu. Even worse, Prince Hardeep would think he'd wasted his time trying to help her.

She took a deep breath. She could do this. Had to do it, even if it was just to prove to herself she could. She scanned the music book, memorizing the complex changes.

Settling on the edge of the chair, she took a deep breath and stared at the strings. This would never work. What was she thinking? She was just setting herself up for humiliation.

Time to get it over with. With a resolute nod, she plucked out the first note.

A beautiful sound emanated from the resonator.

Kaiya's heart jolted and she nearly dropped the pipa in surprise. It couldn't be. It had to be her imagination. She looked up to Hardeep.

Eyes closed, smile broad, he looked enraptured by the sound.

Could it be? She strummed a chord, emitting a wondrous melody. There was no mistake. Heavens, she had done it! Something no one else had accomplished in over two centuries!

Plucking each string, pressing each fret, the music came out inspired. The joyous soul of the song bounded off the page, swirling in seemingly tangible currents.

"Each note raises my spirit higher," he said, yet his own tone was flat. "Maybe do what the book suggested. Adjust yourself in the chair? I think if you straightened your spine, feet flatter on the ground, it would sound even better."

Such strange advice, sounding more like her doctor's counsel than anything her music teachers would ever say. Still, it couldn't hurt. She shifted in her chair and plucked out the tune. Its vibration echoed in her arms.

"One shoulder is higher than the other," he offered.

Adjusting her posture, she continued, and the pulsations merged into her core. With a slight tilt of her waist, they sank to her pelvis, awakening a flare of warmth there. After tucking her tailbone forward, the vibrations reached her legs as well. She looked up again.

Prince Hardeep's expression brightened from his luminous blue irises. He placed a hand over his breast. "Yes! More emotion!"

She closed her eyes and strummed. Her spirit soared to a place only music could take her. Even though she was plain-looking, music made her feel beautiful. And now, playing for this audience of one...her beauty might rival Guanyin, Goddess of Fertility, in her glorious splendor.

Her entire body tingled, from fingertips to toes. Her pulse quickened, roaring loud and torrential in her ears. Her insides writhed like ten thousand fish squirming over each other in a shallow pool. An immense source of energy lay just beyond her reach, like an ocean of power trickling through a pinprick in a wall. There, ready to tap into.

Then her fingers went slack on the pipa and the blood rushed from her head. A dark tunnel in her field of vision narrowed. All went black.

Chapter 8
Conspirators

Trapped like a rat. Avoiding the sailor's gaze, Jie ducked back down among the kegs of sulfur bound for Wailian County. It might be used to cure scabies and ringworm, but there was enough here to put every herb store and acupuncture clinic in the North out of business. No, against the *Tianzi's* law, someone in Wailian was making firepowder and shipping it south.

Getting the message to the clan would be difficult now that someone had spotted her. Near the only exit, seven different voices and hurried footsteps of varying lengths and weights echoed in the cargo hold.

"Are you sure it wasn't just rats?"

"It would have been a huge rat. No, it's an intruder."

"Inform the quartermaster."

Jie sucked her bottom lip. They knew she was here, and there was only one way out.

Winches and gears creaked. The platform to the main deck clunked up, and the door clanked shut.

"Fan out," a male voice called from near the hatch.

Jie leaned forward from between two kegs and peeked out. Three men congregated near the now-raised platform. Four others searched among the crates and kegs. Shadows danced as they raised and waved their light bauble lamps.

Until the hatch opened, there was no escape. At least the patches of darkness allowed her to work her way in that direction. As one man turned his head away, Jie scooted over one crate. When another swept his lamp in her direction, she used the arcing shadow to move to the next.

Child's play. She could keep this up all morning, if need be. Though if information won wars, the time wasted down here could mean the difference between quelling a rebellion in its infancy, and taking years rooting out a well-established insurgency.

A large man near the hatch crossed his arms. "We know you are down here. Just save us the trouble and show yourself."

Oh, she'd give them plenty of trouble. Unless they suddenly figured out a systematic search method, they'd never find her. Still, precious time slipped away.

"Damn stowaway," another muttered.

So they thought her a stowaway. Better that than a spy. It would get her above deck sooner, which would make escape all the easier, as long as the boatswain didn't recognize her as one of the boys he'd recruited. Just better not to let these ruffians know she was a girl. Jie ran her hand through dust and grime and smeared her face.

She then stood and stepped into the light. Lowering her voice, she said, "I'm sorry. I'll give you all my money. A silver *jiao*. Just let me out."

The large man guarding the hatch favored her with a sneer, exposing a long incisor. "Normally we'd take it, brat. Unfortunately, all the gold in Sun-Moon Palace won't buy you out of this situation."

Since when did a sailor not take a bribe? And what did they have in mind? Jie's pulse might have ticked up a beat. Or not. Seven men with more brawn than brains shouldn't be too hard to escape.

A sailor with a scar on his cheek came up and cuffed her on the side of the head, sending flashes through her field of vision. The stubby fingers of another clamped her shoulder.

Jie froze, feigning fear.

"We got 'im." Snaggletooth rapped on the door above with a belaying pin.

The hatch above opened. Standing on the platform as it lowered were two men, one a sailor from the look of his clothes, and a man in robes.

Fat Nose.

Or at least that's what Tian called him. The short sword, which he'd kept hidden in the warehouse, now flashed in his hand. He smelled of coriander. He pointed it at her. "You, boy, what are you doing here?"

Jie threw her hands up. "I ran away from home." Hopefully he wouldn't ask where home was, since Tian, in his usual laconic manner, hadn't bothered to say where the *Wild Orchid* had sailed from.

"What did you see?"

Jie stared at the floor, pretending to be ashamed. "I ain't see nothin'. Just some curry-lovin' brown folk." Right, she could always tell them she'd travelled with the Ankirans, though it wouldn't exactly explain why she'd stayed behind when they disembarked.

With a dismissive wave of his hand, Fat Nose sheathed the sword and turned back to the platform. "Just a stowaway. Not my problem."

"One with a high-pitched voice," Snaggletooth said. "You didn't even bother to check for weapons." He nodded toward a thick-necked sailor.

No Neck patted her down, pausing where no gentleman would. "A girl." His leer left a stain on her clothes. He continued down, stopping again when his hand found one of her three knives. "What is this?"

"A knife?" Jie flashed a guilty grin.

Scarface smacked her on the side of the head again. "You're in no position to make jokes."

Looking at Fat Nose, Snaggletooth harrumphed. "She's been in the hold for Heaven knows how long. A runaway, who might have seen too much. Nobody will miss her. Save yourself the risk. We'll gut her."

"Afterwards." Grinning, No Neck slapped Snaggletooth on the back. "Just like that brownie refugee girl whose little body we threw overboard."

Rapists and murderers! Jie's muscles clenched, ready to break free of Stubby Fingers' grip. Nine men to avoid on her way to the ropes leading out of the cargo hold, though perhaps Snaggletooth and No Neck deserved a knife between their ribs first.

"She's just a girl," Fat Nose said. "Let her go."

"Wait." Scarface held the lamp closer to her face and yanked off her headband.

Jie shot her hands up to cover her ears.

"An elf?" Fat Nose cocked his head.

"Half-elf," Scarface said. "The one we saw on Ayudra."

Stubby Fingers nodded. "Yep. That's her, all right."

"It wasn't me!" Jie shook her head. She'd never left Cathay before. Though trying to convince them might prove difficult, since elves hardly ever left their hidden kingdoms, nor mated with humans like a certain dastard of a father.

"Hah! You want us to believe you have an evil twin?" Snaggletooth looked at his companions, who took up his chorus of laughter.

Jie's fists squeezed tight. They had to be making this up.

"It makes sense now." Stubby Fingers nodded. "She must've stowed away when we docked at Ayudra."

Snaggletooth turned to Fat Nose. "Mister Jiang, no need to waste your time. We'll take care of her."

Fat Nose Jiang held up a finger. "I don't think—"

With a jerk of his hand, Snaggletooth pointed the belaying pin at Jiang. "Our ship, our rules. Now, you can watch if you want…"

83

Jie lowered her chin, loosening his grip. With one hand, she seized his wrist and twisted it; with the other, she whipped her third knife out in an arc, slicing Stubby Finger's wrist tendons. His fingers went limp on her shoulder. Twirling toward the platform, she continued with a backslash through Snaggletooth's wrist.

He stood, staring at his lifeless fingers, his belaying pin forgotten in his other hand. Jie swept under that arm, dislocated the elbow over her shoulder, and caught the weapon as he dropped it. Finishing her spin, she stepped on the platform with the knife pointed at Fat Nose Jiang's flank.

Thank the Heavens. Without the element of surprise, she wouldn't have stood a chance. But now, gaffer hooks, belaying pins, and knives swept out from boots and belts. While Stubby Fingers and Snaggletooth held their wounds moaning, the six remaining sailors encircled the platform.

And exposing her weapon skills would now alert the conspirators that someone might be on to their plans. Time to find out as much as possible. Keeping eyes and ears on the sailors, Jie pressed the tip of the knife into Jiang's ribs. "Tell me, what are you trying to hide here?"

"Silly girl, nothing."

"By now, you've surmised I'm more than a stowaway. Talk." Jie pushed the point through his clothes and ran it over bare flesh.

Jiang yelped. "Okay. I am an inventor." He nodded toward some crates. "I have the prototype for a new repeating crossbow. I didn't want any of my competitors to know."

And Jie's father was a pig. Well, he probably was, but... "Why bother when we have muskets?"

"Muskets have limitations. If it rains. If you need to arc projectiles over your own men."

It was almost believable. Might as well play along; make them think this was all about industrial sabotage. "Then the rumors are true. Open one up and show me."

Jiang nodded toward Scarface. "Go show her one."

Holding his injured wrist, Snaggletooth jerked his head back and forth. "No, that bitch is going to pay!"

"What's going on here?" a voice called from above.

Jie dared a glance. A burly longshoreman stood at the hatch's opening, hands on his hips.

"Nothing," Jiang said. "We will load up soon."

"No!" Scarface leaned into the column of light from above. "We have an intruder!"

Apparently, the two men's agendas had just reached an impasse, and soon her escape route would be compromised. Stowing her knife, she took one step back and leapt toward Jiang. Pop-vaulting off his back, she snared one of the ropes and climbed hand over hand to the tween deck.

The longshoreman's eyes widened.

Jie flashed a grin and bolted through the other workers toward the steps to the upper deck.

"Stop her!" the longshoreman yelled.

One man spun around, too late, and Jie avoided his grasp. Yet two more now blocked her exit. Four came clopping down the steps, broadswords in hand. No easy way out.

Unless… The oar ports provided several not-so-easy way outs. Even if she could squeeze through, it was a long drop into cold water. The winches groaned behind her, likely meaning Jiang, Snaggletooth, and Stubby Fingers were on their way. Right; freezing sounded more appealing than being gang-raped and murdered. She took a sharp turn toward the closest row of benches and then dove toward the oar port.

For once, her flat boy's body proved useful, as she swished through—only to have the hem of her pants catch on the oarlock. She dangled upside down, the drawstring of her pants biting into her waist and hips. Perhaps it was for better, given the narrow rocking space between the hull and the stone dock. The wrong timing would mean being crushed like a cherry. As the gap started to widen, she took a deep breath, drew her knife, and slashed the drawstring.

Into the water she went, wearing nothing more than undergarments. The frigid water sent a chill to her core, almost stopping her heart. Still, she dove deeper, kicking off the dockside and swimming underwater over toward the next berth. The ship's crew would be scouring the waterfront for her, and the longer she remained beneath the waves, the more she could confuse them.

Her lungs burned as she swam near the murky harbor floor. At last, she came to stone steps leading up to the top of a dock. Surfacing, she poked her head out and gasped for air.

She hazarded a glance back in the direction she'd come, ready to submerge again. Sure enough, two berths down, the *Wild Orchid* was at full alert, with sailors running along its dock. It was time to lay low, lest the information about Wailian's illegal firepowder die with her.

She looked at the ship docked here, its dark shadow swallowing up the sun's warmth. The Tarkothi blackship. On deck, a fair-haired man with fine features eyed her.

Her chattering teeth rattled her brain. The foreigners may or may not turn her in, but staying in the water meant death by hypothermia. Waving both arms, she floundered.

CHAPTER 9
Honor in Question

Metal tinkled and chimed as Kaiya's head bobbled in the darkness. Cold seeped into her back, yet warmth cradled her head. The uncomfortable twisting in her stomach seemed to climb higher, almost into her chest. The black in her field of vision faded to a dark orange.

Heat surged through her. Her eyes fluttered open. Above her, the blurry coffered tile ceiling came into focus as she blinked.

Luminous blue irises encroached into her field of vision. Prince Hardeep's tight lips softened into a smile, the air gushing out in a long sigh. "Thank the gods."

The warmth around her head…the way his face hovered above hers…she must be lying in his lap. Her belly twisted into tangles worse than her hair on a bad morning.

Heavens, how embarrassing. And if someone saw them like this, Prince Hardeep might be executed on the spot. She brought her elbows up under her, trying to sit up.

"Slowly now." He placed a hot hand on her forehead.

She looked around. Still in the main chamber of the concert hall. Alone. With him. Her heart fluttered. "What happened?"

"You fainted."

Heat flared in her cheeks. Her body *would* choose such an inopportune moment to faint for the first time ever. How mortifying. "For how long?"

"Only a minute."

Thank the Heavens, there—

He pointed to Yanyan's pipa, lying on the marble floor just out of arm's reach.

"Oh no." Kaiya covered her gaping mouth. She'd dropped it. Dropped a priceless antique, a treasure of her people. She scuttled across the floor and picked it up. Fingers trembling, she ran her hand across the smooth surface of the back. Thank the Heavens, it seemed undamaged.

Hardeep shuffled over on his knees and eased it from her stiff fingers. "Don't worry. The legends claim it survived mighty Avarax's wrath. I doubt such a short drop would do anything to it."

Hopefully. Then again, she should've never touched it in the first place. Never been in this room in the first place. Never been alone with a man, a foreign man.

If anyone found out, Father might marry her off to the most domineering lout of a lord in the realm, one who would make General Lu seem chivalric. No telling what he'd do to Hardeep. Perspiration threatened to seep through the make-up on her forehead.

Setting the pipa on the chair, he clasped her hand. "It's fine. Trust me." His other hand reached behind her neck, and he leaned in.

Heat surged through her. Heavens, he was close. And it felt so right. His eyes were so kind. And he knew music. Of course he was right. The pipa was fine, and as long as nobody walked in—

"Unhand the princess!" Chen Xin shouted from the door.

Heavens, no! The compromising position would give rise to rumors faster than weeds sprouting after a spring rain. Kaiya glanced over Hardeep's shoulder.

Outside the door, the Appointments Ministry secretary looked as if he would faint. Chen Xin and Zhao Yue pushed past him and charged in, blue robes swishing and curved *dao* swords rasping from their scabbards in deadly arcs. The dragons etched into their burnished breastplates appeared to move with a life of their own—their magic, imbued by master craftsmen, would strike poor Prince Hardeep with shock and awe. Even if he had a weapon, he wouldn't stand a chance against that magic, let alone against two of the best swordsmen in the realm.

She had to save him. Pulling his hands for leverage, she staggered to her feet and moved to interpose herself between the deadly blades and her prince.

He resisted her pull. His single footstep blocked her path and spun her around. So clumsy on his part; the guards would certainly slay him on the spot. With her feet crossed and legs still wobbly, it took all her balance to keep from falling.

The imperial guards closed the gap in the blink of an eye, weapons flashing in a synchronous dance of death. Hardeep released her hand and leaped forward into the storm of blades. Kaiya could only stare in horror.

Or amazement.

If he were a poet, his graceful movement would have been his poetry. He dodged Chen Xin's thrust and ducked Zhao Yue's hack, twirling and spinning like a ribbon dancer. In a split second, he had positioned himself so that Chen Xin stood between him and Zhao Yue.

At that moment, he turned his head and winked at her. His blue eyes glittered. Could he be possibly enjoying himself? When one misstep would mean decapitation? Her chest constricted, seizing her breath.

Chen Xin attacked with a horizontal slash, shredding through Hardeep's sleeve and cutting across his arm. No! Kaiya covered her mouth. Chen Xin followed with a downward chop, but Hardeep stepped inside and caught Chen Xin's hands. With a deft twist, he wrenched the *dao* away. Undaunted, Chen Xin drew a dagger while Zhao Yue slipped between them.

"Stop!" Kaiya shook off the dread fascination. If she didn't do something, someone would get seriously hurt. And unbelievably, from the look of it, it wouldn't be Prince Hardeep.

He had taken on not one, but two imperial guards and suffered only a cut. His shorn sleeve didn't even show sign of blood. She spoke again, invoking a tone of authority practiced since childhood. "Chen Xin, Zhao Yue, disengage. That is my command."

Zhao Yue held his sword in a defensive position as he took two steps back.

Lowering his dagger, Chen Xin cast a sidelong glance at her. "*Dian-xia*, are you all right? This man did not try anything inappropriate?"

Heat rose to Kaiya's cheeks. They had done many inappropriate things that afternoon, though probably not along the lines of Chen Xin's question. She shook her head. "No, Prince Hardeep has been a perfect gentleman. He just asked me to play a piece of music for him." Straightening her carriage, she strode over to the prince and held up his wounded arm. "Are you all right?"

Lines formed across his forehead as he looked first at it, then at her. "Yes. It looks like my shirt is the only casualty."

Kaiya parted the tear. No blood at all on the smooth skin over his toned muscle. She dropped his arm and covered her gawp with a hand. "How?"

Prince Hardeep smiled at her, sending her stomach into somersaults, then turned to her guards. With a bow of his head, he presented Chen Xin's *dao* in two hands.

Lips pursed, Chen Xin retrieved his weapon, his eyes locked on the alterations he'd made to Hardeep's sleeve. He sank to his knee and bowed his head. "*Dian-xia*, we have failed you. If it is your command, we will take our lives."

Zhao Yue followed suit, raising his sword above his head.

Such resolve and undeserved dedication! Kaiya shook her head. "This is just a misunderstanding. Wait at the door."

Bowing their heads, they said in unison, "As the princess commands."

Legs shaking, Kaiya scooped up the pipa and traipsed across the floor with Hardeep just a step behind. Hopefully, the guards would not object to her being alone in the storage room with him.

She returned the pipa to its honored place and turned to face him. "I have watched the imperial guards spar, and never before has anyone else come close to defeating even one of them. You fight faster than anyone I have ever seen. How did you do that?"

"Princess Kaiya, your imperial guards might be the most skilled swordsmen in Cathay, but—" He stared out the door into space "—there is a whole world beyond your Great Wall. Wonders beyond your imagination."

And the promise of a world beyond marriage to a suitable lord.

And such an elusive answer. "Are you saying there are others who can fight like you?"

"I am embarrassed to say…" He shifted his gaze to the floor.

"Please."

Eyes still cast downward, he sucked in a voluminous breath. "Well… I started training as a Paladin."

Prince Hardeep was full of surprises. Kaiya fought to keep her jaw from freefalling to the ground. The Order of Paladins, defenders of the Ayuri South, sought out children who showed potential to manifest magic through their fighting arts. Their martial skill bordered on legendary, but to hear about it secondhand paled compared to witnessing it just now. It was like living in the song which recounted the First Paladin, Vanya, dueling with the Orc King.

And supposedly, Paladins could plant suggestions into people's minds. Had he done that to her guards?

Had he done that to her?

Maybe all these feelings were the result of his powers. A pit threatened to form in her gut. No, he had only… "Started?"

He sighed. "Yes. Unfortunately, Madura's aggression cut my studies short. I had to return to Ankira, to lead the defense of my homeland." His eyes searched hers. "I failed Ankira then, just like now, when I could not convince your people to end their trade agreement with Madura."

It couldn't end this way. Kaiya shook her head. Such a selfless, noble man couldn't go home unsuccessful. Not if she had means of rectifying Cathay's misdeeds and helping his suffering people It seemed all the more possible now that she had tapped into the magic of music.

Her hand strayed to Tian's pebble. If a Dragon Song was the only way to convince Father and the lords to do the right thing, so be it. "I will do my best to help you. I will practice more."

A sad smile formed on his face. He pressed his palms together and bowed. "I thank you. Ankira thanks you." He raised his head and his expression brightened. "I have an idea, one that your father might approve of. I want to show you something."

"What?" Kaiya squeezed her sweaty palms together.

"The fabled Dragon Scale Lute. It can supposedly rout an army."

She gasped. A handful of musical instruments appeared in ancient tales, and Yanyan's pipa was the only one known to have survived. She'd never even heard of the Dragon Scale Lute. "How did you—"

"Can you meet me outside the palace tonight? At the first waxing gibbous."

Her heart lurched. She would need a good excuse to convince the Minister of Household Affairs to let her leave at night. Especially with the reception, and the announcement of her betrothal. And once the scholars, steward, secretary, or imperial guards reported her day's highly irregular activities, perhaps General Lu would reject her. Not a bad prospect in itself, but then she might not be let out of the palace until her hair faded to grey.

With a grin, he brought his fingers to her chin and closed her gaping mouth. "Young Lord Peng has Ankira's best interests at heart. I will ask him to arrange something."

She could only nod in a slow bob of her head. Cousin Kai-Long might be Father's favorite nephew, but even he couldn't convince the *Tianzi* to leave her unpunished...let alone to allow her out of the palace to meet a man. A foreign man. Not with her virtue at stake before an important marriage.

He pointed to the book, forgotten near the chair back in the room. "Please keep practicing your music. I hope to hear you again. Maybe as soon as tonight."

Back in the main hall, several booted feet clickety-clacked across the marble floors in rhythmic clops. Kaiya peeked out from behind the corner. At the entrance, the steward, secretary, and her own imperial guards bowed as two dozen imperial guards marched past them in formation.

The Minister of Appointments himself shuffled at their head. A small man in both stature and attitude, Minister Hu was arrogant if nothing else. If his smirk was any indication, the consequences of the day's adventures would not be pleasant. Her stomach churned.

A warm hand grasped her shoulder and pulled her around. Prince Hardeep grinned. "Wait here while I talk to them."

She shook her head. They might not care what a sixteen-year-old girl, princess or not, would say, but she could influence them far better than a foreigner could.

The minister pushed past and walked into the hall. He jabbed a finger at the prince. "There he is!"

The imperial guards surged past the minster and surrounded him.

Prince Hardeep held his hands up, still smiling. "This is my fault. I took advantage of your princess' naïveté."

Naïveté! Kaiya's stomach twisted into a knot. Had all his charm just been an act?

He turned back and winked at her, sending her pulse into a flutter.

Then, the imperial guards grabbed him and thrust him to the ground. If they suspected he'd done anything inappropriate, they'd take his head.

CHAPTER 10:

Nerves taut, Tian rose from his desk, a blank scroll in hand. The Iridescent Moon had just waxed to its second crescent, and Jie would've usually rapped a code on the window frame of the harbormaster's office to let him know she was all right.

"I am delivering these transfer documents to the river wharf overseer's office." He held up the scroll. Dismissed with a wave of his supervisor's hand, he hurried out into the early afternoon sun.

A quick check of the lamp sconce revealed Jie had yet to retrieve his letter for her. He scanned the docks.

In the near distance, the two-masted *White Crane* had come into port since he'd last checked, looking tiny against the enormous Tarkothi blackship. The *Wild Orchid*, where he'd sent Jie this morning, bobbed not far beyond it.

There was no sign of her. Not that he'd expected to find any: she'd be hard to pick out from the milling bodies up close. From this far away, it would be impossible.

Beckoning to a group of urchins, he formed circles with his index fingers and thumbs and put it over his eyes. "Have you seen my friend with large eyes and light skin, very skinny, this tall?" He held his hand at shoulder height, then adjusted it downward to her exact height.

They chattered among themselves, and heads shook.

"What do you need him for?"

"I can do whatever he can. Hire me!"

"Never mind." Tian slipped through the reaching hands, protecting his purse as he went. The children only followed him a short distance before giving up and looking for other opportunities.

He worked his way along the harborfront road toward the *Wild Orchid*, searching among the sailors, dockworkers, and merchants. Across from the ships were offices, warehouses, banks, and bars.

And on a block deeper in, the brothels. Scantily clad women beckoning sailors were like breadcrumbs leading to a street lined by red lanterns.

With no trace of Jie, he swallowed hard, squared his shoulders, and headed to the Celebrate Spring Pavilion. Boisterous laughing and giggles spilled out of its doors.

"Your Lordship." Flashing a shapely leg from where she perched against the wall, Lilac ran a finger down his official silk robes as he passed. "You've come to the perfect place for your afternoon break."

Jasmine squeezed her breasts between her arms as she blinked.

"No, thank you." Tian bobbed his head and entered. Though Lilac and Jasmine didn't remember him, he'd helped teach them Black Lotus ways.

Not well enough, considering they'd failed to attain a minimum proficiency in stealth and fighting to become a full-fledged Black Fist.

Cousins, they were called, serving as eyes and ears of the clan without even knowing it. In all, thousands of men and women raised in the temples, now working as bankers, bakers, bodyguards, scribes, tanners...

And here, like in every major city, as prostitutes. Master Yan had used the *Tiger's Eye* technique to make Cousins forget they'd ever trained in the temple's secret grounds. It didn't erase what skills they'd developed, and that had no doubt protected these girls from abusive clients.

Still, if Tian had worked harder, maybe he could've spared them this life.

Guilt twisted in his gut, even as a mix of perfume and sweat assaulted his nose. If it had been loud from the outside, it didn't compare to the noise indoors. His eyes took a moment to adjust from the bright sunlight. Lanterns hanging from the mezzanine cast the common room in a red hue.

While certainly not on the same level as even a middle-tier House in the capital's Floating World, Celebrate Spring Pavilion catered to the wealthy.

Women in revealing gowns sat in the laps of merchants, laughed on the arms of ship captains, or played musical instruments—though none could compare to Princess Kaiya's talent, of course.

In a private corner, the Madame disentangled herself from the arm of a minor lord. Gaze locking with Tian, she sashayed over, one leg crossing over the other, lace undergarments peeking through the high slits in her blue silk gown with each step.

Unlike the other ladies here, Little Wen was a full-fledged Black Fist. She'd grown up with Jie in the clan, and the two of them, along with a third best friend—whom Tian had never met, and whose name inexplicably escaped him—had entered the Floating World to spy on the aristocracy. While Jie had returned to the temple to help train Tian and the others, Wen had become the most celebrated courtesan in the most famous House.

"Scribe Zheng," she said, voice so sultry, all conversation ceased, leaving only the background music. "I didn't expect you today."

The weight of a dozen envious eyes fell on Tian, and his insides squirmed. He bowed his head. "Miss Wen."

Her fingers slipped into his hand, and she guided him up the steps.

He swallowed hard. The girls and regulars assumed he was one of Little Wen's patrons; and since six months of a government scribe's salary could never afford even a single night with her, rumor had it he accepted bribes.

Even after three thousand, one hundred and forty-seven days having practicality driven into him by the clan, his upbringing as a great lord's son bristled at the idea of corruption.

Little Wen tapped out clan code in his palm. *I have something for you.*

What? He brushed his fingertip over the side of her hand.

Your favorite. She beamed at him.

Wouldn't she just hurry up and reveal it? His lips tightened. *What?*

Evidence. I was going to send Little Ju to deliver it to you, but here you are now. Not like you to break routines.

He frowned. *I sent Jie to investigate a ship, and now she's missing.*

It's Jie. She's fine. Wen continued up the steps. *She would've checked in.*

Wen froze for a fraction of a second before winding around the landing toward the third floor. *There was a commotion at the docks a couple of hours ago regarding a half-elf.*

Jie? Of course it was—

Who else? She pulled him into her room and closed the door. "There aren't any other half-elves in the world, let alone Jiangkou."

Tian bowed his head and set his fist into his palm. "Older Sister."

As she returned the salute, he took a quick glance around the spacious room, and found nothing different in the way she laid out cosmetics on her rosewood makeup table. The ornately carved bed had not been used today, if the smooth sheets were any indication, and there was no indentations to mark male footsteps across the thick Ayuri carpet.

If anything was out of place, it was the shift in angle of an erotic brush painting hanging on the wall. Rendered by a Dragon Artist—like Lamp Man's letter— it would lower the inhibitions of an unsuspecting viewer.

From the size of the room to the furnishings and art, it was a downgrade from Wen's extravagant lifestyle in the Floating World. The cover story was that she'd used her significant earnings to buy the Celebrate Spring Pavilion. In reality, the clan had sent her here to investigate new threats to the realm. While Tian pored over manifests, Wen had ways of getting merchants to brag about what they smuggled in, and captains to reveal irregularities with cargo.

"You'd asked me to keep track of the *Steadfast Mariner*, *Wild Orchid, King of the Sea,* and *Sea Saint's Wrath.* We lured the *Wild Orchid's* captain in this morning." Her movement shifted from sensual to feline stealth as she padded to her bedside table and opened its drawer. She drew out a folded sheet of rice paper and offered it. "I was able to remove this from him."

He took the paper, unfolded it, and scanned.

Apparently, Victorious Trading Company had paid the captain a thousand *yuan* to dump five hundred bales of rice outside a cove not far from here, as the tide was coming in.

Why would they do that? He'd seen the documentation submitted to the harbormaster's office this morning, reporting the loss; the official papers would allow Victorious Trading to make a claim to its insurer and recoup half the value of the rice. Subtracting the thousand yuan they'd paid to the Wild Orchid, they'd lose three thousand, one-hundred and sixty-two yuan at this week's market value.

He sucked in a sharp breath. "Did you read this?"

She nodded. "Are you thinking what I'm thinking?"

Was she? Their minds worked in very different ways, but Wen was smart and insightful. "Tell me."

She beamed. "News of the loss will be reported to the futures traders. It's not a lot of rice to the overall market, but it could influence the price enough for Victorious Trading to turn a small profit once they retrieved their lost bales."

"I was thinking along those lines at first." He shook his head. "But now, I'm wondering: what if they were trying to move supplies? Without the government knowing? What if it wasn't rice at all?"

Understanding bloomed on her face. "I'll send word to Old Chong to investigate the cove."

Just what Tian would've done. "In the meantime, I'm worried Jie got caught."

Wen smirked. "Jie, get caught?"

It wasn't likely. But… "Then where would she be? Could she have fallen into the harbor? She's not a good swimmer."

"Don't worry, she's probably following a lead, and couldn't check in."

Despite her attempt at reassurance, Wen still sounded concerned.

CHAPTER 11
Interventions

Kaiya's silk shoes scuffed on the Hall of Pure Melody's marble steps as she hurried down. The imperial guards' and Household Ministry secretary's robes swished behind her. In the vast central plaza formed by the Hall of Supreme Harmony, the imperial archives, and the Hall of Pure Melody, a contingent of imperial guards surrounded Prince Hardeep.

All weapons remained sheathed, thank the Heavens. The prince might have survived two of the realm's best swordsmen with only a shorn sleeve, but two dozen was another matter. For now, his hands rested on his head in surrender.

Her insides squeezed like a grape in an Arkothi wine press. All her fault. She should've never taken him into the music hall or archives, or at least gone through the proper channels. Really, she should've just seen him off and then gone to meet General Lu, but Prince Hardeep was so, so…confusing.

General Lu was still waiting now, probably wondering if the orc gods would return to Tivara on their flaming chariots before she deigned to greet him. If it were up to her...

Appointments Minister Hu furiously scribbled on a scroll. When he looked up, he spoke in Cathayi. "Prince Hardeep, the *Tianzi* generously allowed you to visit the castle and even dispatched a member of his family to meet with you. You repay his magnanimity by kidnapping his young daughter and spiriting her from building to building."

Kidnapping! How did he come to that conclusion? Kaiya's heart pounded. Expulsion from the palace, perhaps deportation might be more appropriate for what actually happened, but the minister's charges warranted a slow death. Just what had all the scholars and other officials said?

The minister scrutinized her and her entourage before settling on the Household Ministry secretary. "And, Secretary Hong overheard you. You wanted the princess to meet you outside the palace? What did you plan to do? Defile her? Use her as a hostage to secure Cathay's support against Madura?"

Hardeep only smiled. He probably didn't understand the local tongue, let alone the serious accusations and grave consequences. He turned and winked at her again.

Her chest tightened. This ill-advised escapade would never have happened if she hadn't allowed it. She was just as much at fault as he, perhaps even more so for her lack of judgment. Kaiya pushed through the imperial guards, who stepped to the side and dropped to a knee, fist to the ground, as she passed.

"Minister," she said.

He bowed at the waist. "*Dian-xia*. I am glad to see you unharmed. Please tell us what else this rogue did."

She scowled at the minister. "Prince Hardeep did nothing wrong. *I* chose to take him to the imperial archives and Hall of Pure Melody."

The minister sidled in and whispered, "*Dian-xia*, you do not understand. If rumor gets out that you were with the prince alone, it will besmirch your honor and affect your marriage prospects."

"If only it were so easy." Heavens, did she just think that, or say it aloud? Face flushing, she swept her gaze around all the assembled men, making sure all witnesses to her misadventures were now there: the imperial guards, Secretary Hong, Minister Hu, the scholars, and the steward. She raised her voice so all could hear. "Prince Hardeep only wished to save his homeland. I wanted to help him. He did nothing wrong. Any breeches of protocol were *my* choice."

"If I may, *Dian-xia*," called a male voice from beyond the cordon of men. The guards stepped aside to reveal Cousin Kai-Long. He folded a piece of paper as he approached.

Kaiya blew out a breath. If he and Prince Hardeep were good friends, he would surely use his considerable influence to prevent any possible misunderstanding. Kai-Long might only be a second son with little hope of inheriting his father's title of *Tai-Ming* provincial ruler, but all knew the *Tianzi* treated him like his own son.

Minister Hu bowed low, though not as low as he had to her. "Young Lord Peng Kai-Long, this matter does not concern you."

"But it does," Cousin Kai-Long said with an amiable smile. "I am ultimately responsible for Prince Hardeep's presence. It was I who brought him to Huajing, housed him in my family villa, and arranged for his visit to the castle. I even suggested to the *Tianzi* that Princess Kaiya meet him, as a test of her budding diplomatic skills."

Kaiya gaped at him. It had seemed strange that she was the one to greet the Ankirans, and now it was clear. Still, he deflected blame from both her and the prince.

The minister's slit eyes fell first on Hardeep, then on Cousin Kai-Long, and finally on her. "The evidence—"

"Wait." Prince Hardeep stomped a foot on the pavestones as he raised a hand.

Something fluttered in her belly. All heads turned to him. He rotated in a full circle as he spoke, his voice calm. "This is all a misunderstanding. I certainly did not do anything inappropriate with the princess. This is really just a trivial matter."

And he was right. So what if they had visited the archives and music hall? They hadn't damaged anything. Kaiya looked at the men, many who likely didn't speak

109

Ayuri. They might not be convinced, but Minister Hu's expression softened.

He must have realized that with Cousin Kai-Long and her both vouching for the prince, very little would come of it. With a sigh, he said, "Young Lord Peng, I place Prince Hardeep in your care. Please see him out of the palace."

That was it? If Kaiya's mouth could hang any lower, her chin would touch the ground. Surely, somebody would be punished somehow. But Prince Hardeep allowed to just leave? A great resolution, for sure, but a complete surprise.

Something felt off. A resonance hung in the air, an echo from when Hardeep had stomped on the pavestones. Paladins could supposedly persuade others with their righteous magic.

Was Hardeep more than a trainee? It might explain how he'd calmed all those aggressive guards and unreasonable ministers. She, herself, had gone from worried to relaxed.

Her jaw tightened as the guards dispersed. Maybe he'd used magic on her. And not only then, but from the time they'd first met. Had he influenced her decisions?

No, he hadn't finished his Paladin training. He'd asked her to consider the plight of his people, but had not ordered her to do anything. The decision to help the Ankirans was her own. If anything, he'd shown that her unspoken, impossible dreams of rediscovering Dragon Songs were within reach.

"Follow me, Your Excellency." Ayuri rolled off Kai-Long's tongue.

Prince Hardeep flashed a smile at her.

Her heart sank into her stomach. She bowed her head a fraction, as protocol demanded. Maybe the resolution wasn't so great, after all. After the day's debacle, she wouldn't be allowed to see him ever again. Ankira would fall without her ever having a chance to help it. She was nothing more than a plain, gangly girl, to be strategically married off. Never allowed to explore the power of Dragon Songs, even after her breakthrough.

She studied his back, hair, and gait as he and Kai-Long started toward the main gates. Her last memory of him.

Then he turned his head, his luminescent blue eyes fixed her. Her pulse pounded again, just like when she first met him.

Tonight, he mouthed. *At the first waxing gibbous.*
Tonight?

Secretary Hong, that was his name, cleared his throat. "*Dian-xia*, General Lu is waiting."

Kaiya looked back at Hardeep's diminishing form. Tonight... There would be no tonight, at least not with him. He wouldn't be let back in the palace, and there was no way for her to get out. Even if she could grow in her knowledge of Dragon Songs, Father would never let her go to Ankira. Not to mention, there was her own country's stability to consider.

Whatever Hardeep had done to addle her good judgment...well, it had been a fleeting diversion. A three-hour diversion, gauging from the Iridescent Moon's waning toward new. Her future husband, Cathay's savior, waited.

Her lip jutted out, unbidden. If only it could be Hardeep.

CHAPTER 12
Murder Gap

Hiking her gown up and holding her hair in place, Kaiya strode back toward the inner castle. Secretary Hong and her two guards rushed to keep up with her. The faster she could put distance between herself and Hardeep, the sooner she could forget him and accept her fate.

If only it were so simple.

Though abated, the squirming sensation in her belly was a constant reminder of the power and bliss she'd felt while playing Yanyan's pipa. With each step away from Hardeep, the chasm widened between her and *possibility*.

The possibility of being more than just a skinny, pimply political tool. Of being something special. She blinked and found herself at the inner moat. Behind her, Secretary Hong hunched over, hands on his knees, panting. Unlike him, her imperial guards Chen Xin and Zhao Yue managed to maintain a dignified demeanor and appearance.

In the middle of the arching stone bridge, she stopped and found her reflection in the dark water. Heavens, her hair appeared as if a family of songbirds had nested there, and perhaps rearranged her clips and pins as well. The gown, originally folded at an exact angle, now hung awkwardly over her shoulder. She must have looked ridiculous to Hardeep, who inexplicably thought there was even a remote chance she could escape the palace tonight.

"Hurry, Kaiya." With the slightest hint of a frown, Sister-In-Law Xiulan beckoned from the other side of the bridge. "General Lu has been waiting."

Kaiya's paternal cousin Wang Kai-Hua nodded from where she stood beside Xiulan. Several handmaidens bowed in a flash of colorful robes. One of them, Han Meiling, gawked, with wide eyes focused on Kaiya's head.

Kaiya's hand shot up to her disheveled hair. With a sigh, she descended the bridge. Her imperial guards stopped and dropped to a knee, fist to the ground.

"*Dian-xia*, you cannot meet General Lu looking like this." Meiling shuffled over and adjusted Kaiya's hair.

With a deft hand, Xiulan rewrapped Kaiya's sash. "You look like you wrestled a dragon."

"I hope you won." Kai-Hua tugged on Kaiya's sleeves. Though only a year older, she had already flowered with Heaven's Dew and filled out. She now glowed with radiance since her own betrothal to Liu Dezhen, heir to Jiangzhou Province.

Kaiya clenched her clammy hands. Neither Kai-Hua nor Xiulan were malicious, yet neither understood the stress of being sixteen and not yet flowered into womanhood, nor her lack of interest in marriage.

Xiulan stepped back. "General Lu has been waiting anxiously to hear you sing."

Given the general's reputation, he probably cared more about the sound of his own voice. At least today she had been able to sing for someone who *did* care.

"You are so fortunate," Kai-Hua said. "General Lu would make a wonderful husband. So dashing and handsome! With his experience and intelligence, he might rise to head of the Ministry of War."

A path to glory blazed with the dying heart of an imperial princess. Kaiya suppressed a snort. "I am not ready to marry."

Both Xiulan and Kai-Hua stared at her with round eyes. Xiulan said, "You will have to, sooner than later."

Kai-Hua nodded. "Yes, all the girls we grew up with are reaching that age. You know what they say: a woman unwed by sixteen is like a New Year's feast on the third day of the year."

As if a woman were meant to be devoured. Kaiya shuddered. In any case, being all skin and bones, she was more like a nun's rice porridge and tofu than a New Year's feast.

Leaning in, Xiulan said, "I met Kai-Wu's betrothed, Wu Yanli. She is quite...strict and reserved."

Kaiya cocked her head. That didn't seem to fit all the rumors. Second Brother's upcoming wedding hadn't been arranged, at least not in the formal sense. It had been a supposedly chance meeting, followed by a torrid love affair. The handmaidens whispered that the second prince had already partaken of *that* New Year's Feast.

And yet, in affairs of the heart, the *Tianzi* wouldn't extend any leeway to his only daughter. Kaiya stifled a sigh. Prince Hardeep, learning the magic of Dragon Songs: they might as well have been a storyteller's fanciful tale.

"Come along," Xiulan said. "You have made General Lu wait long enough."

Kaiya lifted her chin and squared her shoulders, only for her posture to slump. All the energy she'd put into projecting an imperial image this morning now flagged. Instability in the North had turned a match she'd planned to reject into a *fait accompli*.

What she really wanted, Hardeep—no, reviving Dragon Songs—now lay beyond reach. Each step through the inner castle grounds felt like slogging through knee-high mud toward a funeral.

So unlike Kai-Hua, whose graceful stride might have been skipping for all the effervescence she exuded. So different from Xiulan, the personification of dignity and elegance. Even the handmaidens would make better princesses.

A hand grasped her sleeve, pulling her to a stop. Xiulan nodded toward a gatehouse at the side. "General Lu is in Murder Gap."

How appropriate. A hypothetical invader would believe this the most direct route to the inner castle's gates, only to find themselves trapped in a dead-end

116

courtyard surrounded by high walls. Now, it would be the site of her own proverbial death. But, "Why is General Lu here? I thought we were to meet in the *Danhua* Garden."

Xiulan covered a giggle. "While you were gallivanting about the palace, he took to wandering the castle grounds."

With all her willpower, Kaiya straightened her carriage. She strode through the gatehouse and then down the wide alley. At the hairpin turn, she paused and peeked into the courtyard.

A handsome man in formal court robes sat on a porcelain garden stool next to a bloodwood table. He appeared older than Hardeep, maybe in his early thirties. Long, glossy black hair framed an oval face with the chiseled jaw and high nose of North Cathay. He reached for a teacup on the table, the very motion refined, almost effeminate. An unarmed soldier standing a respectful distance behind him wore blue robes, marking him as an officer in the imperial army.

Xiulan gave Kaiya a firm prod. With no time to prepare herself, she stumbled into the courtyard.

The officer knelt, fist to the ground. General Lu barely rose before sinking to his knee. "*Dian-xia*, thank you for honoring me." His voice echoed off the high courtyard walls.

"Rise," Xiulan said, her voice resonating.

He stood…and barely met Kaiya's eye level.

So short! She bowed her head. "I am sorry to have kept you waiting." Her own words resounded off the walls.

When his mouth opened, he spoke in a high pitch reminiscent of bird chirps. "Your grace and beauty made the wait worthwhile." His contrived smile and rote intonation suggested otherwise. If his insincerity didn't give her a headache, the persistent echo would. He motioned to the garden stool across from him, inviting her to sit.

With as much grace as she could muster under the circumstances, Kaiya shuffled over and settled on the edge of the stool. General Lu sat across from her, and Xiulan and Kai-Hua sat to the side. The handmaidens and imperial guards deployed in positions around them.

Meiling took up the kettle and poured tea.

"Thank you, General," Xiulan said, "for leaving the unsettled North just to meet Princess Kaiya."

He chuckled. "We inflicted heavy casualties on the pale-faced barbarians the last time. I do not think they will be returning soon."

"Pale-faced?" Kaiya ventured. "Don't they stay on their own side of the Great Wall?"

The officer harrumphed, but General Lu silenced him with a wave of his hand. "I am posted in Wailian County, outside of the wall."

That wasn't possible. Surely, Father wouldn't approve of establishing colonies in foreign lands. Kaiya turned to Xiulan, who nodded, then back to General Lu. "What can you tell me of Wailian?"

He laughed. "Had I known we would be discussing the North, I would have come better prepared."

"My apologies for Princess Kaiya." Xiulan bowed her head a fraction.

General Lu waved a hand, the same motion he had used to silence his own underling. "No need to apologize. The Five Classics say a ruler should know the land, and I would be happy to explain."

Heat flared in Kaiya's cheeks. Not like she would be anything more than a political tool, let alone a ruler. No doubt he was thinking of himself.

"We annexed Wailian County nearly a year ago," General Lu continued, "when we discovered abundant reserves of an essential firepowder ingredient. We could not let it fall into barbarian hands. Lord Tong has been building a castle overlooking the mines. A ravine surrounds the castle on three sides, and a sheer cliff drops away on the other side. It is impregnable."

Kaiya's head spun. Cathay had invaded a neighbor, just as the Madurans had attacked Prince Hardeep's Ankira. Though, given the circumstances, it seemed this Lord Tong would be a more appropriate husband than General Lu. She bowed her head. "Thank you for your report."

He laughed again, living up to his reputation for arrogance. "Do not worry, *Dian-xia*. With our guns, Wailian is well-defended."

Kaiya's insides twisted. A lifetime with such a conceited little man, in occupied territory, might be worse than death. If only Avarax could swoop in from the Dragonlands and immolate the courtyard now.

"That's enough politics for the day," Xiulan said. "Princess Kaiya wished to sing for you."

Wished, indeed. As if General Lu even cared; he just played along. Kaiya's face must have flushed redder than Yanluo's Star during the Year of the Second Sun, if her hot cheeks were any indication. Yet what choice did she have? She turned to Meiling. "My pipa, please."

Bowing, Meiling presented the instrument in two hands.

"Thank you." Kaiya extended both arms to receive it. How lifeless it felt compared to Yanyan's. She tilted her head toward General Lu. "If I may?"

"Please." He bowed his head, but not before revealing the tight lips and glassy eyes of boredom.

Sadness clamped her chest. He would never appreciate her beyond the prestige of her lineage. She took a deep breath and plucked.

The sound resonated off the high courtyard walls, sending subtle vibrations into her core. Her stomach coiled again, just like it had in the Hall of Pure Melody when she had played for Hardeep. How had she never noticed the sensation before?

Back straight, shoulders level, feet rooted to the ground, just as Prince Hardeep had suggested. Ah, Prince Hardeep. He was handsome and charming, for sure, but pining over him seemed silly. It must have been those beautiful, hypnotic eyes, convincing her of a happier future than the one for which she was destined.

It must have been how the cobra felt when sung to by an Ayuri snake-charmer. How preposterous to consider such an impossibility.

Closing her eyes, Kaiya plucked out more notes. The book from the Hall of Pure Melody suggested that a skilled performer could project the emotion of a song. Yet for all the happiness this piece embodied, only melancholy trudged in the verses she played. *Align your spine,* the book implored. *Let your heart impel your voice.* Kaiya adjusted her posture, and the vibrations spread throughout her.

There it was, the ocean of power from before, dripping in small drops, the rhythm setting the beat of her music. The song seemed to change of its own accord, and Kaiya's brain somersaulted in her skull. Her vision darkened.

Gasps sheared the air. Robes shuffled. Porcelain shattered on the flagstones.

Lifting her hand from the strings, Kaiya opened her eyes. Though she'd stopped playing, the music trailed off in the echoes.

Tears streaked Xiulan's cheeks, while Kai-Hua and some of the handmaidens freely wept. General Lu…

He gawked at her. With sadness or anger, it was impossible to tell. Bolting up, he spun on his heel and stumbled out of the courtyard. His officer trailed after him, while Chen Xin and Zhao Yue looked on with what could only be described as bewilderment.

A cloaked figure materialized out of nothingness, just on the other side of her guards. The pipa slipped from Kaiya's startled hands and hit the pavestones with a discordant groan. Shaking their heads, Chen Xin and Zhao Yue both swept *dao* swords from their scabbards and backed into a defensive position.

Chen Xin pointed the tip of his weapon at the stranger. "Identify yourself."

The man strode forward. His hands made no move toward the thin longsword hanging at his side.

The guards sprang into action, attacking in a synchronized flash of blades that would have eviscerated even a highly skilled warrior. Yet the intruder blurred through the deadly barrage and arrived on the other side unscathed. Without looking back, he waved a hand at the guards, sending both tumbling to the flagstones.

Interposing herself between Xiulan and the intruder, Kaiya fumbled for the curved dagger tucked in her sash. Not that she stood a chance against someone who could effortlessly defeat two of the realm's best swordsmen. Her chest squeezed around her pounding heart.

CHAPTER 13
Ships and Sailors

Cathay's magnificent sailing ships might have been dinghies compared to the enormous Tarkothi ship Jie found herself on. She huddled under the rough-spun blankets, shivering after her inadvertent swim in Jiangkou's frigid harbor. Even the midday sun on the black wood deck couldn't provide enough heat. No telling how hard Tian would be laughing if he could see her quivering like a maiden on her wedding night.

The only ones looking at her now were the curious faces of light-skinned sailors, likely Arkothi and Estomari from Tivaralan's east. Unlike the local sailors, these smelled like onions.

Some had a darker complexion than the majority, with shorter heights and slimmer builds. Eldaeri humans, the first she'd ever seen. They had traces of elf blood coursing through their veins from millennia before, and perhaps that's why they'd helped her.

Even now, her pointed ears picked up the commotion along the docks. Fat Nose Jiang's henchmen were searching for her, unless the chorus of shouts about a half-naked half-elf girl referred to someone else. Sure, she was safe from them, but minutes slipped by without the clan knowing about the illegal firepowder production and shipments.

A fair-haired man strode over. His broad shoulders and robust frame nearly split the seams of his green uniform coat. She might have been a bug, the way he scowled at her with those snake eyes. With a sneer, he knelt down and thrust forth a mug of a steaming, aromatic tea, which looked and smelled nothing like tea.

"Thank you," Jie said in her best Arkothi. She jutted a hand from underneath the blanket and took it. The cup felt warm, yet did little to chase away the chill from her bones. She took a sip, and nearly spit it out.

Snake Eyes chortled. "First time drinking coffee? You Cathayi don't know what you're missing." He leaned forward, his face taking in her features. "But you're not all Cathayi. A curious girl, really. I would wager you are the reason for all the excitement down there?"

Apparently, no one onboard could speak the Cathayi language, or perhaps they were testing her. She tightened the blanket around her. Sometimes, half-truths worked better than outright lies. "I was hired to clean up their ship, but then the sailors tried to...tried to..." Blinking away crocodile tears, she cast her eyes at the ground, but peeked up through her lashes to see if her best rendition of a traumatized girl had worked.

"A ship is no place for a girl, save for the Pirate Queen herself," a male voice said, the perfect Arkothi enunciated with a tone that bordered on singing.

Jie turned to find the speaker. A slim man with large dark eyes and a high-bridged nose approached, with a marine to either side. Unlike the others, he smelled of musk. The high collar of his own green coat was embroidered in gold. A captain, perhaps, from the way the men bowed, though no sailor spoke so properly. Not only that, a gold circlet adorned his dark hair.

She bowed her head. "An orphan takes what job she can."

"Ah, poor girl." Kneeling down, he lifted her chin and studied her. "A half-elf. There are so few of you in this world, always the result of sad circumstances."

Sad, for sure, but perhaps not what this man thought. At least, not according to the note pinned to her swaddling blanket when she was left at the gates of the Black Lotus Temple. Still, let him believe what he would, if it would help her cause. She nodded.

"What's your name, girl?"

"Jie."

"Jyeh." The man chewed on the sound. His Arkothi might be impeccable, but apparently, his tongue couldn't process Cathayi. "Well, your Arkothi is not bad. Perhaps I can offer you work during our stay?"

Snake Eyes cleared his throat. "Your Highness, we shouldn't be harboring strangers. For all we know, she's a wanted criminal. Let's hand her over to the men looking for her."

Highness. He must be the prince of Tarkoth, here for the imperial wedding. The prince held up a hand,

125

silencing Snake Eyes. "So what do you say about that job?"

She cocked her head. "What kind of job?"

"I need guidance, and I assume you know the waterfront."

More than he could imagine. She nodded.

"The emperor of Cathay will assign me guides and a translator." He grinned. "Since these officials aren't always reliable, I would prefer to have one of my own. We'll pay you a silver crown a day."

With a furrowed forehead, Jie calculated the exchange rate. A silver *jiao* and two copper *fen*. Tian would have known automatically, probably to a fraction of a *fen*.

The prince's lips curved into a crooked grin. "What? No shouts of joy?"

Jie shook her head. "No, it's just that...well... I need to confer with my friends."

"The same ones who got you a job swabbing the deck of a Cathayi trade ship?" The prince stared at the sky.

Jie cast him a sheepish smile. She had to report to the relay station, but it wouldn't take much to slip away if this new job description interfered with her real work. "You are right. I accept."

Snake Eyes cleared his throat. "Your Highness, we know nothing about her. There are men searching for her."

Jie's breath stilled. She looked from the officer to the leader. As long as they turned her over to the authorities, and not the traitors from the ship...

He laughed. "It's not like she could be a spy. Now, tell the quartermaster to check if we have any dresses in our cargo." He spun on his heel and headed toward the forecastle.

Jie turned to Snake Eyes. "Who was that?"

"Prince Aryn of Tarkoth." The rude officer's incredulous tone almost made her feel stupid.

"Why would a prince come all the way to Cathay?"

Snake Eyes snorted. "He will be attending the wedding of your emperor's second son."

The same reason Master Yan himself was three hours away in the capital. It would also explain why a Tarkothi ship had come all the way to the west coast. Now if only she could get off it and share information about the firepowder with Tian.

CHAPTER 14
Challenges

With the reverberation of the pipa and the clattering of metal on the flagstones still echoing, Kaiya pointed her dagger at the intruder. As if that would deter someone who had just dispatched two imperial guards with even more ease than Prince Hardeep had.

Her pulse pattered like a spring rain on the tiled roofs of Sun-Moon Palace. She swallowed the fear and found her tone of command. "Stand back."

The stranger lowered his dark hood, revealing the pointed ears of an elf. Relief washed over her. Lord Xu, her father's aloof councilor.

Though he shared his rarely seen brethren's slight build and delicate features, he stood as tall as a human did. He let his long golden hair flow freely, caring little about fashion trends that might come and go; he'd undoubtedly seen many in his centuries of life. His violet eyes sparkled with mischief. That, and his youthful appearance belied unknown years of wisdom.

Now, as he scrutinized her, he looked just as startled as everyone else.

Behind her, Xiulan and Kai-Hua blew out long sighs.

Kaiya crossed her arms, frowning. "Lord Xu. You have a flair for the dramatic. Was that necessary?"

The elf didn't bother to bow. Her ancestor had decreed that Lord Xu need pay obeisance to no one, not even the *Tianzi* himself. His surprised expression disappeared. "I need to keep my skills sharp. Little around here is more challenging than approaching a princess protected by imperial guards." He looked back and grinned at Chen Xin and Zhao Yue, who staggered to their feet. "Though I guess they hardly constitute a challenge."

Both soldiers dropped to one knee, head bowed. Chen Xin held his sword up in two hands. "*Dian-xia*, forgive our incompetence. If you command it, we will take our own lives as punishment."

Xiulan waved them off. "There is no shame in being bested by the councilor. As you were." She turned back to the elf. "To what do we owe this unexpected visit, Lord Xu?"

He pointed to the pipa, lying forgotten on the ground. "Twice today, the energy of the world has rippled out from Sun-Moon Palace."

Kaiya searched the elf's unreadable eyes. Twice? The first was with Yanyan's pipa, which meant the second was just now. With General Lu. Perhaps that was why he had left so abruptly. Excitement tingled in every nerve.

His stare fixed on Kaiya. "You have finally made a breakthrough in your music."

Kaiya's eyebrows rose. Finally? And where had he been hiding? "You heard it?"

The elf's gaze bore into her, ripping away any mental armor she might have. "*Felt* it. We taught the Cathayi people to manifest magic through artistic endeavor, but the ability to do so with music—Dragon Songs—was lost. Great masters disappeared one by one, after your great-great-grandfather bade them to play Yanyan's pipa. Yet without a teacher, you have intuitively figured out the basics."

Maybe not so intuitively, but Xu didn't have to know about Hardeep. Heat rose to her cheeks.

He placed a hand over his chest. "You have learned to project emotions through your music, though you require an acoustically ideal location like the Hall of Pure Melody. Or this courtyard. However, before you learn to project energy through music, you should learn to listen. Close your eyes. What do you hear?"

Kaiya exchanged confused glances with Xiulan and Kai-Hua, and then listened. The sounds of spring mixed with the rippling of Sun-Moon Lake in the distance. "Waves, wind, and birds."

Xu snorted. "How about your guards' breaths? The beating of your handmaidens' hearts?"

Kaiya gawked. That was impossible, even for her exceptional hearing. Maybe the elf could, with his big ears, but it was too much to expect from a human.

To a collective gasp, the pipa materialized in his hands, looking none worse for the wear after its fall to the pavestones. He proffered it. "Close your eyes and listen."

She received it in two hands and closed her eyes. As if holding a pipa would make difference... But wait, there was Zhao Yue's inhale, barely a whisper over the other sounds. She straightened her spine. Chen Xin's exhale vibrated in one of the strings. The handmaidens' heartbeats were soft puffs in her ear, yet they, too, resonated almost inaudibly in the pipa strings. She looked up at Xu.

"You understand. You hear. Listening is your greatest asset." Ears twitching, he lifted a finger. "What do you hear now?"

Around her, Xiulan and the handmaidens quieted. Kaiya closed her eyes again. There. In the distance. The twang of a plucked instrument and whine of a bow on strings danced with one another.

She opened her eyes. "A pipa and erhu."

"Follow it to its source."

Xiulan nodded. "You go ahead. Kai-Hua and I will look for General Lu."

Kaiya favored Lord Xu with a tentative smile. Even with permission from Xiulan, it seemed inappropriate to wander the castle grounds with an elf. But why not? She'd done worse this day, and nobody

131

would suspect Lord Xu of having any attraction to humans. General Lu had cut their matchmaking meeting short, leaving plenty of time before tonight's reception, where Father would likely *not* announce her betrothal. It wasn't as if she could get in that much more trouble.

It was worth the risk, for the improbable chance to grow in the power of Dragon Songs. With a bow, Kaiya left the courtyard and ambled through the paved alley until it came to a white rock path. She listened as it wound through a garden in the inner castle. Somewhere beyond the budding plum trees, master musicians sparred in an improvised duel between pipa and the two-stringed erhu.

Her imperial guards marched behind her, crunching the stones beneath their boots, synchronizing with the beat of the song in the background. The handmaidens followed with the shuffle of robes. Though the Spring Festival was just a few days away, winter maintained a tenuous grip on the breeze. She tightened the outer gown around her shoulders.

And discovered Lord Xu had not followed.

Her footsteps fell short at the edge of the *Danhua* Garden. Before her, the mottled trunk of a weeping *Danhua* tree curved upward, its willowy limbs cascading downward in strands of red buds. On the ground at the edge of the canopy, almond shrubs formed a circle, their still-grey buds clinging to bare branches. Inside the circle, two of her music teachers sat with perfect posture, playing ornate instruments.

Master Yong Shu ran his bow across the erhu in furious strokes, the whine of its two strings urgent. Master Ding Meihui plucked at her pipa, calm and resolute, waiting. Middle-aged now, rumor had it the two had been involved in a torrid relationship almost three decades before, culminating in their epic performance before her newly enthroned father.

That was then, and age and cynicism had since set in, evident from their strict lessons. Yet at this moment, their performance captured passion and youth, making them seem fresh and vibrant again. Buzzing like a hummingbird's wings, his notes pranced like a fire blazing, while hers churned like the swell of a tidal wave.

Kaiya's spirit soared and her belly fluttered. This was love, made tangible by sound.

Too soon, the duet ended. Master Yong turned to her and bowed low, and Master Ding followed suit.

Finding her breath, Kaiya returned their salute with a low bow. Princess or not, she might as well have been a beggar before her teachers. She straightened and walked into the ring of shrubs. "I have never heard such a passionate performance."

Master Yong nodded. "We will play tonight at a reception in honor of your brother's wedding."

Right, the reception. The one she would have to escape if she had any chance of leaving the castle and meeting Hardeep. Yet with a new world opened to her ears, and General Lu fleeing their matchmaking appointment, the opportunities seemed boundless. Everything fell into place as if Heaven had willed it.

"What made their song so distinctive?" Lord Xu whispered in her ear.

Kaiya's heart might have jumped into her throat. Where had he come from?

"Well?" Xu raised an eyebrow.

There were too many details to mention! Kaiya could barely contain her smile. "The harmony and balance. Two opposite styles coming together to form a whole."

"Very good," Xu said.

Master Ding clapped her hands. "You will soon outshine us."

"Never." Kaiya bowed her head.

Master Ding laughed. "The greatest honor for a teacher is for the student to surpass her."

Wiping sweat from his brow, Master Yong grunted. "Our piece reflects the interaction between Yin and Yang, the push and pull, the mutual creation of harmony."

Xu harrumphed. "Call it what you will, the key is that you listened and understood. Now, try it yourself."

Bowing, Master Ding stood and gestured to her seat. "Please, *Dian-xia*."

Try? Someone who was just learning about love could not imitate that music. To do so would be an insult to what they had just played. She begged them off with a wave of her hand.

With a scowl, Lord Xu nudged her toward the seat with a hand. "Please, *Dian-xia*."

It might as well have been an order, audacious for a lord, but perhaps not for Xu. Kaiya nodded. In any case, Hardeep had asked her to practice. What better way to practice, than with two of her best teachers and an elf wizard?

Master Ding bowed. "Remember what I played, but do not let that constrain you. Let Master Yong guide you, and you will find you are guiding him."

Such curious advice, especially given the rigidity with which both usually taught. Kaiya sat, rooting her feet to the ground and straightening her spine as Hardeep had suggested. Satisfied her posture met his standards, she nestled the pipa in her arms. Like before, it felt lifeless compared to Yanyan's.

"You have to give it life," Lord Xu said.

Kaiya's pulse skipped a beat. It was as if the elf could read minds.

Master Yong laughed and swept his bow across the *erhu*. A jubilant sound burst forth.

The melody would work so well with what Master Ding had just played. Kaiya plucked the strings, copying the beautiful music note for note. The sound resonated inside of her, coiling in her belly again as it had done in the Hall of Pure Melody. Kaiya adjusted her posture, and the vibrations percolated from her arms into her core, and then into the ground. Capture this, and she was one step closer to helping Prince Hardeep.

Seize the song's emotion and make it your own, the book had implored. This song was more difficult than the one in that ancient tome, mixing jubilance with

135

resolve. Opposites. Impossible to grasp both at the same time. What had Master Ding thought of when she was playing?

Love, perhaps? What she might have felt for Master Yong so many years ago? Not like Kaiya could even understand, given her own limited experience. Zheng Tian? They'd talked about marriage at a time when they thought it just meant always being able to play with one another. Hardeep? She barely knew him, even if his eyes twisted her stomach into knots. General Lu? She'd never learn what love was with him.

On the periphery of her vision, Master Ding's tight lips sank into a frown. Master Yong's playing fell out of beat with Kaiya's own. No, she was losing it. Blowing out the breath she held, she lowered her hands.

"*Dian-xia*, if I may." Master Ding held up a hand. "Your playing is technically perfect. It would make a wonderful solo…"

But.

Master Yong lowered his bow. "If I may, *Dian-xia*. We are not playing off each other, as a duet should. Ideally, as my song pushes, yours receives. When you expand, I contract."

Lord Xu nodded. "You are playing what you want, and you are doing it very well. However, you are not listening. That is the key to playing a song like this."

No denying it. So focused had she been on replicating Master Ding's piece, Kaiya had missed the changes Master Yong had improvised. She bowed her head in contrition.

"Keep practicing, keep listening," Lord Xu said. "I will seek you out when you have made another breakthrough." He disappeared, the air popping where he had stood.

Kaiya covered her gasp with a hand. It was surprising to see him disappear just like that, but not nearly so shocking as his certainty that she would make another breakthrough.

CHAPTER 15
Dilemmas

Kaiya listened to the chirping of birds as a cold breeze whispered through new tree buds. Perhaps a garden wasn't the best place to practice the pipa; not when the chill brought goosebumps to her exposed arms. However, Lord Xu had implored her to listen, and it was near impossible to distinguish sounds with the preparations for tonight's reception stirring a ruckus inside the castle.

Never moving from its reliable spot in the halls of heaven, the Iridescent Moon waxed to mid-crescent. Prince Hardeep wanted to meet past sundown at the first waxing gibbous, four hours hence. That left plenty of time to practice. Maybe she could show how far she'd progressed just from the morning. The thought sent prickles dancing through her core.

Focus. She shook the excitement out of her head. The book instructed the musician to *seize the song's emotion* and make it her own. She'd read the lines over and over again since leaving her teachers, and tried to play the song with the happiness it embodied. If she could affect General Lu, certainly she could influence the mood of her handmaidens.

One more try. Adjusting her posture, she lowered her hands to the strings and plucked out perfect notes. Her rendition of the song was so precise, it had to work. She cast a glance at Han Meiling and the imperial guards Chen Xin and Ma Jun. They stood like statues on the veranda, almost blending into the background. Despite her best efforts with the music, they remained stoic as always, the exact opposite of the song's intended effect.

Her lower lip jutted out. Learning from a book was getting her nowhere. The sensation of power she'd felt, first in the Hall of Pure Melody with Yanyan's pipa, then later when playing for General Lu, seemed so distant. Like a dream.

Listen, Lord Xu's voice echoed in her mind, almost too real and with too much of an exasperated tone to be the memory from just an hour before.

She closed her eyes and opened her ears: the battle between spring and winter, played out in the birdsongs, wind, and waves. Spring sang an uncertain song as winter held a tenuous grip. The irregularity of weather seemed just like Prince Hardeep's influence. She had broken more rules this day than she had her entire life, even angered the man Father wanted her to marry.

The uncertainty found its way into her music as she strummed a random tune on her pipa, the hesitant notes reflecting the weather and her emotions. Duty dictated marriage to the general. Her soul wanted to sing with the song of the world. An impossible dream before today, but now her spirit soared. Between Prince Hardeep's promise of the Dragon Scale Lute, and Lord Xu's certainty of a future breakthrough, it now seemed possible.

It also meant leaving the palace tonight, during a formal reception no less, using some lie to meet Hardeep. His Ankira needed her help, but it shouldn't require sneaking behind Father's back. It shouldn't require imposing her will through magic. Even if it were the right thing to do. Surely, there had to be other avenues. Her notes wobbled.

She steadied her breath, and the music with it. Right. It was best to obey the rules. Stay in the castle tonight.

Not that it was even possible to escape. A thousand eyes would be on her, because either the Household Ministry secretary or the Hall of Pure Melody's steward had undoubtedly reported to Father about her unapproved adventures in the palace grounds. Minister Hu had probably spread the lie that Hardeep wanted to take her hostage. Maybe he did.

Father might be too busy preparing for the reception now, but when it did come time to mete out punishment, he would probably forbid any more contact with Prince Hardeep—in addition to any other reprimand she might face.

In the corner of her eye, blue robes twitched in a short blur of motion. Chen Xin and Ma Jun had shuffled, perhaps from the uncertainties in her music.

Another flash of blue and black robes swirled from beyond the veranda. Maybe they were just reacting to that.

No. It was her music. It had to be. It was a sign. All uncertainties melted. She was destined to liberate Ankira.

"Young Lord Peng Kai-Long requests an audience with Princess Kaiya," a male voice cracked from the edge of the garden. Household Affairs Secretary Hong's. He'd been following her around quite a bit today. A spy perhaps, there at his ministry's bidding—or even Father's—to make sure she didn't break any more rules.

Her hands froze over the strings. She set the pipa down and searched for the voice's source. The old man bowed, his lips tight like he had just sucked on sour plums. Cousin Kai-Long stood at his side, folding a sheet of paper.

A letter from Prince Hardeep? Her heart pattered. Another sign.

Kai-Long took the steps down the veranda. "*Dian-xia*," he started, addressing her formally. Even though he was an elder cousin, her position as a princess from the direct ruling line ranked her above him.

Eyes on the letter, she smiled. "Cousin, you do not need to stand on formality."

"As you command, Kaiya." He flashed a devilish grin, his eyes searching hers.

His sarcasm was infectious. She covered a giggle with her fingers, then pointed at the paper in his hand. "Is that…?"

He looked down at the paper and then held it up. *Elephant left three*. "I am playing a game of blind chess. This is my latest move."

Her heart sunk. Instead of a letter from Hardeep, it was just part of a confusing game. Chess made little sense, but Father and Kai-Long bonded over it. "Are you winning?"

"Yes, though it wouldn't be evident." His lips twitched. He cast a glance at the imperial guards, then leaned in and whispered—practically mouthed: "I have a plan to get you out of the palace."

Kaiya stole a glance back at Chen Xin and Ma Jun, who showed no sign of having heard him. Thank the Heavens for her good ears. She held up a hand to stay her guards, and then shuffled a little farther down the path.

At a safe distance away, she turned to face him. "You can get me out during a reception in honor of my brother's wedding? What about General Lu and the betrothal announcement?"

Kai-Long's grin stretched from ear to ear, and he suppressed a chuckle. "When I got back to the palace, General Lu was storming out. His eyes were red-rimmed, like he'd been crying. The servants and officials all say he did not even report to the Ministry of Appointments."

The betrothal remained up in the air. Maybe the general had given up on marriage. Hopefully, someone would tell her something before tonight. "Still, I'm supposed to be sitting at the head of the room, next to Kai-Wu and his bride. Someone will notice my absence."

If Kai-Long shook his head any more, it might wobble off. "Trust me. Old Hong there—" he tilted his head toward the palace official still on the veranda, who ogled them and wrung his hands "—has agreed to help. It took a little convincing. I also called in several favors among the young lords and palace staff."

Kaiya searched his eyes. Nothing but sincerity. Before coming of age and being assigned as a diplomat, Kai-Long had virtually grown up in the palace, had always been close to her and Tian. More than once, he had kept them from getting into trouble. Of course he would have her best interests at heart. Still…. She shook her head. "It risks too many people. It will betray Father's trust in you."

Kai-Long cast his gaze down. In shame, no doubt, considering Father's fondness for him. Before Kai-Long had been sent to Ayuri lands, the two used to share tea on a regular basis, and play Cathayi chess. He raised his head. "That's too bad. Prince Hardeep told me only someone of your talent could use his magical instrument."

Like the Dragon Singers of old. It was her destiny. Was it worth breaking yet more rules? Exposing collaborators to potential punishment? The memory of Yanyan's pipa sent a tingling through Kaiya's hands and into her core. It had caused her to pass out. No telling what a similar instrument could do, with her out in the city without guards.

But oh, the possibilities! And Prince Hardeep would be there with his Paladin skills, to protect her. Her chest swelled. "What would *you* do?"

"Kaiya," Kai-Long said, taking her hand in his. "You must make that decision for yourself. Just know that Prince Hardeep told me you have a gift. He wholeheartedly believes it is like none other since Yanyan herself."

Heat flared, and her hands went sweaty. The exuberant bubble in her chest threatened to choke off her air. Prince Hardeep's kind blue eyes *saw* her. Her potential to do good in this world. He didn't care about how plain she looked. To him, she was more than a stepping-stone to power.

Still, Father also loved her unconditionally. The excitement withered, and the swell of her chest deflated. "Whatever I choose, I will betray someone."

"Not necessarily." Kai-Long squeezed her hand. "I have friends in Vyara City who remember when the Dragon Scale Lute repelled Avarax. If you learn to use it, you can help Cathay. Remember what the *Tianzi* said about the lords of the North. Remember that if Ankira falls, aggressive Madura will be on our border, and I am sure they have stockpiles of firepowder."

It did make sense, and provided a means of getting official permission. She nodded. "I am sure the *Tianzi* will see the logic. I will go to him—"

He released her hand and raised his own. "If you decide to leave the castle—and I will support whatever you choose—the *Tianzi* must not know. Because if he denies your request, all eyes will be on you during the reception, making my plan impossible. It will also be direct disobedience to his order, punishable by death."

Kaiya twirled a lock of hair. If it was just herself to consider, the chance to find her potential, beyond a political marriage, was worth the risk of death. After all, the proverb of marriage being a woman's grave rang even more true from what she'd seen of the short and pompous General Lu.

But what about collaborators? Anyone who helped her escape the castle—from servants, to Hardeep, and even Cousin Kai-Long—would face certain torture and execution. No, asking for permission was out of the question. She searched his eyes again, finding nothing but devotion and support. The Heavens had blessed her with such a confidante. "Tell me your plan. If it endangers anyone besides myself, I cannot go through with it."

"There is magic in the world beyond Paladin fighting skills and our master craftsmen." Grinning, he pulled her behind a large tree, out of the guards' line of sight. He withdrew a red silk pouch and emptied what appeared to be a light bauble into his bare palm.

Kaiya gasped. His face was gone, replaced by her own—or at least, a flattering rendition based off an official court painting. His broad shoulders and muscled frame now withered to her slim, flat build, and his court robes seemed to shrink to size.

Her mouth open and closed in an unladylike manner until a single word could escape. "H-How?"

When he spoke, it was with his own voice, making the situation all the more disconcerting. "An Aksumi illusionist I knew in Vyara City made it."

An illusionist, no wonder. The dark-skinned Aksumi practiced all kinds of sorcery, including the mass production of the ubiquitous light baubles. But, "Whatever for?"

"An emergency. If you ever needed a decoy. Just like tonight, though I don't imagine the *Tianzi* had this sort of circumstance in mind." She—he—stared at the sky.

It definitely wasn't her body language…was it? "This will never work. It doesn't look like me and it certainly doesn't sound like me."

Kai-Long slipped the marble into its pouch and his form snapped back to normal. "My plan takes all that into account. Here's what we will do…"

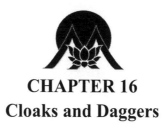

CHAPTER 16
Cloaks and Daggers

Arriving two hours before his appointed meeting with Lamp Man, Tian checked the door's threshold for light and listened for any telltale signs of activity. Unlike the previous times he'd scouted the place out, no guards circled the building. Satisfied no one was there, he picked the lock, which yielded much more easily without imperious half-elves breathing down his neck, and padded in.

At first glance, the warehouse seemed little changed from the morning, but the crates Lamp Man had pointed out to the porter were now gone. They must've already loaded them onto the *Wild Orchid* by now. Jie, unaccounted for since dawn, would probably know, if she were still alive. It was so uncharacteristic of her not to check in with him for such a long time. His gut clenched. If Lamp Man had ill intentions, Tian shouldn't have sent her there alone.

He now climbed a stack of crates, and then shimmied over the dusty rafters to the lone skylight. High-quality glass, likely imported from the Estomari city states in the east. Unlatching the frame, he pushed up on it. The rusty hinges creaked as it opened. Gaining the flat roof, satisfied there was no breeze, he left the skylight open. People never looked up unless they had a reason.

He now stood two stories above the ground, a good vantage point to see if Lamp Man came early to prepare a nasty surprise. The sun had set, and the blue light from Guanyin's Eye mingled with the crescent White Moon to cast the gridded streets and alleys below in an aquamarine hue.

Light bauble lamps crawled along in the hands of drunken sailors as they boisterously made their way around the waterfront. If Jie had received his message, she would stay in the shifting dark spaces between lamps. Her approach would be so quiet, he would never know until she played some childish trick on him.

After an hour surveying the area, he had yet to fall victim to her games. She should've made contact by now. Instead, low voices emanated from the approaching glow of a partially shuttered light bauble. Tian dropped so that he could just see over the half-wall balustrade and crept to the warehouse's southeast corner. Four men strode in unison, their weapons protruding from cloaks. Broadswords. Curved daggers. One cradled a repeating crossbow. The conversation became clearer as they came closer.

"Mister Sha said to meet him here by the second waxing gibbous," Crossbow Man said.

Tian glanced up to the south at the Iridescent Moon. Unless this Mister Sha—Lamp Man, perhaps—made it a point of coming late, he'd be there soon.

"How much is that bastard paying?" the largest asked. "I have some gambling debts."

The one holding the lantern harrumphed. "I told you not to play mahjong with the triads when you're drunk." Monk would make a fitting nickname, given his ascetic guidance.

Gambler stopped midstride, breaking their tight formation. "Mind your own business."

"Both of you, shut up," Crossbow Man said. "We'll make enough to visit to the Floating World afterwards."

"Speak for yourself," muttered the fourth. A short, slim man, his only obvious weapon was a knife.

Their hardened features and confident postures suggested military training. Cathay had too many soldiers past their prime, in need of work. Most hung around the harbor city and capital, employed as guards for rich merchants. Master Yan had identified them as a potential source of instability, if they ever organized.

Footsteps from the other side of the alley drew Tian's attention. The length of the stride matched Lamp Man, and indeed, it was his northern Cathayi features illuminated by a dim light bauble approaching. He hung the same lamp from earlier on a hook above the door and opened the shutters.

The four newcomers turned into the alley and walked to the door. They nodded in greeting.

"Mister Sha," Crossbow Man said. "I hope we have not kept you waiting."

"You did, Mister Gu," Sha lied. He nodded first at Crossbow Man, then the others. "But it is my job to be early."

Gu bowed. "Our apologies."

"You are on time, and you have done good work for my master in the past." Little chance Sha would reveal that master without persuasion or trickery.

Crossbow Gu bowed again. "What's the job?"

Sha looked up and down the alley, and then lowered his voice. "In an hour, I will be meeting with a harbormaster scribe. When we are done, I need him dead and his body disposed of."

Tian's stomach tightened. So Sha planned to kill him.

Gu harrumphed. "A scribe, eh? Easy enough. It will cost you."

"A gold *yuan* each."

Tian's eyes widened as much as the mercenaries' did. Four *yuan* could feed a large family for a month. His life wasn't worth much more than Princess Kaiya's proverbial butterfly, let alone four *yuan*. Sha clearly valued whatever conspiracy he was involved in.

"The terms are acceptable." Gu placed a fist in his hand. "You asked for four of us, so you obviously have a plan?"

"Of course." Sha pointed at the door. "I will maneuver the scribe so his back is to the open door. Slim

Kan can slash his throat from behind. A man will block both ends of the alley just in case he escapes." He pointed up. "You stand on the roof with your crossbow."

Tian stepped back from the balustrade just as Gu looked up.

"How am I supposed to get up there?"

"There's a ladder inside," Sha said, "and a skylight."

Damn! Tian bolted back to the skylight as quietly as he could. He had to close it before they opened the door, lest the creaky hinges draw their attention. In the seventeen and a half long strides, he considered the possibilities. Stay on the roof and Gu would find the closed skylight unlatched…but might not give a second thought to either that or the disturbed dust. Hide in the warehouse, and Tian would have to get back out again to meet Sha at the front door, and worry about Gu's crossbow.

Stay on the roof it was. Tian lowered the skylight, cringing at the hinges' whine. Then he backed to the southwest corner, far from the door below and outside the thirty-two-*chi* glow of Gu's lamp. He pressed his back to the half-wall.

The skylight groaned open. Lantern raised, Gu set the crossbow to the side and climbed up. Now without his cloak, it was clear he was armed with a broadsword and dagger. After giving a cough and brushing dust off his pants, he retrieved his crossbow and clunked over to the edge just above the door. He shuttered his lamp, leaving only glowing cracks.

151

Tian glanced south. The Iridescent Moon had waxed past its second crescent. Below, Gambler's silhouette pressed against the wall near the corner. If Monk had followed Sha's instructions, he would be waiting at the other end, while Slim Kan hid just inside the door.

Five against one, but since they were all separated, Tian could neutralize some of them one at a time. It would be child's play with Jie's help. If only she were here. Closing his eyes, he pressed his hand to the roof to feel for vibrations. Ears perked, he listened for any sign of his irrepressible friend.

Nothing. Time to put his own plan into action. Drawing a knife, he padded back across the rooftop. Gu stood at the edge, looking up and down the alley. As long as he didn't turn around…

Hold the dragonfly with care, for even their fleeting lives have value. Since their parting three thousand, one hundred and forty-seven days before, Princess Kaiya had rarely invaded his thoughts—only at times like this, as a reminder of what his hands could do. Had to do, even if his younger self would have been horrified.

Gu looked back.

Palming a throwing spike, Tian ducked behind the open skylight.

With a yawn, Gu returned to his post. At his distance from the open skylight, he likely saw only a reflection of Guanyin's Eye, whereas Tian could see right through it.

Tian closed his eyes for a split second to erect his mental armor. To banish thoughts of a gentle princess, the best friend he'd promised to marry. Memories led to indecisiveness, and that got people killed. Opening his eyes, he slunk right up behind Gu, covered his mouth, and slashed his neck.

Gu struggled for a second before going limp. The crossbow slipped from lifeless fingers, but Tian intercepted it with his foot and slowed its descent to the floor. A life snuffed out, as easily as crushing a dragonfly. He lowered the body and peeked over the balustrade.

Down below, Sha tapped his foot. Soon, he might join Gu in the netherworld. Tian worked his way back to the skylight. Jie might use a *Ghost Echo*, imitating and throwing Gu's voice to lure Slim Kan into an ambush, but Tian didn't trust his own technique. No, as long as he kept Sha's back to the doorway, Slim wouldn't be able to attack.

Tian continued to the far side of the roof, then lowered himself over the edge. Fingers and toes finding purchase in the cracks between the stones, he descended about a story and then dropped lightly to the street. He dusted himself off and held his knife in an underhand grip to conceal it. Rounding the southwest corner, he walked down the middle of the street. Gambler, leaning back against the building, would see Tian's silhouette, but would likely wait until he turned into the alley before making a move.

Gambler's shadowed form spun, but made no move for the broadsword at his side. Maybe he could be spared, even if Tian would not afford the same courtesy back.

"Good evening." Tian nodded his head.

Gambler lifted his chin and grunted.

Tian leaped forward. With one hand, he pinned Gambler's right wrist; with the other, he drove the knife butt into Gambler's temple, and then set the blade at his throat. "Hands up, turn around," Tian whispered. "Slowly."

Wobbling, Gambler complied. Tian smashed the knife handle into the base of Gambler's skull, and then eased him down as he crumpled. The two successive shots would leave him unconscious for at least six minutes, and he would wake with an excruciating headache.

Stashing his knife in a wrist sheath, Tian turned the corner. Lamp Man Sha had not moved from his spot in front of the door, under the lamp. Their eyes met. He had no obvious weapons.

With a bow of his head, Tian withdrew the copied manifests. "Here, sir."

"Good." Sha beckoned him forward, edging back in an obvious move—at least to a trained eye—to put Tian's back at the open door and Slim Kan's waiting knife.

Tian stood fast. He repeated his lines in his head several times. "All these goods bound for Wailian County. For the new castle?"

154

Sha's eyes narrowed to slits as he received the papers, then opened and shifted from one end of the alley to the other.

Alas, the disconnect between Tian's thoughts and mouth had ruined subtle interrogation, and perhaps even blown his cover. On to the contingency plan, which had to be executed before Gambler came to. Muscles twitching, ready to fire, Tian stepped right where Sha wanted him.

A dagger flashed in Sha's hand. "Now!"

Before it could wrap around his throat, Tian intercepted Slim Kan's arm and twisted the wrist up. Using his shoulders as a fulcrum, Tian dislocated Kan's elbow with a wet pop. In the same motion, he spun and drove Kan into Sha's incoming stab.

Slim Kan screamed. Monk rounded the corner, his broadsword rasping from its sheath. Tian released Kan and seized Sha's knife arm. With a jump back and a yank, he drew Sha into the warehouse, and then twisted his wrist.

Sha went hurtling into the door, slamming it shut, drowning the space in darkness.

Before the image faded from his head, Tian swept the dagger from Sha's hand and pressed the tip to his throat. "Who do you work for?"

"Lord Zu."

Of course, these forms of interrogation were far less effective than subtle ones. "There's no Lord Zu in the North." Tian swept the dagger upward, nicking Sha's chin, before he returned the point to the throat. The door buckled, and Tian pulled the weapon back before the force drove Sha into it. Monk wouldn't be able to push it open, but the threat made for a good incentive. "Tell me."

"Lord Peng."

The *Tai-Ming* Lord? Impossible. "Married to the *Tianzi's* sister."

"No." Sha shook his head. "Not—"

The door slammed open, driving Sha into the dagger faster than Tian could withdraw it. Gambler stumbled into the warehouse, broadsword in hand. Monk stood behind him, holding a lamp and sword. Sha knelt, hands clawing his neck, choking on blood.

Tian glanced at the dagger. It had gone deep enough to puncture Sha's voice box, though whether it had or not would take further examination. For now, it was the dagger and a knife in his other hand against two men armed with broadswords. "Sha won't be paying. Don't risk your life."

Gambler glared back, though his eyes crossed. Two hits to the head and a jolt on a heavy door had taken their toll. He pointed the broadsword at Tian. "I'm going to gut you anyway." He raised the sword and charged.

Backing away, Tian flung the knife. It bit into the upper part of Gambler's chest. Two throwing stars followed, lodging in Gambler's gut. The brute continued undaunted, broadsword swinging in circles. Tian feigned fear—though perhaps it wasn't all an act—retreating deeper into the warehouse.

Gambler's mistake was the regularity of his swinging pattern. As his weapon swept up for the fourth time, Tian vaulted forward and sliced behind Gambler's elbow. Spinning to the side, Tian continued the downward slash to sever Gambler's knee ligaments. A shoulder-butt created distance for Tian's side kick to his shin. He spun to find Monk's sword starting a swing.

Decapitation was unavoidable.

The hack came up short, and the blade clattered on the floor as Monk sank to his knees and gripped his side. Behind him, a lantern on the ground lit a short silhouette in a one-piece dress with a frilly border. With a knife. His savior—but who? Tian slammed his heel into Monk's head, knocking him to the ground. A quick glance at Gambler found the man lying on the floor, holding his knee.

Tian circled around to get the light out of his eyes. Which immediately rounded so wide, his eyeballs might've fallen out of the sockets.

The strapless pink dress clinging to Jie's lithe body was far more suited for one of the fair-skinned merchant princesses out of the East. She actually looked like a girl, despite the color mismatch. It was the first time he'd seen her in a dress since their initial meeting in the Floating World.

She pointed a bloody knife at him. "Don't laugh."

He opened his mouth—

"Not. A. Word." Her tone left no room for negotiation, even as her scowl dared him to speak.

157

"Right." He leaned over Monk, whose unconscious wheezing rattled the air. Jie's knife had caught him in his flank, puncturing his lung. He would not be saying much, if he ever woke at all. Gritting his teeth, Tian slashed his throat. A quick, merciful death.

Jie's eyes roved from Slim Kan to Gambler to Monk to Sha. "Who are these people?"

"Mercenaries." Tian pointed to Sha, likely dead, since blood no longer squirted from his throat. "Hired by him. From Wailian County."

Jie nodded. "The *Wild Orchid* held several kegs of sulfur, bound for Wailian. Domain of Lord Tong. He is making firepowder."

Tong was a long-time confidante of the Emperor, who'd stayed out of the last insurrection. Was he making a move now?

"Sha might work for Lord Tong himself." Squatting by the corpse, Tian examined the body. Sometimes, forensic clues yielded more information than interrogation. A grey crust lined the sole of Sha's shoe, while traces of what looked to be sawdust flecked his coifed hair. Tian lifted Sha's still-warm hand. Traitor or not, Tian had passed his death sentence.

Sha's smooth hand did not speak of a life of hard labor or frequency in wielding weapons. The index finger bore a gold ring shaped in the form of a coiled dragon, perhaps a replica of the Guardian Dragon of Cathay itself. More curious was the pink grit under his fingernail.

Tian held up the hand for Jie to see. "What do you make of this?"

She leaned over and sniffed, no doubt her keen elven senses picking up more than his nose could. "It has a fishy smell."

He withdrew a fine lockpick and scooped out the pasty substance. "Fish paste? He seemed too cultured to eat with his hands." He held up the pick to her for confirmation.

"I'm *not* going to taste it." Jie sucked on her lower lip. "Perhaps he was a sloppy eater."

He glared at her, prompting her for her real answer.

She released her bottom lip with a smack. "Yutou Province is famous for preserved pink fish paste. Fat Nose Jiang has a Southern accent, and the *Wild Orchid* stops in Yutou on a regular basis."

And fish paste could keep for a year, or more. Tian tapped his chin with a finger. The problem was that Yutou Province exported a lot of fish paste, to all over the country. Now if only it were possible to find out how much fish paste Lord Tong in Wailian was buying. And rice. Five thousand bales of rice and five hundred barrels of pink fish paste could feed his army of five thousand for a year. Then there was the firepowder.

He looked up at Jie. "You—"

"I have already sent word about the illegal firepowder. I would imagine Master Yan will be interrupting the imperial reception to brief the *Tianzi*."

159

Tian tapped his chin. What had appeared to be a brewing insurgency now threatened to boil into a full-blown rebellion, destabilizing Cathay for the first time in three centuries.

CHAPTER 17
Not the Brightest Moment

Kneeling at the far end of the dais in the Golden Dragon Room, Kaiya listened to the music ensemble that played in the background. Master Ding on the Pipa, Master Yong on the Erhu, accompanied by famous musicians playing *the guzheng*, *ruan* guitar, and recorder. All mingled in choreographed harmony, all technically perfect as would be expected at an imperial reception.

Though the sound didn't carry the same emotions as her masters' earlier duet, it resonated through rice wine-fueled conversation among the hereditary lords and ladies. Dressed in their finest gowns and robes, they all sat on the imported sablewood floors around low tables, enjoying delicacies prepared by the finest chefs in the realm.

Each place was set with some of her favorite dishes, though Cousin Kai-Long's embarrassing plan had killed her appetite: a bowl of royal red rice, a low-rimmed bowl with jade asparagus and immortal mushrooms sautéed with royal-ox butter, a small saucer of soy sauce-braised golden pork belly cubes, a small plate of fried finger-length whitefish, a medium-sized plate of chopped crispy quail, and a lacquer bowl of shark fin soup. A small cup for rice wine sat on the right side, next to a pair of chopsticks. The Imperial Family's symbol of a blue five-clawed dragon decorated each white porcelain dish.

Insides twisting, Kaiya looked through the sliding doors. Painted with dark golden dragons flying among the clouds, they stood open to the garden beyond, thankfully allowing cool air off Sun-Moon Lake to percolate in and alleviate the stifling air. Facing north, they did not provide a view of the Iridescent Moon, so she would have to rely on Kai-Long to keep time. Going along with his potentially humiliating plan might tarnish the hard-to-maintain façade of Perfect Princess.

And she had been far from perfect today. Surprisingly enough, the Minister of Household Affairs hadn't approached her about her transgressions, nor had Father summoned her regarding the betrothal to General Lu. She shifted in her seat. Certainly, one of the witnesses would have reported everything by now.

Or perhaps they'd been too busy preparing for this reception to deal with a naughty sixteen-year-old. Tomorrow might be another story, but for now, Second Brother Kai-Wu and his soon-to-be bride took center stage.

Everyone took turns approaching the dais where the Imperial Family ate from small individual tables. Second Brother, never one for ceremony, slouched beside his bride-to-be. Wu Yanli, the daughter of *Tai-*

Ming Lord Wu of Zhenjing Province, might have been a porcelain doll with her cold elegance. She almost rivaled Xiulan in beauty, and rumor had it she had enchanted Kai-Wu with the magic of her tea ceremony.

Young Lord Chen Qing, a *Yu-Ming* heir to a county in Jiangzhou Province, approached with a dumb smile on his face and a wine saucer in hand. He dropped to his knee. "*Dian-xia*, congratulations on your new sister-in-law. Let us toast." His eyes swept to the porcelain decanter at her side.

The one filled with water, part of Cousin Kai-Long's plan. She nodded. She filled Young Lord Chen's saucer and set the decanter down. He then took it and filled her saucer.

She took a dainty sip and her eyes widened. Hot and spicy, it stung her throat. She covered her cough. That was not water! There must have been a mistake. And now, an unprecedented line of young lords had formed up behind Chen Qing, all with feral grins.

Oh no. She craned her neck. Hopefully, Kai-Long was out there somewhere. Or a servant, who could swap out the decanter...but for what? Nobody knew it was supposed to be water. The next young man, Young Lord Fen of Fenggu Province, already knelt before her, filling her saucer with rice wine.

The alcohol burned her mouth, and showed no signs of abating even after several more young lords toasted her. She was to have feigned drunkenness and retired early, but now, it looked like her poor acting skills might not be needed.

Her stomach heaved. Head spinning, she covered her mouth, and luckily, nothing came up. Eyes rounding like the wine saucer, Young Lord Zi, the seventh to serve her, scuttled back several steps. Humiliating for sure, made worse by actually being drunk.

Still, no one could blame her. It would appear just as Kai-Long had planned: a bunch of potential young suitors trying to make an impression on her, but gone too far. At a reception like this, even a prince or princess was fair game, and Father could forgive a sixteen-year-old for not holding her wine.

Kai-Long appeared at her side, hand on her elbow. "Easy, *Dian-xia*. Come, let me help you." Releasing her, he walked through the crowd gathering in front of Eldest Brother Kai-Guo and Xiulan and bowed before Father at the center of the dais.

Father was engaged in discussion with a middle-aged minister, his brow furrowed in an uncommon show of public emotion. The minister shook his head and held up two fingers. Father actually frowned, but then stayed the minister with an innocuous hand, and turned to Kai-Long. Kai-Long leaned in and whispered into Father's ear.

Turning and meeting her gaze, Father nodded.

Permission to leave, with Cousin Kai-Long, his favorite nephew. Subtle enough to save face. With a bow of apology to the waiting young men, she rose.

And wobbled. Her head spun. Again, a firm hand grasped her arm.

164

Kai-Long leaned in and whispered, "You are doing great."

Great? If only he knew it was no act. Placing each foot in front of the other felt like a toddler's first steps. "Who is that speaking with the *Tianzi*?"

"Deputy Yan. One of his most trusted advisors."

She looked back to where Father still conferred with this Deputy Yan. "What were they talking about?"

Kai-Long shrugged. "I'm not sure. They quieted as soon as I came over. Now come along."

With his support, they made it to the garden, all under the watchful eye of imperial guards. Guanyin's Eye hung low in the night sky. At its most open this year, it seemed to scrutinize her foolishness.

Cold air filled her lungs, clearing her head, if only a little. "That wasn't water!" She spun and shoved him with two hands. It would have knocked herself over if he hadn't caught her.

"No!" He shook his head. "The servant must have made a mistake. It's okay though, the plan will still work."

Plan? Right. To see gorgeous Prince Hardeep and try the Dragon Scale Lute. It would certainly improve what had become a mortifying evening.

He draped a silken shawl over her shoulders, and then beckoned a servant. "Bring us some hot tea."

He then guided her along the courtyard paths, their feet crunching in the white pebbles. Where were they? No matter how familiar the inner castle was, everything appeared the same through her bleary vision

165

and spinning head. Up ahead, a small octagonal pagoda overlooked the moat between the inner castle and the main palace.

Holding her hand, he helped her up the steps. Inside she plopped into a seat, the marble cold on her behind. She scanned the far end of the path, where two imperial guards kept a respectful distance.

"Are you all right?" Kai-Long asked.

"I think so." No. With heat flaring in her cheeks, Kaiya fanned her face with a hand.

He leaned back and stretched his arms over the pagoda's half-wall. "I want you to bend over, so the guards can't see you, take off the shawl, and pretend to dry heave. Loudly. Stay down, then give the shawl and your outer robe to her." His head tilted down, to the side.

Kaiya jerked her head in the direction he indicated, the sudden motion making her brain twist and flip.

A palace maid was hunched over there, below the line of sight of anyone outside the pagoda. The dark partially shrouded her face, but she bore an uncanny resemblance to Kaiya. Probably from the illusion bauble.

Taking off her outer robe in front of a man, cousin or not, wasn't part of the plan. Dry heaves weren't either, and the way Kaiya's stomach twisted, things might not be particularly dry. "Who is she?"

"Someone who owes me a favor." Kai-Long chuckled. "I know a lot about many of the handmaidens and palace servants."

Curse the buzzing in her head. Why did this feel wrong?

"Hurry," Kai-Long said. "When the servant comes with the tea, you will swap places."

"How did you come up with this plan?"

Kai-Long grinned. "I've snuck a few ladies out this way in the past. More than a few. And it will work even better than ever this time with the magic." He held out his palm. Cradled in a silk kerchief was a marble, similar to the magical light baubles that lit the palace and probably every other house in the world. "Don't touch it directly. Not yet."

It must be another illusion bauble. Kaiya took up the kerchief, nearly knocking it out of his hand. "What will this one make me look like?"

"Just a plain girl. Trust me, everything will be all right. Nobody is going to get in trouble."

There'd been a little too much magic for one day already. Kaiya took a deep breath. The cool air did little to clear the alcohol-induced haze. She glanced toward the imperial guards, just shadows in the distance. The servant approached, holding a tray with a teacup and kettle in trembling hands.

It would be okay. Kai-Long had done this many times.

"All right." She motioned for him to turn his back. When he did, she gritted her teeth, leaned over, and did her best approximation of dry heaves. She ripped off the shawl and shrugged out of the robe, then passed

167

them to the girl, who stood up, hand over her mouth, coughing.

"Good," Kai-Long whispered, patting the girl on the back. "Cough a little."

As the girl complied, the other servant, now cloaked against the chill, stepped into the pagoda with tea. She poured it into a cup and set the cup and kettle on the table. How wonderful tea would be right now! Kai-Long placed himself in the guards' line of sight and motioned Kaiya to her feet.

When she stood, the second servant dropped to all fours. Kai-Long pulled the cloak off and draped it over Kaiya's shoulders. The girl who now resembled her reached for the tea and took a sip. It happened so fast, a blur to Kaiya's addled head.

"Now," Kai-Long whispered to her, "Thank me and tell me to take my leave while you rest here."

Kaiya fought the urge to bow her head, lest the guards see the switch. "Thank you, Cousin Kai-Long. I am feeling a little better now. I am just going to sit for a while. You may take your leave."

"It has been my honor." Kai-Long bowed, then pulled the hood over her head and placed a hand on her shoulder. He whispered again, "I am going to report to your imperial guards. In about ten minutes, meet me on the other side of the bridge. Remember, the bauble must touch your bare skin at all times. Try to walk in a straight line, with the body language of a servant."

Whatever that meant. She watched as he left and walked up the path to where her guards waited.

"Princess Kaiya is feeling better," he told them. "The cool air is doing her well, and I think after sitting for a while with several cups of tea, she will be fine." With a nod of his head, he disappeared around a hedge.

Kaiya looked down at the girl pretending to be her. Who was she beneath the illusion? And had they crossed paths in the palace before? She must be new. Not to mention, her posture appeared much too stiff, the motions too jerky as she reached for the teacup.

The tea smelled good, and it probably would help allay the throbbing in her head. Still, a servant would never dare drink after a princess. With the guards watching, thinking Kaiya to be the servant, it would ruin the illusion to drink the tea.

"Now, *Dian-xia*," the girl whispered, lips trembling.

Kaiya stood. With deliberate care, she took one step after another. As she approached the bridge over the moat, she glanced in the direction of the guards. Their dark shapes didn't move. Heavens, this plan was actually working.

On the other side, Kai-Long waited.

They hurried through the palace grounds, his pull on her hand forcing a quick pace. The twists and turns along the corridors between the buildings would have all been familiar with a clear head, but they might as well have formed a maze tonight. Light from the three moons made it even more disorienting.

At last, they came to the central plaza formed by the Hall of Supreme Harmony, the Hall of Pure Melody, and the imperial archives. Aksumi light baubles hung in strings from the dozens of espaliered fruit trees, casting hypnotic shadows in all directions.

Despite the particularly large crowd of palanquin bearers, palace guards, and provincial soldiers and staff, the courtyard still seemed vast. Hundreds of eyes fell on them as they neared Kai-Long's Nanling provincial contingent, congregated near the main gates.

"Young Lord Peng," someone cried out. Soldiers snapped to attention.

Stopping in place, Kaiya peered back at Kai-Long. Even through her muddled head, everything was now clear: this wasn't right. If it was just her escaping the palace with no help, the risks barely outweighed the rewards. Now, it involved several people, many likely blackmailed. If this plan failed, any accessory to this ill-advised adventure would face severe punishment. She gripped Kai-Long's sleeve. "No, we can't do this."

"It's too late. If we head back now, it will draw too much attention. Don't worry."

She looked at his entourage. The porters prepared the two-person palanquin.

A palanquin, no...the narrow confines, the stuffiness... She skidded to a halt and nearly tripped over her gown. Her head spun and chest tightened. She squeezed Kai-Long's elbow. "We can walk."

He faced her, the light baubles casting webby shadows over his grinning face. "You won't be spotted this way."

She fixated on the palanquin…just one. Come to think of it, "Where is your family? I didn't see them at the reception."

"The horse-relay messengers said their ship was delayed. They are expected in Jiangkou harbor tomorrow morning."

His villa chamberlain shuffled over and bowed. "Leaving so soon, Young Lord? With a…friend, I see."

Kai-Long nodded. "Yes. I already paid my respects to Prince Kai-Wu, and my…friend…wished to depart early."

"To the Floating World, then?"

Kaiya's heart jumped into her throat. The Floating World, where men's dreams took flight, was so far away, it would take half the night to get there. And though it boasted a variety of entertainments from exotic music to theater, the most common diversion was…*that*. It certainly wasn't a place for a woman of high standing. She clutched Kai-Long's arm and shook her head.

He leaned over. "Don't worry. We are headed in that direction, but we won't go in. Come, lower your head." He stood by the palanquin door, blocking the chamberlain's sight of her.

With a sigh, she ducked in. The walls seemed to squeeze all the air out. Head in a fog, her pulse raced. Her throat tightened. This was such a bad idea.

Cousin Kai-Long dipped in to the palanquin and settled across from her. She sucked in a last breath of the outside air and the coolness filled her lungs. The door snapped shut.

171

She pressed Tian's pebble, firm and resolute beneath her sash. It would be all right. Handsome Hardeep's guidance would help her revive a long-lost art, and with it, she could save a beleaguered people. Just like the Dragon Singers of old. It would benefit Cathay as well. Father would understand. Someday. Maybe.

The palanquin pitched upward, threatening to send her stomach into rebellion. She wouldn't be saving anyone tonight. As the men fell into a rhythm, the ride smoothed. From the sounds, the palace's front gates opened, and a throng of guards marched out.

She was outside of the palace. For this first time in her life, it was unscripted, with no imperial guard protection.

Kai-Long smiled at her. "Is everything okay now?"

She gulped. "I think so."

He reached across and clasped her hand. "We will have you back before anyone knows you are gone."

And when would that be? It wasn't like the decoy could sit and drink tea until dawn. She squirmed. "Heavens, this is a horrible idea. What do the girls who wait in the pagodas usually do?"

"Not to worry. Eventually, when no one is watching, they just head back to their own quarters."

"Someone is *always* watching me!" Everything was so clear now, even if alcohol burned in her veins. "She might look like me, but the poor girl doesn't know the secret imperial language or the codes that will get her

172

into the Imperial Family's sleeping quarters." How hadn't she seen it before?

His expression did not look the least bit concerned. "Don't worry. All she has to do is drop the bauble and no one will be the wiser. I—"

The palanquin lurched to a stop, sending Kaiya's stomach into a flop. Only with supreme effort did she keep everything down. Still, any hope of meeting Hardeep was now dashed. Her shoulders slumped.

Outside, swords rasped from sheaths.

"Identify yourself," someone said.

CHAPTER 18
Conspiracy Theories

Jie slipped out of the ridiculous pink dress in a side room of the clan safehouse in Jiangkou. It had been tempting to intentionally stain the satin in one or five places during the hasty clean-up of Tian's mess at the warehouse, but maybe she'd return it to the Tarkothi instead of burning it.

First, the possible rebellion in the North took precedence, and in their rush to organize information, they hadn't been able to completely scour the warehouse. If a conspirator with a trained eye came looking for the now-deceased Sha, they'd know their treachery had been compromised. Maybe they'd move their plans for rebellion up, before the *Tianzi* could preempt it. Tugging on her utility suit, Jie slid the door open and went into the main room.

As always, Tian was working on his convoluted mess of strings and paper notes and evidence, crisscrossing the room like a web spun by a spider addicted to gooseweed. He'd probably devised this visual method for organizing information not so much for himself, but for the sake of others: a glimpse into all the disjointed goings-on in his head.

His lips drew a tight line as he furiously scribbled more notes. Knowing him, the deaths of five men weighed heavily on his gentle soul. So smart, so skilled, yet so hesitant to use those skills. It's what made him so attract—endearing.

He looked up from his scraps of paper and presented Sha's shoe. "The dry mud on the sole is greyish."

Jie nodded. The only place around here with that color mud was along the Jade River, which emptied into Jiangkou Harbor. "Unless he was fishing in the Jade River shallows with those, I would bet he recently visited the quays near the river."

He held up a folded packet labelled *sawdust*. "Near the lumber mills."

"And the river barges," she said. "And then, there was the pink fish paste under his nails. Assuming he wasn't a sloppy eater, he must have been checking out barrels of it."

"It will keep for a year. Or more. Perfect for surviving a long siege."

The door whispered open and Huang Zhen, a boy of ten, slunk in. The initiate's stealth skills were improving, though not enough to assign him dangerous missions. "Eldest Sister Jie, Elder Brother Tian. We investigated Victorious Trading. It's a stock corporation, owned in part by Lord Chu, Lord Xi, Lord Qin, Lord

Tong, and Evergreen Trading. And guess what?" His face brightened.

In contrast, Tian's face might have been the dark side of the White Moon. He jotted the names down on a sheet of paper. "None of those lords have arrived in the capital. For Prince Kai-Wu's wedding."

Jie followed his gaze into the web of notes. "What's the connection?"

"Lord Tong claims the barbarians are threatening the saltpeter mines." Tian pinned up the name list to one of the strings. "The others are all *Yu-Ming* lords of the North. A combined twenty-one thousand, three hundred provincial soldiers under them."

Jie outlined a map of the realm with her finger in the air. A quite accurate one, in all modesty. "And those counties are the major saltpeter producers. Working together, it would cut off fresh firepowder supply from the rest of the country."

"Aren't imperial stocks large enough to overwhelm those counties?" Huang Zhen asked.

"Maybe," Tian said, oblivious to the smudge of ink on his nose. "But Wailian Castle is impregnable. The *Tianzi* would have to commit ninety-two percent of the national army and seventy-three percent of the loyal provincial armies to a long siege."

Ninety-two and seventy-three? Exactly? Jie stifled a chuckle at his precision. "And that is assuming the rest of the *Yu-Ming* are loyal. Lord Tong is one of the *Tianzi's* favorites."

"He had close ties to Lords Shi and Yang, both who rebelled."

Jie nodded. Ten years ago, during her assignment as a courtesan-in-training in the Floating World, she and Tian had helped uncover Yang's treachery. Two years ago, they'd quelled Lord Shi's rebellion. Lord Tong's name had come up often in both incidents, but she'd never even seen him.

"What else do we know of Lord Tong?" she asked.

Tian shrugged. "He is fifty-four. His wife died in childbirth three years ago. He hasn't remarried."

"Strange he hasn't," Jie thought aloud.

Huang Zhen's face flushed a red bright enough to light a dark room. "Little Sister Feng Mi says he likes young girls, and is very rough."

Jie shuddered. She'd all but forgotten about those rumors. Feng Mi was only eleven, a quarter-Nothori *Black Fist* adept planted as a Night Blossom trainee in the Floating World. Jie and Tian had rescued her as a toddler from the Trench, a formerly-mob infested ghetto just outside Huajing's city walls. If Lord Tong had harmed her, Jie would make sure he paid for more than rebellious intent. She shook the idea out of her head. "No, a hereditary lord marries not to sate his appetite, but rather to build alliances."

"Suspicious." Tian set down the list of potentially rebellious lords. "What about Evergreen Trading?"

"I researched it." Huang Zhen flashed an impish grin. "It's a stock corporation, held by other companies, all in the South."

"The South," Tian repeated, pointing to the bottom of her imaginary map. "Where Lord Tong is illegally shipping firepowder."

On her air map, Jie traced the highway up the central valley. "If the *Tianzi* sent the bulk of the army to pacify the North, it would leave the capital vulnerable to a surprise attack from the South."

Huang Zhen looked from one to the other with rapt attention. "How do we uncover Lord Tong's allies in the South?"

"Well, to start," Jie said, "which lords from the South have not yet arrived in the capital for the imperial wedding?"

"*Yu-Ming* Lords Chi, Shen, and Bai from Yutou Province." Huang Zhen counted his fingers. "From Nanling Province, *Tai-Ming* Lord Peng—"

"That's it," Tian said. "Sha mentioned Lord Peng."

Jie shook her head. "He's married to the *Tianzi's* sister, and Nanling Province didn't get firepowder from Wailian."

"Not that we know of. And the *Wild Orchid* is registered to Nanling. So just in case..." Tian wrote Lord Peng's name on his list. "Let's scout the trade offices and warehouses near the river docks. Zhen: send every available adept in the area to meet us there."

"But first," Jie added, "Use the horse relays to send our suspicions to Master Yan. And I'll send a cleaner to that warehouse. The *Tianzi* will need time to formulate a response before Lord Tong can act."

CHAPTER 19
Blades of the Night

Head buzzing with rice wine, Kaiya listened as boots clopped and weapons rasped outside the suffocating confines of the palanquin. She squeezed her fists tight. Despite Kai-Long's reassurances, the servants who'd helped her risked torture and execution. Now, there might be a more immediate threat. This debacle couldn't get much worse. She didn't even have a dagger to defend herself.

Neither did Kai-Long. Still, he snapped open the door and jumped out. "Stay here."

No, that wasn't an option. Someone had to take responsibility for this mess. She crawled on all fours out of the palanquin, without any semblance of imperial grace. At least the hooded cloak and illusionist's bauble hid her identity. Legs quavering from alcohol and sitting too long, she staggered to her feet.

The surroundings didn't look familiar. Lined by two-story wood buildings, with storefronts on the first floor and residences on top, it could be virtually any side street in Huajing. Kai-Long's provincial soldiers all stood with broadswords drawn. He, himself, took a sword from a guard and strode toward the newcomer.

A lone figure with a curved blade in hand blocked the procession's way. He stepped forward into the light, both hands raised.

Prince Hardeep! His chin was now bare, the pointed beard gone in the hours since they met. His beautiful blue eyes found hers in the crowd. Though the hooded cloak hid her face, recognition dawned in his expression.

Trying to stand straight, Kaiya lowered the hood and smoothed out her dress.

"Prince Hardeep." Speaking perfectly in the Ayuri tongue, Kai-Long locked his gaze on Hardeep's backpack. "This is not where we had planned to meet."

Adjusting a pack, the prince shifted his intense gaze from her to her cousin. "Yes. I fear the Madurans have learned of my visit to the palace." He glanced back in the direction he'd come. "I was followed. I've lost them for now, with the help of my men. I thought you were bringing the princess. Who is that?"

Oh, the magic bead. Kaiya started to stuff it in her sash when Kai-Long placed a hand on her wrist.

Pulling her along, he sidled up to the prince and whispered in his ear. "This is her. Aksumi magic."

Hardeep's mouth gaped…though he had seemed to recognize her before. If only she had a mirror to see what the magic made her look like. He nodded in a slow bob.

"Are you unharmed?" Kaiya asked.

Shoulders squared, Hardeep made a single, resolute nod. "I came to warn you. You should return to the safety of the palace walls." Though his body language suggested confidence, his beautiful eyes fixed on the ground in defeat.

Kai-Long's brow furrowed. "What about the Dragon Scale Lute? What about her potential to save your country and protect ours?"

What about her accomplices back at the palace? Kaiya clenched and unclenched her fists. Her alcohol-addled mind made the dilemma even more confounding.

"I can't risk her life." Hardeep looked up at her. "Not even for my beloved homeland."

The trembling in his voice struck a chord, making Kaiya's legs wobble even more than her weak tolerance for rice wine. Even through the drunken haze, all indecision faded. Like the Dragon Singers in the epic songs of old, she would save his beleaguered nation. It was her choice, not his. "I—" She stumbled forward a few steps.

Arms outstretched, he caught her. Warm and enveloping, his embrace felt safer than a full complement of imperial guards. His luminous eyes gazed into hers. "No. You don't know the Madurans. They don't care about your noble intentions or your gentle soul. They don't care if you are just sixteen. If they think you are meddling in their affairs, they won't hesitate to kill you."

A moment of unadulterated clarity pierced through the mental fog. In the brevity of that moment, it all made sense. She pushed herself out of his arms. "No. My country's sale of guns and firepowder brought on your country's misery. Our classic texts on governance teach that we must rectify wrongs we have caused."

His eyes widened as he leaned back. "But…"

Her voice flowed more steadily than expected, reflecting the certainty in her heart. Maintaining defiant eye contact, she gave a decisive nod. "I *will* help."

Kai-Long shuffled on his feet. "This is wonderful, but how long will it take?"

Her moment ruined, she tried to glare at him, but wasn't sure which of the two Kai-Longs in her wine-blurred vision was the real one.

Hardeep looked up at the Iridescent Moon, now waxing to its third gibbous. "I can have Kaiya back at the palace in two hours."

More than enough time to swap out with the servants. Maybe even to return to the reception, since that would last until all hours of the morning.

Kai-Long clasped her hand. "Please be safe."

"I'll be all right." She leaned into the prince. "Prince Hardeep has Paladin training."

Kai-Long searched her eyes. With a sighing nod, he took a sheathed dagger from his guard and passed it to her. "Very well." He bowed to Prince Hardeep. "I entrust you with the princess' life. My uncle would be devastated if anything happened to her."

"As would I." Hardeep pressed his palms together and bowed his head.

Kaiya squared her shoulders. "I will be fine."

He then took her hand in his. The heat coursed through her. "Let's go."

Walking down the street, Kaiya glanced back at Kai-Long. His lips drew into a tight line. She would owe him quite a favor. He'd done so much already, helping to get her out of trouble. Unless…

She turned to Hardeep. "May I ask you a question?"

"Of course. Anything."

"When you were surrounded by all the angry guards, you stomped on the ground and told them everything was all right." She stopped, so her drunken legs wouldn't send her tumbling into an embarrassing heap, and met his gaze. "Was that Paladin magic? I felt the echo."

His smile broadened. "You noticed! The stories from the War of Ancient Gods claim Yanyan could sense when Vanya used her Paladin skills. You have already grown more in a day than most Paladin trainees."

Her face flushed hot. Still, she had to ask the next question, the one that ate her. "You…you didn't use it on me, to convince me to help Ankira?"

His jovial expression turned serious. He took her hands in his. "Paladin magic doesn't work that way. Even if it could, I wouldn't use it to make you do something against your will."

Studying his face, she found nothing but sincerity. She hung her head. "I'm sorry. I should have never asked."

He lifted her chin. "Don't apologize. You are right to question magic. As I told you before, there is a world beyond your Great Wall."

She swallowed hard, even as relief mixed in with her embarrassment. It was time to change the subject. Her hand ventured toward his jaw. "What happened to your beard?"

Maybe it was the rice wine, but when he guided her fingers along his smooth chin, it sent her belly erupting in a swarm of butterflies.

"I shaved it, so that my enemies would have a harder time recognizing me."

Her smile formed, unbidden. It made him look even younger, more handsome, though his unique blue irises were a dead giveaway. "Where is the Dragon Scale Lute?"

Hardeep looked around the street, and then leaned in. He spoke Ayuri in a low voice. "I don't have it. But I carry with me an old journal from my uncle's visit to Vyara City, twenty-nine years ago. He was there representing my country when your emperor dispatched a mission to negotiate the sale of muskets and firepowder with both Ankira and Madura."

Her alcohol-muddled mind took a few seconds to grasp the significance. Kaiya sucked in a sharp breath. Cathay had played both sides of the conflict and profited. Anger churned inside her.

"I don't blame you for your nation's past sins." He squeezed her hand fondly. "I am just glad you recognize them."

185

"How does the journal relate to the Lute?"

"Twenty-nine years ago, the dragon Avarax awoke from a millennium of sleep. He descended on Vyara City and threatened to immolate it with his fiery breath."

Kaiya shuddered. A peninsular city of spires, domes, canals, and fruit trees, Vyara City was home to hundreds of thousands of people. They would have all perished in dragonfire. "What happened?"

"An elf prince played a song on a lute which repelled Avarax."

Repelled a dragon with just a lute, the Arkothi equivalent of a pipa! Kaiya gasped, and then cocked her head. "The Dragon Scale Lute?"

Prince Hardeep's grin spread from ear to ear. "Its resonance plate was made from one of Avarax's scales. Its strings were made from his whiskers. If it could scare away the mighty Avarax, it could certainly rout a human army. I have tracked it back here, to your capital."

Kaiya's brain swam in circles. All this time, she thought he had it. Even without rice wine, the revelation would have confused her. "How did it get here?"

Prince Hardeep's grin faded. "My uncle noted in his journal that it fell into the hands of Rumiya, the Grand Vizier of Madura. He gifted it to one of your trade officials after he helped negotiate the firepowder deal. We're going to his house now."

"Whose?" she asked. Chief Minister Tan, probably, given his defense of the agreement. He'd benefitted personally. Anger boiled in her chest.

"Wait. Something feels wrong." Hardeep fell silent and beckoned her along.

At this hour, they encountered only a handful of people, mostly laborers on their way home. Prince Hardeep held her right elbow and hand, supporting her shaky steps. On occasion, he took a furtive glance around. After a few minutes, they headed into a side street.

"Do you feel it?" he asked. "Someone is watching us."

She hadn't felt anything. There was no one around. Kaiya started to turn her head.

"No," he whispered. "Keep your attention forward."

At the intersection up ahead, a large man dressed in a black shirt and pants stepped into the street. He pointed a broadsword at Hardeep. "Give me the backpack."

Hand on the hilt of his curved *talwar* sword, Prince Hardeep stopped in place, jerking her closer to him. The magical bead slipped from her fingers and tinkled to the ground.

Click, swoosh, click, swoosh. The rhythmic clicks came from behind.

Prince Hardeep pushed her to the side. Something—no, two things—zipped through the space where they had just stood and thunked into a house. He whipped out his sword, his backpack not seeming to affect the fluidity of his motion.

If only her head were a little clearer! Fumbling for her dagger, Kaiya searched for the source of the clicks. Another large man leveled a repeating crossbow at them. He pressed the trigger and cocked.

"Come on!" Kaiya pulled Prince Hardeep out of the line of fire and ran toward the swordsman. If they lined up with the other assailant, the crossbowman would likely think twice about shooting.

A pair of enormous men in black hoods turned the corner, joining the first. They all sank into attacking stances. Behind her, two more charged in. Six against two. Or one, considering she was just a drunk girl with a dagger.

"Help!" Kaiya yelled. Screaming might be all she was good for. With lights shining behind sliding windows, many of the citizens had to be awake.

Though she had pulled Hardeep, now he hauled her forward, moving so fast her drunken feet nearly entangled each other. What was he doing?

Above, windows opened and heads poked out. In a city famed for its safety, the fighting must have come as a surprise.

The three in front leaped in with curved swords, cutting in deadly coordination. Prince Hardeep edged to one side while deflecting one of the blades and prodding her past the attacks. Cloth sheared open and one of the would-be-assassins buckled to the ground. Hardeep yanked his hooded mask off.

A boy about her age, perhaps younger despite his huge size, stared back at her.

"Come on!" Hardeep said, pulling her through the opening. On the other side, they broke into a run.

Eyes glinting, Hardeep mumbled something unintelligible, though the foul tone suggested some sort of curse. The sudden rush of blood to her head, combined with the alcohol, sent her vision blacking at the edges. A cold wind blasted through her hair. Her legs gave out and she staggered, nearly falling to the ground.

Hardeep propped her up and slowed to a stop. Stopping? It wasn't as if she ran that fast, and those men—boys—had long legs. She blinked a few times and searched for the assailants.

There was no sign of them.

Panting, she looked up at Hardeep. "How did we escape them so fast?"

"I'm not sure, but listen."

There were no sounds of pursuit, just the sound of several muted conversations behind second-floor windows. They couldn't have run that far, but maybe her muddled brain had warped her perception of time and space. Where were they now?

"I think we are safe now." He ran a hand through her hair. "You did well. I owe you my life."

"How so?" She tilted her head. He'd saved both of them, when her stumbling had slowed them down.

"The crossbow bolt would have hit me had you not pulled me out of the way." The sincerity in his tone and intensity of his gaze her pulse flutter.

189

"I've never heard of anything like this happening in the capital." She frowned. The gravity of it all felt like a ship anchor on her shoulders. Something was wrong, but she couldn't pinpoint what.

He harrumphed. "I would expect nothing less from the Madurans."

She shook her head. "I don't think they were Madurans. They didn't look Ayuri." No, with the brown eyes and black hair… "They were definitely Cathayi."

"The Maduran trade office probably hired some mercenaries. They sure picked some large ones."

Very big, probably among the largest humans she'd ever seen. "And young, too."

"Well, we are safe for now. And we're here." He pointed.

She followed his gesture to the sparkling granite walls surrounding a good-sized villa. A fountain bubbled behind the walls, pouring into what was likely a pond. As a whole, the house looked too large and elegant to belong to even a high-level official. Not even a secretary or minister could afford such opulence.

Though maybe Chief Minister Tan could, with his ill-gotten wealth. It was corrupt men like him who undermined Father's moral authority. She might not be a Dragon Singer yet, but she could live by their principles. She squared her shoulders and started toward the gate.

"Wait." Hardeep seized her hand.

She turned and looked at him.

"We need a plan."

Oh, she had a plan. No one would dare deny an imperial princess. "Whose residence is this?"

"Lord Tong Baxian. He was one of the architects of the trade deal with Madura."

The name sounded familiar. A rich and powerful hereditary lord, given the size of the villa. If he'd sold Madura out, he'd sooner turn her over to Father for a reward than surrender the Lute. Liquid courage drying up, she paused and listened.

CHAPTER 20
The Dragon Scale Lute

The gurgle of water churning in the pond beyond Lord Tong's villa walls might have just as easily come from Kaiya's stomach. And not because of the rice wine.

She and Hardeep would have to trespass and steal, like common thieves. This plan was a far cry from the lofty ideals of the Dragon Singers. Her hand strayed to Tian's pebble. He'd never condone this.

Or maybe he would, considering how Lord Tong had acquired the Lute by selling out a small nation and its people. Swallowing down her mortification and replacing it with righteous indignation, she looked.

Two guards flanked the ornate iron gates. To think she'd almost marched right up to them and demanded entrance.

"There has to be a servant's entrance." She pulled Hardeep to the alley formed by the stone walls of this and the adjacent compound. As suspected, there was a plain wooden side door.

Unguarded.

Exchanging glances with her, Hardeep gave it a pull, and found it locked. He turned back to her. "I could break it down."

"His guards would hear it. I have another idea." A drunken one, but one which might actually work. She knocked.

His eyes widened. "What are you doing? You're letting them know we're here."

"Trust me." She flashed a smile full of confidence she wasn't really feeling.

The eye slot snapped open, revealing dark eyes framed by crinkles. "What do you want?"

She held up a jade bracelet, her favorite. Worth a small house, it was a small sacrifice to make if this bribe could benefit the Ankirans. "Let us in, and this is yours."

The eyes locked on the bangle, evaluating.

Kaiya held her breath. Maybe this wasn't such a good idea, if this lord inspired loyalty among his soldiers and servants. If whoever was on the other side alerted the rest of the villa, it would slam the door on any chance to get in.

Shaking his head, Hardeep frowned at her and reached for his blade.

The door opened. A middle-aged man in green livery stepped through, and snatched the bracelet. After a visual once-over of them, he started down the alley.

"Wait," she said, alcohol haze fading a fraction. She held out a gold ring, a treasured gift from Mother. "Tell me where I can find the Lute."

Licking his lips, he looked at the ring, then pointed to Hardeep's ornate *talwar*. "Give me the sword, too, and I'll answer your question."

Without a moment's hesitation, Hardeep unhooked his scabbard.

Kaiya placed a hand on his wrist. "Wait. What if we are attacked again?"

"No sword, no information." Crossing his arms, the servant jutted his chin out.

"It's all right," Hardeep said in Ayuri. "I can disarm anyone who doesn't have Paladin magic."

This was a bad idea. Still, Hardeep had been unarmed against the imperial guards and escaped with only a shredded sleeve. She retracted her hand.

With a smile, Hardeep presented his weapon in one hand.

The servant took it with greedy eyes. "What about the ring?"

"After you tell us what you know." Kaiya tried to glare, but the alcohol probably made her appear cross-eyed.

His brow creased for a moment. "The chamberlain plays the lute. Strange, foreign instrument."

Kaiya shook her head. "Impossible. Only a Dragon Singer could play it. It is made from a dragon scale."

"Oh, *that* lute." The servant's mouth rounded. "The lord shows it off sometimes. He keeps it in the vault in the northeast corner of the compound."

Northeast? Hopefully, Hardeep had a better sense of direction than her. Kaiya frowned, but offered the ring.

The man snatched it up and scampered down the alley.

Kaiya swallowed hard, partially regretting the loss of her jewelry.

"How did you know that would work?" Hardeep beamed.

"The lord must be at the reception, with most of his guards. Without good reason to deny us, a servant wouldn't turn down the equivalent of a lifetime of pay."

The appreciation and admiration in his nod sent flutters into her belly.

She fanned her hot face. "Let's find the vault."

With Prince Hardeep one step behind her, Kaiya squared her shoulders and walked through the servants' door with as much grace as the alcohol allowed. Which was to say, she almost tripped on her borrowed cloak.

Cream paper lanterns with light baubles hung from a central string across the courtyard. Sharply pitched eaves of green tile capped a spacious two-story residence and several side buildings. Red latticework framed windows in the white walls. At the center of the manicured courtyard, a carp pond bubbled. The compound seemed devoid of activity, though the pluck of some stringed instrument echoed from within the main residence. The musical scale sounded foreign. Could it be?

It wasn't in the direction the servant had said. Her gaze locked on a small one-story building with a wooden door on the near side of the villa. After a quick visual sweep of the yard, she started toward it.

Hardeep grabbed her arm. "That's the servants' privy. The vault is that one." He pointed toward the far end.

Kaiya swallowed hard. They'd have to cross the entire compound without being seen. Unless... She pulled him along the shadowed wall, toward the privy, with the stealth of a legendary Black Fist.

"Do you have to..." he gritted his teeth. "...relieve yourself?"

Heat flared in her cheeks. "No. We can hide behind the privy, and use the shadows between the other buildings to get there."

The silence between them was punctuated only by the plucks of the foreign-sounding instrument.

He grinned. "You're good at this sneaking around."

Her face flushed hotter, and she chuckled nervously. "I'm secretly a Black Fist."

"A what?"

Of course he wouldn't understand. "They're the boogeymen, stealing naughty children at night."

His brow furrowed.

"I'm joking; they're just a myth."

With a shrug, he followed her through the shadows.

Even on the outside, the privy stank worse than anything she'd ever smelled. How pampered her life was, to have servants taking care of every inconvenience. She held her breath as she peered around its corner.

A servant in green livery hurried down a path between the residence's two wings, but he wasn't facing them. She dashed toward the next building.

And tripped.

She fell face-first onto the light-colored gravel. Curse the rice wine. Biting her lip, she suppressed a squeak and looked toward the servant.

His eyes swept back and forth. His gaze paused right where Hardeep was.

Kaiya's chest tightened.

Then the man's head turned, and he continued on his way.

She let out her breath as quietly as she could, and allowed Hardeep to help her up. Her stumble now proved more humiliating than painful or frightening.

With only the instrument's sound and the occasional voice in the distance, they reached the vault without further incident. It was almost too easy. Surely, the Heavens must be smiling upon their task. Like the Dragon Singers, they were correcting a historical mistake.

Hardeep studied the heavy door and lock. He grinned. "I don't suppose a Black Fist could pick that?"

"Maybe if they really existed." She snorted and peered at the lock.

"Then we will need to hurry." Closing his eyes and taking a deep breath, he lowered his shoulder and slammed into the door.

The timbers shuddered with an ear-splitting crack.

The musical instrument in the distance went silent, then voices erupted in chatter.

Kaiya threw up her hands. Even in her drunken state, she knew... "The door opens outward!"

He gave the door a hard tug, and it opened.

"How?" She gawked.

With a grin, he pointed at the mangled locking mechanism. "Paladin training. I focused my power into that spot. Now let's hurry!"

They raced in. When he closed the door behind them, the room fell into darkness.

"Keep quiet," he whispered. "They won't notice the lock unless they look carefully. We just need to hide here until they pass. Now..."

They were about to lay eyes on the Dragon Scale Lute. Kaiya blinked as Hardeep opened his palm to expose a light bauble. Pulse racing with a mix of apprehension and excitement, she looked around.

The vault was empty.

How could that be? Had the servant lied? Then again, it didn't make sense for there to be nothing in here at all. She turned to Hardeep.

His eyes took in the vault without seeing.

Had this all been for naught? Her jewelry, gone. And now they'd have to hole up in this stuffy, narrow room until Heavens knew when. How long before the court realized she wasn't in the palace? This night couldn't possibly get worse. Panic rose in her voice. "Where...where could it be?"

"Wait." He took her hand and placed it on his chest. "Let me think." He felt hot, even through the smooth, thick cloth of his *kurta*. His heart thumped. Slow. Resolute. It seemed almost audible.

Like her guards and handmaidens earlier today.

Listen. Lord Xu had implored her to listen. She closed her eyes.

The heavy door and thick walls partially muffled voices and footsteps outside, but Hardeep's heartbeat now sounded clear.

And there was something odd—foreign and ominous—among the multitude of sounds outside. One hand on his chest, she placed the other on the door.

A symphony of vibrations echoed through the wood.

Then, the door opened.

Kaiya's heart leaped into her throat. Though the break in contact with the door had severed her link to the vibrations, sounds now poured in. Boots crunching on gravel. Shouts. And that nearly inaudible, ominous pulse. Three guards burst in, weapons bared.

If Heaven had smiled on them before, it now pointed and laughed. Behind them followed a young man with beautifully coifed hair and swishing green robes. He cradled a stringed instrument, like a pipa, in one arm. The light bauble lantern in his hand shined on the white powder on his face, which gave him an ivory complexion. He might be wearing more foundation than she had been this morning.

199

About her age, he was handsome, bordering on beautiful, with dignified features that might belong on a member of the imperial family. And of course, there was the lute in his arm.

Made of wood, not dragon scale. Its strings resonated, but it wasn't the source of the foreboding thrum.

"Who are you?" His voice came out high-pitched, tremulous, and effeminate, eliminating any resemblance to her brothers. Holding the lantern higher, the young man's eyes roved over them, then to a spot in the vault, when they widened. Panic made his voice crack. "What did you do with the Dragon Scale Lute?"

What? The servant hadn't misled them, then. The Lute was supposed to be here. She exchanged glances with Hardeep, who shrugged. She looked at the instrument in the man's hands.

Gaze following hers, he snorted. "No, not this lute. *The* Lute."

She shook her head. How did this happen? And how were they going to get out of this predicament? The room was so stuffy, and one of the guards stank of rice wine, exacerbating her drunken haze. "We don't have it."

The leader beckoned to the soldiers. "Take them."

The men surged forward.

Hardeep's hand reached toward his sword hilt.

Which wasn't there, after their trade for information.

Kaiya stared, wide-eyed.

Undaunted, Hardeep twisted and weaved through their attacks. They pursued him deeper into the vault.

Leaving her near the entrance, with the leader. He wasn't that much larger than her.

She stepped to help Hardeep, but he waved her off. "Go! Find the Lute!"

Surely he'd be all right. These were two soldiers, certainly not the equal of imperial guards. Head still buzzing, she pushed past the leader.

His thin fingers clamped down around her left wrist.

Though she'd never taken it seriously, the contact reflexes from her Praise Spring Fist training kicked in. She rotated her left palm up, exposing the soft inside of his forearm. She dragged her fingernails across the flesh.

Crying out, he yanked his hand back.

She hiked up her skirts, turned, and ran. Her heart pumped, and for that moment her head felt nominally clear.

Not daring to look back, she dashed across the courtyard and rounded a red column on the residence's veranda.

Breaths heaving, she peered around the column toward the vault.

The three soldiers and their leader emerged, heads turning left and right.

There was no sign of Hardeep. Had they slain him? Kaiya covered her mouth.

"She can't have gotten far," the young man said. "They must have had an accomplice who took the Dragon Scale Lute. You, go get the captain. He's at the imperial reception."

She ducked back, closed her eyes, and took several deep breaths to fight down the rising panic and despair.

That haunting resonance pulsed between the thumps of her heart in her ears. Though nearly imperceptible, it sounded louder than before, and seemed to be taunting her. The source was close. Inside the residence.

Through her slippers, she gripped the stone veranda with her toes and straightened her spine.

The soldiers' footsteps spread throughout the courtyard, though none approached. She opened her eyes and scanned the area.

The armed men were marching along the wall. Their little leader, lute still cradled in his arms, swept his gaze over the compound.

He was still by the vault, making it impossible to check on Hardeep without getting caught.

Could he be bleeding to death?

Think, think. There had to be a way to create a diversion and double back. Drawing deeper onto the veranda, Kaiya edged toward a door. She pressed her ear to it, and heard nothing save for the eerie thrum that answered her heart.

She slid the door open and slipped in.

Heat washed over her as she left the cool night air. Bloodwood stands, porcelain vases, and hanging scrolls all decorated the central hall. The quiet moan came from somewhere nearby.

It had to be the Lute. Find it, and she'd threaten to smash it unless they let her help Hardeep. She closed her eyes and, with one hand in front of her, followed the sound.

A dozen paces down the hall, the thrum's intensity blared from the left. The sound of her heartbeat echoed off of...she turned her head and looked through the circular archway into a side room.

Like an insect drawn to a light bauble, she ventured in. A red, blue, and white wool carpet from the Ayuri South felt soft beneath her feet, and covered much of the marble tiles. Calligraphy and paintings by famous artists evoked a sense of calm and welcome.

Bloodwood chairs surrounded a low table with a marble top, and on one of them rested a lute. Similar in appearance to a pipa, its fretted neck tilted at a sharp angle. It had at least a dozen strings compared to a pipa's four. Its soundboard was the color of cinnabar, and had a texture similar to leather.

Avarax's scale. Why would the chamberlain have expected it to be in the vault, if it was here?

Kaiya's eyes widened as she picked it up. It had a vibration, a life of its own, like Yanyan's pipa and so unlike her own. So ancient it must be; it smelled like rust. The several pairs of twisted strings shimmered like wet lines of spider silk in the morning sun. She ran her hand over the resonance plate. With its countless ridges, it resembled the cross-section of a tree stump.

"She's in here!" a high-pitched voice yelled from the doorway.

Kaiya's heart jumped into her throat. She turned to find the leader. So entranced had she been by the Lute, he'd come upon her unawares.

He stared at the instrument, mouth agape. "You! So you had it all along. Where did you get the strings? Do they work?"

Strings? Work? Kaiya looked down at them. They certainly looked new... She faced the man and studied him.

He didn't have a weapon. With his thin build and the way he wrung his delicate hands, he couldn't possibly be a soldier. Still his eyes looked at her, calculating.

Standing only half a head taller, he was still more than a match for any princess, save for little Lin Ziqiu, who took the Praise Spring fighting more seriously. He apparently came to the same conclusion, and took a step closer.

Her pulse raced. She raised the instrument above her head, though the very act sent her muddled head spinning. "Stay away, or I'll smash it."

He froze for a few seconds, then took a step closer. "Go ahead. I'd hoped the strings would remain forever lost, anyway."

Why? She lowered the Lute and took a step back.

Boots hurried across the wood floors in the hall, and a guard appeared at the doorway.

"We didn't find anyone else, Chamberlain Li," he said, his eyes on her.

A chamberlain? At such a young age? Kaiya studied his made-up features again. It would be a surprise if he were a day older than her.

The guard favored her with a curious expression. "Isn't that Princess Kaiya?"

"How do you know?" Chamberlain Li asked, now looking at her with renewed curiosity. "Have you seen her?"

"I had the impression she was prettier, but this is undoubtedly her."

Kaiya gritted her teeth.

"You're right." Li gave a slow nod, then narrowed his eyes. "*Dian-xia*, why did they send *you* to steal Lord Tong's lute? Now that I think about it, *who* sent you?"

Pulse skittering, hands shaking, Kaiya lifted the Lute again. "I'll smash it."

"Go ahead." Li waved a dismissive hand.

"No!" The guard stretched out a staying hand. "Chamberlin Li, it is you who is supposed to…"

Kaiya looked from one to the other. With Li's expression scrunched up into apprehension, he didn't appear to be bluffing. Or maybe the rice wine was still muddling her judgement.

"Bring her friend over. She'll be more inclined to negotiate."

Friend… Hardeep! He was alive! Hope rose in Kaiya's chest.

The guard turned on his heel and clacked down the hallway, leaving her with Li.

"There's no need for us to be uncivil." He gestured to a side table, where a porcelain decanter sat with several small matching cups. His fingers quivered. "Have some rice wine."

Tea, an inner voice implored.

Even as she kept the Lute cocked like a club in her own trembling hands, Kaiya gave a polite nod. She wouldn't drink another drop of alcohol for the rest of her life, but for now the request would get the chamberlain a few steps away.

He poured the rice wine into a cup, his grace in every motion that of a musician.

"Where did you learn to play a foreign instrument?" she asked with genuine curiosity.

He looked up from his work, eyes narrowed, searching hers. His expression softened. "My mother was a famous pipa player and singer in Yanhu, and she taught me. When Lord Tong hired me, he bade me learn. I taught myself."

What a strange demand of a chamberlain. "I would like to speak with Lord Tong."

The chamberlain wet his lips as he offered the cup. "He…he, uh… Barbarian uprisings have kept him busy in the North. He was unable to visit the capital for the prince's wedding."

Kaiya stayed back, ignoring the wine.

Two sets of bootsteps bracketed staggering footfalls in the hall outside. A pair of guards turned into the room, Hardeep draped between them.

Kaiya's heart leaped as they thrust him to the floor. He showed no outward sign of injury, and his breathing was light.

"The turtle egg is heavier than he looks," the one guard from before said.

Kaiya bristled at the insult, and fought the urge to run to Hardeep's side.

"Now, *Dian-xia*, turn over the Lute and I'll let you and your friend leave." Despite his offer, he still eyed the Dragon Scale Lute as if he'd just sucked a lemon and a bitter melon at the same time.

Could he be trusted? Probably not. Kaiya looked at the dwarf-made water clock, now indicating that the Iridescent Moon waxed to its third gibbous. One hour had already passed since she left the palace. They needed to get back before anyone realized she was gone. Her gaze shifted to Hardeep.

Chamberlain Li followed her eyes. "If you don't hand it over now, I'll have my men kill him."

Chapter 21
Treachery Afoot

A cool sea breeze blew through Tian's hair as he reached the top of the lighthouse, at the head of the seawall that separated the harbor from the mouth of the Jade River. Jie was briefing the four Black Fist adepts gathered there.

Looking up, he found the Iridescent Moon in its usual spot, now waxing past its third gibbous, indicating less than two hours before midnight. Only a little more than an hour had passed since he'd killed Lamp Man Sha, and they'd already found Fat Nose Jiang. With the evidence on Sha leaving a trail here, it had been almost too easy.

Below, light bauble lamps hung from posts on the seventeen riverside docks, mingling with the soft blue light of Guanyin's Eye. Twenty-two men armed with broadswords stood guard as thirty-seven longshoremen and boatmen worked to load eleven privately owned river barges.

Fat Nose Jiang oversaw the operation at the head of one of the quays, personally inspecting twelve barrels of fish paste, and eight kegs of sulfur, and six hundred and forty-two bales of rice,

He'd wager that some of the rice had been the bales dumped in the cove.

They were nearly done, and no doubt the barges would push off at first light, bound upstream for Lord Tong and his allies. Whatever else could be said about the conspirators, they were efficient.

Tian unfurled his official robes and passed them to Chong Xiang, a forty-two-year-old adept with a crook nose. "Put these on. You know the plan."

Chong beamed. "Brilliant. Just like the Architect."

Tian snorted. Chong must've just been a green recruit when the legendary Black Lotus strategist died on a secret mission thirty years before. He'd have no basis for comparison. Still, if Chong wanted to wax nostalgic… "That makes you the Surgeon," Tian said.

"Then that leaves me as the Beauty?" Jie peered at Guanyin's Eye, the Blue Moon.

Her reference to the last of the ill-fated trio would have made sense, except there would be no baiting gullible men. "No, you're the lookout and runner."

She sucked on her lower lip and released it with a pop.

He studied Chong, who shrugged into the official robes. "Have Jiang at the dock overseer's office in ten minutes."

With that, he started his mental countdown. He and the adepts descended the lighthouse. Jie motioned them to assigned lookout points as they snuck along the south end of the docks toward the overseer's office.

Its weathered plank siding afforded plenty of handholds, and in seconds he had gained the rooftop. The terrace provided a commanding view of the river wharfs, just a throwing star's toss away from where Jiang was now unfurling a scroll and reading. Stairs descended to the office below. Tian tested the door. Unlocked and well-oiled.

Slipping in, he padded down the steps. The overseer's office was only a twelfth the size of the harbormaster's and sparsely decorated, probably because the overseer was busy overseeing his own finances. Tian worked his way between several desks, taking note of the shuttered lamps, and came to the door. He unlocked it. Five minutes to spare, assuming Chong kept to the timeline. Cracking the wooden window shutters, he squinted out.

Jiang pressed the scroll to his chest while Chong crossed his arms. A guard flanked Jiang, hand on sword hilt.

"I don't recognize you from the harbormaster's office," Jiang said.

Chong's booming voice carried the chill air. "Look, I don't want to be out here at this hour any more than the harbormaster, but since I'm just the new deputy, he sent me. There's a minor clerical error we need to resolve."

Jiang leaned in toward Chong and whispered something beyond Tian's hearing. Something shiny glinted in his hand.

A weapon?

"A bribe," Jie whispered, her breath hot on his ear.

Tian whipped around. She'd snuck up on him, yet again. "Is everyone in place?"

She yawned. "Very soon."

He turned back to the crack between the shutters.

"I see everything is in order." Chong gestured toward the overseer's office. "You'll have to sign an affidavit."

Jiang threw up an arm. "Can't it wait?"

"My sleep is worth more than a gold *yuan*."

The guard's sword hand twitched. Chong settled ever so slightly in his stance, his hands reaching across into either sleeve. Jie placed one hand on the shutters while the other palmed a throwing spike.

"Very well." With a sigh, Jiang motioned for his guard to follow.

Tian blew out a long breath. It had worked just as he expected from what Jie'd told him about Jiang not wanting to hurt her on the *Wild Orchid*.

She tapped on his arm. *Guard is mine.*

Non-lethal, he tapped back.

Of course.

The men's footsteps came closer. Light feet pattered on the roof. Tian's grip tightened on his knife. The door pushed open.

211

"I'll get the light." Chong stepped in.

Jiang and the guard followed.

Pushing the door closed with his foot, Tian yanked Jiang's hair back and pressed a knife to his throat. "Not a word."

Across from him, a large body crumpled to the floor.

"You!" Jiang said. "I recognize your voice. You're the boy from this morning. I guess you didn't take Sha's bribes. Where is he?"

Dead, but Jiang didn't have to join him as long as he cooperated. In all likelihood, he wouldn't divulge much, not without time they didn't have. Tian spoke in Jie's direction. "Prepare the intoxicant. Chong, dim light."

A light bauble spilled a brittle light from between Chong's fingers, revealing Bu and Li's silent arrival. A cork popped off a snuff bottle. The sweet fragrance of *yinghua* flowers filled the air. The contact toxin affected only men, making them even more malleable to a woman's suggestion. It would also leave them with a splitting headache and little memory.

"Put him in a chair and take one step back," Jie whispered.

Tian dragged a chair over with his foot and then shoved Jiang into it. Keeping the knife at Jiang's throat, he backed off.

"What are you doing?" Jiang's voice quivered.

"Making you more comfortable." Casting a broad smile, Jie straddled Jiang and pressed her lips to the divot below his nose. In two seconds, the tension in his body melted. With a hand, she pushed Tian's knife hand away. "That isn't necessary. Mister Jiang will be cooperative, right?"

"No…" Jiang mumbled. "Yes…"

"Good boy." She ground into his lap and pressed her chest against him.

Disgusting. Tian's jaw twitched as he focused on Jiang's back, which would look better with a knife in it. Maybe if it were Wen doing this kind of interrogation it would feel less inappropriate, since she wasn't so young.

But no, even if Jie looked thirteen, and had for as long as he'd known her, she was three years, two months, and eighty-seven days older than Wen: ten years, three months, and two days older than him,

Jie shifted back. "So Mister Jiang, who do you work for?"

"I really shouldn't say…"

"No, you shouldn't, but you will." Her voice was so…sultry. So wrong.

"Evergreen Trading." No surprise there.

"What do you do?"

His voice began to slur. "I have a budget to make sure things get to where they need to go."

"What things?"

"Turmeric." His hand reached to Jie's buttocks.

The son of a turtle egg deserved to have his manhood decapitated for lusting after…well, Jie might be twenty-nine, but she was still a girl, maybe not yet flowered for all that she let on. Knife flipped to an underhanded grip, Tian took a step forward.

She waved him off with one hand and moved Jiang's hand off her butt with the other. "Eight kegs of turmeric? Is Lord Tong opening up a chain of curry shops throughout the North?"

Jiang chuckled nervously. "Firepowder to Yutou, sulfur and food stores to Wailian."

So that was the connection. Tong was using sulfur from the faraway nation of Pelastya to make firepowder, which he traded to Yutou Province for fish paste.

"How much food so far?" Jie ran fingers through his hair.

"Twelve thousand *shi* of rice and twelve hundred *jin* of pink fish paste." It would explain some of the lost rice bales. All that was enough to feed Lord Tong's five thousand men for two years, four months and eight days, if the fish paste kept that long. Or less, if there were more soldiers.

She kissed his ear. "Why so much?"

"I don't ask questions; I just do what I'm told." Try as he might, Jiang's hand couldn't get past Jie's as he tried to grope her.

Tian sighed. Jiang was nothing more than an accessory. Not even a bad person, save for salacious proclivities and putting money ahead of nation. "What about Lord Peng? Is he involved in Evergreen Trading?"

Jiang's hands paused in their futile efforts and he snaked his head around. His words came out more and more slowly. "The *Tai-Ming* lord? No, he's the *Tianzi's* lapdog. He wouldn't dream of skirting the laws of interdependence."

Tian looked at Jie. She'd defended Lord Peng and now wore a smug look to prove it. Peng was clearly innocent, unlike the conspirators who paid little heed to the three-hundred-year-old rules set up by the Founder himself, which ensured everyone prospered but stayed dependent through specialization. Maybe Lord Tong and his allies were jealous that only the capital province was allowed economic diversification. Or, they were planning on outright rebellion.

Jiang's head jerked and his eyes blinked.

Jie slapped him lightly. "Stay awake. I don't want you falling asleep before the fun begins."

"I...won't." The last word came out as a mumble, and his eyes rolled up into his head. They'd get no more out of him for another ten hours.

Two sets of footsteps, an adult's and juvenile's, brushed across the roof and down the stairs. Bu and Li turned around, hands on their concealed weapons, but eased when Qu and Little Huang appeared.

Despite the chill air, sweat glistened on Little Huang's forehead. "We have an emergency! Princess Kaiya has gone missing."

Tian's stomach flipped. Princess Kaiya...as children, they'd been best friends. They'd promised to marry each other. Silly, for sure, and three thousand, one hundred and forty-seven days had passed since their last meeting, but still. Now she was missing while a rebellion brewed. "Who knows about it?"

"That's all I know," Little Huang said. "Master Yan ordered all available agents back to Huajing to search for her."

Tian exchanged glances with Jie. If the rebellious lords found out, they'd spare no effort to take the princess hostage. "If we ran, it would take us three hours to reach the West Gates."

"*You* can't go back." Jie picked herself off Jiang.

He frowned. If anyone could find clues to Kaiya's whereabouts, it would be him.

Jie seized his arm and searched his eyes. "They'll execute you."

Banishment or not, he had to help. Kaiya was his oldest, dearest friend. His last connection to a more innocent, idealistic time. "It doesn't matter."

"It does. And you need to make sure the river barges stay docked. And what if Jiang's men coming looking for him?" What was that look? Pleading?

Tian sighed. She was right. There was still a mission here, and anything could happen in three hours. Still, "We can't just let the rebels capture her."

"We don't even know if the traitors know. I will go back by horse relay, tell Master Yan what we've found out. You take care of things here."

Fists clenched, Tian nodded. She was right, of course. He still needed to complete the last part of his plan: go to the harbormaster, tell him about the contraband, and have him come to the docks with soldiers to impound the cargo. He looked up at Jie, his own eyes undoubtedly begging, *Please make sure she is safe.*

CHAPTER 22
Uncommitted Resolve

Standing in Lord Tong Baxian's receiving room with the Dragon Scale Lute in hand, Kaiya's heart roared in her ears. Give up the instrument, and maybe Chamberlain Li and his henchmen would let them go.

Maybe not.

And if she gave it up, she couldn't use it to help Ankira. Not only that, who might Lord Tong use it on? Could Li even play it? That would mean he was also becoming a Dragon Singer. Maybe he already was one.

A mix of jealousy, indecision, and fear stirred inside her. The lute buzzed of its own accord. With a trembling finger, she made a tentative pluck on a bass string.

The barely audible sound came out low and desolate, like the lament of an exiled ruler over the fall of his kingdom.

Despite the lack of resonance, a tremor coursed down Kaiya's spine. The chamberlain's eyes widened. The two soldiers took hesitant steps back.

At their feet, Hardeep stirred.

Fighting the urge to still the string and quell all the misgivings building in her heart, she picked at a treble string.

The wail keened like a small child, alone and hunted.

The chamberlain turned and ran, his footsteps fading down the hall. One of the guards dropped his blade and covered his ears. The other froze in place, mouth open in a silent scream.

Hardeep swept up the fallen broadsword and jumped to his feet. In a fluid motion, he whacked both men with the flat of the blade.

Both collapsed.

Shuddering from the Lute's horrific notes, Kaiya placed a hand over the strings to silence their keen, then ran over and wrapped Hardeep in an embrace. She'd never been so close to a man before, and after the eeriness of the Lute's sound, it felt comforting. Its ominous echo still resonated in her mind.

He pushed out of her arms and held her shoulders, beaming. "You did it. With practice, you'll be able to project its sound."

Not like she ever wanted to hear it, ever again. She studied the sound plate. "How did they acquire one of his scales?"

He scratched the back of his neck, brow furrowed and eyes looking up at his own lashes. "A legend from before the War of Ancient Gods has it that Aralas himself dislodged that scale from Avarax's neck."

"How? I have never heard such a legend."

"Perhaps the stories in the South differ from Cathay's." Hardeep scratched the back of his neck. "He used an arrow made of pure light."

Kaiya nodded. Paintings of that era did depict the elf angel's bow, shooting lightning.

"We need to flee before more men arrive. Come." He opened the bag he was carrying and gestured for her to put the Lute into it.

She did so, happy to be relieved of the instrument and its fell music. Cinching the drawstrings, he bent over and retrieved a scabbard for the sword he'd taken. Then he took her hand and guided her toward the front door.

Despite the horror and misgivings, her heart swelled. She'd coaxed a sound first out of Yanyan's Pipa, now out of the Dragon Scale Lute. It hadn't seemed possible this morning, but now, she might really be able to help Hardeep. Then again, just those two plucks gave birth to more misgivings than any of the day's other misadventures. Was it worth hearing the Lute's moan again? She shivered.

Outside, Prince Hardeep turned and took both her hands. "Thank you so much. I could never have done this by myself. You found the Dragon Scale Lute, and even plucked out a sound. I have more hope now than I have in a very long time."

His hands, on hers, drew her closer. The warmth was reassuring, mingling with the rice wine dancing in her head. Maybe she'd abused her position, but it was for the right reasons. The liberation of an occupied people. The revival of a lost art. The chance of being more than just a political bride. All possible because this one man saw true potential in her.

He placed one hand on the small of her back and cradled her nape with the other.

Fire erupted all through her. Never had a man held her like this. Her stomach buzzed like a hummingbird's wings. All three moons seemed to shine on only them. She closed her eyes and tilted her chin up to him, parting her lips to offer him her first kiss.

Nothing.

Then, a finger touched her lips. She opened her eyes to meet his sigh.

"We must stay focused," he said. "For now. I can't lose myself in you." His arms released her.

The warmth fled her body as the cool night air rushed in. The alcohol haze still fogged her mind, but at least now, things were a little clearer. She'd been about to kiss a man! How could she even consider something so inappropriate?

That, on top of breaking several rules, risking servants so she could escape the palace, and intimidating a chamberlain.

Now, the rejection.

Of course he would. She was plain and lanky, and all he really needed was a gullible princess to find and steal a magical artifact.

"Please, Kaiya, come with me." The manipulator took her hand and tugged her along.

Pulling back, she held her ground. "No, this is wrong. I understand your need to help your country, but maybe there are better channels. Let me present the case to my father again."

He let out a long sigh. "You are right. I am so sorry. I was so excited at your breakthrough earlier today, and again, that we so easily retrieved the Dragon Scale Lute. I will take you home now, before anyone gets in trouble."

His beautiful eyes seemed so defeated. He was placing her concerns over the welfare of his own people. Guilt clawed at her chest. She stared down at the pavestones until he tugged her into a walk.

Kaiya kept her head down as they plodded in somber silence. At her side, Hardeep mumbled something unintelligible. She looked up and found the profile of his sharp chin. The sudden motion sent her head spinning again, a black tunnel narrowing her field of vision. She stumbled.

His arm shot out and caught her. "Let me support you. We are fairly close to the palace."

Blinking away the blurriness, she leaned into him. Oh, if only she could help him without having to break so many rules.

Up ahead, low voices muttered in Ayuri. Hardeep jerked to a stop, pulling her closer. If they had returned the way they had come, it might mean more Madurans, ready to ambush them again. Her hand strayed to Cousin Kai-Long's dagger as she scanned the surroundings.

Hardeep's hand patted her on the shoulder. "It's all right. They are my people."

"How can you tell?"

They turned a corner and he pointed. Dozens of men, women, and children huddled around tables in the middle of a street between two rows of dilapidated buildings.

Guilt knotted in her throat. So much poverty, while she never wanted for luxury.

"Your father, in his generosity, allowed refugees from Ankira to stay on this block."

This block, out of sight. She'd never heard of such a decision, nor had she ever seen such a run-down place so close to the noble's district. Then again, her processions always stuck to main roads, and the distance between the houses here suggested tertiary streets. No lord would come this way. They'd pretend it didn't even exist.

If everyone else would sweep these people under the rug, Kaiya would see them. Validate their suffering.

Lit by the plump Blue Moon and the half-White Moon, barefooted children wearing threadbare *kurta* shirts chased each other in raucous circles. At the tables, where light baubles cast domes of light, women in faded *saris* gossiped among each other as they ate a meager meal. The few men were all middle-aged, dressed in tattered clothes, sitting on rickety chairs as they chatted.

Guilt squeezed Kaiya's belly. They all had to be hungry and freezing, while her people feasted in the warmth of the palace.

At her side, Prince Hardeep sighed. "Lord Peng understands our plight. He suggested bringing you here to meet me, but the Madurans' hired knives were waiting. That's why I met you closer to the palace. Come."

His hand, so large and reassuring, released hers. The lingering warmth in her fingers tingled away, leaving a hollow sensation in her chest. He beckoned her to follow. Up close, the pungent scent of turmeric hung in the air, mixing in with a cinnamon aroma, which swirled from steaming cups. Children stopped running and the men and women all looked up.

Hardeep leaned in. "Most of these people had ties to the Cathayi trade office in Akira. Your officials there helped many escape. Now, they work as laborers and servants for wages so low, they can barely feed themselves. Some of the prettier girls end up in the Floating World for rich men with exotic tastes."

Kaiya's chest constricted. How horrible. She'd compared marriage to death, but what these girls suffered… She studied their expressions. All bore lines of worry on their proud faces. One young woman in particular looked striking. Her features were less round, her complexion lighter, speaking of some Cathayi blood. She lowered her head.

"Prince…Hardeep?" The oldest man pressed his hands together. "Thank you for your assistance. Please, bring your guest to join us." He scooted over and gestured to a pair of seats.

Hardeep extended an open hand, inviting her to go first. "Please, Kaiya. You must be hungry."

Her belly rumbled its assent. Heat flared in her cheeks. She'd had at least six or seven cups of rice wine, and never had a chance to actually eat anything solid. With a nod of her head, she settled in the indicated chair.

And nearly fell, again.

Hardeep grabbed her arm, sparing her yet more embarrassment.

"Poor girl." One of the middle-aged women clucked, placing a cup of dark liquid in front of her. "Here, drink some chai. It will warm you up on this chill night."

Kaiya accepted it, savoring the warmth the cup radiated into her hands. Certainly not as intense as Hardeep's warmth, but comforting, nonetheless. She took a sip. The smooth tea slid down her throat, dancing in a burst of spices. Heat percolated through her.

"Eat, eat!" Another woman slid a cracked porcelain plate in front of her. Another ladled what appeared to be shredded chicken in a yellow sauce on top of a round disk of flatbread.

Kaiya looked at the center dishes from which the refugees served. Her own plate must have accounted for half of what remained. She shook her head. "No, I can't possibly…"

Hardeep laughed. "In my homeland, even beggars will treat their guests as royalty."

How ironic. Kaiya forced a polite smile.

He leaned in and whispered, "Eat. Otherwise, you will offend them."

Kaiya swept her gaze around the table. Expectant eyes met hers. Very well, she would eat. Her stomach certainly demanded it, and it would be bad manners to decline. However, there didn't seem to be any chopsticks or any other kind of utensils. She fiddled with a lock of hair.

"Use your hands," Hardeep said. "Tear the flatbread, eat it with the chicken."

Hands. Kaiya studied hers, which had touched ancient musical instruments, dirty shirts, jewelry, furniture, and princes' hands. Gulping air, she reached out and ripped off a piece of sauce-covered bread. It smelled wonderful. Bad manners or not, she pushed the whole thing in her mouth and chewed. Turmeric, sugar, and other spices swirled over her tongue. Piece after piece disappeared as her stomach urged her on.

Around her, the Ankiran refugees broke out into laughter.

One woman clapped her hands. "She is hungry!"

"Your Excellency, you can't afford to feed her," one of the men said.

Prince Hardeep laughed. "Not with what is left in the national treasury, no."

Kaiya paused on a bite. Ankira was bankrupted because of Cathay's avarice, which she put on full display now. Perhaps her dress, possibly worth more than everything on this block combined, was paid for on the backs of the Ankirans. The guilt weighed like a dwarf anvil in her gut.

He placed a hand between her shoulder blades. "The way you are eating, you might deplete your own country's treasury."

Blood burned in Kaiya's cheeks.

"A song!" Hardeep rose from his seat and beckoned one of the middle-aged men. "Bring me a sitar."

The man disappeared into one of the houses and brought out what resembled a long lute with a bulbous resonator. It had so many strings, including several underneath the top ones that didn't look accessible to the player. Hardeep received it in two hands.

Beaming, he started picking at the strings. The sitar whined in high-pitched shifts, with the lower strings echoing the main refrain with harmonic resonance. Some of the other men began beating on the table with their hands as the pace picked up, bobbing their heads to the rhythm.

Upbeat, the song spoke to Kaiya's soul, and it was all she could do to keep from standing and dancing.

"The drumming refrain is called a *tala*," one woman told her.

Blue eyes locked on hers, Hardeep began to sing. His low voice, rich like the chai, sent Kaiya's belly fluttering in a storm of butterflies.

> *Ankira, my home.*
> *Land of rich soil and verdant valleys,*
> *Home of the ten thousand gods on earth.*
> *Warmth of the heart*
> *My heart yearns for my homeland.*

The others joined in, their voices rising as one. The resonance surged inside of her, coiling just as it had in the Hall of Pure Melody. Prince Hardeep flashed a smile, beckoning her to join in.

She dropped her gaze to the street, shaking her head. The sentiment, she understood, and yet, it was her country that helped oppress his. How could she let her voice meld with theirs?

Their song came to a slow, melancholy end, and the sitar trailed off into a somber hum. These people missed their homeland, wanted to return, wanted to be free.

Hardeep sighed. "It is getting late. We must get you back before anyone realizes you are gone."

The power of music, flourishing in her as the Ankirans had sung, still spiraled throughout her core. It tingled in her fingers and toes, and she aligned her body. "No. Let's test the Lute."

"No," Hardeep said. "No, I have already caused you too much trouble."

"I want to. For you. For your people." She studied her feet. "For myself."

He lifted her chin. His eyes searched hers, rocking back and forth in mesmerizing sweeps. "Are you sure? Please, don't feel obligated just because a bunch of old men sang for you."

She nodded with heartfelt passion. "Yes. Yes. It is in my power to do so, and I shall."

Prince Hardeep looked from her to his people. "Her voice holds the key to our salvation!"

The men and women broke into a cheer, a genuine appreciation that no one in the court had ever shown her.

Beaming, Hardeep took her hand. "Let's go. Somewhere acoustically perfect, to magnify your voice."

Heat mingling into the echo of the song, she rose. Thanks to the trip to the archives, she knew just the place. "The Temple of Heaven."

He raised an eyebrow. "Are you sure?

Was she? To enter the sacred tower without a blessing from its priests invited a death sentence. She searched his eyes again.

Her heart swelled. Yes. Better to die than to give up on rediscovering the lost magic of Dragon Songs when she was so close. She nodded.

The Ankirans all pressed their hands together and bowed their heads as Hardeep led her down a street. Headed south, according to the Iridescent Moon's position.

After a few blocks, he stopped. His head swept from left to right and back, pausing at an empty wooden produce stand outside a shuttered green grocer.

"What is it?" Hand on her dagger, she peered through the dark at the stand.

He pulled her closer. "Our friends from before. They must have tracked us back here." He stomped a foot on the street, sending vibrations rippling out. After a second, he said, "Only two this time, one behind the stand, and one there." He twisted behind her and swept a sword out of its scabbard. Wood shattered with a loud crack.

He spun around to her front. Metal clinked against sword, and then clattered on the ground. The dark outline was shaped like a star. She squatted down to pick it up. Pain bit into her fingers as a sharp edge cut her.

"Stay down," Hardeep said. His blade whizzed, again cutting projectiles out of the air with clanks and thuds. As he moved, the silk bag containing the Dragon Scale Lute slipped from his shoulders. It hit the ground with a discordant groan, like the keen of a murderous beast in its death throes.

The villains stared at the bag, wide-eyed.

Fear crawled up Kaiya's spine. She shuddered at the sound. It was just like at Lord Tong's villa. If it evoked fear in those men, and now her, maybe… She reached for the bag and fumbled with the drawstrings. Pain bit where the star had cut her thumb. Still, she managed to fish the Lute out.

She rose from her low squat to a level horse stance, similar to the one Doctor Wu taught for breathing exercises. Spine straight, thighs parallel to the ground, she cradled the Lute and plucked one of the treble strings.

A sound like a widow mourning her dead husband wailed from the Lute, twisting in her core and then resonating into her limbs. Unlike her first attempt, it was louder. The barrage of attacks stopped and the two large men in the shadows lowered their weapons.

Kaiya strummed across all the strings. The dissonance of high and low pitches must have sounded like the chorus of souls tormented by Yanluo in the pits of hell. The would-be assassins dropped their weapons. One's crossbow crashed onto the pavestones, sending a loaded bolt soaring toward them.

With a low mutter, Hardeep jerked back, his hip jarring into her head and knocking her back.

Pain flared in her temples and white flashed in her field of vision. Just when the alcohol had begun to clear. She blinked away the cobwebs.

Hardeep knelt beside her, his brows furrowed. "Are you all right?"

Was she? Her head ached, her thumb stung. Her chest hurt from the Lute's echo in her heart. She gawked at the thin line of blood on her thumb.

Tearing a strip of cloth from his shirt, he wrapped the wound. Tight and firm. He helped her to her feet with a chuckle. "You must be lucky, to survive two attacks with just a small cut on your thumb."

It didn't seem lucky, nor a laughing matter. She pouted.

His smile flattened. He turned to the side and pointed. "We are here."

Already? And where had their attackers gone? She looked at him, and then followed his gesture. An eight-tiered stupa, its colors indistinct in the night, towered above white stone walls. Two soldiers in ceremonial robes and breastplates flanked the metal gates.

There was only one place in Huajing like this: the Temple of Heaven, which housed a chunk from a fallen star, brought to Cathay by the Wang Dynasty Founder at the bidding of the gods.

And if the story from the geomancy book was true, it was built around dragon bones, on the spot where the elf angel Aralas revealed himself to Yanyan, the mother of musical magic.

Her pulse quickened. There was one last chance to leave before risking a capital offense.

CHAPTER 23
Gone Rogue

While Jie had long grown used to the smell of humans, horses were another story. She'd never ridden one by herself before, and would hopefully never have to again. How the ruddy-skinned Kanin plainspeople spent all day in the saddle was beyond her. Their purebred swifthorses were part of the relay system that she used now.

It dated back to before the Hellstorm, during the Hundred Years of War between the Arkothi and Ayuri Empires. Though horses and messengers were meant to change at waystations every twenty miles, she only changed horses. A trip that normally took the better part of a day on foot lasted only an hour, but left her butt and thighs so sore, she'd almost welcome Fat Nose Jiang's groping.

Or maybe Tian's. Not as if he'd even shown the least amount of jealousy when she used her feminine wiles on Jiang.

Dismounting in the broad, moonlit plaza outside Sun-Moon Palace, outside a perimeter of imperial guards, she wobbled over to where several officials gathered. Every joint and muscle ached with each step.

Blue robes swished as a familiar imperial guard officer blocked her way. Either the horse had given her away, or perhaps sore muscles compromised her stealth. The five-clawed dragon on his breastplate sent a shiver through her spine. "You!" he said. "Who are you to commandeer an imperial swifthorse?"

Disguised as a court official, Master Yan shuffled over, bowing. "General Zheng, this is my daughter Jie. She has hurried all the way from Jiangkou to join in our task." He spoke in a loud whisper as his eyes roved past the perimeter.

Jie followed his gaze, her elven vision locking in on the armed men across the moat, their robes showing no symbol of allegiance. She turned back and bowed, looking up through her lashes at the commander of the imperial guard; Zheng, Tian's cousin, which explained the familiarity. Only a handful of the senior-most imperial guards knew of the Black Lotus Clan and Master Yan's true identity.

General Zheng favored her with furrowed brows. Lowering his voice, he beckoned her past the cordon, across the plaza and into the ring of officials. "Thank you for coming. Master Yan has told me about your particular abilities."

Pretending to pay attention to the general's pleasantries, Jie leaned in to her adoptive father and whispered, "Tian thinks Lord Tong Baxian has gone beyond the illegal production of firepowder. He might also be plotting a rebellion with Northern Lords Chu, Xi, and Qin. All own part of a suspicious trading company, and none have arrived for the imperial wedding. He has also been stockpiling food. Also absent are Lords Chi, Shen, and Bai from Nanling Province, and much of the illegal firepowder has ended up there."

Without breaking stride, Master Yan bowed toward General Zheng. "I must brief the *Tianzi* on an urgent matter. I entrust Jie to you."

"What have we learned so far?" Jie asked.

General Zheng grunted. "The princess left the reception four and a half hours ago at the first waxing gibbous with Young Lord Peng Kai-Long of Nanling Province."

Jie sucked on her lower lip. Tian had adored Peng as a child, though a mistake by Kai-Long had led to Tian's banishment. As confirmed by Fat Nose Jiang, the Peng family was unquestioningly loyal to the *Tianzi*. "Do we know where they headed from there?"

"Young Lord Peng left her near a pagoda in the inner castle. She disappeared right after that, and nobody has seen her since."

Leave it to imperial guards to lose a princess. Jie swept a hand toward the palace walls. "Sun-Moon Palace is vast. Are you sure she is not here?"

General Zheng gave a perfunctory nod. "Everyone, including members of your clan, has swept the grounds thrice over."

The girl wasn't trained in stealth, so… "How did she get past the imperial guards?" Besides the fact they

235

were witless strong-arms. "Surely someone would have seen her?"

"Magic." General Zheng spoke the word with a tone that suggested he had just eaten a bitter melon. He held a glass bauble, like an Aksumi magic light, cradled in a silk kerchief. "When it touches bare flesh, it makes someone look like her. The servants found it in the pagoda."

Jie took the bauble in hand.

General Zheng nearly choked. "That is disconcerting. Please, don't touch it. It makes you look a little like her."

If only she had a mirror. Jie had never seen the princess up close, but had heard she was a plain-looking girl. Whatever Tian had seen in her... She wrapped the bauble up as she thought. Tian's recollections of Princess Kaiya suggested a sweet and obedient girl, who would never dream of breaking any rules. Where had she acquired Aksumi magic baubles and what prompted her to run away? "Was there anything out of the ordinary in her schedule today?"

General Zheng harrumphed. "She met a suitor, but only after an interruption from a foreign supplicant to the *Tianzi*. She was quite smitten by him."

"The suitor?"

"No, the foreigner. General Lu broke off the matchmaking meeting halfway through."

Jie stifled a sigh. General Lu had served a northern rebel eight years ago, but had betrayed him and helped a lord loyal to the realm put down that rebellion.

When that lord conspired against the throne two years ago, she'd convinced Lu to proclaim loyalty to the *Tianzi*.

He now commanded the national armies in the North. Posted in Lord Tong's Wailian County, no less, where he'd earned the nickname *the Guardian Dragon of Cathay*.

Another conspirator? Maybe she was still suspicious after he'd led troops that had tried to kill her during that uprising eight years ago, and didn't trust him for his repeated opportunistic side-switching. "What do we know of the foreigner?"

"Prince Hardeep Vaswani of Ankira. Nineteen years old according to the archives, and apparently trained in Ayuri Paladin arts."

Paladins could supposedly plant suggestions in the gullible, and if the Founder's Dictionary of the Cathayi Language were illustrated, it would probably show a picture of a sixteen-year-old princess in the entry for *gullible*. "Where would we find Prince Hardeep?"

"He was staying with Young Lord Peng Kai-Long."

Young Lord Peng again. Also something of a vainglorious narcissist based on Tian's childhood recollections, but unquestionably loyal. Perhaps Prince Hardeep had duped him, too. "Where is Young Lord Peng right now?"

"He is at the *Tianzi's* side, taking blame for this debacle. He said Prince Hardeep was visiting the Ankiran ghetto."

237

"I've never heard of such a thing." And Jie heard a *lot*.

"It's fairly new. Young Lord Peng petitioned the *Tianzi* to allow the Ankiran refugees to stay there."

With no other clues… "Then that's where I'll start. Where is it?"

"I will send Princess Kaiya's most senior imperial guards with you." He gestured toward a gaggle of blue-robed men who would stand out anywhere in Huajing.

Jie pursed her lips. It would far easier if he just told her. "Do you think they're reliable after they let the princess slip through their fingers?"

General Zheng's frown mirrored her own. "I charged them with watching the reception tonight, not the princess."

"They will only slow me down." Though as sore as her muscles burned, she might not be moving that fast.

Five imperial guards, all in their mid-to-late twenties, marched over. The dragons etched into their burnished breastplates scowled, sending the little human hairs on her arms prickling. In unison, they saluted General Zheng with a right fist in a left palm.

He gestured toward her. "This is…what is your name again?"

"Jie." She hopefully contained the roll of her eyes.

"Right. She will be searching for clues. You will accompany her. Jie, this is Captain Chen Xin, Zhao Yue, Ma Jun, Xu Zhan, and Li Wei."

Jie examined each. Even with her elven vision and Black Lotus training, little differentiated the five dour men. They might as well have been moving statues, bowing their heads and barking in unison, "Yes, General."

With an affable smile, Li Wei—or maybe it was Ma Jun—beckoned her, with his left hand. Unlike the others, he wore his sword on his right. "I know a fast way to get there."

Nodding, Jie followed him. The other four pushed past her, through the perimeter and east into the city's northeast quadrant. For all the interest they showed, she might as well not have been there.

"I thought he'd never let us go," said Chen Xin. Definitely Chen Xin, clearly the oldest with his rough skin and salt-and-pepper hair. The three gold stripes on his cuffs marked him as the leader. Tian had said something about a run-in with him years ago, before his banishment.

"Too bad we're stuck with *her*." Xu Zhan—or was it Zhao Yue—jerked a thumb at her.

Now away from the general, there was little need to hide the rolling of her eyes. "I'm right here."

"May I speak freely?" said Xu Zhan...yes, it was Xu Zhan. His knuckles were flat and worn, the mark of a brawler. "You might be an elf, but we'd be better off with scent hounds."

Jie's pulse roared in her ears. "I'm not an elf, and while a dog might have a good nose, it lacks my brains to connect all the clues. I doubt the five of you combined could compensate for that."

Xu Zhan's flat-knuckled hands closed into tight balls.

Laughing, Ma Jun, the one with the boyish face, clapped Flat-Knuckle Xu Zhan on the back. At least one of them *did* have a personality. "Never mind him, he's just worried."

"We'll never find her." Lefty Li Wei shook his head, sending the scar on his chin zigzagging. "Not before ruffians do, and do horrible things to her."

Zhao Yue, the one with a triangular head like a fox, held up a hand. "Everyone in the capital knows what she looks like. They wouldn't dare touch her."

Ruffians didn't fear the law, and rebels would do worse. Jie would never underestimate an imperial guard's idiocy again. Any more of their banter and she'd tear her hair out. "Is it much farther? Wait." She paused at an alley, where something sparkling in the three moons' light caught her eye.

The men all came to a stop and followed her gaze down the alley.

"What is it?" Salt-and-pepper-haired Chen Xin crowded over her shoulder like a monster from a horror novel.

Jie took in the alley. With the bright moons, her night vision hadn't taken over, but her visual acuity still picked up on details these five buffoons would miss. She pointed at the splintered wood of a two-story house.

"Two holes, from crossbow bolts. The size is too big for standard-issue Cathayi bolts."

One eye closed, fox-faced Zhao Yue leaned toward the wall while Xu Zhan pushed past him and tested each hole with his finger, like a bear pawing for honey.

"Bring a lamp over here." Jie knelt down and picked up the cracked glass bauble that had originally drawn her attention. She withdrew the one General Zheng had given her. In boy-faced Ma Jun's lamplight, the texture, color, and size were close to identical. "Maybe the princess came this way."

Grinning and making himself look more like a fox, Zhao Yue elbowed Xu Zhan. "She's definitely better than a dog."

"Blood." The coppery smell drew Jie to a line of blood droplets. She leaned over and touched it. "Fairly fresh, two or three hours old. The spray pattern suggests blades—" she moved to the place where the wielder had likely stood and swung her arm as if holding a sword "—cut through an artery."

Lefty Li Wei fisted his hair with both hands. "This is horrible."

Chen Xin cleared his throat. "Citizens! Come out in the name of the *Tianzi*."

Perhaps they weren't that dumb after all. In the second stories, windows opened, and faces peeked out.

"What happened here?" Chen Xin yelled.

Voices erupted all at once.

"An assault!"

241

"A girl and a man."

"A foreign man."

"Attacked by six masked men."

"Big men."

"Very big men."

Jie blew out a whistle shrill enough to wake ghosts. "One at a time. Were the man and girl harmed?"

"No."

Thank the Heavens. "How long ago? Which way did they go?"

Fingers pointed out the north end of the alley. "Two hours. They turned the corner, and that was that."

"That's the general direction of the Ankiran ghetto," Ma Jun whispered.

"Did the attackers give chase?" Chen Xin said.

"Yes."

Flat-Knuckled Xu Zhan took off in the direction they pointed, with Lefty Li Wei close on his heels. Not like it would make much difference given the two hours that had passed.

Jie started to join the rest of the imperial guards following them, but paused and grabbed Ma Jun's elbow and Chen Xin's wrist. "Wait. Captain, go retrieve your men. I have an idea." If someone was trying to capture the princess… She looked up at all the people. "I need a dress, large enough for him—" she thumbed at Ma Jun "—and four sets of male clothes. I'll pay a gold *yuan*, and we'll even return the dress when we're done if he doesn't like it."

Ma Jun snorted as commotion buzzed. "What are you trying to do?"

"You will be bait for anyone who is trying to harm the princess."

His forehead scrunched up. "I don't look anything like her."

Jie withdrew the magic bauble and pressed it to her skin. She didn't feel any different, but…

Ma Jun gasped. "It's just like Princess Kaiya, only pretty."

"Now *you* look like her." She pressed the bauble into his hand.

His appearance changed in a blink. He no longer towered above her, but now stood just a head taller. Gone were the broad shoulders and boyish face, replaced by a thin, pretty girl on the edge of womanhood. Perhaps prettier than the real princess, based on descriptions; and even in the imperial guard uniform, which had shrunk to size, it was clear how Tian could find her attractive.

Insides twisting, she plucked the bauble from Ma Jun's grasp. "But first, we need to size you."

"Why can't *you* do it?" A tight-lipped frown replaced his usually jovial expression.

"Because it will look strange for Princess Kaiya to sniff blood stains and examine weapons." Not to mention she'd already worn enough dresses today to last a lifetime.

A crowd of commoners gathered, pushing gowns into her face.

Jie shook her head. "Too coarse. Too small. Too plain. Too conservative. Yes!" She snatched up a light blue gown of silk, which must have belonged to a large woman, and held it up to Ma Jun.

His wide eyes protested. "I'll look fat in that."

"The magic will bring out all the right parts and hide the many wrong ones." She coughed. "Many, many wrong ones."

When the other guards returned, they occupied a citizen's foyer and changed into the disguises. The guards all poked fun at Ma Jun, even the curmudgeon Xu Zhan. Yet when Ma Jun pressed the bauble to his bare skin and transformed into Princess Kaiya, they all dropped to a knee, fist to the ground.

Reflex, no doubt, just like the temple dogs responding to a treat. Jie gave herself a mental pat on the back. The disguise might work better than expected. "Now, we are going to continue to the Ankiran ghetto. Princess Ma Jun and I will walk ahead, and the rest of you hang back. If the attackers are still out there, and they don't already have your princess, maybe we will draw them out."

After some grumbling, they set off again. Ma Jun's muttering about the dress leaving him cold and constrained made Jie grateful that she hadn't had to wear formal gowns since her stint in the Floating World. In any case, his body language appeared too stiff, too…male. The Northern lords' agents would never take the bait.

After several blocks, Jie called for a halt in front of a greengrocer's empty cart. She knelt down and picked up a crossbow bolt with black fletching and a round point. At first glance, it seemed to match the hole in the wall from before. And there, under the wheel of the cart...no, it couldn't be. She reached over and retrieved a throwing star, lacquered black. A Black Fist weapon. Beneath it was a thin line of blood, fresher than the last.

"What is it?" Chen Xin knelt down next to her.

He couldn't know about the throwing star, not until she found out more. Jie stashed the weapon in her sleeve with a flick of her wrist, then wiped her finger across the blood and held it up. "Fresher blood here. I think we are getting close." Closer to a potential betrayal on Master Yan's part? No, never. A renegade, perhaps? Or an adept who tried to help the princess, but had not reported back?

Princess Ma Jun sashayed over. She—*he*—pointed north as he spoke with a deep voice mismatched for a young woman. "The Ankiran ghetto is a few blocks that way."

A scream pierced the night, right where he pointed.

Jie broke into a run. Even without Ma Jun's guidance, the disjointed chorus of screams, yells, and shouts might as well have been a beacon. That, and as she neared, the coppery scent of blood mingling with curry. She turned a corner into a side street lined by poorly maintained row houses.

From the far end of the block, three dark-clothed men with repeating crossbows pelted bolts into a mess of overturned tables and chairs. Bodies of men, women, and children sprawled in the jumble, blood slickening the pavestones. A few still lived, cowering behind splintered furniture.

Two more large men stood with their backs to her, swords in hand. Their form-fitting clothes resembled those Black Fists wore on missions. From the bodies at their feet, which bled from ugly gashes, it appeared they had cut down anyone who tried to escape.

With each hand, Jie reached across and pulled three throwing stars from either sleeve. In the same motion, she flung them at the nearest two. One dropped to his knees with a grunt as three stars lodged in his back.

The other man took one star to the left shoulder—she'd need to practice more with her off hand—and spun around. Snarling, he loped over with his broadsword raised.

Better not to test her knife against that. She spun around to run...and slipped on a stray crossbow bolt. How had she not seen it earlier? She landed on her butt, already sore from the horseback ride. The huge man's blade came down.

It clanged against a curved *dao* sword just a fingerbreadth from her head. In the same motion with which Xu Zhan brushed away the incoming broadsword, he countered with a two-handed slash. The *dao* sliced through the murderer's neck and sent his head rolling to the ground in a swirling blood trail.

Jie popped up to her feet. The crossbowmen ran and the other imperial guards, save for Ma Jun in his dress, gave chase. Her short legs would never keep up. She turned to Xu Zhan and pointed to the headless body. "We needed to keep him alive for questioning!"

"You're welcome." With a smug smile, Xu Zhan examined his weapon.

Perhaps thanks were in order, but he didn't need to know that. Jie harrumphed. "I had everything under control."

Lip curled, he sheathed his blade. "Instead of risking yourself, you should've let soldiers take care of them."

"I did take care of one, and wounded the other enough to make him easy to apprehend. Not kill."

Xu Zhan cocked his head. "Was that you? I thought the other one got hit by friendly fire."

Right, the Black Fists and their weapons were secrets that not even the imperial guard knew of. For all he knew, she was just some kind of investigator. It had to stay that way, even at the cost of a bruised ego. She bent over the corpse, technically not face-down given his decapitation, and retrieved the star with a deft swipe. "Since this one won't talk, I'll see if the other one is beyond interrogation."

Ignoring Xu Zhan's smug face, she hurried over to the one she'd hit. Blond—blond?—locks of hair spilled out from his hooded mask. He lay on his side, chest heaving with labored breaths. Two of her stars had dug deep, likely puncturing both lungs. He wouldn't be answering any questions either.

She retrieved her weapons and went over to help survivors. They were all bronze-skinned Ayuri, likely Ankiran nationals since this was their domicile. No, definitely Ankiran. The husband and wife she'd seen disembarking from the *Wild Orchid* that morning lay among the dozens of dead and mortally wounded. Jie's gut twisted. The cold-blooded murderers hadn't even spared women or children. And why? Nothing like this had ever happened in Huajing.

She followed the sound of whimpering and the stench of voided bowels. Three boys, maybe ten to twelve years of age, huddled under a table, tears in their eyes. At first glance, they appeared to be the only survivors. They must've had enough sense to hide just as the massacre began.

Poor boys, to have witnessed something so horrible. Still, they might have valuable information. She knelt down and pointed over at Ma Jun, still magically disguised as the princess. Using her halting Ayuri, she asked, "Was she here earlier?"

One of the boys nodded. "But she wore a different dress."

An observant one...perhaps worthy of training. "How long ago?"

He looked up at the Iridescent Moon, now waxing past its fourth crescent. "Maybe an hour?"

The trail would be getting colder. "Was she with someone?"

His voice trembled. "The noble."

"Where did they go?"

The boy pointed south, back in the direction she'd come.

"Look at this." Ma Jun held up the murderer's straight broadsword. "I've never seen a weapon like this."

Jie had. It was a Black Fist sword. Just like the throwing star she'd retrieved. And the men wore close-fitting but mobile utility suits. If the clan were helping enemies of the *Tianzi*... Certainly, Master Yan would have said something.

She swiped it from his hands before he could share the evidence with others. "You'll ruin the disguise."

Something was afoot, but now wasn't the time to think it through. The watch needed to be called, and a princess needed to be found.

A keening wail filled the night. The dreadful sound sent a spear of ice down Jie's spine.

CHAPTER 24
Foreboding Melodies

Whether the low buzz was in her head, echoed in the Dragon Scale Lute's strings, or emanated from the Temple of Heaven, Kaiya couldn't tell. Her spatial relations and sense of direction must have sunk to the bottom of Sun-Moon Lake. They couldn't have possibly reached the Temple of Heaven, in Huajing's south.

Maybe she and Kai-Long had ridden the palanquin farther than she thought; or she and Hardeep had just run a lot faster and longer than her drunken, jarred brain could register. She shook her head in hopes a clear thought would surface. No such luck, and no point in sounding like a fool.

Still, an inner voice that sounded suspiciously like her brother's soon-to-be bride reminded her: entry into the sacred grounds without a blessing was far worse than wandering the palace without permission or gallivanting through the city.

Another voice, which sounded like Crown Princess Xiulan's, rose above the warning. The Dragon Singers of old would risk death to do the right thing.

She closed her eyes and thought back to the Ankiran refugees. Impoverished. Downtrodden. A result of her country's profiteering. A wrong she had to rectify. Heart swelling, she edged back a step and studied Prince Hardeep.

Staring at the Temple of Heaven's eight-tiered stupa tower, his head bobbed in a rhythmic beat, as if listening to a song in his head.

He was so courageous, like the Dragon Singers in her favorite songs. Like she could be.

With one hand on Tian's pebble, she pointed at the walls. "How do we get past the guards?"

Prince Hardeep flashed a conspiratorial smile. "We'll climb over the walls."

She covered her mouth. He'd probably never worn a dress. Not to mention, "Patrols walk around the perimeter at regular intervals. It will be impossible to get over the walls without being seen."

His eyes strayed to the Lute, still in her hands.

How could he even suggest it? Using it on thugs was one thing, but on loyal soldiers… Shaking her head, she thrust the instrument into its bag and offered it to him.

A hint of a frown formed on his lips. "All right, I have an idea."

"What?"

"Trust me." He grinned. "Everything has worked so far."

Getting ambushed twice didn't seem to be part of any successful endeavor. Still, they had gotten out of it with little more than a cut on her thumb. Not to mention they had escaped the palace, itself a difficult proposition. "All right."

With his always-charming smile, he squeezed her hand and crept toward the Temple of Heaven's walls. As she had told him, guards in ceremonial breastplates and armed with broadswords circled the perimeter, always within line of sight of each other.

Again, he mumbled under his breath in sounds so foul, it could only be a curse. Not like she hadn't warned him that it was impossible.

Serendipitously, both guards stopped in place and turned away from them. Had they heard something?

Hardeep tugged her forward to the wall. At the base, he cupped his hands together. "Your foot," he mouthed.

Kaiya stared at his hands, forming a makeshift stirrup. How unladylike.

An unexpected grin tugged at her lips. It was like being a child with Tian again, far more fun than having tea with a dumpy general who only wanted her for a trophy.

She stepped into his hands, and he lifted her up, all the way to his shoulders. At that height, her hands just barely reached the top. Head spinning, she hopped and pushed her weight up to the top. Skirts and propriety be damned, she swung a leg over.

Below, the stone wall circled in an ellipse, with the stupa sitting on a three-tiered white marble base at one focus. An identical base stood at the other focus, with walls partially formed by dragon bones. Brittle leaves scattered across the empty grounds, unswept since Father's visit during the last Spring Festival.

"Your hand!" Hardeep hissed from the outside.

Right, Hardeep. Shaking her foggy head, she leaned back and extended a hand.

Hardeep backed up, and then bolted into a quick run and jump. He caught her hand, his weight nearly dragging her back down to the ground. Luckily, his other hand slapped up on top of the wall. Leaning back, she pulled him to the top. The yanking burned her arm and shoulder muscles. Heavens, he was heavier than he appeared. Down below, the guard was just then looking forward again.

Safe! Hopefully, their run of luck tonight would continue. She swung her other leg over and shimmied down to the marble ground. Hardeep leaped down after her, landing with nary a sound.

"Now what?" She scanned the compound, which she'd never seen from the inside. In just a few days, on the New Year, Father would come here for his annual prayers to the gods. How beautiful his voice always sounded, audible from almost anywhere in the city.

Hardeep pressed up against the wall. "Any guards? Priests?"

"No, the temple remains empty until just a day or so before the New Year, when priests from the Jianguo Shrine sweep it and prepare for the emperor's visit."

"Well, then." Walking toward the marble base at the near focus, he unshouldered the silk brocade bag and opened it. "According to your archives, this is where Aralas revealed himself to Yanyan."

Kaiya nodded, but, in retrospect, coming here just because of a chance meeting a thousand years before didn't make as much sense now as it had earlier in the day. So the elf angel had met the mother of Dragon Songs here. It wasn't as if he'd taught her here...unless he had? "Now what?"

Up a few steps, they arrived at the top of the base's three tiers. Hardeep stepped in the direct center and closed his eyes. "Our legends say Aralas met his Ayuri lover Shivani on Shakti's Hill in what is now Palimur City. It was there that martial magic flared in her." He offered the Lute.

Kaiya received it in two hands. "Our magic calligraphers, painters, and other artisans do not have to visit holy sites to gain their power. It just takes dedicated practice over many years."

"I see." He scanned the surroundings, his gaze pausing briefly at the top of the stupa. "There is something special about this place. Perhaps if you played, we might discover something?"

She shrugged. They had nothing to lose, except maybe some sleep from the haunting melody of the Lute.

He scooted off the center spot and gestured to it with an open hand. "A beautiful performer like you will need a stage."

Beaming at his compliment, she stepped onto it. The ever-present hum echoed louder in her ears.

"Don't let any other sound distract you," he said. "Concentrate only on the Lute. Maybe try that posture from before."

She lowered herself into a horse stance and gripped the marble with her toes, then looked up at him expectantly. "I don't knowhow to pluck out specific notes on this instrument."

"You are so talented, I'm sure you will figure it out quickly." He tapped his chin with a finger, again invoking the image of her childhood friend, Tian. So cute. And reassuring. "Now, where in this compound does the emperor go to say his annual prayers?"

With an open hand, Kaiya gestured toward the stupa.

"I am going to take a look. From the shape of the ellipse, I would wager the sound is strongest there."

Inside the stupa was sacred territory, where the fallen star was kept. Only a select few were ever allowed to visit. If a foreigner entered, no telling what would happen. Perhaps another Hellstorm. She shook her head. "You mustn't."

He searched her eyes. His gaze was mesmerizing in the way it seemed to explore her soul.

But no, they had done too many things she shouldn't have today, culminating in the chance at a death sentence, and this would be a monumental mistake. The consequences would be borne not by her, but perhaps the entire nation. She broke eye contact and stared at the ground.

"Very well," he said. "I do want to get closer and admire the architecture. I promise I won't enter." His smile was reassuring.

Of course he wouldn't do something against her wishes; he had yielded to her will time and time again.

Or would he? They'd already committed capital crimes. As he walked across the compound, she tentatively tried a string while pressing a fret. Though she kept the pluck light, its eerie moan came out loud. Even Hardeep turned his head, his irises reflecting the blue Eye of Guanyin in the heavens above.

Several more plucks reverberated louder than they should, given the amount of force she used. The descending heptatonic scales all made logical sense, and even if each note seemed to evoke the feeling of an emperor's betrayal, a queen's execution, or the outbreak of a plague, the sound was tonally perfect and frighteningly beautiful. No wonder that in the hands of an elf, it could compel a dragon to flee.

She experimented with chords and descending scales. Confident she could play, she increased the force of her plucks and strums, improvising an Arkothi marching song she'd once heard. The vibrations fluttered and twirled in her core, spreading through her arms and legs.

Outside the walls, dogs howled and birds cawed. She picked up the tempo, weaving bass and treble notes into a web of harmony. Her entire body tingled, her insides wriggling like the Guardian Dragon of Cathay chasing after his Flaming Pearl. The power from earlier in the day, which had felt like an ocean dripping from a hole in a wall when she played Yanyan's pipa, now trickled through her.

If Yanyan's pipa made her beautiful, the Dragon Scale Lute transformed her into the embodiment of might and power. What would Hardeep think? She looked up.

He stood, pressing his back against the doors to the stupa, his expression one of awe...or perhaps, like her, exultation? They were here, together. He'd brought her and the Lute. Without him, this feeling wouldn't now be resonating in her chest, urging her to sing.

Behind her, the gates to the temple grounds rattled. From her music? Or maybe someone trying to get in? She started to turn her head.

Don't look back! Hardeep mouthed, or maybe spoke. No matter how, his message rang clear. *The power is within you! Sing!*

Yes, sing! No, someone was there, ready to expose this latest, worst transgression. Some of her fingers sped up while others slowed. The lute's song wobbled into a staccato, along with the vibrations inside her. Her heart thumped at irregular beats. The crushing pain felt as if a phoenix from the imperial aviary sat on her chest.

Everything blurred, bleeding into greys and blacks until darkness and silence overtook her senses.

Chapter 25
Loose and Open Ends

With Princess Kaiya in danger, and Tian too far away to help her, every one of his nerves stretched taut. Burying his worries, he ordered the team to return the overseer's office back to its original state.

Qu used his forging skills to create documents that would stall the otherwise legal shipment to Wailian County.

Li gestured to Fat Nose Jiang and the bodyguard, both unconscious. "On to the next stage?"

"We should kill them," Ju said, a knife flashing in his hand. "Threats to the realm."

Tian shook his head, Princess Kaiya's words in his mind. *Hold the butterfly with care, for even their little lives have value.* If traitors caught her, would they value her life? "If they go missing, it will tip their employers off. We will proceed as planned."

"On to Wen's, then," Li said, patting Fat Nose Jiang on the shoulder. "Lucky bastard will wake thinking he'd slept with her."

Tian nodded. He'd planned as much, since Celebrate Spring Pavilion was close. Still, there were some uncertainties: a simple bodyguard couldn't afford a night at Celebrate Spring Pavilion; and though Fat Nose Jiang had tried to grope Jie and clearly liked women, they didn't know whether or not he procured the services of prostitutes.

Still, it was a reasonable cover story. Tian gestured to Ju. "Did you bring the gentlemen's clothing for you, me, and Li?"

Ju gave a curt nod and produced a satchel.

Satisfied, Tian turned to a ledger he'd found inside of Fat Nose Jiang's robes. The notes within were meticulous, and Tian's mind savored the challenge of translating the procurer's code. Working backwards from today's shipment, he figured out the icons for rice, fish paste, sulfur, and other materials.

Just as Fat Nose Jiang had said, his papers showed that Lord Tong of Wailian County had ordered twelve thousand bales of rice and twelve hundred barrels of fish paste, in addition to other supplies hard to come by in the North. They'd been sent in small shipments almost daily over the last three months, with some items like the sulfur declared as sesame seeds on official documents.

There was more to this simple duplicity: Lord Tong wasn't just taking advantage of market prices to acquire these supplies cheaply. No, it looked as if Fat Nose Jiang, Victorious Trading, and Evergreen Trading had actively bought and sold these commodities among themselves to depress the prices. Using futures contracts to prevent a surge in costs, they'd taken losses on small transactions in order to buy larger quantities for less.

It wasn't unheard of for the trading companies to collude on these types of trades, but it usually coincided with weather reports and harvest predictions. Without a doubt, Lord Tong was skirting the realm's interdependence laws. He would soon be in open rebellion, and was building up his supplies in expectation of a siege.

Tian's heart clenched at other possibilities dancing in his head. What if Lord Tong had kidnapped Princess Kaiya to use her as leverage?

Once all was in order, he, Ju, and Li all donned the silk gentlemen's robes. Tian took Qu's forged documents and stuffed them into his clothes; he'd deliver it to the Harbormaster's office early in the morning, which would lead to a bureaucratic nightmare for the river barges.

Li and Ju hoisted the bodyguard between them; and Chong, still dressed in official robes, helped Tian with Fat Nose Jiang.

Once Qu, at lookout, gave the clear signal, they headed out.

Clearing the river docks, they rounded the bend to the ocean port. Between Tian and Chong, Fat Nose Jiang wasn't that heavy, even if his feet dragged.

The *Indomitable*, the enormous Tarkothi ship docked at the twenty-sixth berth, looked and sounded alive with activity, even at this late hour. Light baubles illuminated the deck high above, where some sailors laughed, while others sang to the accompaniment of some foreign instrument.

Whether their prince was onboard now, or out in the city, it was impossible to tell; he'd come around the continent for the imperial wedding, but also to meet with trade officials about acquiring more cannons and firepowder. Jie had apparently gotten her pink dress from him.

A pair of their marines strolled along the road nearby, laughing.

"Your friends had a little too much to drink?" one said in Arkothi, pointing at Fat Nose Jiang.

Pretending not to speak their language, Tian smiled and bobbed his head. The rest of his cell followed suit.

"Stupid Cathayi, can't even speak a proper language," the other marine said.

The first gestured out into the harbor. "Well, even the Serikothi speak our language, and they're short-cocked, inbred shits."

Tian continued, Fat Nose Jiang still slowing them down. When they cleared the Tarkothi ship, he looked past the docked vessels.

The Serikothi ship, the *Intimidator*, bobbed in the waters, its gargantuan size making it look closer than it really was. Their Crown Prince Koryn had also come for the imperial wedding; and, like the Tarkothi Prince, he planned to negotiate the purchase of cannons and firepowder. They wouldn't be able to come into dock until dawn, when the local tug crews and dockworkers started their shifts.

That might've been for the better. Given the enmity between the Tarkothi and Serikothi—despite them once being one people of a single empire—their marines meeting on Jiangkou's waterfront, possibly with alcohol involved, could lead to chaos and bloodshed.

Prostitutes in revealing garb caroused by the intersection to the road which led to Celebrate Spring Pavilion. None tried to accost the cell members, likely wary of the two unconscious men dangling between them.

Tian gestured to an alley, then reiterated their plan in clan signs, *Leave the bodyguard there, pour some rice wine on him. Make sure no one disturbs him. Be there when he wakes with the cover story.*

With quick acknowledgements, Li and Ju did as they were told. Tian and Chong continued to Celebrate Spring Pavilion with Fat Nose Jiang hanging between them.

At the door, the ladies gawked.

Chong grinned. "I've contracted a night for our friend with Madame Wen, but he drank too much."

They made way, while one bowed and opened the door.

Inside, perfume and smoke cloyed the air, and Tian fought the urge to cough. Only a handful of patrons lounged with ladies in the common room. The muffled grunts and moans from the upper levels suggested most of the guests had already found company for the night.

Disentangling herself from one of the Tarkothi officers, Wen rose and sauntered over. Tian had to reach across Jiang poke Chong to keep him from gawking.

Just keeping up the act, Chong traced clan code on Tian's arm.

Right.

Chong cleared his throat. "Madame Wen, here's my guest. We hope he'll wake up soon."

"I'll see that he is entertained when he does," she said in a sultry voice.

The few men in the bar all squirmed.

She batted her eye-lashes and gestured up the steps. "Please take him to my room, I'll be there momentarily."

Drag-carrying Fat Nose Jiang along the docks had been taxing enough, but taking him up three flights of steps left Tian winded. He heaved a deep breath after they lowered him onto Wen's bed.

"He's heavier than he looks," Chong said, wiping his brow. "I'm stuck here all night?"

"At least until he wakes. You and Wen can corroborate the cover story."

Chong grinned. "It's a tough job, but someone needs to enjoy the scenery."

"The clan appreciates your sacrifice," Wen said as she slipped in and closed the door behind her. She came over to the bed and studied Fat Nose Jiang. "A Southerner, working for the North?"

Tian nodded. "Just a middle-man for Victorious Trading. Maybe you can coax some more information about of him when he wakes."

"Leave him to me." She sat down beside him. She ran a finger over his neck, eliciting a moan.

Chong shivered as Tian pulled him out of the room.

"Wait," Wen said.

Tian turned.

She held up two metal cylinders, each about two inches long. "This was sewn into his collar."

He'd missed them. He came back into the room and took them. They were identical, and too light to be steel.

Bronze trigger pins. He'd seen ones just like them in repeating crossbows, three thousand, one hundred and thirty-four days ago. The size was a quarter-inch longer than the imperial standard.

"What do you make of it?" she asked.

"Trigger pins for a Repeater."

She covered her mouth. "It's like the murder you solved eight years ago."

He nodded. "Fat Nose Jiang had told Jie something about a new prototype, but why would he be carrying a part?"

She pressed up against Tian and blinked innocently. "How could I ever find out?"

How indeed.

The need to figure out this conundrum almost made him forget about his concern for Princess Kaiya.

Almost.

CHAPTER 26
Aftermath

Metal tinkled and chimed as Kaiya's head bobbled on a cold, hard floor. Her body lurched. Something dug into the back of her head, over and over again. Her hairpins.

"*Dian-xia*," a female voice called. "Wake up."

A jolt of pain flared in the divot under Kaiya's nose. Her eyes fluttered open. Above her, the star-studded night sky came into focus as she blinked.

Luminous blue eyes encroached into her field of vision. Hardeep...

No, a woman.

Barely-visible lines of wisdom framed a familiar, matronly face. Pulled up into a tight, austere coil, her long silver hair seemed to have a faint bluish tinge to it, perhaps reflected from her eyes.

Those eyes. Pale blue like the moon Guanyin's Eye itself, unique in a Cathayi woman. Their depth and serenity evoked a soothing calm rivaling Sun-Moon Lake on the clearest of days. Kaiya loved those eyes as she adored the *Daoist* master to whom they belonged.

Struggling to sit up, Kaiya coughed a few times before finding words. "Doctor Wu. What are you doing here?"

"An awe-inspiring song pulsated through the city, coming from the Temple of Heaven," said the ancient woman—nobody knew her actual age, though some speculated her longevity rivaled that of a dwarf or even an elf. As a master of an art that sought the secret to immortality, she didn't look particularly old. That, despite the fact she eschewed the pearl creams and other make-up that most Cathayi women used as the passing years magnified the effect of gravity. "The question is what are *you* doing here?"

What *was* she doing here? Playing enchanted musical instruments in the middle of a forbidden area, with a foreign prince.

Foreign prince!

Hardeep must've been nearby. Kaiya scanned the surroundings. They were outside the gates of the temple compound. There was no sign of him or the Dragon Scale Lute, only a man whose blue-and-gold robes marked him as the Jianguo Shrine's high priest. He craned over her while several other priests huddled beyond, whispering among themselves as their judgmental stares fell on her. How mortifying.

One of the priests ran past, probably headed for the palace to report to Father. Once he learned about her sneaking out and entering the Temple of Heaven, on top of disobeying his initial order to send Prince Hardeep away...

She looked around again. "Where is Prince Hardeep?"

"Who?" Doctor Wu raised a perfectly sculpted eyebrow. She turned to the growing crowd of murmuring men. "Who is Prince Hardeep?"

The most charming and handsome man Kaiya had ever seen. The only one who ever truly knew her. "A foreign supplicant to the *Tianzi*."

"Where is he now?" General Zheng, Commander of the Imperial Guard, shouldered his way to the front, several imperial guards in tow. The other men bowed and made way. He beckoned the hall steward and her guards. "Was he alone with the princess? Here?"

Kaiya's stomach churned. When the truth came out, Prince Hardeep would lose his head, foreign dignitary or not.

The priests all exchanged glances. Apparently, Hardeep had escaped without anyone seeing him. Which meant she had fainted, and he had just left her there.

To get help. He must have risked his life to get help. And he was safe.

General Zheng turned back to the priests. "Where is Prince Hardeep now?"

The men all looked among themselves, shrugging.

"I…I am not sure." The high priest squinted and blinked like a child testing new spectacles.

The general pointed to three imperial guards. "Go find the foreigner."

Kaiya twirled a loose lock of her hair. Maybe Prince Hardeep had just abandoned her to save his own skin. And like some silly daydream, she'd believed music made her beautiful in his eyes.

How gullible she'd been. Breaking rules, acting like a love-struck fool. And now, possibly getting servants and Cousin Kai-Long executed. Her, too. Cold seeped into her hands, and her vision faded at the edges.

"Steady, *Dian-xia*." Doctor Wu placed one hand on Kaiya's back, the other on her wrist, feeling her pulse. Her eyebrows clashed together like charging goats. "Show me your tongue."

Kaiya glanced up at a different kind of audience than she was accustomed to. How embarrassing. Heat flared in her cheeks.

Doctor Wu swept an imperious gaze over the assembled men. "Turn around."

Like a temple's revolving storm door shutters, the men spun and snapped into place. Jaw tight, General Zheng nodded and turned around as well.

Thank the Heavens. Kaiya nodded to the doctor in thanks and stuck out her tongue.

"I see." Doctor Wu's lips pursed. She spent the next several minutes poking and prodding at her, while soldiers jogged around the temple walls and nervous priests shuffled at a respectful distance. How mortifying, to have so much attention for all the wrong reasons.

Just when Kaiya's heart was about to stop, a middle-aged man slunk through the wall of imperial guards. The white-and-red symbols stitched into his blue robes marked him as a member of the Ministry of Household Affairs. "*Dian-xia*, the *Tianzi* commands you to present yourself before him."

Heavens, no. Kaiya resigned to humiliating herself in front of all the hereditary lords. The *Tianzi*— Father—had no choice but to pass harsh judgment.

Doctor Wu's hand squeezed hers, sending a reassuring warmth coursing through her body. "Don't worry, *Dian-xia*. I will accompany you."

For whatever good that would do. No matter Father's respect for the doctor, he couldn't afford to appear weak and overlook a capital offense. Not when the North was unsettled. Not when she couldn't prove her budding skill at Dragon Songs. Hopefully, when meting out punishment, he would take into account that she had never done anything wrong in the past.

Doctor Wu helped her to her shaky feet. The men around her all bowed. Imperial guards formed up behind her. The Minister of Household Affairs led her from the Temple of Heaven's front gates to where a palanquin and a several dozen imperial guards awaited.

Kaiya peered at the palanquin, all vibrations of power from the Lute melting away from her core. She gritted her teeth and ducked into its narrow confines. It rose off the ground and lurched into a steady pace. Outside, the imperial guards marched in tight formation.

How foolish she'd been, believing Prince Hardeep wanted to help her. An accomplished musician himself, he'd probably taken the Lute. He might have already chartered a ship back to Ankiras, where he would scatter the Maduran armies with the instrument's fell magic.

Leaving her here, on her way to a possible death sentence. The palanquin walls seemed to close in around her. Memories of being locked in an armoire sent her pulse skittering. Kaiya took a deep breath of the hot, stuffy air in hopes it would calm her. She should be grateful for the privacy. Now hidden from prying eyes, salty-hot tears trickled unchecked down her cheeks.

An eternity in the bobbing coffin dragged on until the procession finally ground to a halt. Kaiya dried the tears with her sleeve. Her eyelids felt heavy and swollen. Herald calls and the swoosh of opening gates indicated their arrival at Sun-Moon Palace.

"*Dian-xia*," Chen Xin said from outside, reassuring her with a familiar voice. "We have passed the front gates of Sun-Moon Palace. Would you like to alight?"

The guards and servants knew her habits well, predicting she would want to walk the rest of the way to the castle. Not tonight. The Iridescent Moon neared full, ready to shine light on her shame. Her voice caught and she cleared her throat. "Take me to the Jade Gate. Take your time."

Kaiya shuddered, worried her cracking voice had revealed weakness. Nonetheless, the ride from the palace's main gate to the Imperial Family's residence would afford her just enough time to regain her composure. If she were to present herself before Father,

271

she would hold her head high when accepting his judgment.

To calm herself, she envisioned her ride as a walk. Past the Hall of Supreme Harmony. To the Dragon Bridge between the palace grounds and the castle. Through the winding alleys of the inner castle compound.

The palanquin came to a gentle stop, and the porters lowered it to the ground. The doors slid open and a hand, smooth as phoenix feathers, took hers to help her out.

Her legs quavered. The imperial guards by the gatehouse dropped to one knee, fist to the ground.

Doctor Wu released her hand.

The palace chamberlain shuffled forward and bowed. "*Dian-xia*. The *Tianzi* summons you to his quarters immediately."

Kaiya nodded. She forced herself to achieve a semblance of grace as she crossed the covered stone bridge from the keep to the Imperial Family's walled-off, hilltop residence. Moonlight sparkled off the gold leaf of the one-story pavilion's tiled eaves. Surrounded by moats, the building was further protected from magical intrusion by an ancient ward.

Her personal retinue of handmaidens and guards stopped and knelt as she approached the gatehouse connecting the family's restricted bedrooms to the rest of the residence. There, eight imperial guard sentries stepped aside while the gatekeeper—an old nun from Praise Spring Temple—held up a light bauble lamp to Kaiya's face.

The woman spoke in the Imperial Family's secret language, her voice hoarse as she asked one of the hundreds of questions needed to validate Kaiya's identity. "What land did the Founder and his consort come from?"

"Great Peace Island," Kaiya answered, using the secret language's name for Jade Island.

"How many patron saints watch over Cathay from Jade Island?"

"Eight," Kaiya said, "though some include The Dwarf as the Ninth."

"What are their names?"

"The Water Saint, The Metal Saint, The World Saint, The Fire Saint, The Wood Saint, The Earth Saint, The Heavenly King, and The Sea King. The Dwarf is King of the Underworld."

Without looking back, the gatekeeper rapped a code—changed hourly—on the heavy ironwood doors. They slid open, revealing the shaved pates of nine bowing nuns, armed only with the empty-handed *Yongchun* fighting style.

The Founder had established these security protocols, after having barely survived his most trusted vassal's surprise attack, just before he came to post-Hellstorm Cathay. In his time, the nuns had used daggers. Later, his consort taught them her own unarmed combat skills.

Kaiya walked to the *Tianzi*'s quarters, surrounded by an escort of nuns and with Doctor Wu one step behind.

273

Her brothers and Crown Princess Xiulan, all kneeling on cushions, turned their heads toward her as she stepped into the bedroom antechamber. From where he sat on a cushioned bloodwood chair, Father fixed her with a severe gaze.

Belly tight, Kaiya dropped to her knees and pressed her forehead to the ground.

"Rise," Father said.

Straightening, she looked up to focus on something else. The ceiling was coffered, with jade insets carved to depict scenes from the Wang Dynasty's glorious history. Lacquered wooden panels with mother-of-pearl inlay adorned the red walls. Lanterns with bloodwood frames around paper-thin white jade and dangling red silk tassels hung from the ceiling, providing a soft light from the Aksumi baubles.

His dignified tone remained the same as if addressing dinner plans or a devastating flood. "I am told that you left the palace without permission, unprotected, and entered the Temple of Heaven."

Kaiya bowed her head. There was no point in denying what everyone knew. However, beyond that, she had to protect Hardeep, Kai-Long, and all the servants, even if it meant bending the truth. "Yes. Please, I acted on my own accord. I tricked the servants and imperial guards. I was selfish and foolish."

His eyes narrowed for a split second. "Did you enter the stupa? Did you behold the fallen star?"

She shook her head.

"Then we have some leeway in meting out punishment." He let out a long breath, so uncharacteristic of him, and then looked from Eldest Brother to Second Brother. "It seemed everyone in the city was drawn to the unique song emanating from the Temple of Heaven, like moths to a light bauble. With your ear for music and perceptive hearing, you must have gone first. Yes, you are undoubtedly the victim of evil magic. Luckily, you did not enter the stupa."

Kaiya tilted her head a fraction. He was fabricating an excuse to protect her, glossing over the fact that she did enter the compound, if not the stupa.

But apparently, no one considered that *she* could have created that music. And as much as she should have told the whole truth, including the attacks on her and Hardeep, it would risk too many people.

"Doctor," Father said, "perhaps with your broad understanding of the world, you could tell us what kind of instrument makes that sound?"

"I am not entirely sure." The doctor shifted on her feet, lips pursed. "Magic and music are Lord Xu's expertise."

Father turned back to Kaiya. "Now, I have heard some disturbing news about your actions from earlier in the day."

From earlier in the day? Was the issue with the Temple of Heaven resolved so easily? Something was wrong. "Yes." Kaiya pressed her forehead to the dark wood tiles. "I—"

275

Doctor Wu held up a silencing hand. "If I may, *Huang-Shang*, I have more pressing news. Good news."

More pressing than her directly disobeying his order and nearly damaging a priceless artifact? More important than the capital offense of breaking into the Temple of Heaven, even if Father glossed over it? Kaiya fidgeted on her knees.

Father's eyes shifted from Kaiya to the doctor. "Speak."

"I have felt the princess' pulse and studied her tongue. She is about to blossom with Heaven's Dew. I would guess in a few days, on the new White Moon."

Heat rose to Kaiya's head as she sucked in a breath. Such a private consideration, at least for most girls, was now dragged out for her brothers to hear. Not like they wouldn't know soon, anyway. They'd likely been privy to this particular topic of speculation among the servants—and through their loose lips, among the hereditary lords and ministers as well. Curse her good ears for overhearing the furtive whispers.

Xiulan leaned past Eldest Brother Kai-Guo and winked. As usual, Kai-Wu showed little interest in state affairs, which apparently included her soon-to-start monthly rhythms.

At least it was finally coming. Most of the palace girls her age had already taken that step into womanhood. Even her spunky cousin Lin Ziqiu, two years younger, had already started. Kaiya dared a quick glance up.

A rare smile flitted across Father's face before his expressionless demeanor returned. "This is most welcome news. A marriage might help pacify the rebellion in the North."

Kaiya twirled a lock of hair. Just this morning, the North had been merely unsettled. Now it was a rebellion? And if what Doctor Wu said was true—and she was never wrong in matters of health—Kaiya would be eligible to marry in less than a week. "What rebellion?" she ventured.

"Yes, this is fortuitous," Father continued, seeming not to have heard her. "Especially with Kai-Wu's wedding so close. I hope to see grandchildren before I join your mother, and the realm will certainly be reassured by the birth of heirs to the Mandate of Heaven." He looked to Eldest Brother Kai-Guo and Xiulan.

Xiulan averted her gaze while Kai-Guo fidgeted. A year into the marriage and the Crown Princess' private considerations were under even more public scrutiny than Kaiya's. And with their quarters right next door, she knew their lack of success had little to do with a lack of trying.

Kaiya bit her bottom lip. She might be jealous of Xiulan's peerless handwriting, perfect posture, impeccable manners, pearly complexion, doe eyes, and hair where no strand ever fell out of place; but Kaiya didn't envy the pressure to conceive an heir. Her own future sons would be far down the line, after her brothers' sons, after Father's younger brother and his sons. Poor Xiulan withered under Father's stare.

It wasn't fair. Clearing her throat, Kaiya set aside all questions about the rebellion and pressed her forehead to the floor. "Father, I apologize for the trouble and embarrassment I have caused. I should not have accompanied Prince Hardeep to the Hall of Pure Melody and nearly ruined Yanyan's pipa." Or violated the sanctity of the Temple of Heaven, but if he had forgotten about it, there was no need to provide a reminder.

Doctor Wu clucked. Yes, her earlier deflection had gone to waste, but someone had to rescue Xiulan from her awkward position. At least nobody's monthly cycles were under scrutiny for the moment.

The weight of Father's stare pressed her into a deeper bow. "Rise," he said.

Kaiya sat up. In the corner of her eye, Xiulan mouthed, *Thank you.*

The *Tianzi* said, "My daughter, it is good you recognize your mistakes and have made yourself accountable. However, as I rule by the Mandate of Heaven, if I were to show leniency, it would be perceived by the palace staff, officials, and hereditary lords as preferential treatment. Do you understand?"

"Yes, *Huang-Shang.*" Kaiya bowed her head.

Jawline set, he nodded. "In four days' time, the day after Kai-Wu's wedding, you shall present yourself before me with the hereditary lords in attendance. Until then, you shall be confined to the castle with limited visitation. I am assigning Secretary Hong to vet all who call on you."

Bowing again in acknowledgement, Kaiya suppressed a sigh. That list of visitors would certainly *not* include Prince Hardeep, if he even turned up. He probably wouldn't, since she was of no use to him anymore.

Kai-Guo said, "Father, perhaps you should assign a Black Fist to follow Kaiya."

As if at sixteen years old, she still believed in the boogeymen that stole unruly children from their beds and forced them into a life of thievery. Kaiya would have rolled her eyes if Father weren't there to see it.

Father waved off Kai-Guo's empty threat. A smile formed on his face. "People in and around the Hall of Pure Melody report that your music this morning bordered on the divine."

What would they say about her song in the Temple of Heaven, if they knew?

Doctor Wu snorted. "If I may, *Huang-Shang*, she played with forces she did not understand or know how to control. It has thrown her energy out of balance, perhaps beyond the ability of the palace physicians to treat. She is fortunate that I came from Haikou to deliver herbal medicines to your family."

Father tilted his head a fraction, the appropriate recognition for a *Tianzi* to show someone as respected as Doctor Wu. "You shall be her first visitor then." He turned to Kaiya. "Now, off to bed."

Jie watched from the shadows as Princess Kaiya rose. Without a doubt, the magic bauble image was much prettier than the real deal, which cast Tian's taste further into question. Crown Princess Xiulan stood as well, and both ladies and the mysterious old woman bowed and shuffled out of the *Tianzi's* room. At the last second, Doctor Wu made direct eye contact.

Holding her breath, Jie froze in place. The old woman, with undoubtedly equally old eyes had picked her out of the shadows. Or had she? Without any sign of acknowledgement, Doctor Wu followed the princesses out.

The *Tianzi* cleared his throat. "Continue."

Master Yan melted out of the shadows and beckoned Jie to join him behind Prince Kai-Guo and Prince Kai-Wu. "Tell the *Tianzi* what you have seen."

The whole story? She'd already briefed Master Yan on the attackers' Black Fist weapons, and he insisted the Black Lotus only served the Son of Heaven. Now, he nodded, answering her unasked question.

She turned to the *Tianzi* and pressed her forehead to the ground. Was that the right protocol? She'd never reported directly to the throne before. "*Huang-Shang*, the attackers were all large young men. They used Black Fist tools but were not Black Lotus adepts. One was Cathayi, but another had blond hair and fair skin."

"The answer appears clear to me," the *Tianzi* said. "One of your own has trained others in your ways."

Master Yan shook his head. "Impossible. All masters, past and present, living and dead, are accounted for." Such audacity to be so direct!

The *Tianzi* just chuckled. "My old friend, perhaps it wasn't a master. In any case, I am more concerned about who they work for."

An enigma, to be sure. Jie let her lower lip smack as she released it. "With the rebellion in the North, I thought they might be hired by Lord Tong. But—"

Crown Prince Kai-Guo raised a hand. "But why would Lord Tong have the Ankiran refugees slaughtered?"

Jie said, "Guests of Young Lord Peng Kai-Long."

The *Tianzi* sighed. "Maybe they are sending a message to Young Kai-Long."

"Perhaps Cousin Kai-Long made enemies when he worked as a diplomat," Crown Prince Kai-Guo said. "Madurans?"

Master Yan raised a hand. "Remember, they targeted the princess, too. Until we gather more evidence, we cannot rule out anyone."

The Crown Prince nodded. "In the meantime, we must address Lord Tong's rebellion. Kaiya will flower soon. If she marries General Lu, that would send a message."

Master Yan shook his head. "General Lu was offended by the princess. He has already departed for the North."

"Lord Tong himself, then," the Crown Prince said. "Offer her as a bride, and in return, have his son brought to court as a hostage. That should secure his loyalty."

Jie searched the prince's expression. Marriages were preemptive, and Lord Tong looked to have already made his move. "*Huang-Shang*, if I may, Lord Tong plays, shall I say, both sides of the chessboard. With females, his tastes have a sharp edge. I am not sure you would want to expose your own daughter to such humiliation."

The *Tianzi's* face might have been chiseled out of stone for all the emotion he showed. Though there it was, the vein in his temple bulging. "We will consider other options first. In any case, the hereditary lords will see her value as a bride as a good reason not to execute her."

Perhaps death would be better than marriage to Lord Tong. Jie sucked on her lower lip. No telling how Tian would react if the princess married such a degenerate. She composed her expression when the *Tianzi* settled his gaze on her.

"You will shadow her," he said.

If Jie's stomach could sink any more, she'd have to pick it off the floor. Babysitting would be such a waste of her skills. There had to be a way out... Right. "*Huang-Shang*, today I was hired as a guide and translator for the Tarkothi prince, Aryn. I must return to his ship in Jiangkou by dawn." Her butt ached at the thought of the horse ride back, and then having to wear that outrageous dress, though even that would be better than having to keep an eye on a stubborn girl.

The *Tianzi's* eyes shifted to Master Yan, who nodded. He turned back to Jie. "I find it quite the coincidence that a blond Black Fist appears the same day a Tarkothi ship arrives. Look into it."

Crown Prince Kai-Guo nodded. "Also, a prince from Tarkoth's rival, Serikoth, will be arriving to negotiate trade. He will be attending Kai-Wu's wedding, as well."

Prince Kai-Wu's eyelids fluttered open. Apparently he had been dozing.

"Perhaps," the Crown Prince continued, "you could find ways to fan the hostilities. It would tempt them to order more cannons and firepowder."

Master Yan might have a point, but fanning hostilities didn't seem relevant to the impending rebellion. Still, it was certainly better than shadowing Princess Kaiya, even if it meant wearing that ridiculous dress again. Now if only her rear end could survive the night.

CHAPTER 27
All Paths Lead to Music

Eyes closed, Kaiya listened as spring sang its song through bird chirps and the wind rustling in fruit tree buds outside the Chrysanthemum Chamber. One of the many multipurpose rooms in Sun-Moon Castle, it had been appropriated by Doctor Wu for an acupuncture treatment.

Kaiya lay absolutely still, for Heavens knew how long. Gold needles protruded from points all over her body, throbbing and buzzing and blossoming as if her body hosted a fireworks display. It might as well have been one, given all the palace physicians who came and went, all bobbing their heads at Doctor Wu's wisdom. At least a dozen hands felt her pulses, and she had to stick her tongue out each time for their examination.

Had they been treating her themselves, they would have had to insert the needles blindfolded; but today, they held hand mirrors up to politely and indirectly see the points Doctor Wu had chosen. Not that it mattered; her lanky body might have just as easily belonged to a boy.

Not for long, though, if what Doctor Wu had said was right. And she was never wrong.

Thank the Heavens. Maybe the news of her blossoming would stifle the rumors and jokes behind her back. Of course, it also meant her wedding to General Lu, or perhaps some rebellious Northern lord, might happen in less than a month. That future did not include Prince Hardeep or Dragon Songs. She let out a long sigh.

"Breathe more deeply!" Doctor Wu said, the shift in her position revealing the jagged scar on her neck. "No sighing. It constrains your *Qi*, just like when you tried learning to play magic from a book. You were too excited, weren't you?"

Yes. Although the needles didn't allow her to move or speak at the moment, the omniscient doctor didn't need to hear the answer to know it.

Doctor Wu harrumphed. "I have taught you about energy flow since you were a child. You should know better. And using *that* instrument."

Yanyan's pipa, nearly ruined by her own hand. If the doctor knew about the Dragon Scale Lute, she might be even more horrified. The needle in her belly sent a jolt radiating out in a wave.

"You might be as stubborn as Yanyan, herself."

Doctor Wu was old, but couldn't possibly be old enough to have known the first master of Dragon Songs. Could she?

"You can get up now."

Get up? Kaiya shuddered. Even the smallest motion caused her muscles to twist around the needles, sending surges along her body's energy paths.

From right above her, Doctor Wu's voice bordered on exasperation. "Quickly now. I already took all the needles out."

Kaiya opened her eyes. Stretching out her arms and legs, she wiggled her fingers and toes. Though she could move again, her body still sang from the symphony of Doctor Wu's treatment.

The doctor hovered above her, twisting a dozen needles between her fingers. "Now, get dressed. I will be back." She pointed toward a folded robe and left the room.

Groaning up to her knees, Kaiya retrieved the gown and held it up. The coarse brown cloth looked nothing like her usual embroidered silks, let alone the extravagant robe she'd worn to meet General Lu. Prince Hardeep had seen her in that, along with the thick layer of foundation, drawn-on eyebrows, and extended lashes. If he saw her now…

Blotches of pimples or not, her face certainly felt better without the cosmetic mask. If only she could be naturally beautiful like Xiulan. Catching her sigh, lest Doctor Wu hear it in the other room, Kaiya slipped the plain robe on. It could only mean one thing: one of the doctor's tortuous lessons.

No sooner had she tied the sash than Doctor Wu slid open the door and marched back in. Her eyes darted from up to down in a cursory evaluation before she nodded. "Good. You may not be particularly pretty, but you have a strong spirit."

Kaiya's chest tightened. The doctor's words probably hadn't been meant to hurt, but still...at least Tian had always adored her, no matter how plain she was. And Prince Hardeep...

"Straighten your spine," Doctor Wu said. "Good. Now listen, when you played *that* song with *that* instrument, you opened connections inside your body like the great musicians from the past. However, you were too excited and lost control of it."

Kaiya's mouth gaped of its own accord. Doctor Wu hadn't even heard her play, yet somehow knew.

"Close your mouth. I might not know Dragon Songs, but for your health, you have two paths: either master it, or give it up altogether."

The doctor could have just said to give it up and get married. Maybe the fact she mentioned mastering it first offered a hint as to what she thought was best. And to think it was even a possibility! Kaiya shuffled on her feet.

The doctor pointed to one of the east-facing windows. "No decision should be considered without meditation. Stand there, face Jade Mountain."

What did she want? What was best for Cathay? Kaiya took short strides to the designated spot. Snow-capped Jade Mountain, dark green in the mist, rose over Sun-Moon Lake.

"Now, focus on your breathing, anchor yourself with the energies of Mother Earth."

287

Kaiya suppressed a shudder. It was one of the first exercises Doctor Wu had taught her eight years before, at the *Tianzi's* bidding, to treat childhood anxiety. The calm had helped her get over Tian's banishment. It also left her legs shaking in pain. She sank into a deep horse stance, her thighs parallel to the ground, spine straight, and attention locked on the mountain. The pose was thoroughly unladylike. Nonetheless, it had helped develop the strength and balance she needed for the most graceful dances.

Doctor Wu regarded her with a furrowed brow. With a nudge of a hand, she lifted Kaiya's chin to further straighten her back. "Now breathe, tongue on the roof of your mouth, in through the nose letting your belly expand; out through your mouth, pushing your belly in."

Gripping the floor with her bare toes, Kaiya did as told. Cool air settled into her lungs, and the tingling from the acupuncture spread and dispersed.

Doctor Wu afforded Kaiya a cursory glance. "Good. Your inherent Fire energies rage, fueling your creativity, but you must contain them with nourishing Water. Visualize your weight sinking deeper and deeper into Mother Earth as you exhale. Draw her life-giving energy through your *Yongquan* points in your soles as you inhale and bring them to your *Dantian* below your navel."

Kaiya obeyed, imagining the energy of the world as tangible. A deep breath in, a slow breath out. Thoughts of Prince Hardeep settled, replaced by a calm drawn from the resolute vibration of the earth. The cool sensation seemed almost like the tranquility she felt when lost in her own music.

Which, in turn, felt nothing like playing Yanyan's pipa or the Dragon Scale Lute.

The doctor clucked. "You practice too much of that *Praise Moon Fist* fighting. Its nature is Wood. It easily transforms into Fire and rises to your head. If you do not nurture your Water energies, your inherent Fire will burn out your *Sea of Marrow*. No wonder you lost control of the song's power."

Kaiya's knees burned from the strain, yet she almost forgot about them as she mulled over the doctor's perplexing words. The power of Dragon Songs didn't seem at all related to medicine.

Then again, Prince Hardeep, a non-Cathayi who shouldn't be able to channel magic through artistic endeavor, had told her to straighten her body and put her feet on the ground. If it came from just his love of music, then maybe her music teachers had left something out of their instruction. With no sign of the prince, she might never find out. He was probably on the first ship bound for his besieged Ankira, Dragon Scale Lute in hand.

"Focus." Doctor Wu pressed Kaiya's back, straightening her spine. "Remember to root yourself next time you decide to play with things you don't understand."

Kaiya might have cowered had she not been concentrating on the stance.

The doctor harrumphed. "In fact, maybe you shouldn't play these songs of power at all. That music last night…a frightening energy coursed through it, one that did not belong to Mother Earth. Lose control of such power in such a place, and it might have dire consequences. For you. For the world."

For the world? One song having dire consequences for the entire world…the very idea of it was overwhelming.

Doctor Wu came around and shot her an imperious look. "If you ask me, you should find a real instructor."

"There are none," Kaiya said. Her voice came out as a squeak, probably from not having spoken for the last few hours. She straightened out of her stance. "At least not for music."

Doctor Wu shrugged. "I don't know much about magic, but at its core, artistic endeavor is all the same: the expression of intention."

"I don't know…" Not that she had any reason to learn anymore. The whole idea of using a Dragon Song to change the minds of the lords and Father, which felt so right last night, was clearly treason. And Hardeep's other hope, expelling an invading army with fear, apparently involved powers that might be too terrible to invoke.

"You have always had the potential. I have long felt it in your pulse. You must make a choice."

Such revelations; why now? And if it was always there, maybe this was a chance to rediscover her people's lost art.

"You are prettier when you smile," Doctor Wu said.

Kaiya covered her mouth. "If I wanted to learn, what would you recommend?"

Doctor Wu tilted her head like a cobra. "Observe others who can evoke magic through their art."

"I can't go out into the palace grounds for two days." Kaiya sighed.

"There is always the Crown Princess."

Right. as a Dragon Scribe, Xiulan could manifest magic through her calligraphy, and appeared even more radiant when doing it. After rescuing her from the uncomfortable discussion of unconceived heirs, she owed Kaiya a favor.

"Start there. Small steps," Doctor Wu said.

Kaiya caught herself before she sighed and earned another rebuke. "If only Lord Xu would teach me more."

"More?" Doctor Wu's lips twitched. "I would be wary of that rascal. Wherever he is in the world right now, I would wager that Lord Xu heard the song last night. It would not surprise me if he makes an appearance soon."

***

Kaiya knelt on a silk cushion on the veranda in the Gardenia Courtyard, listening to the smooth swoosh of Xiulan's brush across rice paper.

Her sister-in-law sat at the bloodwood table with her back straight, soles flat on the ground. She held her hanging sleeve with her left hand as the brush danced across the page. The posture looked similar to the way Hardeep had suggested Kaiya sit when playing the pipa.

The slow, graceful motions and steadfast whirr of the brush were lulling, hypnotic. Kaiya almost forgot how her legs still ached from the low stance hours before.

Several handmaidens stood at the edge of the veranda, all craning their necks to see the Crown Princess write. Four imperial guards flanked the doors, including her own Chen Xin and Xu Zhan, so still they might have been statues themselves.

Xiulan set the brush down and held up her paper. The handmaidens clapped.

Kai. Victorious, just like the first character in Kaiya's name, shared by her brothers, as well as cousins Kai-Long and Kai-Hua.

Kaiya's chest swelled with pride, and a smile tugged at her lips. For all her mistakes, she'd already accomplished more with music than any human had in two hundred years. "I feel it," Kaiya said. "How did you do it?"

"My master emphasizes getting in the right mood by sitting straight and grinding the inkstone. I held a sense of pride and satisfaction in my heart and wrote."

Once you have seized the song's emotion and made it your own, the music book from the Hall of Pure Melody had said, *you must project it. Rooted to the ground, your spine aligned, let your heart impel your voice.* Kaiya glanced back at the beaming handmaidens and stoic guards. None seemed as affected as her. "Why did it affect only me?"

292

Xiulan bowed her head. "I remembered the gratitude I felt when you saved me from embarrassment yesterday."

Kaiya nodded. While not exactly a lesson from a master, at least it was a small step in understanding. If only Prince Hardeep were there. When she was near him, it felt like she could do anything.

Appearing at the door, Secretary Hong creaked into a low bow. "Young Lord Peng Kai-Long has come to meet with Princess Kaiya."

Cousin Kai-Long stepped past the secretary and sank to his knee, fist to the ground. A large embroidered silk bag slipped from his shoulder. Could it be? He looked up to the Crown Princess. "If you would excuse me, *Dian-xia,* I would like to walk with Princess Kaiya."

"As you wish, Young Lord Peng." Xiulan gestured toward the garden.

"Thank you, Eldest Sister." Peering at his silk bag, Kaiya rose and nodded toward Kai-Long to take the lead.

White pebbles crunched beneath their feet as they wound along a path lined with glossy green gardenias. She lowered her voice. "Thank you for your help last night."

Kai-Long nodded. "I took full responsibility, even offered to cut my own throat. The *Tianzi* will withhold judgment for two days, and until then, I am confined to either the palace or my family villa."

"I am sorry." Kaiya bowed her head.

"It's all right. My role has been kept secret so as not to influence the opinions of the hereditary lords. I will prove my loyalty and worth to the *Tianzi* by leading the vanguard in an assault of Wailian Castle if we need to put down the rebellion."

Kaiya gasped. The impregnable fortress, if what General Lu said was true. And Kai-Long was confirming that the insurgency had indeed intensified.

He took her hand and patted it. Casting a glance back at the two imperial guards following several steps behind, he leaned in and whispered, "I managed to get Prince Hardeep to safety."

Hardeep! Alive and safe. Kaiya's pulse skipped a beat, and she almost stopped in her tracks. She turned away from Cousin Kai-Long and looked forward. "Where is he now?"

"Hiding at my pavilion. He apologizes for disappearing so quickly, but his life is in danger."

Kaiya sucked in a sharp breath. "The *Tianzi* must already know the entire story, not just about the morning, but the night, too. He would have Hardeep killed, wouldn't he?"

This time, it was Kai-Long's turn to stop and face her. "No—or at least, I do not think so. I have already spoken on Prince Hardeep's behalf."

"Then why is his life in danger?"

Cousin Kai-Long resumed his walk. "The Madurans received word that he is meddling with their trade agreement. My father's province shares a border with Ankira, and we have witnessed the refugees from

Madura's brutal occupation. Madura is a warlike nation, and when they act, they rarely do so in moderation."

Kaiya's chest constricted. No doubt they were behind the massacre last night. And to think Cathay sold these violent people firepowder. "Wouldn't Hardeep be safer in the palace?"

"I am working with palace officials to allow it. In the meantime, he asked me to give you this." He unslung the bag and presented it to her in two hands.

The Dragon Scale Lute? Kaiya stared at it for a few seconds before receiving it. She loosened the drawstrings and peeked inside.

A lute.

Though not the one made from dragon scale. Who would've imagined there would be three of these foreign instruments in the capital? She cinched the drawstrings and bowed. "Thank you."

He flashed a conspiratorial grin. "I would be happy to pass messages for you."

A smile came unbidden to Kaiya's lips. "Thank you, Cousin. Please tell him that I want to help him."

"Be wary," Kai-Long said. "If the Madurans think you are meddling in their affairs, they won't hesitate to snuff out your young life."

Prince Hardeep had said as much. And they had already snuffed out so many. Kaiya's breath hitched. How awful, to be murdered for doing the right thing. And to think the Madurans acted with impunity on Cathayi soil. She straightened her carriage, not wanting to show fear. "The prince and I were ambushed last night, twice."

Kai-Long stopped, spun, and faced her. His eyes could not open any wider. "Did you tell the *Tianzi*?"

She shook her head. "Everyone believes I was lured out of the palace by the music."

Kai-Long blew out a long exhalation. "At least you won't get Hardeep in trouble for *that*. Still, the *Tianzi* must know, so he can increase your guard."

"Don't worry. He assigned a Black Fist to watch me." Kaiya rolled her eyes.

"A what?" Kai-Long's gawk, combined with his wide eyes, made him look like a caricature she'd once seen. His hand strayed to a folded piece of paper in his sash.

"Preposterous, right?" As though an imaginary boogeyman could do anything against Madura's very real hired knives.

Kai-Long offered a nervous laugh. "If I didn't know how much the *Tianzi* treasured you, I would say he is being lax with your protection."

"I always have at least two imperial guards whenever I am out of the residence."

Kai-Long glanced back at the two men, and then leaned in again. "Have you heard of the Golden Scorpions?"

Of course she'd heard of the evil warriors with expressionless masks, though mostly as scary bedtime stories. Cast-offs and deserters from the Order of Ayuri Paladins that Hardeep had almost joined, the Golden

Scorpions used their martial magic in the service of Madura's aggression—including assassinations. Fear crawled up her spine like a spider.

She tried to keep her voice confident. "The *Tianzi* forbids them from entering Cathay. It's grounds for terminating the trade agreement."

"They don't always wear masks. Just be careful."

Her chest squeezed around her heart. What if Hardeep, trained in Paladin ways, wasn't really a Paladin...

CHAPTER 28
Eldaeri Princes

Between the lack of sleep, her aching thighs and butt from riding a horse, and the ridiculous pink dress, Jie hoped she would have little need for her physical Black Fist skills today. Just like the day before, she picked her way north among the longshoremen, sailors, and boys crowding the docks at dawn—the difference being that today, she wasn't disguised as a boy, and she waddled like a duck.

And these types were not known for their chivalry. If she castrated every man who catcalled her in the first two blocks, Cathay's next generation of foul-mouthed, flea-ridden sailors might never be born. Instead, she ignored them, walking toward the five-mast Tarkothi ship moored at the twenty-sixth berth.

Or was it the twenty-third berth? That's what the sign at the head of the dock indicated. Had they taken the time and effort to move it three berths up overnight? The enormous black ship filled her visual field, and would have needlessly clogged up the harbor.

She walked up the dock to the gangplank. Two marines stood guard, cutlasses dangling at their sides.

They looked too small to be soldiers, and their features were almost effeminate. Eldaeri, in all likelihood. The nine-pointed silver sun emblazoned on their crimson surcoats...

Crimson?

The Tarkothi livery had been forest green. Unless they'd moved the ship and dyed their wardrobes, this was their rival, a Serikothi ship bearing their Prince Koryn all the way from Tivara's far east.

Fan hostilities, Crown Prince Kai-Guo had said. As if she knew enough about these northerners' customs to do so.

"We have no need for whores," one of the marines called in Arkothi.

The other elbowed him. "The way she walks, I'd bet my mama's teats she serviced the entire Tarkothi ship last night."

The first laughed. "You'd lose that bet, since Tarkothi peckers are so small from crossbreeding."

Both men chortled.

Jie rolled her eyes and spun on her heel, but not before looking up at the deck. Unlike the Tarkothi, who employed the larger ethnic Arkothi and Estomari, all the Serikothi appeared to be the elf-blooded Eldaeri. If the two countries' rivalry were limited to trading insults about manhood sizes, Cathay wouldn't sell many cannons from her fanning hostilities.

Ignoring their continued jeers, she went back to the harbor front and continued north. Past the Serikothi giant, the Tarkothi behemoth loomed over the three-mast Cathayi ships.

Jie paused and scanned from north to south and back, comparing. The two foreign vessels, with their black wood hulls and sheer size, might have been twins. Perhaps the size of their ships compensated for...

She blew out a sigh. Serikoth and Tarkoth— along with a third kingdom, Korynth—had once been a single Eldaeri empire, divided over a century ago by a greed-driven civil war. That made it a lesson for Cathay to learn from, given present circumstances.

"Hurry up, girl," a male voice called.

She turned to find the large, belligerent Tarkothi officer from the day before. Snake Eyes, the one who had begrudgingly found her the dress that she now begrudgingly wore. Her attempt at an Arkothi-style curtsey met with a chuckle. "I am sorry, sir."

"We will be departing for the capital when the Iridescent Moon wanes to its second crescent."

Jie looked south to the moon. Just three hours before subjecting her poor body to yet more travel, back to the capital, *again*. Hopefully, it didn't involve horses. "I will be—"

"In the meantime, His Highness would like to see how the Cathayi river-barge system works." Snake Eyes' gaze paused on the *Saint Gong*, now completing docking procedures at the twenty-eighth berth, before he pointed past it. "I understand they start on the other side of the lighthouse? Go to the harbormaster's office to arrange a guide."

Jie nodded. What a coincidence that Prince Aryn wanted to visit the scene of last night's escapades. If Tian had done his job, there wouldn't be anything out of the ordinary to see. "My friend works for the harbormaster."

Snake Eyes stroked his bare chin. "Very well. Bring him here, but make it quick. I will inform the prince. And you—get yourself together and stop walking like a maid the morning after her wedding."

Heat rose to the tip of Jie's ears. No more boats, no more sailors after this. If only there were somewhere clean to sit that wouldn't wrinkle the dress. Right, no more dresses either.

She turned back toward the harbormaster's office, which might have been abandoned for all the activity going on outside. Usually, merchants and ship quartermasters crowded near the doors at this hour.

From the entrance, she poked her head into the huge room. The rows of low tables, each covered with papers, brushes, and inkstones, suggested two dozen people worked there, but today only a handful of clerks and officials were on duty.

Tian included. He looked up, eyes meeting hers, a smile blooming on his face. She beckoned him out.

He reached her side almost before she could blink. "Was the princess all right?"

Not *good morning* or *I'm glad to see you're safe*. For show, Jie squeezed her mouth into a tight frown. Make him squirm a little. "Come, walk with me."

He glanced back into the building, and then nodded. "What happened?"

Jie started back toward the Tarkothi ship. "She was attacked by large men, using Black Fist weapons."

He sucked in a breath. "So is she unharmed?"

For someone so smart, so able to draw connections, he missed the obvious. "The port would be on high alert if she were hurt. Yes, she is fine."

He blew out a sigh. "They had our tools?"

"Throwing stars, Black Fist swords, cat claws, and smoke packets. They also used repeating crossbows, though with a larger magazine and bolt head."

"Our weapons and tools are secrets." Tian tapped his chin. "There must be a traitor to the clan."

Yet everyone was accounted for. The clan had made a thorough audit eight years earlier, after an old operative, long presumed dead, turned up quite alive. In fact, she'd been Madame at the Floating World House where Jie had been training.

She set the thought aside. "Master Yan is devoting significant resources to uncovering the mystery. In the meantime, what did you do with Fat Nose Jiang and his henchman?"

"We drugged them. They won't remember a thing. I presume they are at the river docks arguing with the harbormaster."

Right, the docks. She pulled his sleeve. "I need your help."

"All right. Let me tell the official on duty." He disappeared into the office.

Jie glanced at all the ships, each representing Cathay's dominance in international trade. Its lifeblood. So much wealth, and so many people vying to control it.

"Lead the way," Tian said.

Had he snuck up on her? That would be a first! She nodded and headed north with Tian at her side.

"You are waddling. Like a duck. You shouldn't have grinded up against Fat Nose Jiang."

Concern? Even if the tone was matter-of-fact? She grinned. "Consider yourself lucky you're not a Black Lotus sister." The chorus of longshoreman and sailor whistles punctuated her point.

Tian glared at them, only to meet with laughs.

"Come on little girl, you can do better than a skinny clerk. I can show you what it's like with a real man."

Jie reached over and took Tian's hand in her own. He started to yank it away, but then stiffened up. The sailors laughed.

At the dock twenty-three, three Serikothi men in polished steel cuirasses and scarlet capes assessed a herd of some thirty horses led by three merchants. No doubt the stodgy harbormaster would have taken issue with the beasts blocking the way and leaving stinking piles in the roads, had he not been busy at the river docks.

One of the Eldaeri men shook his head. "Is this the best you have?"

"The best in Cathay," a merchant said in Arkothi with a thick Cathayi accent. "The Dongmen Provincial cavalry buys from me."

303

Jie glanced at Tian. His father ruled Dongmen, and his eldest brother was an officer in their cavalry. If he thought anything about the horse trader's comments, his expression revealed nothing.

"The *national* cavalry buys from me," said the second trader.

Another Serikothi harrumphed. "Then they are getting ripped off."

The third Serikothi laughed. "We make better ships, breed better horses."

"But no firepowder," Jie muttered.

"What is the commotion, lieutenant?" A Serikothi man in a crimson uniform approached from the docks. He walked with a confident gait and bore a strong resemblance to Tarkoth's Prince Aryn. Two other officers flanked him. He smelled of cinnamon.

The second Serikothi crossed his arms against his chest and bowed his head. "Your Highness, none of these horses meets our standards. We would look foolish riding them into the capital."

Highness. Yet another Eldaeri prince. With the rebellion in the North, maybe having all the foreigners around was a bad idea. Not just for their own safety, but... Jie leaned in to Tian. "You don't think any of these foreign governments are helping Lord Tong? Perhaps in return for firepowder, funneled through Yutou Province?"

Tian tilted his head toward the Serikothi black ship. "According to the *Intimidator's* manifests, it stopped in Yutou. We'd have to sneak on board to find

304

out more, but I don't know the first thing about Eldaeri ship layouts."

She didn't either. "Maybe—"

"You." The Serikothi prince beckoned Tian.

Bowing, Tian shuffled over. "Prince Koryn Vardamcar, welcome to Cathay. How may I be of service?"

"You look like an official. When did the Tarkothi dock?"

Why so curious? Jie studied the prince's fine features.

"Yesterday, Your Highness," Tian said.

"Be a good man and see to it that when your emperor sends our guide, we ride ahead of the Tarkothi. Pay the man, Captain Damaryn." He bent his head toward his aide, even more handsome than the rest.

And blond. Eldaeri supposedly didn't come fair-haired. With his thin eyebrows and full lips, he might even be considered beautiful. Looking at the prince with fervent devotion, the captain crossed his arms in front of his chest and bowed. He withdrew two foreign gold coins and presented them to Tian.

Shaking his head, Tian held up a dismissing hand. "I am just a scribe. For the harbormaster. The Imperial Foreign Ministry will be in charge of assigning a guide."

Prince Koryn stroked his beardless chin. "Perhaps we shall take it up with the Tarkothi, then. Scribe, who leads them?"

"It is not my place to know." Tian said.

In all likelihood, he did know, even if his official position didn't require it. Still, Crown Prince Kai-Guo had given the order to spit in rice bowls, and if there was any chance either of these rival nations were in league with Lord Tong's rebellion, this might be a way to find out. Jie bowed. "If I may, Your Highness, that would be Prince Aryn."

Prince Koryn turned and scrutinized her. "What a pretty girl. Thank you."

Even if his words carried no emotion, heat flared in Jie's cheeks. Tian had undoubtedly heard the compliment. Still, his face remained blank. She said, "Prince Aryn hired me to translate for him. We are headed there now, where Scribe Zheng will give him a tour of the river docks. Perhaps I can facilitate an introduction." And instigate trouble.

Tian's brows clashed together. "What—?"

Apparently, Prince Koryn had a similar idea. "What is Prince Aryn paying you?"

"A silver crown a day, Your Highness." She curtseyed, or at least tried to.

"I'll pay you two silver crowns a day to be our guide."

To be a guide, and not a spy? This seemed more a battle of one-upmanship than a serious conflict. In any case, it might be a way to get aboard the ship. "I...I... Let me think about it."

Tian's brows furrowed, his lips drawn into a rigid line.

Prince Koryn peered at her. "Don't take too long. In the meantime, I'll take you up on your offer to introduce us." He turned to the first three men. "Choose the twelve best horses for your cavaliers. Captain, bring eight marines with us."

"What are you doing?" Tian hissed.

"Finding a way onto his ship." And seeding trouble, per the prince's orders, but Tian didn't have to know it.

His eyes widened for a split second, his beautiful brown irises darting toward the approaching Serikothi marines.

They all carried repeating crossbows. With a larger magazine, just like the murderers last night.

"Lead on." Prince Koryn gestured toward the Tarkothi ship.

Jie exchanged glances with Tian, then bowed her head. There had to be some way to get ahold of one of the crossbows.

When they reached the Tarkothi ship, Prince Aryn was waiting with Snake Eyes and several marines dressed in green and silver livery. Hands crept toward weapons, though Prince Aryn himself yawned.

Snake Eyes growled. "Look what flotsam the tide brought in."

"Now, now, Peris," Prince Aryn said. "No need for hostilities to ruin a joyous occasion."

"It could hardly be joyous with *that* filth," Snake Eyes Peris growled.

Prince Koryn straightened, drawing himself to his full height, not even as tall as Tian. "Had I known the Cathayi had invited Tarkothi mutts, I wouldn't have considered our own invitation such an honor."

Peris pulled his sword a quarter of the way out of his scabbard. Marines on both sides all shouldered forward, cutlasses flashing and crossbows leveled. Jie would have rolled her eyes at men and their toys, but Jiangkou harbor was about to become the scene of an international incident.

"At ease, General." Prince Aryn stayed Peris' hand. "We are guests here."

Prince Koryn snapped his own longsword back, though not before revealing its strange grey metal. "Prince Aryn is right. Maybe when we leave, we can settle this outside of the harbor, ship to ship."

"You'll need firepowder," Jie offered. "Maybe extra cannon fitted to your deck. You know what they say about a ship and its number of cannons."

Tian nudged her. *What are you doing?* his eyes asked.

Neither of the princes appeared to have heard her. Prince Aryn's lighthearted demeanor melted away, replaced by eyes fixated on his counterpart's sword. "I am afraid you have me at a disadvantage. You are?"

Maybe the Serikothi Crown Prince paused for dramatic effect, or maybe he didn't plan to answer at all.

"Crown Prince Koryn," Jie supplied, ignoring a glare sharp enough to cut through steel.

A grin forming on his lips, Prince Aryn crossed his arms and bowed his arms. "Well met, Cousin. Distant cousin." He turned to the blond aide. "And you must be Captain Damaryn. Your reputation precedes you. Even in Tarkoth, it is said you have bedded half the noblewomen in Serikoth."

With his nonchalant expression, Prince Aryn sounded like the drunken uncle at a New Year's feast; not that Jie had any uncles to compare. His lip twitched for a split second. Had his words been premeditated?

Coughing, Captain Damaryn exchanged glances with Prince Koryn, then crossed his arms and bowed his head. "It is my honor to meet you, Your Highness."

"I'm sure." Prince Aryn yawned at his Serikothi counterpart. "You seem to have found my guide. Feel free to join us on our tour of their river docks."

The Serikothi prince held a finger up. "I came to discuss the order in which our parties will enter Cathay's capital."

"If it matters that much to you, the Serikothi may go first." Prince Aryn shrugged. With his unflappable nonchalance, it would be hard to instigate troubles between the two.

Whatever else, their mutual enmity likely discounted *both* the Eldaeri kingdoms conspiring with Lord Tong. Jie waved northward. "Didn't you want to see the docks? This is my friend, Scribe Zheng, who works for the harbormaster."

"Pleased to meet you." Tian placed his right fist into his left hand and bowed.

"Lead the way," Prince Aryn said. He looked over his shoulder at the Serikothi prince. "By all means, join us."

Prince Koryn's eyes shifted from Prince Aryn to Tian and back. "We have other matters to attend to." He turned to Jie. "Remember my offer."

Crossing his arms, he bowed his head. The captain and Serikothi marines saluted as well, and then followed their prince back to the *Intimidator*.

Harrumphing, Prince Aryn resumed his walk toward the river docks. "I thought we'd never be rid of them. Now, Jyeh, what is this offer he mentions?"

She feigned a shy smile. "He offered to pay me two silver crowns a day to act as his translator and guide."

He laughed. "Prince Koryn may be a capable field general, but in matters of state, he only cares about appearances. If it matters that much to him, then by all means, take up his offer. Just know that if you do your work well, I have a long-term job in mind."

Tian raised an eyebrow. Whatever Jie was up to with these Eldaeri princes, it had little to do with rooting out traitors or uncovering a conspiracy. It was also wasting his time. *The Saint Gong*, which had just docked when he joined Jie, was almost tied down to the moorings at berth twenty-eight, right beside them. According to the manifests, *Tai-Ming* Lord Peng and his first son were aboard, and deceased Lamp Man Sha had named him as one of the conspirators.

"Scribe Jung." Mispronouncing Tian's name, stout Peris' voice grated like a knife dragged across a whetstone. "The prince asked you a question."

Tian looked up. "I'm sorry. Question?"

Prince Aryn pointed toward the mouth of the Jade River, emptying into the harbor. "Why put the lighthouse so far inland?"

"To ensure oceangoing vessels don't run aground."

"I bet that seawall helps with that, too." Was that sarcasm in the prince's voice? It was hard to tell in Arkothi.

Tian nodded. "Jiangkou was established as close to the capital as possible. The Jade River gets shallow fast. There's a lot of silt from its tributary, the Iron River." Which flowed from the hotbed of rebellion. And the seawall ensured the shallowness, to prevent larger ships from getting *too* close to the capital. It was curious that the Tarkothi would be interested in the river barges. "This is as far as a ship can travel inland. That's why goods have to be transferred to river barges here."

Prince Aryn pointed. "So what is going on there? I'd wager the commotion is what kept me awake last night."

Tian looked past the lighthouse, where officials, the local watch, and imperial soldiers swarmed over the river docks like ants. His own doing, in an effort to impound the supplies bound for Wailian County and its allies. There, arguing with the harbormaster and overseer, was Fat Nose Jiang, looking much worse for the wear. Jie's intoxicant would have left him with an awful hangover and only vague recollections based on the suggestions Tian planted in his addled head.

He cast a sidelong glance at Jie. She'd gone beyond the call of duty, grinding her nether regions up against Jiang's lap when a simple kiss on the neck would have sufficed. Surely she hadn't needed to go that far.

Grasping the prince's sleeve, she pointed at the chaos. "It looks like they are seizing rice and whatever is in those kegs."

Now she was blathering on. He'd said he wanted to see the river docks, not get a blow-by-blow account of cargo impoundment procedures. The lack of sleep must have really dulled her edge. Thankfully, Prince Aryn showed little interest. Tian interposed himself. "It might be dangerous to go down there. I advise waiting here."

Prince Aryn yawned at Peris. "Satisfied?"

So it was the large aide who actually wanted to see the docks. He crossed his arms over his chest. "Yes, Your Highness."

The prince waved a dismissive hand. "Your emperor's representatives should be arriving soon to escort us to the capital. Let's head back."

Tian studied Peris. What was this man's interest in the docks? Tapping his chin, he followed the Tarkothi entourage back toward their ship, the *Indomitable*.

Jie's ears twitched. She pulled him down. "Get down, get down!"

Prince Aryn's guards formed up around him, cutlasses drawn and crossbows leveled. Screams and crashes erupted nearby.

Tian followed her eyes to the source: the wharf to their side, berth twenty-eight, where the *Saint Gong* was docked. *Tai-Ming* Lord Peng Xian's honor guard of sixty-two men broke ranks. Two palanquins lay on their sides, a man clutching his neck in front of one. From behind the second, a set of legs sprawled out. Soldiers drew weapons while dockworkers and longshoremen cowered or fled.

"Repeater crossbows." Her eyes roved over the surroundings. "Same sound frequency as the ones used last night. Fired twice from two different locations."

On the dock, soldiers formed up around the palanquins.

"Lord Peng Xian is dead!" someone yelled.

"Young Lord Kai-Zhi is hit!"

"Call a doctor!"

Tian's gut knotted as he scanned all elevated points. The attackers would need to have sightlines high enough to shoot above the guards. Not only that, but they would have needed to know Lord Peng and his firstborn had arrived on the *Saint Gong* today.

"There." Jie pointed toward the Tarkothi *Indomitable*.

Tian squinted. A large man strolled down the gangplank, no visible weapons. "He's unarmed. Why him?"

"He's big. He's calm. Get him. I can't run in this stupid dress."

Tian hiked up his own robes and sprinted, undoubtedly compromising his cover in the process. Dockworkers, sailors, and longshoremen ran about yelling. Jie was right; whoever it was, now on the dock, he didn't seem to be in any hurry.

Until their eyes met.

He was a Cathayi boy, perhaps only fourteen despite his larger size.

Just ten feet away to start, the suspect's long stride gained distance faster than Tian could take it away. For someone so large, he effortlessly weaved through all the panicked people. And now he'd disappeared.

A fist caught Tian in the side of the head, but he ducked under the second and swept his leg out. The boy jumped over the leg and shot out a side-kick which Tian had to lie back to avoid. Popping back to his feet, he exchanged several strikes with his opponent, none of the blows landing. It was as if they each knew what the other was planning.

The boy leapt back, grabbed a dockworker, and shoved him into Tian.

Tian spun away, but his quarry broke into the open and ran south. With his long legs, there was no hope of catching up. He looked back at Tian, grinning. But maybe...up ahead, ten crimson-garbed Serikothi cavaliers were already mounted. Three imperial officials in blue bowed before Prince Koryn, who stood with Captain Damaryn at his side.

"Assassin!" Tian yelled.

Prince Koryn swung up into a saddle and drew his sword. In what could only be described as poetry, the Serikothi men unslung their bows, notched arrows and maneuvered their horses in a precise curve around the officials and their liege. They loosed three volleys in quick succession, even as their horses advanced and encircled the assassin.

All thirty arrows found their mark. There would be no questioning the boy.

Jie sidled up to Tian, a repeating crossbow looking huge in her hands. "Next time, maybe use the word *pickpocket* instead of *assassin*."

Not like he knew that Arkothi word until just then. Cathayi words were hard enough to speak without rehearsing. Because of that, the assassin was dead, and the audacious plot of murdering a *Tai-Ming* lord in broad daylight became that much harder to unravel.

Here was yet another crime scene to process, on the eve of Prince Kai-Wu's wedding, with a rebellion brewing in the North.

CHAPTER 29
Father Figures

Kaiya sat atop the castle parapet, dangling her stick legs over the edge despite the silent protests of her imperial guards. Long shadows cast by the setting sun yawned out over Sun-Moon Lake, whose gentle waves lapped up against the base of the stone walls. The lake stretched to the horizon, its placid surface broken only by a few small islands.

If only her thoughts could be so calm.

A day remained until Kai-Wu's wedding, two until her judgment for wandering the palace with Hardeep. What if he was really one of Madura's Golden Scorpions, and he'd used her to steal the Dragon Scale Lute for his evil country? Niggling doubts remained.

No, it couldn't be. She'd sent Secretary Hong to the Foreign Ministry, and he'd confirmed Ankira indeed had a nineteen-year-old Prince Hardeep. Kai-Long had reassured her that he'd met Hardeep at the Ankiran palace. He'd taken her to the Ankiran refugees, who welcomed him as their ruler. And, of course, he was fighting to liberate Ankira *from* Madura.

She turned Tian's pebble over in her fingers, its smooth coolness comforting. She knew every imperfection by touch; cherished it as a talisman of a more carefree time. Eight years had passed since she last saw her childhood playmate, the one with whom she could always share her deepest secrets.

If only she could share the secret of Hardeep! And her dreams of reviving lost magic. Tian would understand. But no. Although he might be the son of a first rank *Tai-Ming* lord, Father had banished him long ago for a stupid prank. Who knew where he was now?

"*Dian-xia*," her handmaiden Han Meiling said from behind her. "Here is the lute you requested."

Kaiya closed her hand around the pebble and turned.

Her handmaiden knelt, with Hardeep's lute nestled in her arms.

Stowing the pebble into her sash, Kaiya received the instrument with both hands. She flipped it around and straightened her back. Her toes gripped the stone ground. Taking a deep breath, she strummed.

The vibration of the strings flitted through her arms. Each note came together in technical perfection, yet her uncertainties and doubts wavered through the melody.

Xiulan had thought of her when writing calligraphy, which apparently guided the magic in the script to her; Kaiya looked to Han Meiling.

317

The handmaiden averted her gaze, then soon shuffled and tugged at her gown. Her fidgeting increased as uncertainty clouded her expression.

Could it be the effect of the song? An excited shiver coursed through her.

The lute disappeared into thin air, taking its song with it. Kaiya's heart leaped into her throat. Meiling gasped. Her guards all drew their *dao*.

"An interesting choice of instrument." Lord Xu stood there, her lute in his hand. The slight rise of an eyebrow and the tone of his voice asked for an explanation.

"You told me to practice."

He lifted a hand in a swift motion. All sound around them silenced, leaving only his voice. "I told you to practice your listening."

Mouths agape, her guards charged forward, only to hit an unseen barrier. Their palms circled against it, looking much like the Estomari mime who once entertained the court.

They might not have even been there for all the mind Lord Xu paid them. "You were responsible for the song at the Temple of Heaven. Even there, this lute could not make that music."

He knew! Kaiya shook her head. "I…no, it wasn't this instrument, but rather one made from a dragon scale."

Xu's eyes narrowed. "How did you acquire it?"

"It was in Lord Tong Baxian's possession. My understanding is that he received it during a trade mission to Vyara City."

The elf lord's face betrayed nothing. "Where is it now?"

As if she knew. Maybe Hardeep had stolen it, but there was only risk in telling Xu about the foreign prince at all. She shook her head. "I don't know. When I awoke, it was gone."

"I see." His gaze bored into her. "I am glad you revealed this to me. In any case, listen first. In order to project your sound farther, you need to hear and borrow the energy around you. To have the greatest effect, you must listen for the most opportune moment."

She shook her head. "I can't learn that by myself, I—"

He placed his index finger over her heart. "Most importantly, you must trust what you hear, to know if using the skill warrants the dangers of using it."

She stared at his finger for a few seconds, and then looked up. "Dangers?"

"Magic ripples out from its source, its strength greatest at the time and place of invocation. However, its echo spreads throughout the world and diminishes through the ages. Even the song Yanyan sang to Avarax a thousand years ago persists, hidden among all the other sounds of the world. In any case, magic serves as a beacon to those who know what it is. Not all of those people—and I use that term loosely—are as benign as I."

A shiver went down her spine. "Avarax."

319

He nodded. "Yes. He now knows there is again someone with the potential to affect him with her song."

"Will he seek me out?"

The elf shrugged. "Who understands the heart of a dragon? Perhaps he will entice you to seek him out, instead. I could not tell you whether he would kill you or twist your skill to his own benefit."

Kaiya shuddered. Perhaps the revival of lost magic was no longer worth the cost. "I will forget about music."

"You might forget about it, but he won't. If he has not already felt last night's song, he will soon." He tossed the lute back.

Maybe letting it smash against the pavestones would be better. Kaiya caught it nonetheless. "What can I do?" To think she had considered being devoured by a dragon favorable to marriage.

"Listen." He swept his hand down; the sounds of spring resumed, and her guards tumbled forward. Without even looking, Lord Xu caught Chen Xin with one hand and supported Zhao Yue with the other. Letting go, he then pointed far out into the lake.

The two guards dropped to their knees and started to raise their swords above their heads.

Waving them off before they offered their lives in penance yet again, Kaiya followed the elf's gesture. In the distance, lumber herders guided felled trunks of eldarwood trees through Sun-Moon Lake's placid waters. Laboring during the early spring melt, they had already begun their annual transport from the forests of the empire's inner valley to the shipyards on the coast. Since commoners were prohibited from coming too close to the palace, the workers kept their distance. They seemed like children's balls bobbing on the waters.

"Can you play loudly enough for them to hear?"

Forgetting all sense of propriety, Kaiya gaped at the preposterous challenge. The castle parapet wasn't the Hall of Pure Melody, let alone the Temple of Heaven. "That's…that's impossible."

The elf shrugged. "Not for Yanyan."

Kaiya shook her head. As though her paltry skill could compare to the legendary slave girl. Nonetheless, she plucked a string as hard as she could, emitting a loud, disjointed note.

Lord Xu burst out laughing.

Chagrin and anger washed over her. No telling what shade of red her face was.

After stifling a chuckle, Lord Xu deftly swiped the lute from her hands and strummed.

The series of notes sang in jubilation, tangible in its clarity. It was as if all the heroes of Cathay's past had marched into the present, urging her forward with their battle cries. Kaiya's uncertainties and embarrassment melted away. Her spirits rose, and even Chen Xin and Zhao Yue squared their shoulders and smiled. Out in the lake, the herders looked in their direction.

The elf turned back, face inscrutable. He returned the lute to her. "It is not the strength of the pluck that matters, but the intensity of your emotion. Only the power of your intent can compel the sound

321

beyond its physical limitations. Hear the waves of Sun-Moon Lake and allow them to lend you their strength. Now try again."

Kaiya's focus shifted from Lord Xu to the lute. Her musical talents were renowned throughout Cathay. Yet neither her own performances, nor any other she'd heard from famous musicians, could compare to the elf lord's improvisation.

She took a deep breath, aligned her posture, and listened. Waves sloshing against the walls below seemed to set a rhythm for the wind rustling through the ripening buds on tree branches. Birds joined in, their melody harmonizing with the song of spring.

Without conscious thought, her fingers danced over the lute strings, melding with the symphony of natural sounds. Perhaps her hands created the music, or maybe the music moved her hands. Clear and resonant, the melody filled the garden and blossomed out across the lake and palace grounds. The lumber herders looked back at her.

A hollow pop startled her, bringing her song to an abrupt halt.

The elf was gone. Only her guards and handmaidens remained, all shaking their heads and blinking as if waking from a trance.

"Keep listening," Xu's voice whispered on the wind.

Still staring at the lute in her hands, Kaiya turned as footsteps approached along the parapet. She looked up.

Flanked by two men from his native Nanling province, Peng Kai-Long dropped to a knee, fist to the ground. "*Dian-xia.*"

"Kaiya," she corrected.

He nodded. "Yes, Kaiya." His voice...did it wobble? It sounded abnormally somber, maybe something she wouldn't have picked up just a day before.

"What's wrong?" She motioned the handmaidens and guards to step back.

His lips tightened into a tight line. "How did you know something was amiss? I thought I hid it well."

She shrugged. "Something in your voice." Or was it his short breaths? They sounded loud in her ears, even if he showed no sign of labored breathing.

His shoulders slumped, so unlike his usual dashing demeanor, his pulse pattering like a tentative rabbit. "I have come to the palace to swear my loyalty to the *Tianzi.*"

For harboring Prince Hardeep? Kaiya's palms felt cold and clammy. "I am sure my father trusts you implicitly." Kai-Long was his favorite nephew, after all.

He shook his head. "No, formal vows. I have been elevated to *Tai-Ming* lord of Nanling Province."

"I don't understand." Kaiya's brow furrowed. Kai-Long's father was the ruler of Nanling. Something must have happened to him. But Kai-Long's brother would have inherited. And Kai-Long was supposed to lead an army to take Wailian Castle.

"My father and brother were on their way here to attend your brother's wedding." Kai-Long's voice

323

cracked, his shoulders slumped. "They had just docked at Jiangkou when they were…were murdered."

Kaiya sucked in a sharp breath. How was that even possible? A *Tai-Ming* lord, undoubtedly travelling with a full entourage of unquestioningly loyal armed guards, would make for an intimidating sight.

Poor Kai-Long, he must be in shock. He'd never been groomed to lead a province, never wanted to be anything more than a trade official, and now… She took his hand in hers. "I…I am so sorry."

A tear formed in his eye, which he wiped away. "It's so sudden."

"What happened?"

"We don't know yet. The *Tianzi's* agents are sorting through conflicting eyewitness accounts and uncovering evidence. They think rebels in the North are behind it. But I know." His fist tightened. "The Madurans knew of my friendship with Prince Hardeep. I am sure they have a spy in our villa in the capital, and knew he was staying with me. They are behind this, even if they don't dare to get their own hands dirty."

More evidence that Hardeep wasn't a Golden Scorpion. Of course he wasn't; and now, Kai-Long's family had suffered. She placed a hand on his shoulder. "I am so sorry."

His eyes met mine. "Be careful. They slaughtered a dozen Ankiran refugees in a ghetto last night. They must surely know about your meeting with the prince."

Blood drained from her head. Her legs wobbled. Kaiya reached out to keep from falling, and he caught her.

All those poor people, killed. Maybe because of her. To think that just two days ago, her main concern was having to meet potential suitors. Now, it looked like she'd made enemies in Madura. And maybe even a dragon.

Kai-Long turned to leave when Secretary Hong appeared at the entrance to the garden. He bowed low. "*Dian-xia*, the *Tianzi* has requested your presence in the Hall of Supreme Harmony."

She was technically confined to the inner castle, but the *Tianzi* did not make requests. Of course, the unprecedented assassination of a *Tai-Ming* lord and the massacre of foreigners in the capital changed the circumstances.

Bowing her head, she passed the lute to Han Meiling. With a nod to her imperial guards, she stumbled over to Secretary Hong. He guided them through the castle bailey, past the courtyard where she'd embarrassed General Lu.

She walked in a haze as they continued across the moat and into the central palace grounds. The alleys between the buildings and walls had seemed like a maze to her rice-wine-induced haze the night before, and it was no easier to keep track of the directions today. The faces of all the innocent Ankirans haunted her. They'd been living, breathing, laughing. Treated her like an honored guest. Now, they were gone.

325

At last, they arrived in the central plaza, the scene of too many misadventures yesterday morning. Up the one hundred and sixty-eight steps to the Hall of Supreme Harmony. She fought to breathe evenly.

Inside, the rows of kneeling officials and hereditary lords nearly filled the floor. It was so rare to see the hall so full. As she walked down the central aisle, toward where her father sat on the Jade Throne, many murmured among themselves. Behind her, Kai-Long's booted footsteps clopped across the marble floors.

At the front, she turned and walked to a space on the other side of her brothers. Kai-Guo's fists clenched tight, while Kai-Wu barely kept his posture straight. Kai-Long's footsteps stopped in place just behind her.

Father looked somber, even more so than usual. How could he not be, with the murders of his brother-in-law and nephew on Cathayi soil? And then in two days, he'd have to dispense punishment on her. He seemed to have aged since yesterday. If his health were failing, she might be to blame.

From his place a step behind the *Tianzi*, Chief Minister Tan cleared his throat. "*Tai-Ming* Lord Peng Kai-Long, step forward."

She tilted her head a fraction to find Kai-Long in the corner of her eye. He cast a somber smile toward her and rose. Striding to the place just before the dais, he sank to his knees and pressed his forehead to the ground.

"Rise." Father's voice shook with fatigue. When Kai-Long straightened, he continued. "Nephew, as pleased as I am to see you elevated to *Tai-Ming*, I

326

convey my regrets for the loss of your father and brother."

"Thank you, *Huang-Shang*." Kai-Long bowed his head again.

"Swear your loyalty to the *Tianzi*," the Chief Minister said. He placed the jade seal of state in Father's left hand.

General Zheng strode forward. With both hands, he placed the Broken Sword into Father's right.

Kai-Long's swordbearer shuffled down the central aisle and presented a ceremonial *dao* to his lord. Imperial guards stepped in closer to Father, their hands resting on their own swords. There was little need: by custom, only imperial guards were allowed to carry weapons in the hall, and the ceremonial *dao* was only a hilt and scabbard.

Bowing his head, Kai-Long held the blade up in two hands. "Under Heaven, I swear eternal loyalty to the Jade Throne. I serve at your pleasure. My sword is your sword."

He set the sword down on the floor before him, while another page came forth, bearing a seal on a silken cushion. Usually, the jade provincial seal would be used, though the immediacy had required a replica.

Again, Kai-Long bowed his head and lifted the seal in two hands. "Your command is my command."

Father beckoned him out of the bow. "You have trained as a diplomat and served magnificently in that capacity for the last few years. However, ruling a

327

province will prove challenging. I will send advisors with you on your return to Nanling."

"Thank you, *Huang-Shang*." Kai-Long pressed his forehead to the floor. He straightened. "*Huang-Shang*, if I may, I am certain that agents of Madura perpetrated this act."

The assembled men broke into a chorus of murmurs.

Kaiya's belly clenched. Kai-Long would undoubtedly bring Prince Hardeep into the conversation, which would in turn remind Father of her own transgressions from the previous day.

Father silenced them all with a twitch of his mustaches. "After you informed me of your suspicions, I sent my own agents to investigate." He faced the Chief Minister.

Tan cleared his throat again. "The Maduran trade mission vehemently denies involvement. They convey their regrets."

"Lies." Kai-Long's voice carried an edge of anger.

The Chief Minister gestured to an old man in the first row, on the other side of the central aisle. "Deputy Yan, please report."

Kaiya tried to find Deputy Yan in the corner of her eye. He only very rarely appeared at the palace; last night at the reception; the last time before that being when her childhood friend Tian had been banished. Then, as now, his head moved whenever she tried to study his features. All she could say was that his face was plain. If

328

foreigners had paintings of Cathayi faces in their encyclopedias, surely his would be the one.

The official bowed his head and stood. "*Huang-Shang*, my agents scoured the scene and followed up with eyewitnesses and the Jiangkou city watch. We recovered two of these." He held up two bloodstained crossbow bolts.

Kaiya looked at Kai-Long's fists, so tight the knuckles blanched. He must have known the Madurans had not used crossbows in nearly thirty years. They had Cathayi muskets, after all.

Deputy Yan continued, "The first penetrated Lord Peng through the throat. The second punctured his son's lung. Also, several eyewitnesses claim seeing five large Cathayi men fleeing the scene."

Just like the large men who had attacked her with crossbows. They might be the ones responsible for murdering the Ankirans, as well. Kaiya fiddled with one of her sleeves. All Kai-Long had to do was mention Prince Hardeep to give the Madurans a motive.

He glanced back at her, his eyes begging like the small court dogs. He then looked back to Father. "Thank you for devoting resources to the investigation, *Huang-Shang*."

Kaiya let out her breath. Kai-Long had spared her the embarrassment, at least for now. Still, that expression of his…

Father nodded a fraction. "We will keep you apprised, Little Peng. Now…" He turned to the Chief Minister.

No, poor Kai-Long had lost his father and brother. He could have exposed her secret to give the potential killers a motive. He'd protected her, to his own detriment. Summoning resolve from the firmness of Tian's pebble beneath her sash, Kaiya rose. "*Huang-Shang.*" Her voice came out as a mouse's squeak.

The collective sucking in of breaths might have rid the room of half its air. The lords and ministers, already surprised by a girl even being present in this meeting, must have been shocked that she dare speak.

Chief Minister Tan gaped at her, his lips moving but no sound coming out.

Father's face showed no surprise. "Speak, Princess."

Kaiya glanced back at all the hostile scowls. Swallowing her nervousness, she straightened. "*Huang-Shang*, I believe Lord Peng's suspicions—"

"*Believe?*" The anger in Chief Minister Tan's voice almost silenced her.

"—because I was attacked last night, too."

A second collective gasp would certainly rob the room of air, or maybe it was just her head spinning with apprehension. The ensuing jumble of sudden conversations was disorienting.

The *Tianzi* showed not even the least amount of surprise at her revelation. Did he already know? He raised his hand and the room once again fell into silence.

She peeked over her shoulder. Behind her, the lords all gawped. Kai-Long, sitting at her side, nodded with a smile.

"On my way to the Temple of Heaven—"

Murmurs rumbled again. *Tai-Ming* Lord Liang of Yutou's voice sputtered above the rest. "The Temple of Heaven? Did she enter the stupa without a blessing from the priests? If not, to view the fallen star is punishable by death."

Apparently, her visit to the Temple of Heaven had been kept secret, and she'd just revealed it. Her belly tightened.

Kai-Guo jumped to his feet. "It was that eerie music, drawing her like a moth to a flame. It was not her fault."

Kaiya shifted on her knees. This lie, too, would one day be exposed. Probably today. Right now.

Eyes raking over the assembled men, silencing them again, Father fixed his gaze on her. "Continue."

She bowed her head. "Several large Cathayi men attacked me. Six the first time, two the second."

Father showed no sign of surprise, though he rarely revealed any emotion.

Lord Liang of Yutou scoffed. "Are you saying you were able to defend yourself against six armed men?"

The *Yu-Ming* lords from his province nodded, followed by several others.

Kaiya lowered her finger, which had unconsciously twirled a loose lock of her hair, and took a deep breath. "I was with Prince Hardeep of Ankira, who was trained by the Ayuri Paladins. He fended them off."

More murmurs. No telling what they thought about a young princess, alone with a man, wandering the city streets at a late hour.

She swallowed hard. "I went to Lord Tong Baxian's villa—"

Father raised a hand to halt her. "Lord Tong's?" He looked to his advisors.

Why the interest in Lord Tong? She gave a tentative nod. "I st… I retrieved an artifact there. An Arkothi lute, made from a dragon's scale. When I played it, two of the assailants fled. The song the city heard last night, I played it myself. I am sorry to say that I lost the Lute when I passed out."

"It concerns me," Father said, "that Lord Tong had such an instrument."

Foreign Minister Song, kneeling among the other high officials, cocked his head, a look of confusion on his face. He turned to Father and pressed his forehead to the ground. "*Huang-Shang*, I do recall Lord Tong Baxian receiving the Dragon Scale Lute directly from Madura's Grand Vizier."

Chief Minister Tan nodded. "There were many things which we received as gifts from Madura after a successful trade agreement. We all did." He nodded to Minister Song. "I do seem to recall the musical instrument from Grand Vizier Rumiya did not have strings."

"But it does now?" Father asked.

Kaiya nodded. "Even his chamberlain was surprised that it did."

332

"If the Lute does what you say, it could be a dangerous weapon. Where is it now?" Father's lips pressed tight in rare show of public emotion.

Kaiya cast her eyes down. "I think Prince Hardeep took it."

Chatter broke out among the assembled men, stayed by Father's hand. He turned to his ministers. "Deputy Yan, investigate the princess' claims. It may not be the Madurans, but I find it suspicious that large men would target the Ankiran refugees, the late Lord Peng, and the princess."

"As you command, *Huang-Shang*." Deputy Yan bowed.

"General Tang." Father gestured toward one of the armored men. "Report on your men's seizure of Lord Tong's villa."

Seizure? What had Lord Tong done to forfeit his land?

Sinking to a knee, General Tang placed a fist to the ground. "*Dian-xia*, we found it abandoned."

"Mobilize your men. Coordinate with the city watch to scour the streets for Prince Hardeep and the Dragon Scale Lute. I want it found, and him brought before me."

General Tang bowed his head. "As the *Tianzi* commands."

Kaiya's heart rattled in her chest. She might've just sacrificed Prince Hardeep and herself to help Cousin Kai-Long. Still, it was the right thing to do. A princess shouldn't hide behind others' lies.

"Lord Peng," Father said. "You may return to your place among your peers."

Kai-Long bowed his head, rose, and strode back to his place among the *Tai-Ming*. Kaiya started to sit.

"Wait." Father's gaze locked on her. "Since Lord Peng has been elevated to *Tai-Ming*, all the first-rank hereditary lords, and many of the second rank, are now here. With their advice, I will pass judgment on your transgressions yesterday, as it has bearing on how we deal with the rebellion in the North."

CHAPTER 30
Unenviable Choices

A hundred disparate breaths rustled behind Kaiya as she knelt in the front row of the Hall of Supreme Harmony. Apparently, her public humiliation would not wait until after her brother's wedding after all.

Chief Minister Tan cleared his throat again. "Princess Kaiya, step forward."

Rising, Kaiya kept her shoulders straight and chin high as she walked over to the place Cousin Kai-Long had just vacated. She focused on that spot, lest the curious faces of all the lords and ministers reduce her to a quivering mass of nerves. More than a few murmured, mostly showing appreciation for her poise. If only they knew how contrived it was.

She stretched her arms out to straighten her long-hanging sleeves and brushed her gown to her shins. Sinking to her knees, she placed her forehead to the floor.

"Rise." Father's voice quivered. If anything, the tone sounded like the one he'd used at Mother's funeral.

"*Huang-Shang*," she said, acknowledging his command and straightening.

"Yesterday, you entered the Hall of Pure Melody without permission and handled Yanyan's pipa. Last night, you left the palace without permission and entered the holy grounds of the Temple of Heaven."

There was no honor in denying what everyone in the room knew. "I did." She bowed low.

"What do you have to say in your defense?" His voice sounded imperious, as if he were addressing one of the rebellious lords of the North and not his own daughter.

So much for the rare smile he had afforded her the day before. Keeping her head down, she took a deep breath to settle herself. "I wanted to help the beleaguered people of Ankira."

"In the Hall of Pure Melody? In the Temple of Heaven?" Though he was undoubtedly expressionless, his voice hinted at a rise in his eyebrow.

It'd made so much sense yesterday, but sounded so stupid now. She'd let Hardeep's enthusiasm get the better of her. "I thought by learning the magic of Dragon Songs, I could use the Dragon Scale Lute to liberate Ankira." Her own voice squeaked in her ears.

Chuckling broke out among the assembled men. No doubt they thought her naïve to believe she could revive a long-lost art.

Then the hall fell silent.

She dared a glance up. Her father's lip hinted upward just a hair to one side, his tacit message ordering the men to silence. His voice swept from left to right, something she'd never noticed before. "We are a nation

336

governed by the Mandate of Heaven, and everyone, including myself, must follow the laws set forth. Princess Kaiya has courageously confessed to her transgressions. For her punishment, I will hear counsel."

Someone—from the weight and motion, Kai-Long—rose to a knee. "*Huang-Shang*, if I may. The princess' intentions were good and selfless, even if her methods were misplaced. I would recommend lenience."

"Lord Peng," the *Tianzi* said, using Cousin Kai-Long's new title. "As the newest member of the *Tai-Ming*, you show bravery and initiative to speak first. We must remember, however, that horrible crimes have been committed in history with the best intentions. The Teleri Empire justifies the gang rape of every woman in its realm to breed an army of so-called peacekeepers."

Kaiya's heart lurched. Since when did rape become the moral equivalent of trespassing?

"*Huang-Shang*." Another man, Xiulan's father Lord Zhao from his voice, rose to a knee in a shuffle of robes. "The Five Classics state that a subject may learn more from forgiveness than punishment."

Father responded, "The classics also state that a ruler who is too gentle with his people invites rebellion. Just think if the Sultanate of Levastya had censured the priests who abandoned their patron god. Perhaps their king would not be living in exile and his people subjects of a foreign conqueror. With a rebellion now bubbling over in the North, wouldn't it be better for a ruler to make an example of those who disobey him?"

Kaiya's heart went from lurching to racing. Father really was going to make an example of her. If she was lucky, the penalty would be banishment. Then, she could follow Hardeep to Ankira. Maybe free the people from the yoke of Maduran oppression, if he still had the Dragon Scale Lute. However, if any of them mentioned the Temple of Heaven again, a death sentence could be warranted.

Just behind her, Eldest Brother Kai-Guo shuffled. He probably wanted to speak on her behalf, but he never went against Father. Second Brother Kai-Wu would certainly say something in her defense, but the light sound of his breath suggested he was dozing. Not surprising, given his lack of interest in these functions of state.

"*Huang-Shang.*" The voice of Tian's father, Lord Zheng of Dongmen Province, echoed in the hall. "The princess has never shown any sign of defiance before today."

"As the classics say," the *Tianzi* said, "without correction from a parent for a first offense, no matter how mundane, a good son might one day become a rebel, a good daughter a whore. Such impertinence—"

Kaiya bristled inside, a roaring in her ears drowning out the rest of Father's words. All she had done was try to help a persecuted people. Apparently, that was the first step to selling her body and instigating a rebellion. It wasn't like she had offered herself to the prince.

Impertinence, was it? Let them all see impertinence.

Gasps erupted as she rose from her bow. "If I may, *Huang-Shang*. The Five Classics also say that when no one acts to correct a moral wrong, a minister should remonstrate those who would turn a blind eye."

The *Tianzi* stared at her, expressionless. "I am glad you have studied the Five Classics. Are you now a minister in addition to being a priest and a Dragon Singer?"

Each word might as well have been a slap. Even though every fiber of her upbringing urged her to bow in contrition, Kaiya squared her shoulders. "*Huang-Shang*, I may not be a minister, but none have spoken on behalf of a people downtrodden by our open trade policies."

The hall fell utterly silent. She looked around. The Chief Minister had dismissed her plea to terminate the trade agreement just a few days ago. Now, he gawked.

Her mind raced through memories of the past few days. Each image felt like a fresh burn, fueling both her anger and courage. Her voice grew bolder and firmer. "I may not be a priest, but even the eyes of a girl can see the immorality of our ways."

The faces of the Ankiran refugees refused to fade from her vision. The smiles that welcomed her into their humble home, fed her when they had little to spare, and performed songs for her when they had little to celebrate. The faces of the innocent. "In the hands of an aggressive foreign army, our guns have widowed women.

339

Our firepowder has orphaned children." Her voice broke toward the end.

The deafening silence of the hall carried the broken notes all the way to the far ends of the room. In the corner of her eye, the lords and officials gawked. A grim satisfaction grew inside her.

For the first time in her entire life, she held every person's attention. Heart swelling, she delivered her final words as gently as a prayer. "We profit from others' suffering. And last night, their people were murdered on our soil. Surely Heaven would not condone it."

The lords and ministers erupted in whispers. Father's withering stare fell on her.

Courage waning, Kaiya added the honorific address to the end of her tirade: "*Huang-Shang*."

She pressed her forehead back down to the floor. What had possessed her to speak, to embarrass Father in front of all the lords and ministers like that? Maybe before her rant, she would have been confined to quarters until marriage. Now, she'd left the *Tianzi* no choice but to administer a more serious punishment. The Founder of the dynasty had stripped titles, cut out tongues, even executed families to five generations for such outbursts. Her palms clammed up.

"Chief Minister Tan," the *Tianzi* said.

"*Huang-Shang*." The Chief Minister's voice sank, suggesting his bow.

Her insides twisted, comforted only by the cool marble against her forehead.

"Let it be noted that we shall not extend the trade agreement with Madura."

Another collective gasp might have finally sucked the last bit of air out of the room. It had, if her spinning head were any indication. She ventured a glance up.

"As the *Tianzi* commands, so shall it be noted." Chief Minister Tan beckoned toward a scribe.

"For her many crimes, I sentence Princess Kaiya to a quick, merciful death." Father held up a hand, silencing the hall before any protests started.

Of course this would be the punishment. Insides turning to jelly, she pressed her head to the floor again. At least her blood would pay for a respite for Ankira.

"Let it be further noted that Princess Kaiya's death sentence shall be suspended as long as she remains obedient, and shall be entirely revoked if she proves worthy to the realm."

Barely in control of her body, Kaiya looked up. Father was smiling. A real smile. Even more than when Mother had still been alive. "Very good, Kaiya," he said. "I knew you could do it. You acted out of compassion, and you defended your decision even at risk to yourself."

Her cheeks flushed. Praise from Father was rare, and in public was unheard of. There must have been a reason.

He continued, "Even if you one day learn to sing Dragon Songs, do not use it as a crutch when a moral argument, spoken from conviction in your heart, will suffice."

Especially if magic was a beacon for a dragon, as the elf Xu suggested. She bowed again. "Yes, *Huang-Shang.*"

"Remember this lesson well, for even though a woman will never sit on the Jade Throne, she may one day rule as regent."

Regent? Such a strange thing for Father to suggest. There had been no regent since the Founder's Consort, who ruled for eighty years in that capacity before dying at the unprecedented age of one hundred and twenty-four.

Kaiya would never assume such a title, but still, Father had offered her rare praise, in front of all the ministers and hereditary lords. Emboldened, she straightened. "What about the remaining year on the trade agreement?"

The *Tianzi's* smile faded. "As Chief Minister Tan said, the treaty was negotiated under the imperial plaque. To renege outside of the proscribed stipulations would be tantamount to me forsaking the Mandate of Heaven. Perhaps it would invite another Hellstorm. Do not fear. Less than a year remains."

Kaiya sighed. Ankira did not have a year. "And if Lord Peng's suspicions are confirmed, that the Madurans assassinated his father?"

"Of course, such an action would void the agreement." Father's gaze lifted from her and settled over the room. "However, my agents believe it is Lord Tong of Wailian County."

Kaiya sucked in a sharp breath. Lord Tong was the leader of the rebels. That's why the army had seized the villa. Not only that, he had expected it, emptying his vault and holing up in the impregnable Wailian Castle.

Father scrutinized her before addressing the assembly. "The rumors many of you have heard are true. Chief Minister."

Chief Minister Tan stepped forward, prompting Kaiya to kneel. He unfurled a scroll, cleared his throat, and read:

"To Wang Zhishen, Emperor of Cathay. The four counties of Wailian, Tieshan, Jinjing, and Hongzhou have long been exploited by the rest of the realm. Our pleas for fairness have fallen on your deaf ears. Therefore, we hereby declare ourselves the independent Kingdom of Fengshan. Withdraw imperial troops from our sovereign land. Not only will any incursion on your part be faced with fierce resistance, we will cut off your firepowder supplies and share the secret formula with your enemies. From Tong Baxian, King of Fengshan."

A cacophony of angry protests echoed throughout the hall. Kaiya covered her ears to dull the roar.

After a moment, Father silenced them with a single glance. "I will hear your counsel."

Uncle Han, *Tai-Ming* lord of Fenggu Province, slammed his hand down on the marble floor. "*Huang-Shang*, we must crush them immediately."

343

Several of the *Yu-Ming* nodded in agreement, but *Tai-Ming* Lord Liang of Yutou Province shook his head. "Wailian Castle is impregnable, and those counties monopolize firepowder ingredients. If they sell to potential enemies…"

Kaiya twirled a lock of her hair. This must have been how Ankira felt so many years before.

Tai-Ming Lord Zheng of Dongmen Province cleared his throat. "*Huang-Shang,* we can blockade the Iron River and cut off their access to ports."

Lord Liang shook his head again. "*Huang-Shang,* if Wailian establishes direct trade with the northern barbarians in Rotuvi, they could access the deep-water port in Iskuvius and use the ships of Serikoth, with whom we do not have a sphere of trade agreement. It would tempt Tarkoth to end its own treaty with us. I advise we normalize relations with this Kingdom of Fengshan and levy tariffs so they can use Jiangkou."

"Appeasement!" Lord Han tugged his beard. "*Huang-Shang,* if you let those four counties go, you will only encourage others."

Xiulan's father, Lord Zhao, turned back to the lesser nobles. "Almost all the hereditary lords are here. I trust none of them would rise in arms against the Mandate of Heaven?"

All the assembled lords bowed like ripples gliding across Sun-Moon Lake.

"Good," Lord Han said. "Our combined provincial and imperial soldiers outnumber those four paltry countries thirty to one. Let us crush this rebellion."

The chamber shook with the confident roars of approval. Kaiya looked up at Father. His face betrayed nothing, which meant there was a possibility of civil war. Thousands would perish. Others would end up in poverty like the Ankiran refugees. Certainly there was another way. She peeked back at Lord Liang, the lone dissenter up to now, and Kai-Long. Their expressions might have been mirror images, staring off into the distance, jaws relaxed. Pensiveness, perhaps, and neither appeared ready to intervene.

And who would? Their voices would fall unheard, drowned out by the roar of bloodlust. Those robust chants, a symphony of voices speaking as…one? She closed her eyes and listened. Yes, there it was, a rhythm in the disparate voices. The pulse of fervent men.

Only the power of your intent can compel the sound beyond its physical limitations, Lord Xu had said not an hour before. *Hear the waves of Sun-Moon Lake and allow them to lend you their strength.* Holding the rhythm of the men in her heart, she stood. "*Huang-Shang.*"

The shouts swallowed up her voice. Even standing, she went ignored. No, she could not fail, not now. Toes gripped to the floor, she straightened her spine. Beneath the shaking marble dwelt a resolve, that of the earth, preventing the excitement from descending into cacophonic disorder. Seizing that resolve in her soul, she spoke again. "*Huang-Shang.*"

345

The din of men subsided. Father looked at her, eyes wide for the first time she could remember. Yet now that she had everyone's attention, what had she planned to say? She surveyed all those men, the ones who surely resented a woman—no, a girl not yet blossomed—in their midst. A few started to mutter.

Now was the time to speak, lest her single voice get lost. *Speak with the conviction of your heart*, Father had said. Tian's pebble squeezed tightly in her fist, she bowed her head. "*Huang-Shang*, allow me to marry Lord Tong on the condition that he submit to the Mandate of Heaven."

Silence.

Enough to consider the weight of her words. She knew nothing of Lord Tong. He was a stodgy Northerner, like General Lu. What if he were even worse? If he were the domineering type, all she'd learned about sound and music these past two days would go to waste. And no matter what, she would never see Hardeep again.

Lord Liang broke the silence. "*Huang-Shang*, the princess' suggestion is sound. It will allow us to bring the four counties back into the realm without conflict."

"Appeasement!" Lord Han said.

Locking eyes on her, Kai-Long—Lord Peng— nodded. "*Huang-Shang*, I agree with Lord Han. If another lord decides to rebel, there are no more imperial daughters left to marry out."

Kaiya stared at him. As a diplomat, he'd never advocated war.

346

"*Huang-Shang*," said *Tai-Ming* Lord Wu of Zhenjing Province, father of Kai-Wu's bride-to-be. "This is a special case. While no other place in Cathay can repel your armies, we could never take Wailian Castle by force."

Father's lips curved downward for a split second. "Chief Minister Tan, send a messenger bearing an imperial plaque to Lord Tong. If he agrees to submit to the Mandate of Heaven, the four counties in rebellion will be incorporated into a new Fengshan Province with him promoted to *Tai-Ming* lord." He turned and held her gaze, his eyes drooping in defeat. "He will also wed my daughter, placing their future sons sixth in line to the Jade Throne."

Kaiya stopped herself from twirling a lock of her hair. With an imperial plaque, representing the honor of the *Tianzi* himself, there was no escaping this marriage. The one she'd volunteered for.

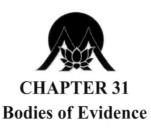

CHAPTER 31
Bodies of Evidence

Tian paced in the shadow of the Tarkothi ship *Indomitable*, reconsidering all the evidence they had uncovered over the course of a day. As a mere scribe in the local authorities' eyes, he'd remained at the periphery of an investigation that both the city watch, and the imperial commander quickly deemed the act of a lone assassin.

A boy. His face hadn't looked much older than twelve, but he was easily taller and broader than a grown man.

Ignoring the snickers and snide comments of passersby, Tian repeated his side of the martial exchange in the air while picturing the boy's responses in his head. Without a doubt, they were Black Fist fighting skills.

Which didn't explain the murder weapons. Tian held the image of the two crossbow bolts in his mind. The heads were too large to shoot from a Cathayi repeater, and Jie had heard two crossbows loosed from different positions. Unfortunately, the echo off the water had prevented her from pinpointing the second assassin's hiding spot. The crossbows used in the attack had yet to be uncovered, and could have belonged to any of the Serikothi or Tarkothi marines. Little Huang Zhen had taken an Eldaeri crossbow Jie'd stolen from the Tarkothi ship back to the safehouse. If only they still had one of the bolts extracted from *Tai-Ming* Lord Peng's body to test if it fit.

Cathayi boy. Eldaeri weapon. Two precise shots. Had either Serikoth or Tarkoth hired the assassin and provided the weapon? And for what purpose? Perhaps to frame the other, so Cathay would demand changes to the navigation treaties.

In this, the Serikothi seemed the more suspicious. Claiming danger, Prince Koryn had refused to cooperate with the investigation and instead returned to his ship and anchored at the mouth of the harbor, guns pointed toward shore. But how could either of those two parties, both arrived the day before, have known when Lord Peng's ship would dock?

Tian looked toward the *Saint Gong*, still cordoned off by the city watch. The palanquins remained where they'd fallen, even though the bodies of Lord Peng and his son had already been conveyed to the capital. Lord Peng had always been kind, before and after Tian's banishment. The other lords admired him. Maybe his murder had been a message to the *Tianzi*, and Peng had only been a target of opportunity.

Now, a few men gathered at the head of the dock where the *Saint Gong* was moored. From the jerky gestures, it appeared to be a merchant arguing with the guards. No closer to an epiphany than before, Tian went to intervene. At least he could fulfill some of his harbormaster office duties, and get a second, better look at the crime scene.

Up close, the merchant might have been one of the plainest-looking Cathayi men ever. Middle-aged, brown silk robes, not too short, not too tall... He wouldn't stand out in a group of plain men. He pounded his walking staff onto the road. "Please, it is just one box."

"For the tenth time, no." A lieutenant of the city watch waved a dismissive hand. "No one except city watch or a government official can board this ship until the lead investigator approves. Now move along."

Tian bowed. "Perhaps I can help?"

The merchant studied Tian's robes. "Ah, a harbormaster official. Yes, thank you. My company shipped some wares on the *Saint Gong*. One item is needed for Prince Kai-Wu's wedding tomorrow."

"What is your company's name? And your position?"

"Golden Fu Trading. I am Fu Jinxian, the owner." He bowed.

Right, the *Saint Gong's* manifest had indicated Golden Fu Trading's three crates and a box. "The Levanthi spice or Ayuri gooseweed?"

The merchant gawked. "All of it. Heavens, you have a good memory. Maybe I could entice you into leaving the harbormaster's office and entering the private sector."

"No, no." Tian waved both hands. "My family sacrificed a lot to get me this job. Let me see what I can do for you."

"Thank you." Nodding, Fu kept his eyes on Tian.

Tian turned to the guards, yet peered beyond them at the overturned palanquins. "May I?"

"You can go onto the dock, but not the ship." The lieutenant pointed at Tian's sleeve, where the embroidered badge showed his low rank.

Tian frowned. "When will they open this dock?"

"Ask the investigator." The lieutenant shrugged.

"Where is he?"

"Who knows. Maybe whoring."

Another young man pulled up in a rickshaw. His fine silk robes and jade rings suggested a life of luxury, and his smooth skin and soft-looking hands belonged to a boy who had spent too much time studying, not enough time in the sun. The silk pack slung over his shoulder suggested a traveler, yet flaunting so much wealth with no bodyguards was just asking for trouble. A Prodigal Son, wasting his father's wealth on adventure, in all likelihood. He looked from a piece of paper to the three-masted trading ship. "Is this the *Saint Gong*?"

Merchant Fu sighed. "You won't be boarding anytime soon."

The Prodigal Son alighted, paid the rickshaw driver, and sent him on his way. He straightened out his robes. "I'll be working as the quartermaster's assistant. I'll just wait until—" His eyes locked in on the fallen

351

palanquins. He pointed at the bloodstains. "What happened here?"

Tian studied him. He didn't look like the type to survive a day at sea, and must have been travelling all day not to have heard the news. "*Tai-Ming* Lord Peng and his son were murdered."

The Prodigal Son covered his mouth with a hand. "Heavens. Have they caught the killers?"

The lieutenant nodded. "Kill*er*. There was just one. Of course we caught him."

Of course *not*. Not both of them at least, and the city watch had arrived well after the Serikothi had slain the one. Tian evaluated the deck of the *Indomitable*. At that distance, the boy must've been an expert with the specific murder weapon. Perhaps he'd been a Cathayi child raised among the Tarkothi, trained to use an Eldaeri repeater. Yet why would the Tarkothi want Lord Peng dead?

The Prodigal Son motioned to the palanquins. "There had to be at least two assassins, shooting from opposite directions."

Tian's eyes darted left to right. How could this newcomer—of course. Why had no one seen it earlier? Lord Peng had fallen on the south side of his palanquin while his son fell on the north. Tian nodded toward the lieutenant. "You said I could go onto the dock?"

Scoffing at the Prodigal Son, the lieutenant motioned Tian by, but stopped Golden Fu and the young man from following.

"Come on, let me through," Prodigal Son said. "I am Foreign Minister Song's son."

The lieutenant snorted. "If you aren't Foreign Minister Song himself, you're going to stay off the dock."

Tian knelt by Young Lord Peng's blood, now dried into the dock's stone. He'd been shot in the chest, the bolt lodged deep. The assassin would have had to fire from the north...the deck of the *Saint Gong*? No, much too close, too sharp of a downward angle, and the bolt had entered...at a rising angle.

Tian cursed himself. He'd seen the body from the head of the dock, but hadn't processed that until now. Neither had the lead investigator or anyone else. It had taken an observation from some wealthy brat, who saw the aftermath and drew conclusions. If the Black Lotus had discovered this kid years before, he might have been recruited.

All the pieces of the puzzle were coming together. Two shooters. Two firing pins in Fat Nose Jiang's collar. Were they the same? With Wen too conspicuous with her beauty, Little Huang and Chong had tailed Jiang after he'd left Celebrate Spring Pavilion.

If so, he could've prevented this by neutralizing Jiang.

Guilt churning in his stomach, Tian walked toward the *Saint Gong*, and estimated the space between the hull and the dock. Certainly wide enough for someone to fit, but how could they hold on to the side and shoot? Without being seen, no less. He would have had to levitate.

Or…if the slain assassin had used Black Fist skills, perhaps the second one had similar training. Tian peered over the side of the dock again. If any of the mortar between the stones had been disturbed, it would be a sign of cat claws. Evidence of foot spikes would be down on the side of the dock, some five to six feet. Hard to tell from here—

A glint of sunlight flashed in Tian's eye from just beneath the waterline, fourteen and a half feet below the top of the dock. He looked back toward the head of the quay, where the guards didn't seem to care but both Fu and Song were watching with rapt attention.

Tian took off his shoes, robes, and pants, leaving him only in his undergarments and some concealed tools. Hands gripped to the side of the dock, he lowered himself down and probed the stones with his toes. There it was: dust from scraped mortar, and above it, deep indentations in the mortar itself. Evidence of cat claws. Taking a deep breath, he let go and plunged into the icy water, below the spot where whatever it was glinted.

He reached out and caught ahold of a fine cord in the water. With rapid kicks, he dove deeper, grasping the line and counting twenty-one feet to the seafloor, where it wrapped around a stone. Lungs burning, he returned to the surface and gulped air. There, right beside him just beneath the water, floated a repeating crossbow, tied to the cord.

Now, at low tide, the metal cocking mechanism caught the setting sun's light. At the time of the attack, the tide had been close to high. The planner had been no legendary Architect, hadn't taken into account the tides or the fact that the cord fibers would expand in the water. In all likelihood, the crossbow that'd fired the bolt that killed Lord Peng also floated between dock twenty-three and the hull of the *Indomitable*. It was now a matter of retrieving both weapons before the city watch investigators ruined the evidence.

It would be much easier if Jie were around to help.

CHAPTER 32
Party Crashers

The horse-drawn carriage's cushions softened the jostling to Jie's poor aching butt as she accompanied Prince Aryn and his aide Peris from Jiangkou to Huajing. Snake Eyes Peris had protested her place of honor in the prince's cabin, but Prince Aryn just waived off the complaints. The more Jie talked to him, the more likable he became, and the less likely it seemed the Tarkothi were involved in *Tai-Ming* Lord Peng's murder.

Even before their departure, he'd opened up the ship to investigators, shown inventory logs of crossbows and bolts. Certainly, those could be misrepresented. However, as Tian had said, the Tarkothi had no way of knowing Lord Peng would arrive at that time, nor did they have any clear motive to kill him.

The Serikothi, on the other hand, had been far less accommodating to the imperial officials. Instead of joining this procession from the harbor, they sat safely aboard their ship at the mouth of the harbor. It looked a lot like a blockade. Jie sighed. If only she could be investigating in Jiangkou with Tian instead of stuck with a foreign prince.

By the time they arrived at Sun-Moon Palace, the sun's last rays illuminated the sloping blue roofs and high white walls. Jie stared out at it, admiring the beauty.

Prince Aryn leaned over. "I'd wager you never imagined getting so close to your imperial palace, let alone entering it."

At least not in the last twenty hours. Still, appearances had to be maintained. She nodded with her best approximation of enthusiasm.

Peris yawned. "Be sure she doesn't steal anything."

Prince Aryn fixed him with a severe gaze, and Peris returned to staring at his own feet.

The carriage slowed to a stop near the palace's front gates. Up ahead, an open carriage bore the bodies of *Tai-Ming* Lord Peng and his son, draped in black war banners emblazoned with Nanling Province's red wolf. Imperial officials reverently transferred them to biers, and an honor guard of imperial soldiers came out to escort them into the palace.

Prince Aryn blew out a sigh. "The assassin shot from our ship. I feel as if we bear responsibility for the lord's death. I am still trying to figure out how he got past our guards and boarded."

Jie had a good idea: with Black Fist skills. The boy had been large and skilled, like the men who slaughtered the Ankirans the night before. Perhaps Peng Kai-Long's suspicions about the Madurans were well-founded. At war with Ankira, perhaps they'd tracked

Prince Hardeep and stumbled on the refugees. The Peng family helped Ankira, making Lord Peng a target.

Still, Lord Tong couldn't be ruled out, and perhaps Serikoth's suspicious actions hinted at collusion. Jie found herself sucking on her lower lip.

"Come on, Miss Jyeh," Prince Aryn said.

She turned to find the carriage door already open, and the prince extending his hand to help her. Peris frowned.

Ignoring his glare, Jie accepted the help. With her other hand on the annoying skirts, she jumped down. Their official guide—a secretary from the Ministry of Appointments—took the lead, and six Tarkothi marines fell in behind them. They passed over the arching bridge. Imperial guards lined the sides, their *dao* drawn and held in salute. At the gatehouse, imperial officials bowed. Black Lotus brothers snickered at her from the shadows.

"Prince Aryn of Tarkoth," announced the Minister of Appointments.

Their guide took them to the central plaza, now being decorated for the wedding ceremony. He pointed out the buildings in better Arkothi than Jie could muster. Around them, other parties of foreign dignitaries looked around, mouths agape.

They arrived in the tree-lined Nine Courtyard on the east side of the palace, named for its nine guest pavilions. A veranda wrapped around the tree-filled yard, connecting three buildings on each side. Light illuminated their paper windows.

Jie took note of the imperial guards on either side of each door, as well as the half-banners hanging above. Several countries were represented. The Foreign Ministry apparently had the good sense of placing rivals Serikoth and Tarkoth as far away from each other as possible, though Madura's gold scorpion banner hung just two buildings down from the twenty-one-pointed sun of the Ayuri Confederation. Curiously, one banner depicted the red star of Tivar, symbol of the turquoise-skinned Tivari who had enslaved humankind until their loss in the War of Ancient Gods.

The guide bowed low and held a hand toward the door. It opened into a central room with an Ayuri wool rug and bloodwood furniture. Several sliding doors stood open to bedchambers.

"Please make yourself comfortable, Prince Aryn," the guide said. "We shall bring you dinner soon. Afterwards, the *Tianzi* has arranged for Night Blossoms of the Floating World to entertain you."

She sucked on her lower lip. It'd been eight years since she left the Floating World in disgrace. A Blossom from that time would certainly recognize her; and as the only known half-elf in the realm, she would be a cautionary tale to younger Blossoms.

The Eldaeri, on the other hand, had no idea what the guide was talking about, given their blank expressions.

Jie tiptoed and whispered into Prince Aryn's ear. "Ladies of the night."

A slight grin formed on the prince's face, and he leaned over and whispered to Peris, whose eyes rounded before he frowned. The guide bowed again. "If you have any other needs, please let me know."

Prince Aryn plopped onto a plush cushion at the head of the central table. Stretching his legs out, he gestured at his entourage to relax. He patted the cushion next to him, inviting Jie to sit. She knelt and dutifully poured some rice wine. The sooner he passed out in a drunken haze, the sooner she could investigate the Madurans to see if they were involved in Lord Peng's murder.

Little did she expect him to pour her wine and insist she drink. It burned her throat and warmed her to the core.

Maids delivered a feast of roasted meats, quick-fried vegetables, and cold noodles, as well as Arkothi-style forks, knives, and spoons instead of chopsticks. Though the prince might be too dignified, his marines wouldn't be above pilfering silver cutlery. Sitting cross-legged around the table, the men attacked the food as only men could, with plenty of noise and mess.

"I bet you never ate so well," Prince Aryn said. Gazing at her through heavy lids, he rested a calloused hand on her thigh.

So much for his charm. Perhaps his interest had little to do with her ability to translate. Never mind that by human standards, she didn't look much older than twelve or so.

She brushed his hand away. "Your Highness, I'm sure you'll find your dessert much more filling."

Pouting, he held out his cup. "I doubt dessert will taste as sweet."

"Then you have never seen a Night Blossom." She filled his cup to the brim.

He drained it with a single gulp and pointed at a mirror on the desk. "Look at yourself. Once you washed your face and put on a pretty dress, you took on a beauty no human could hope to emulate."

Even *in* that dress, Tian had laughed at her. Jie brushed her hair behind her tapered ear. Though the way the prince now gazed at her, perhaps the problem wasn't her immature body as much as Tian's cluelessness. That, despite his uncanny ability to make connections.

She studied Prince Aryn's face. Tian might be handsome, but he couldn't compare to the prince's fine features. And charisma...well, Prince Aryn had more in his pinkie than Tian could accumulate in two lifetimes.

Jie leaned into the prince and placed his hand on the small of her back. She tilted her head and closed her eyes, inviting his lips to take hers. Why not? In her thirty-one years, she'd never given herself to a man for her own pleasure, always in the line of duty.

His other hand nestled her nape, and he brought his mouth to hers. He tasted of rice wine and need, and she parted her lips, welcoming him in. Her insides fluttered with either nerves or alcohol, and heat flared in her, from desire and maybe a little too much wine. Ignoring the marines' whoops and hoots, and Peris'

361

frown, she swung a leg over and straddled him. His hardness pressed against her.

The doors slid open. In the corner of her eye, Jie saw two gorgeous Night Blossoms in provocative silk robes. Their maid carried several folded blankets in her arms. Both were unfamiliar, though their style suggested they came from the Lilac Estates. That maid, though! Feng Mi, a Black Lotus initiate. Jie and Tian had rescued her from the crime syndicates.

One of the Night Blossoms covered her giggle. "It looks like the prince has little need of our services."

Jie's cheeks burned. Had Prince Aryn understood? Yes or no, his attention never left her. The Night Blossoms might as well have not been there for all the attention he paid her.

Feng Mi flashed subtle clan hand signals. *Master needs you. Castle. Half hour.*

Half an hour! The walk to the castle would take half that time, which left barely any time to enjoy Prince Aryn, or spy on the Madurans. Sighing, Jie pushed back. "Your Highness, your entertainment has arrived."

Only then did his eyes stray to the Night Blossoms before returning to her. His voice was breathy in her ear. "I want *you*."

Despite the heat and need surging through her, she shook her head. "I mustn't interfere with the emperor's arrangements." A half-truth.

His shoulders slumped, and for the first time, he seemed more a man than a prince. "Understood. Well, get some rest. If it pleases you, you shall sit next to me at the wedding tomorrow."

Peris let out a sigh that could only be relief. The man either had a stodgy adherence to appearances, or adoration for the prince that went beyond that of a devoted retainer.

"Don't you have somewhere to be?" Aryn glared at him before turning to her. "How about tomorrow?"

Jie stood and curtseyed. "You honor me, Your Highness. I'm going to stroll around the courtyard and clear my head." And eavesdrop on the Madurans. She looked back at the prince, whose attention never left her. She turned around to find a bundle of black cloth in her hands.

Feng Mi winked.

Her utility suit. Jie tapped a code on the girl's arm as she passed. *I watch Madurans.*

Outside, the cool spring air filled her lungs and helped unscramble Jie's head. Heavens, to think she'd almost slept with a prince. It could've been explained off as duty; yet another half-truth in a life full of half-truths.

Striding down the veranda as quickly as her dress would allow, she headed toward the Madurans' villa. She paused midstride as three altivorcs emerged from their guesthouse.

The Maduran's invitation to an imperial wedding made sense, but the Tivari...it wasn't as if Cathay had trade routes with their subterranean cities, nor a need for their only product: mercenaries. Shorter, stockier than humans, their booted feet clopped on the

363

wood terrace like horse hooves. Though the centermost altivorc might have been as beautiful as an elf, with coifed black hair and a black surcoat, his two guards were prototypically hideous.

One froze in place, grabbed the leader, and pointed at her. Three sets of Tivari eyes met hers and they broke into an animated series of grunts that vaguely resembled a language. While the leader and the right guard headed into the Maduran pavilion, the third came lumbering in her direction.

Not to share a recipe for post-dinner sweets, from the snarl on his face. Unless the main ingredient was half-elf ears and tongues. Jie ducked into an alley between pavilions, clenched her utility suit between her teeth, and then spider-climbed her way up. The dress got in her way, undoubtedly making her stand out like a prince among Black Fists.

Now where did that thought come from?

Before she reached the top, the altivorc turned the corner.

And rumbled through, without looking up. Predictable, like humans. The whiff trailing after him smelled of swine.

Once he went around back of the pavilions, Jie continued up to the roof. Keeping close to the steeply pitched tiles, she shrugged out of the dress and into her stealth suit.

Now properly dressed for the tasks at hand, Jie worked her way along the rooftops, jumping from pavilion to pavilion until she came to the Madurans'.

She peeked into a second-floor window, and finding the room unoccupied, slipped in.

Angry voices argued in the central room. Jie crept across the sleeping chambers and slid the door open a crack. Light shone from below, leaving the mezzanine shrouded in shadow. She eased the door open wide enough to squeeze out and then parked herself near the guardrail.

Down in the central room, the third altivorc had joined the others. The handsome leader crossed his arms, addressing someone out of her line of sight. His Ayuri was heavily accented. "So Prince Dhananad didn't respond to our request to negotiate? His invitation to the imperial wedding would have provided the perfect cover. Instead, I find *you*."

Dhananad...that name... Jie scrunched her forehead, trying to remember why it sounded so familiar.

The unseen Maduran, a male, answered, "Prince Dhananad does not have fond memories of the Cathayi."

The altivorc rumbled off a soliloquy of garbled sounds, with *Dhananad* the only intelligible word. The raw anger in the tone suggested nothing flattering, though it could have been Tivari romantic poetry for all Jie knew.

However, Dhananad's dislike of Cathay sparked a memory. Thirty years before, a young Prince Dhananad had been a collateral target of a Black Lotus operation—carried out by the famed Architect, Surgeon, and Beauty—to retrieve a secret artifact. The ill-fated mission had led to the deaths of those three, and Master

365

Yan had used the *Tiger's Eye* technique to block the memories of all clan members, ensuring that only he knew their real names or the nature of the relic.

Below, the altivorc switched back to Ayuri. "I assume you, in your capacity as Master of the Golden Scorpions, will act on behalf of Madura?"

Jie suppressed a gasp. A Golden Scorpion, a cast-off of the Paladin Order, here in Huajing. Against the laws of the realm. A master, no less. She edged forward, but no angle provided a good line of sight on the man.

"I will consider it."

"You have a reputation for sowing chaos and bringing down empires. I assumed you enjoyed it."

The Golden Scorpion laughed. "You know me too well."

"We are brokering a deal between Lord Tong and the Teleri. It's success depends on Madura's involvement."

Jie's head spun. The faraway Teleri Empire was busy gobbling up Arkothi city-states in Tivaralan's northeast. Their next target was likely to be Serikoth. However, an alliance with Lord Tong would allow them a way through the Wall in the North.

The man yawned. "You should know better than to rely on Madura. The Grand Vizier kept the royal family stupid for a century, leaving them ill-prepared for life after his sudden departure."

"Indeed." The altivorc scoffed. "Left them inept for nearly three decades. I am sure he is gloating as we speak."

"Indeed."

"So, you will take part in the attack?"

"You will know when I have decided."

Jie pictured a map in her head. In order for Madura to even consider invading the South through the Wall, they'd need to divert considerable resources from the siege of Ankiras and the occupation of Ankira.

Unless the attack referred to something else. A target of opportunity. A soft target.

Like the imperial wedding, where Lord Tong and his allies could wipe out the imperial family and any number of hereditary lords. Did they have the numbers and weapons to do it? A Maduran Scorpion could even the odds against a dozen of imperial guards and the Black Lotus.

Jie snuck back into the room and took a deep breath. Master Yan needed to hear this, and the Madurans and altivorcs needed to be monitored.

CHAPTER 33
Ulterior Motives

The silence in the Hall of Supreme Harmony allowed Kaiya to hear the collective breaths and heartbeats of the assembled lords and ministers. None breathed more rapidly than she, and her pulse pattered faster than anyone else's.

After all, none of those men would be marrying a traitorous lord in the coming weeks. Perhaps days. And she'd resigned herself to this fate. Hopefully, Lord Tong was not like other Northerners in their dislike of the arts. He'd made his chamberlain learn the lute, after all.

Father gave the slightest of nods, and all the men pressed their foreheads to the ground.

Chief Minister Tan cleared his throat. "Distinguished lords, you may retire."

Around her, the lords stood, many of them discussing the implications of her impending marriage. Several approached and bowed their heads, offering their congratulations.

As she rose, she looked to Father. Cousin Kai-Long—Lord Peng—stood before him, whispering, his voice too low for even her keen ears to pick out from the surrounding conversations. He turned toward her, and Father's gaze followed. Father nodded.

They were discussing her. Kai-Long opposed her wedding; maybe it had to do with that. She'd know soon enough, with the way he approached her wearing a broad grin. He bowed his head. "Congratulations, *Dian-xia*."

"Thank you, Lord Peng."

He started to laugh, a breach of protocol in the Hall of Supreme Harmony, but contorted his face into a smile. "Come with me. I would like to introduce you to the wife of Ambassador Vikram of the Ayuri Confederation. She is in the guest pavilions. The *Tianzi* has already approved."

Why bother with extending pleasantries, when now she was nothing more than a bride-to-be? She looked to the Jade Throne. Father, now barely sitting straight, nodded.

Cousin Kai-Long gestured toward Secretary Hong, who hovered nearby. "Go find the princess' handmaiden Meiling, and have her meet us in the central plaza with the princess' lute."

Prince Hardeep's lute, not hers. It was a cruel reminder of how much she was sacrificing. Her belly felt hollow. But why would an ambassador's wife care about a foreign instrument Kaiya couldn't even play?

Secretary Hong wetted his lips. "I am supposed to—"

"Hurry." Kai-Long leaned his head toward the doors. "I will take responsibility for the princess until you return."

The hapless secretary bowed his head. "As you command, Young Lord... I mean, *Jue-ye*."

Kai-Long beckoned two imperial guards, ones she recognized but who were never assigned to her. "Come."

They had started out of the hall when Appointments Minister Hu ventured into her path. His eyes narrowed like a snake. Perhaps he still bore resentment for her contradicting him the day before. "The princess has a dinner with the Crown Princess in two hours."

Kaiya suppressed a shudder. This sudden dinner, on the eve of her wedding announcement, could only mean one thing. *That* discussion. It was typically a mother's responsibility to discuss the arrival of *Heaven's Dew* with a daughter who was soon to blossom, but Mother's passing meant that duty had fallen to the elder sister-in-law.

Undoubtedly, a pillow book would be involved. Her younger friend Lin Ziqiu had already shown her the collection of graphic woodblock prints before, and it had made her blush hotter and brighter than Tivar's star during the Year of the Second Sun. Soon, Kaiya would be acting out those pictures, with a lord she'd only recently heard of. Now instead of blushing, her insides squeezed into a painful knot.

Cousin Kai-Long stepped forward, at an angle which interposed himself between her and Minister Hu like an imperial guard would do. "The *Tianzi* has approved Princess Kaiya's meeting. Two hours is more than enough time."

Eyes shifting from Father to her to Kai-Long, Minister Hu smiled with about as much warmth as a burnt-out hearth at midwinter. He spun on his heel and went fawning over to another *Tai-Ming* Lord.

Cousin Kai-Long grinned. "I think I could get used to this new position."

Kaiya would have at least faked a laugh if not for the reality of her situation. She was getting married to a stern man who might not even let her play music. She would never see Hardeep again. Not only that, it had been her own choice, for the realm. Her lips tightened into a straight line. Thankfully, Cousin Kai-Long spared her embarrassment by turning around and leading her out of the hall.

Secretary Hong and Han Meiling met them on the far end of the central plaza, the handmaiden bowing with the lute in her hands, then joining the retinue two steps behind. Kaiya's belly writhed, like the twists and turns they took through the alleys between buildings. Somewhere up ahead, musical notes danced on the winds, plucked from…a lute?

The sound grew louder, taunting her as a reminder of what she would be losing. They rounded a corner into the Nine Courtyard. Carefully manicured by imperial gardeners, the open space featured a central pond bordered by soon-to-blossom flowers. Plum trees already bloomed, their white and pink petals drifting on a light breeze like snow. It might have been a metaphor for her own impending blossoming and deflowering.

She froze in place. One of the banners above the pavilion door was emblazoned with a golden scorpion, the symbol of Madura. The ones Prince Hardeep suspected of trying to kill them last night. Heart seizing, she clutched Kai-Long's sleeve. "How could the Foreign Ministry house the Madurans here?"

"It was my doing."

"Yours?" Her heartbeat resumed, only to roar in her ears. If the lute still played, its melody didn't make it through the veil of her shock.

Kai-Long squeezed her hand. "As the Founder wrote, keep your friends close, your enemies closer. In any case, their crown prince refused to come, so the pavilion is empty. Come along." He gestured toward a banner with a twenty-one-point star.

Thoughts clearing, she listened. The lute's melody came from inside the Ayuri Confederation's guest pavilion. The Ayuri South had many musical instruments, though the lute belonged to the Arkothi north. What a coincidence that Meiling now carried one as well.

No, it couldn't be just a coincidence, but rather a sign from the Heavens. Maybe her dreams weren't dead. Kaiya resumed her walk, stride lengthening.

The sound intensified when the bowing servants slid open the doors. Kaiya stepped over the high threshold and into a central room that vaulted two stories high. Standing along the walls, six Ayuri men in white *kurta* shirts with gold embroidered collars all turned and met her gaze, then pressed their hands together and bowed their heads.

A man lounged on the wool carpet in a copper-colored *kurta*, and a woman in an orange sari knelt beside him. Both rose and pressed their palms together. White wisps streaked through his black hair, which framed a deep brown face so dignified, he could only be Ambassador Vikram. His lighter-skinned wife looked old enough to be Kaiya's mother, yet maintained a lustrous beauty all the same.

However, neither drew her eye more than the blindfolded man sitting cross-legged at the head of the room. Several musical instruments, both from the Ayuri South and Arkothi North, surrounded him. He paused with his hands above a lute and bowed his head.

"Good evening, Lord Peng," Ambassador Vikram said.

Cousin Kai-Long bowed his head. "Good evening, Ambassador. Princess Kaiya, may I introduce you to Ashook Vikram and his wife Shariya."

Pressing her palms together, Kaiya bowed her head in Ayuri fashion. "I am pleased to meet you."

With a smile, Lady Shariya gestured to a cushion. "Please, Your Highness, sit."

"Thank you." After Kaiya's adventure with Prince Hardeep, the Ayuri words came out smoothly, almost as perfect as Kai-Long's. She brushed her skirts to her shins and knelt on the cushion, and the ambassador and his wife followed.

Head bobbling, reminiscent of Hardeep, Ambassador Vikram bowed toward Kai-Long. "Lord Peng, I cannot thank you enough for introducing us to the Blind Musician."

Kaiya studied the lute player, who wore Cathayi-style robes, yet whose dark skin tone marked him as Ayuri or Levanthi. The wide blindfold covered most of his forehead and nose.

Still standing, Kai-Long grinned. "Did you test him?"

Lady Shariya placed a hand over her chest. "Yes. I felt cruel at first, but then amazed. Your Highness, you must see this. Musician, please play."

With a bow of his head, the Blind Musician plucked out a forlorn melody on the lute: a low thrum, descending so low it might have been to the depths of hell.

Kaiya sighed. It was as if he could feel her sadness.

Removing some of their rings, both the ambassador and his wife flung the jewelry at the poor man. Kaiya covered her mouth. How could they do such a thing to a blind person?

Yet even as he played, he shifted in place, deftly avoiding each ring. The music not only remained steady, his movement seemed to shift with the ebb and flow of the notes.

Kaiya sucked in a breath. With practice, she had finally learned to hear heartbeats. That skill paled in comparison to the Blind Magician, who seemed to *see* with his ears.

Secretary Hong and Han Meiling also gasped. Kaiya found the imperial guards in the corner of her eyes. Even if they did not audibly express their shock, their gawking mouths betrayed rapt attention.

"This is the real reason I brought you here." Kai-Long's breath tickled her ear. "To meet the Blind Musician."

Kaiya's mind somersaulted. First Prince Hardeep, then Lord Xu, Doctor Wu, and Xiulan. In the last two days, they had all taught her abilities applicable to Dragon Songs. If she could learn the Blind Musician's skill...but alas, there was no time. Not with an impending marriage.

"My song resonates with your heart and comes back to me. It tells me your desires." The Blind Musician's low-pitched voice crackled like logs in a fire. "I will teach you what I can tonight. Bring your lute." He pointed to the instrument in Han Meiling's hands.

Kaiya could only stare. Perhaps Cathay's Dragon Songs weren't dead after all. Yet the Blind Musician's bronze skin tone could not belong to a Cathayi person. She dipped her head in slow nods.

Kai-Long chuckled. "Let us take our leave of the ambassador and his wife. We do not have much time before your dinner, *Dian-xia*."

Dinner...and the talk, the one that Kaiya's mother would have given had she not died already. Yet that appointment seemed insignificant in this moment, save for the time constraints it presented.

She bowed her head. "Ambassador Vikram, it was an honor to meet you. I thank you for your hospitality. Please allow me to steal away the Blind Musician and leave you to the entertainment my father has arranged."

Both the ambassador and his wife rose, pressed their hands together, and bowed their heads. The Blind Musician stood as well. Playing his lute in smooth plucks, he navigated around the cushions and rings and came to the door.

Was this the right thing to do? After all the rules she'd broken the day before? Kaiya glanced at the imperial guards, who showed no sign of protest. Han Meiling chewed on her lower lip, but said nothing. Kai-Long only smiled.

Pressing her palms together, Kaiya bowed to the ambassador and his wife. Her pulse raced as she turned and stepped over the ghost-tripping threshold. Behind her, the Blind Musician seemed to have no issue negotiating it, either.

"Where to?" she asked.

Kai-Long pointed to the guest pavilion designated for the Madurans.

Kaiya's pattering heart almost stopped even as her feet shuffled toward the entrance. It seemed so...wrong. Even if the Madurans weren't there. The imperial court allowed her dear Prince Hardeep's enemies a place of honor, while his own nation suffered. And there was nothing she could do. Not anymore. Not when her own homeland faced fragmentation. She was just as selfish as the advocates for unlimited firepowder trade.

"You'll be fine," Kai-Long said with a smile. "No Golden Scorpions will ambush you tonight. And you have two imperial guards to protect you."

"What about you?"

Kai-Long looked up to the Iridescent Moon, now waxing to its first gibbous. "I have another matter to attend to, but Secretary Hong will make sure you are on time for dinner with Crown Princess Xiulan."

The last line was delivered with enough emphasis that poor old Hong cringed.

Kai-Long leaned in and switched to Ayuri. "I handpicked guards who can't speak Ayuri, and Hong will do anything you say."

Why would that matter? Unless the Blind Musician intended to tell her something not meant for prying ears? Maybe news of Hardeep, since Kai-Long had apparently arranged this. Pulse skipping again, Kaiya stepped over the threshold and into the guesthouse. Meiling hurried ahead to unshutter the light bauble lamps. The Blind Musician and the guards followed.

Striding across the carpet faster than even someone who could see, the Blind Musician sat cross-legged at the head of the vaulted central chamber. Then he removed the blindfold.

Blue eyes danced in front of her.
Prince Hardeep.

CHAPTER 34
Hot and Bothered

Secretary Hong's breath wheezed in the background as Kaiya gawked at Prince Hardeep. The guards showed no signs of surprise; Kai-Long had probably chosen them not only for their lack of fluency in Ayuri, but also because they had not seen Prince Hardeep the day before.

Now, his eyes danced with mirth, sending Kaiya's mind spinning. Despite her best efforts to control them, her own lips quirked into a grin. When he spread his arms, inviting an embrace, she ran towards him as quickly as her gown would allow.

Dao rasped out of scabbards as the imperial guards closed in.

"Stand down." Kaiya stopped midstride and held out a halting hand. She locked an imperious gaze on them. Hopefully, as long as she did not fall into his arms, they would hold back.

One of the guards bowed his head. "*Dian-xia. The Tianzi* commands that no man touch you until your marriage."

Chest tightening, Kaiya offered Prince Hardeep a conciliatory smile. Even if he might not understand the Cathayi language, the swords and body language needed no translation. Still, to be absolutely sure, she said, "I am sorry, Prince Hardeep. For everyone's safety, you must not touch me."

Hands raised, Prince Hardeep looked from the imperial guards' blades and back to her. "I will do my best to obey the order, but my style of teaching is very...hands-on. I might not survive our lesson." A flirtatious smile formed on his lips.

Kaiya's belly fluttered like a dragonfly's wings. "Lesson? Do you really know how to see with your ears?"

He shook his head. "If such a feat of sound perception existed, it would have belonged to your people's Dragon Singers."

"Then how did you avoid the rings?"

"Paladins can sense attack trajectories."

All excitement drained away as Kaiya's heart sank into her belly. His was a different type of magic, one that a budding Dragon Singer could never learn.

Not only that, if a Paladin could accomplish such an act, so could one of Madura's Golden Scorpions. It was time to end all doubts, once and for all. Subtly, so he wouldn't see through her questions. "Why the ruse with the Ayuri Confederation ambassador?"

His lips formed a tight line. "I didn't want them to recognize me. I have no love for them."

Not helping. "Why not?"

He shook his head, shoulders slumping in defeat. "In Ankira's time of need, when faced with Cathayi guns and the sting of the Golden Scorpions, the Confederation refused to send aid."

Neither the anguish when he spoke of Ankira's plight, nor the venom with which he named the Golden Scorpions could've been contrived. The defeat in his posture was real, unless it was the inspired performance of an unparalleled stage actor with thousands of years of experience. And, of course, Kai-Long had vouched for him. How could she have ever doubted?

If not for the watchful eyes of the guards, she would've taken his hand. "Maybe there was a reason they couldn't help?"

"The Confederation's Paladin protectors claimed to be too busy containing the ravages of the great Avarax." The awe in the prince's voice when he mentioned the dragon could only come from deep-rooted fear. "Speaking of which, I was serious about the lute. You should learn, so that when the time comes, you can play the Dragon Scale Lute."

"Do you have it?" Not that she ever wanted to play it again.

"One of our pursuers took it while I fought the others."

She sighed. "There won't be a chance for me to help you, anyway. I am betrothed. I will marry Lord Tong in a few weeks."

"The same Lord Tong?" Hardeep cocked his head. "It doesn't matter. We don't know what fate holds for us, only that it has brought us together."

Fate. The closest word in Cathayi, *yuan*, suggested that mountains and deserts and oceans could not stand between those fated to be together, while those without *yuan* could pass each other every day and never meet.

"Let us begin." As he approached, one slow step in front of another, his blue eyes seemed to look straight into her soul.

Kaiya's breath hitched. Every muscle froze in place, like a doe facing a hunter's arrow.

He stopped as the imperial guards strode forward with hands on their swords. "Sit." He motioned to the floor beyond.

"On the floor?" Her voice came out as a squeak.

He nodded. "Have you seen a painting of the Goddess Saraswati?"

She'd seen so many paintings of the Ten Thousand Ayuri deities: Surya, Lord of the Sun, riding his flaming chariot drawn by white horses. Beautiful Shakti, Goddess of Fertility, holding auspicious symbols in her many hands. Black-skinned Yama, dragging sinners down to Hell. And of course, Saraswati, sitting cross-legged with an Ayuri-style lute cradled in her arms.

The pose might be appropriate for an Ayuri goddess, but a Cathayi woman of noble standing would never sit with her legs so…open. The constricting inner dress might not even allow it. Her blush must've now been illuminating the room better than the light baubles.

He smiled again, this time less flirtatious, more understanding. "Correct posture is important for everything in life."

Just like Doctor Wu had said. Kaiya glanced at the imperial guards, and then, with a deep breath, held the folds of her outer gown together while hitching up her inner dress. With the amount of heat her face put off, she might be able to warm the entire palace on this chilly evening. She met Hardeep's gaze again.

He gave her a perfunctory nod.

Reassured, she settled into a cross-legged seat on the floor. She arranged the outer gown, as much for modesty as to conceal her stick legs and enormous feet. No telling what the guards and handmaiden were thinking at this moment. Better not to even look in their direction. She kept her eyes focused on the prince as Han Meiling presented the lute, the one he'd given her through Kai-Long yesterday.

"Do you like it?" he asked.

"Yes." Mundane conversation. It was good. It would keep her mind off the unladylike pose. Maybe.

"I would have rather given you a lute that has been in my family for decades. Unfortunately, I had to borrow this one from the refugees."

Kaiya ran a hand over the wood. The varnish had faded in some places, and several scuffs scarred its belly. She shook her head. "You gave this one with the best of intentions. I will treasure it for that alone." Even if she might never be allowed to play it in her new husband's home.

He pressed his hands together. "You are too kind. Now—"

Secretary Hong cleared his throat. "If I may, Your Excellency, why did you abandon the princess at the Temple of Heaven?"

Prince Hardeep shook his head. "I had to draw away the assassins who wanted to harm us."

So that's why he had abandoned her. No, not abandoned her, but protected her. Again.

"Now, Princess," he said, "straighten your back, let your shoulders relax. Rest the resonator on the floor."

She looked at the foreign instrument in her hands. He had not been nearly as meticulous at the Temple of Heaven two nights before.

"In the Ayuri South, just as a warrior must become one with his weapon, we believe the performer must become one with her instrument."

Kaiya nodded. Her teachers had said pretty much the same thing.

"Cradle it as if it were your own baby."

She nearly dropped the lute. As if she had ever held a baby before; and to think she might very well be cradling her own in less than a year. Truth be told, the bawling babies brought to court by the great hereditary lords provided plenty of disincentive in that regard. Even when they had grown a little older, the snot-nosed brats lacked manners.

384

Hardeep cleared his throat, drawing her attention to him. He wore an amused smile. "Your arms are too rigid, and if that is holding a baby...you are choking its neck. Relax."

He drew in behind her. His body heat radiated into her back as he adjusted the instrument's position. She closed her eyes and listened for his heartbeat. Slow, powerful, like a spring-fed river sloshing against a dam. Fireworks burst in multiple explosions all through her core. So much for relaxation. It would be easier holding the low horse stance under Doctor Wu's glare than to concentrate with him so close.

Around her, the imperial guards' tension wound tighter than a dwarven coil. Hands gripped sword hilts. His head craned over her shoulder, his chin just a hair's breadth away from her neck. "Here," he said, breath warm on her ear. His hand covered hers as he loosened her fingers around the lute's neck. The jolt from her hand went up her arm and into her heart. It might have skipped a beat or three.

Blades swept out as the imperial guards closed in as fast as a viper strike.

Prince Hardeep jumped back, hands in the air. "I am sorry."

"He was just helping me hold the lute correctly." Kaiya waved the guards off.

They froze in aggressive stances, a sword's distance away from the prince. A low growl emitted from deep in one of their throats.

Secretary Hong's voice wobbled, whether from nervousness or his halting Ayuri or a combination of both. "Your Excellency, you may instruct, but do not touch."

Prince Hardeep pressed his palms together. "I apologize. I will do my best, but I must say that it is very hard to teach if I cannot help the princess feel the instrument."

Yes, feel the instrument... Kaiya banished thoughts of Hardeep caressing her like his lute.

"You will have to make do." The rigid line of Secretary Hong's lips, along with the lack of apology in his tone, left no doubt as to what he really thought.

The residual heat from Prince Hardeep's closeness clung to her back, tingling and percolating through her with the same slow, resolute pulsation. Maybe distance was for the better. If the prince remained so close, there would be no way she could concentrate on learning how to play.

The next hour dragged on like sweet torture. Hardeep would come tantalizingly close, making her pulse race and palms sweat. It took all her effort to keep her fingers from slipping on the lute's neck. Never before had she felt such a connection with a man, and to have him so close. Oh, for him envelop her in those strong arms, to brush his lips across her neck! A primal heat erupted deep inside her, making her squirm.

Each time he got too close, the imperial guards reacted within a split second, assuming offensive stances. He would ultimately raise his hands and back away with a bow. The constant tease left every one of her nerves on edge. It was nothing short of a miracle she learned anything.

If her nerves were on edge, the guards' must be even more so. Instead of the near-motionlessness and stoic expressions, their fierce scowls could have rivaled the dragon etched into each of their breastplates. Poor old Secretary Hong hunched over, and Meiling shuffled on her feet.

Still, in the short time, she managed to learn a few simple folk songs, as well as parts of a far more complicated piece. When he played it himself, the complex chords, rapid changes in pitch, and extreme key ranges left her head spinning.

Limbs languid, her bony bottom aching from sitting for so long, and her entire body still hot with desire, she looked up at him. "Your Excellency, it is almost time for me to go."

He offered an encouraging smile. "Maybe try it one more time. Do as the book you read says. Let your heart project your emotions into the song."

She held back a sigh. The only emotion she could project right now would be embarrassingly wanton lust. Or maybe irritability and exhaustion. She looked around. From their slouching, Secretary Hong, Meiling, and the imperial guards felt equally irritable and fatigued.

"I would wager since they already feel tired, it would make them more so." He grinned.

Perhaps. Kaiya closed her eyes and listened for their hearts. There…a cacophonous chorus of erratic thumps. She had never noticed before, at least not until Lord Xu had pointed them out on the castle walls earlier in the day. Among them, Hardeep's heart remained steady and powerful.

"Don't tax yourself," he said. "Relax. Listen to nothing except your own music."

Opening her eyes, she nodded. Still, though he might enjoy music, and might have read that single passage from the book, he certainly would know nothing of projecting power through borrowing other sound as Lord Xu had taught.

She closed her eyes and listened again. The collective heartbeats rung in her ears, all waves for her exhaustion to ride on. Loosening her stiff, tired fingers, she played the first frame of Hardeep's song. The chords came out crisp. The changes in pitch resonated clearly. Aligning her spine and joints, feeling the ground through her behind, she continued. The sound filled the hall.

Behind her, Secretary Hong yawned.

She continued strumming and plucking, her own fatigue percolating through her core. The minister's robes ruffled as he dropped to a knee. The imperial guards wobbled in place. Heavens, it was working!

And there, among her own music and the beating of all the men's hearts, Hardeep's own heart throbbed with strength. Borrow that, as she had the sounds in the garden earlier, and it might be possible to magnify the effect.

"Sing!" Hardeep said. "Let me hear your beautiful voice."

Sing! Yes, the lute begged for an accompaniment, like the interplay between her masters' pipa and erhu. She raised her voice in song, letting the lute's melody guide her. Energy welled inside her, climbing toward the crescendo. Her spirit soared with it.

Hardeep smiled, his blue irises twinkling.

No! Breath hitching on the notes, her voice cracked. It was like trudging up the snowy slopes of Jade Mountain on an empty stomach. Her own heart refused to maintain the power. All energy drained from her arms. Her spine, held erect for so long, finally gave out. Gasping, she slumped over the lute.

Her gasp echoed the others around the room. She turned to see many of them crumpling over as well. The imperial guards knelt on one knee, their fists on the ground not in salute, but rather to prop themselves up.

She'd done it! This time without the use of a musical instrument imbued with an innate power, no longer in a place with perfect acoustics. A cool wave washed over her, and she filled her lungs as if it would help keep her sitting straight.

Hardeep crawled over to her side, panting. His words came out in gasps. "Very good, princess. Perhaps with more practice and the Dragon Scale Lute, you could repel even Avarax." He slumped over, the side of his head plopping on her lap and his hair splaying out in a blossom of silky tendrils. The warmth—no, the blazing heat—burned through the silk of both gowns and into her legs. A fever?

Behind her, the imperial guards stirred, but made no move to intervene.

She pushed the lute over and rested it on the floor. Running a hand through Hardeep's glossy black hair, she brushed it aside to reveal the bronze tone of his neck, smooth, save for a dark oval scar in one spot. So smooth, and…kissable. His eyes were closed, partially concealed by yet more of his voluminous hair.

She swept it over, pausing on his forehead. It was hot, for sure. Too hot. She beckoned Secretary Hong, now just regaining his feet. "Call a palace physician. No, Doctor Wu, if she is in the palace."

Secretary Hong said, "*Dian-xia*, she is searching for the Dragon Scale Lute."

That didn't make sense. Why would a doctor look for a musical instrument? She fixed him with an imperious stare. "It doesn't matter, any doctor then. Prince Hardeep needs help. He has a fever from the fatigue. He needs acupuncture."

Hardeep's eyelids flapped open. "No. No acupuncture."

With a giggle, Kaiya brushed a hand over his cheek. To think an almost-Paladin, who had dared face two imperial guards unarmed, would be scared of thin little needles. "It's okay, Prince Hardeep. They don't hurt. Your fever will break with just a few needles."

Behind her, the guards muttered. They were finding their feet.

"I will be all right." Prince Hardeep pushed himself off her lap and scuttled back. "I just need some

390

rest. You, too. It has been a long day of hard practice. Rest and don't practice again tonight. I will find a way to meet you tomorrow."

Secretary Hong looked at them. The wrinkles around his eyes and jowls stood out in lines of black against his wan complexion. He turned, shuffled back toward the entrance, and beckoned someone in.

A palace official, a Foreign Ministry secretary from the markings on his robes, entered and bowed low. "Lord Peng petitioned the *Tianzi*. He has graciously allowed the Blind Musician to stay in these guest quarters."

Outside the doors, other officials were taking down Madura's banners. Such an honor! Guest quarters were usually reserved for visiting dignitaries from Cathay's largest trading partners, and certainly not for a musician with no name. If Hardeep were on the palace grounds, there might be some way to meet again tonight. Even if this pavilion was a good walk from the inner castle and imperial residence.

Gaining his feet, Hardeep pressed his palms together. "I thank you for your hospitality, but my effects are in Lord Peng's villa. I will retire there for the night."

The secretary clucked his tongue. "To refuse The *Tianzi's* hospitality would be in very poor form. We have a fine meal prepared for you, as well as several Night Blossoms from the Floating World."

Kaiya's stomach twisted into a tight knot. Renowned for their beauty and grace, the Night

391

Blossoms would make Hardeep forget all about her. Not to mention they would freely offer what she could not.

Or could she?

CHAPTER 35
Women's Secrets

Approaching the Phoenix Garden with the two imperial guards and Secretary Hong, Kaiya listened to the stream rustling toward the courtyard's central pond. Still, all she could hear were her inner insecurities. The beautiful and elegant Night Blossoms would make her Hardeep forget all about her flat body and plain face. Maybe he was already wrapped in their arms, preparing to personally hand her to Lord Tong.

She blinked away the tears blurring her vision. Another beauty came into focus, rubbing salt into her self-confidence's open wound. Wearing an elegant floral gown, Crown Princess Xiulan sat in an open pagoda overlooking the pond. Several handmaidens, including Meiling, stood at a respectful distance. Two of her imperial guards at the edge of the garden melded with the background. The scent of roasted pork and garlic-steamed vegetables wafted on a breeze.

Gently illuminated by a shuttered light bauble in the pagoda ceiling, Xiulan stood with a smile. "You're late," she called.

Because of Hardeep's lessons. If only there had been more time. While Secretary Hong and the two guards came to a stop at the garden's edge, Kaiya lowered her head as she walked up the path to the pagoda. "Forgive me, Eldest Sister."

"Your handmaiden informed me of your…visit. Come, sit." With a graceful wave of her hand, Xiulan indicated a porcelain garden seat by a stone table built into the center of the pagoda.

How much had Meiling said? How many ears had heard? How many people knew that a just-betrothed princess had allowed a foreign man so close? Almost close enough to touch. The memory of his lips within a hairbreadth from her neck sent her heart fluttering.

Kaiya shook the image out of her head and looked at the meal. Artfully arranged food graced porcelain dishes. Her stomach rumbled in the most unladylike fashion. Playing music much of the day, and then the audience with Father in front of all the lords, had left her hungry and drained. With no semblance of grace, she plopped down.

In contrast, nonchalantly graceful as a weeping willow, Xiulan settled on her own seat. She lifted a teakettle and filled Kaiya's cup. When she set the kettle down, Kaiya picked it up and poured tea into Xiulan's cup. Some of it splashed.

How embarrassing! Kaiya bowed her head in apology.

"It's okay." Xiulan placed a hand on hers. "You have had a long day."

And the last hour had felt like a full day of sweet torture. Kaiya's face flushed at the thought of Hardeep. Thank the Heavens her head was down to hide it.

"You are thinking about him, aren't you?" Xiulan's voice carried concern, but no accusation. How did she know?

Kaiya let out a long sigh. "I have never met any man like him. Beyond his handsomeness, his voice is so sweet. He might be a foreigner, but his eyes hypnotize me." Making her feel beautiful. She looked up.

Xiulan gawked, all her usual poise scattered to the four winds. It was if they were holding two different conversations. Oh, Heavens, Xiulan must not have been referring to Hardeep.

Covering her mouth, Kaiya turned to the handmaidens and guards. If they had heard... Well, Xiulan already had, Meiling already knew, and Kaiya's confession had left no ambiguity.

"Oh, Heavens," Xiulan said with a stuttered whisper. She placed a hand on her chest. "You are enamored with the foreigner."

Enamored? It sounded so shallow. It had to be love. Yes, she admitted it. If Kaiya could lower her head any more, her face would be in the food. And her appetite had just fled with her last vestige of dignity.

Xiulan squeezed her hand. "I was mistaken." Surprisingly, there was no rebuke in her tone.

Kaiya hazarded a glance up.

Xiulan smiled. "Let me tell you a secret. Before I was betrothed to your brother, my father's most trusted

Yu-Ming wanted me to marry his first son. He was a handsome young man, and our parents had arranged a chance meeting so no one would lose face if things didn't work out." She took a deep breath and let it out. "They did."

Kaiya's pulse quickened. Kai-Guo and Xiulan made such a beautiful couple, even more so considering the imperial nature of their marriage. If any relationship provided even a semblance of hope, it was theirs. To think there had been someone before. Kaiya edged forward on her seat. "What happened?"

Xiulan sighed. "The *Tianzi* asked to strengthen the ties between our families. How could my father refuse?"

"And the *Yu-Ming* heir?" Kaiya tried to keep her voice low through her excitement.

"My father forbade him from contacting me." Xiulan leaned in with a conspiratorial smile. "But we maintained correspondence through one of my handmaidens and his page. It was a passionate exchange."

Was that a suggestion to defy the *Tianzi's* orders and maintain an illicit communication with Prince Hardeep? Kaiya cocked her head. "And now?"

Xiulan laughed. "As soon as Kai-Guo and I were married, the lord's son broke contact. Not for fear of punishment, but because of his integrity. He would have ended things whether my husband was Crown Prince or a beggar."

"Why are you telling me this?" The mixed signals made frustrating knot puzzles look simple in comparison.

"No reason, except to share a secret with my little sister." Xiulan covered her giggle. "The decision is yours. Though realistically, as an imperial princess, you would not be allowed to marry a foreigner, even if you weren't already betrothed."

Kaiya let a sigh escape. Of course that was the case, no matter how much she might want to believe otherwise. She and Hardeep would never be together.

"Kaiya, I used to think about that young lord in the first months of my marriage. However, I soon grew to adore your brother."

After meeting someone as charming as Hardeep, Kaiya didn't think she could ever love another. She peered into her teacup. "What do you know of Lord Tong?"

Breath hitching, Xiulan shifted in her seat. Kaiya looked up. Dear Sister-In-Law's lips pursed. Her expression darkened.

"Tell me." Kaiya's voice cracked. Rebel or not, he might still be a kind man.

"His late wife was a friend of my mother. She was spirited in her youth, but marriage broke her."

"Marriage is a woman's grave." Kaiya's sweaty hands tightened into fists.

Xiulan shook her head. "It doesn't have to be. No, Lord Tong is well-known for his depravity. Several of the houses in the Floating World have banned him for fear of what he might do to their Night Blossoms."

Kaiya's chest tightened. What had she gotten herself into? She summoned the memory of Hardeep, so close, nearly pressed against her back as he taught her the lute.

Run away. There was still time to run away.

"Which brings me to the reason the *Tianzi* asked me to meet privately with you tonight." Xiulan reached back to the seats built into the pagoda's sides and retrieved a silk-wrapped package. "Doctor Wu said Heaven's Dew will arrive soon. I think that might explain your sudden interest in foreign princes."

Yes, better to think of Hardeep. Kaiya eyed the vermillion silk bundle as Xiulan placed it on the table with two hands. No doubt a pillow book. With a shy tilt of her head, Xiulan gestured toward it with an appropriately delicate wave of her hand, inviting Kaiya to pick it up.

Feigning the disinterest she would have had just a few days before, Kaiya bowed her head and lifted it with the formality of a minister accepting an imperial decree. Hidden beneath her silk gown, her heart pounded. She unwound the red cord bindings, then the silk wrapping. The light green cover was innocuous enough, save for the title *Cloud Rain*, emblazoned in gold characters.

"It's fairly new," Xiulan said. "By imperial palace woodblock artist Gao Liang. It was presented to your mother thirty years ago, when she married the *Tianzi*. Open it."

Cheeks hot, Kaiya spread it somewhere in the middle. She sucked in a sharp breath. The imperial archives might boast the largest collection of books in the world, but no doubt, this particular book wasn't kept there.

Glimmering in vibrant colors, a man and woman were locked in an embrace with lifelike radiance. Not only that, their mutual affection spilled off the page. Just looking at it brought labored breaths. Heat surged inside of her.

It seemed remotely similar to the emotions Hardeep stirred in her. If it were the two of them, acting out the image in the book...his weight on top of her... Biting her lip, Kaiya tried not to squirm.

Pulling her gaze away from the page, Xiulan wiped her brow. "Palace artist Gao Liang could infuse his art with emotion-evoking magic. When I say how I grew close to the Crown Prince so quickly, I would credit this book for part of it."

How dangerous was that? Both dangerous and helpful, depending on the circumstance of a marriage. Thoughts of Hardeep's closeness earlier in the day mingled with the book's magical impact on her. Him, behind her, chest nearly pressed to her back. Kaiya shut the book and fanned herself with it. "Thank you for your gift."

Xiulan bowed her head. "Perhaps this will make your marriage to Lord Tong more palatable."

Him again. Faceless up to now, her inevitable destiny loomed in the recesses of her mind like the mythical Black Fists stalking their prey.

Kaiya set the book down as if it were a hot plate. If it couldn't be with Hardeep, perhaps it would be better to take the tonsure and live life out as a nun. Though it was unlikely anyone would let her do it, since her value as a princess was determined by whom she could marry.

Unless she could revive a long-dead art. Something she had already started, with Hardeep's help. On the table, the pillow book's gold lettering beckoned her. Heat and desire cascaded through her. Tonight, she'd confess her feelings to Hardeep. Maybe even steal one true kiss just once before marrying Lord Tong, and no one would have to know. She just had to get to him before the Night Blossoms did.

CHAPTER 36
Spies Like Us

As Jie slipped into the solarium of Sun-Moon Castle's residential wing, Master Yan turned his head a fraction. Somehow, even at his old age, he still sensed her arrival when no other clan member could. With a subtle hand signal, he ordered her to stay in the shadows, out of sight of the nine *Tai-Ming* lords, the Chief Minister, and War Minister Shan.

Oblivious to the existence of the Black Lotus, they all knelt on silken cushions on the stone floor. They faced the two princes and the *Tianzi*, who sat in a cushioned bloodwood chair with his back to the night sky.

"When Lord Tong arrives," the *Tianzi* was saying, "take him into custody. It doesn't matter how many guards he has."

"*Huang-Shang*." Lord Peng rose to a knee. "So offering Princess Kaiya as a bride was just a ruse?"

Crown Prince Kai-Guo nodded. "Yes. She is our bait, to lure him into the capital."

The poor girl. Jie sucked on her lower lip. Perhaps it was far better to be an orphaned half-elf than a princess.

Lord Liang of Yutou rose to a knee. "*Huang-Shang*. Your messenger bore an imperial plaque. To renege on your offer is tantamount to forsaking the Mandate of Heaven. Another Hellstorm…"

"Lord Liang," the *Tianzi* said. "Our messenger bears a piece of jade artwork and the missive was written with a magic that will distract Lord Tong from questioning its authenticity. I will not allow my daughter to marry a traitor, and I would sooner take his head than elevate him to *Tai-Ming*."

Jie suppressed a snort. Why bother to ever use a real plaque if it risked the wrath of Heaven?

Boots clopped in the hallway and heads craned to the solarium entrance. A messenger ran in and dropped to a knee, first to the ground. Head bowed, he proffered an envelope. "*Huang-Shang*, a message from Lord Tong."

The rebel certainly hadn't wasted any time in responding; the horse relays would've taken four hours to reach Wailian and return.

General Shan strode forward and swept the message away. He marched back to the *Tianzi,* where the Crown Prince received it. He unwrapped the cover and snapped it open. A messy script, reminiscent of Tian's careless hand.

The Crown Prince's eyes darted back and forth, his face darkening before finding the *Tianzi.* "*Huang-Shang*, Lord Tong agrees to the marriage, but insists that the matchmaking meeting occur in Wailian Castle. The wedding will take place before Prince Kai-Wu's so that Lord Tong may attend as brother-in-law."

The room rose in uproar. Jie slipped through the shadows to the side to better gauge the lords' body language.

"Impertinent!" Lord Han of Fenggu slammed a hand on the floor.

"The audacity!" shouted Lord Wu, whose daughter's marriage to the second prince might be affected.

Lord Liu's forehead furrowed, his look one of confusion. A slight smile formed on Lord Liang's face.

402

Lord Zhao of Ximen, father of the Crown Princess, tightened his fists.

"It comes as no surprise," said Lord Peng. "We are dealing with a traitor, after all; an ambitious man with no honor."

Perhaps even more ambitious than they all suspected. Jie closed her eyes and thought of the voice in the Maduran guesthouse. If Lord Tong, in league with the altivorcs, Madurans, and other untold allies, attacked the imperial wedding, his marriage to Princess Kaiya would give him substantial standing in the aftermath.

The *Tianzi* swept his gaze over the men, silencing them. "I will hear your counsel."

Lord Liang rose to a knee. "*Huang-Shang*, unless we want a costly civil war where we could potentially run out of firepowder, we must acquiesce to Lord Tong's dem—requests."

Jie studied his expression. So much of Wailian's firepowder ended up in Lord Liang's province. Perhaps he, too, was in league with Lord Tong, a mole in the *Tianzi's* inner circle.

Lord Peng Kai-Long rose to a knee again. "*Huang-Shang*, I think Lord Liang is correct. However, maybe we can bend this to our advantage. Send Princess Kaiya to Wailian County with an appropriate honor guard of a thousand men. As her cousin, and now *Tai-Ming* myself, I will lead. Once inside Wailian Castle, the honor guard will weaken its defenses from the inside while General Lu leads the imperial armies in the North to assault it from the outside."

The room fell silent as the lords nodded. Jie shook her head. Leave it to military men to suggest cutting off an arm to remove a wart when a surgeon's knife would do. Only warlords could fathom this harebrained plan actually working.

Master Yan shared her opinion. "*Huang-Shang*, what if Lord Tong does not allow so many in the entourage to approach the castle?"

General Shan's white mustaches quivered. "All we need to do is capture the gatehouse and hold it open long enough for reinforcements."

"General Shan," the *Tianzi* said, "were the plans for Wailian Castle submitted to the War Ministry?"

The general's jaw set at a hard angle. "No, but we can rely on General Lu."

Jie sucked on her lower lip. Maybe it was not a coincidence that the princess had met General Lu for a matchmaking meeting.

"We will keep the pretense by adhering to Lord Tong's demanded schedule." The *Tianzi* sighed. Actually sighed. "General Shan, how long will it take to reach Wailian Castle?"

"By forced march, nine hours to the Great Wall, another two to reach Wailian Castle."

"Then Princess Kaiya's procession must depart tonight. Mobilize a thousand of your best soldiers and send word to General Lu. Chief Minister, provide logistical support so we can depart in two hours. Deputy Yan, have your people ride ahead and learn of Wailian's defenses."

404

Jie rubbed her poor butt. It looked like another horse ride lay ahead.

Master Yan bowed his head. "Might I suggest instead you send an imperial phoenix rider? It will arrive sooner and get a better view."

"So it shall be done." The *Tianzi* peered around the room. "The rest of you withdraw and mobilize your vassals, in case Lord Peng's idea does not work."

The men pressed their heads to the floor. When the *Tianzi* released them from their bows, they rose and filed out of the room. Jie waited and watched. Once they left, the *Tianzi* would need to hear of the exchange in the Maduran guesthouse.

The Tianzi raised a hand. "Lord Peng, Deputy Yan, wait."

Both men knelt. The room cleared, save for them and the two princes.

Shoulders slumping, the *Tianzi* seemed to age. "I cannot have Kaiya marry Lord Tong. His late wife was always happy in her youth, but looked terrified after just a month of marriage. We know how he treats women. If the plan should fail, and there is no means of escape..." His voice choked. "She will have led a happy life."

Lord Peng bowed his head. "I shall take care of it myself. Quickly, mercifully."

"There is another way." To avoid revealing her identity Peng Kai-Long, Jie reached into a pouch and touched the magic bauble. Appearing as Princess Kaiya's idealized image, she stepped out of the shadow and bowed.

405

The *Tianzi's* eyes widened, while the princes gawked. Lord Peng covered a gasp.

Master Yan offered her a rare smile. "With this disguise, *my* daughter will be able to get close enough to the traitor to kill him. The princess needn't even go to Wailian."

"But the…" Lord Peng coughed. "She looks similar, but not exactly alike. And Lord Tong will have her checked for weapons."

Jie grinned. Not like she needed a weapon to kill a man. "That is not our biggest problem. I overheard our altivorc guests say Lord Tong is coordinating some attack with the Teleri Empire and Madura. At first, I suspected it was an invasion of Cathay, but I wonder now if they plan to attack Prince Kai-Wu's wedding. They have smuggled a Golden Scorpion master in. I overheard him, but could not get a good look at his face."

"I will assign assets to every Ayuri in the palace," Master Yan said. "What about…"

The *Tianzi* turned to Lord Peng. "The Ankiran prince. Hardeep. Do you trust him?"

Face blanking, Lord Peng's head rose and fell in slow bobs. "Yes, *Huang-Shang*. I've known him a long time, and trust him implicitly."

"Any other collaborators?" Master Yan asked.

"When I meet Lord Tong," Jie said, "I will find out how many traitors conspire with him."

Face blanking, Lord Peng's head bobbed in slow nods.

The *Tianzi* tilted his head a fraction. "Master Yan, your people are resourceful."

"Daughter," Master Yan said, "go trail the princess and learn her voice so you can imitate it with the *Mockingbird's Deception*."

Crown Prince Kai-Guo raised a halting hand. "This must all be kept secret from the princess. She must not know the procession leaving tonight is meant for her. She might think to interfere."

With the two crossbows used to assassinate Lord Peng and his son in a rice bale, Tian paused at an alley. With the authorities considering the case solved, it had been easy to retrieve the murder weapons.

It was only slightly less easy setting a trap for the young man tailing him now.

Especially since the large boy might know Black Lotus hand signs and silent codes.

Still, using night's darkness to cover his signals, Tian had walked past Chong, Bu, Li, Wen, and Little Huang in his circuitous route from the harbor to the safe house. From their bird calls, they were ready to act. All he had to do was walk into the alley and have his tail follow him in.

He turned in and walked toward the end. Sure enough, the boy followed, talon dagger in hand, creeping in with his back pressed to the walls.

Dropping the bale, Tian spun around and drew his knife. At the other end of the alley, the dark shapes of Chong and Bu dropped to the ground from above.

The boy's head whipped from Tian to the men behind him and back again. He raised his weapon, whether to throw it or slash his own throat it wasn't possible to tell.

A rope dart shot out from the rooftop and encircled the kid's knife hand. With a yank, his arm jerked upward. Tian followed the line with his eyes. Up on the steeply pitched roof, Wen twisted the rope around her elbow and then her waist for leverage.

The target had other ideas. Probably twice her size, he pulled back. Her feet started to slide on the tiles. Tian raced forward. Chong stomped through the boy's knee while Bu wrapped him into a chokehold. With just one free hand, no leverage, he clawed at Bu's arm. Then his eyes rolled up into his head and he crumpled to the ground.

A shadow darted through the street, at the near end of the alley. Tian blinked. It hadn't been as large as this boy or the one the Serikothi had killed earlier in the day, but whoever it was had seen the trap.

Tian pointed. "Elder Brother Chong and Elder Sister Wen, give chase. Elder Brother Bu, Little Huang, bring him back to the safe house. I'll go ahead."

408

Hefting the rice bale, Tian hurried back, constantly checking to ensure he hadn't been followed. Inside his room of strings, he dumped the two crossbows onto a table next to the Eldaeri crossbow Jie had stolen and a standard Cathayi repeater. Side by side, the Cathayi model was clearly smaller than the other three, which all appeared exactly the same.

He popped open the magazines of the murder weapons. The one used to kill the *Tai-Ming* lord still held two bolts, while the one used to murder his son had one. Their heads were too large to fit the Cathayi repeater, while the shafts were as short as the Eldaeri ones. Either the Serikothi or Tarkothi must have provided the weapons.

Except... the Eldaeri used sablewood, whereas the bolts used in the assassination were made of ironwood, a tree that didn't grow in Eldaeri nations thanks to their forestry programs. And the bolt heads, the same width, were cast instead of wrought—a Cathayi technique that allowed for mass production. And the firing pins were exactly the same length, width, and weight of the two they'd found in Fat Nose Jiang's collar. These crossbows posed more questions than they answered.

And Fat Nose Jiang likely had those answers.

Back in the safehouse's main room, Chong and Huang discussed their prisoner. They'd have to wait for Little Wen to return. Her male-targeted contact toxins, combined with feminine wiles honed during her time in the Floating World, should have no problem drawing information out of a strapping young man. That left some time to see if the crossbows themselves were as different as the bolts they fired.

With deft hands, Tian first disassembled the Serikothi crossbow. The articulating wood joints used wax to help with the cocking motion—an old technology, from when the Eldaeri first conquered the eastern coast nearly three centuries before, and which they apparently still used today.

In a side room, it sounded as if Little Wen had returned and had already started working her magic. Let her use her special skillset; Tian would use his. He took apart one of the murder weapons to look for any internal differences.

He sucked in a breath. Though it might look like an Eldaeri repeater on the outside, its internal mechanisms were Cathayi improvements. Oiled steel ball bearings for a smoother motion. Cogged gears to minimize the jerking of the cocking lever. An exact channel for the bolt. That, combined with the longer barrel, would improve its accuracy. Just as the Cathayi had reverse-engineered the Eldaeri repeater and designed a superior weapon, Fat Nose Jiang had taken the guts of Cathayi innovations and made an even better weapon.

Turning away from this new piece of the puzzle, Tian went to the main room, where Chong and Huang combed through the boy's effects—all Black Fist tools. From the side room, the boy's deep panting suggested a large lung capacity.

Tian lifted his chin to the kid's items. "Find anything interesting?"

"If I didn't know any better, I would swear he was Black Lotus."

So would Tian. Sliding the door into the interrogation room open a crack, he peeked in. The scent of *yinghua* flowers percolated out. Bare back to him, Little Wen tilted her head a fraction, enough so that she could probably see him in the corner of her eye, and then returned her attention to the sweating boy she straddled. With a stupid grin, he sat bound to a chair, naked save for undergarments, which strained against his excitement.

Clad in only lacy underpants herself, Wen rubbed against him while pressing her ample bosom into his face. She pulled back, just out of the reach of his craning neck. Her voice came out pouty, breathy. "Why did Lord Tong want Lord Peng dead?"

"I swear I don't know. He just gave the order."

"You're sure?" Her sultry tone stirred Tian's pulse.

The boy nodded like the seals that wintered in Jiangkou. "I swear."

"I will be back." Covering herself with crossed arms, she lifted herself off him and turned around.

Tian averted his eyes more out of politeness than because any of the Black Lotus cared. Indeed, Little Wen had been the first woman he'd ever seen naked, three thousand, one hundred and thirty-nine days ago, during his first weeks in the clan.

411

Finding a cloak hanging next to the door, he draped it over her shoulders before making way for her into the main room. "What did you find out?"

"He claims they belong to a Black Fist clan known as the Water Snake, trained by a Black Lotus defector."

A new clan didn't seem possible. Tian searched her eyes. Black Fist interrogation methods could be painful or pleasurable, but none were completely reliable. "All Black Lotus members, past and present, are accounted for."

She shrugged. "They work for Lord Tong. He ordered the assassination of Lord Peng and his son. There were three in Jiangkou for the operation, and they know about *us*."

Now one was dead, this one captured. A third remained at large. "How much do they know?"

"This one saw you retrieving the crossbows, and was tracking you, hoping to find this safe house."

"And their own base of operations?"

"Wailian Castle."

Tian tapped his chin. "Try to find out how many there are and if they had anything to do with the attacks in the capital last night. Chong, Little Huang, go find Fat Nose Jiang."

Bu slipped in, panting. "Word from Master Yan, on the last horse of the night. Jie is disguised as Princess Kaiya and heading to Wailian Castle tonight."

"What?" Tian's heat jolted. It might keep Princess Kaiya out of danger; but if Water Snake Black

412

Fist cell defended Wailian Castle, it would be hard for Jie to infiltrate and even more difficult to attack. But how could he get word to the capital without use of the horse relays?

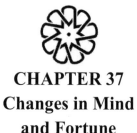

CHAPTER 37
Changes in Mind
and Fortune

From where she stood just outside the double doors to the Hall of Pure Melody, Kaiya listened to the arrhythmic clops of boots across the central courtyard. There marched a contingent of imperial guards, casting long shadows from the Blue and White moons.

Every nerve tingling with desire for Hardeep, she couldn't return to the imperial residence. Not tonight, or at least not now. Once behind those walls, there would be no getting out until morning, and he'd forget all about her.

Her stomach twisted into a knot again, as her better sense warred with the primal urges brought on by the pillow book's magic. She'd strong-armed Secretary Hong into allowing her to come here, ostensibly to retrieve a book from the music library. From his wringing hands, no doubt he thought her insane given the trouble caused by visiting the day before. The poor old man seemed tired all the time, but ever since she played the lute for Hardeep, he looked as if he might keel over and die.

The two guards, as well, lacked their usual composure. Shoulders slumped and heads hanging, they resembled the crude illustrations of the Yu Dynasty laborers who built the Great Wall six hundred years before. She closed her eyes and listened. Yes, their hearts were beating slowly and sluggishly. If they were all so tired, perhaps it wouldn't take much more to put them into a sleep. There had been a song like that in the music book...

Light, slippered feet pattered up the Hall of Pure Melody's marble steps. Kaiya opened her eyes to find Han Meiling, cloak in hand. Bowing, she presented it.

"Come." Legs trembling, Kaiya stepped over the ghost-tripping threshold and into the main corridor.

Secretary Hong and her two guards followed. She shuffled toward the performance hall's open double doors. If she entered without permission, it would be the second time breaking the same rule in as many days.

Was this worth the risk? Father had only suspended her death sentence as long as she remained obedient.

No, she was protected. They needed her to marry Lord Tong. Kaiya hummed the musical notes, considering. The Night Blossoms were the epitome of Cathayi beauty and grace, the exact opposite of her. Prince Hardeep wouldn't be able to resist their charms.

Then again, that's what men did. The Floating World wouldn't exist without men's urges. No, she couldn't let it happen, at least not before she confessed her feelings. With a deep breath, she entered and swept across the performance hall's floor.

Near the center, Kaiya stopped and listened for the heartbeats of her small entourage. In this acoustically perfect chamber, they all pulsed loudly in her ears, the rhythm slow and tired.

Drawing in a quick breath, Kaiya gripped her toes to the floor and straightened her posture. She hummed the tune more loudly. Like a lullaby, it dipped and rose in gentle waves, slowing with each refrain. The men wavered in their spots.

Her own stamina guttered. Maybe it wouldn't hold out. Maybe she would pass out before they did. She forged ahead with her hum, despite her wobbling legs and heavy head. Just a little more. Like a flame burning the last of its wax, she gasped out one last stanza.

Secretary Hong, the imperial guards, and Meiling all slumped to the ground. Kaiya, too.

She propped herself up on her elbows to find their eyes closed, breaths shallow.

Asleep? Summoning her last drop of energy, she picked herself off the ground and trudged over. Her feet might be disproportionally large, but now, they also seemed to be encased in Estomari concrete.

She started to bend over to confirm they were asleep, but thought the better of it. She might very well fall over and not stand again until morning. If this were the cost of magic, it didn't seem possible for the legendary Yanyan to sing Avarax to sleep.

Several more paces and she reached the door. She rested against the doorframe, letting her flagging strength grow little by little. She took a few minutes to consider this foolishness. In the courtyard, she'd stick out like a cloud on a sunny day.

But past the courtyard, it was all alleys between the buildings, and the guest pavilions weren't that far away. Her heart pumped faster, replacing her fatigue with nervous energy. A few more deep breaths, and she was ready to try. For Hardeep.

Vitality returning by the moment, Kaiya tiptoed down the corridor to the hall's entrance. She paused at the threshold and peeked out. A few officials walked through the courtyard, but there were no imperial guards.

Donning the cloak Meiling had brought, Kaiya pulled the hood over her head and peeked out of the hall again. The officials from before had walked even farther away, and still, no imperial guards appeared to be around. She started to step out.

Across the plaza, a large, dark shape flashed near the entrance of the Imperial Archives.

Freezing, Kaiya peered in that direction.

Nothing.

Just her imagination. Unless there really were such a thing as Black Fists. She hurried down the steps, nearly tripping on her gown along the way.

Running would certainly draw the attention of any eyes she had missed in her initial scan, so Kaiya walked at a moderate pace. South and east towards the closest alley off the courtyard. When she turned the corner, she let out a sigh of relief. It didn't seem as if anyone had seen her, or at least noted it was her.

She would be reunited with Prince Hardeep soon. The fatigue from before seemed to melt away, replaced by a renewed vigor and excitement.

And need. She shuffled quickly through the alleys, pausing to look around each corner for any stray official or guard.

After several minutes, she came within two turns of Nine Courtyard. Soon, very soon! Hugging the pillow book to her chest, Kaiya took a step into an alley. She caught an imperial guard in her peripheral vision and quickly ducked back the way she'd come.

How stupid of her! In her excitement, she'd forgotten to check, even forgotten to use her ears. The guard would surely challenge a cloaked and hooded stranger, carrying a mysterious bundle to the chest.

Holding her breath, she pressed back against the wall and listened. The booted footsteps…

…headed in the opposite direction.

Not daring to let out a breath, Kaiya loosened her sweaty fists. In the future, if she were to make a habit of sneaking around, it would be worthwhile to learn the patrol patterns.

When the footsteps turned a corner, she edged forward…and paused again. Another sound lurked in the symphony of the night, somewhere behind her. She spun around to find its source.

Nothing. She surveyed the space for a few more seconds. She was becoming paranoid. Shaking the doubts out of her head, Kaiya continued into the alley, stopping again at the edge of the courtyard and looking at the pavilion where she'd left Prince Hardeep.

No! Girls giggled from within, mingling with a deep male laugh. Kaiya's shoulders slumped. Perhaps he'd already started drinking, already started acting out pictures from the pillow book with the Night Blossoms.

Hollow in her belly, she crept from tree to tree, deeper into the garden, and then tiptoed up to the veranda that connected all the pavilions. Curiously, no guards stood watch outside. Perhaps they were posted inside.

At Hardeep's pavilion, she pressed her ear up against the closest window's latticework.

"Yes, lower," Prince Hardeep said, to the giggles of at least two Night Blossoms.

One of the ladies let out a primal moan. Voice panting, she said, "Your Excellency is so well-endowed."

If Kaiya's stomach could twist any more, it could be used as a New Year's knot decoration. She meant nothing to him beyond her ability to save his own homeland. She held a hand over her mouth.

"I didn't know the foreigner could speak Cathayi," a high-pitched girl's voice said from behind.

Kaiya's heart leapt into her throat. She whipped around.

There was no one there. The courtyard was empty.

"Show yourself," she commanded.

419

"Is that even the prince's voice?" The voice changed, now sounding suspiciously similar to her own, and came from...the stone dragon overlooking the pond?

A ghost, perhaps? A chill crawled up Kaiya's spine. But no, it couldn't be. Sun-Moon Palace's layout confused ghosts, herding them out through the alleys' twists and turns.

"Who are you?" she hissed. Closing her eyes, she listened for a telltale breath.

There, in the eaves. Hidden in the trickling of the palace stream and the Night Blossoms making the clouds and rain with Hardeep, breathed a slow, light breath. Kaiya looked up, just in time to see a shadow flutter away. The breath disappeared.

Black Fist? Kaiya shook the silly idea out of her head. Regardless who the mysterious girl was, she was right: that wasn't Prince Hardeep's voice in the pavilion, and up to now, all his words had been spoken in the Cathayi language. Steeling herself against what she would inevitably see, she burst through the doors.

There, a Night Blossom mounted the Minister of Appointments himself. Her gown hung loosely at her elbows. Another almost-naked Night Blossom lay on her side, head propped on an elbow, a hand hidden somewhere beneath the first's gowns.

Kaiya cast her eyes at the floor. "Where is Prince...the Blind Musician?"

"*Dian-xia!*" The minister pushed the woman off. Covering himself, he rose and bowed.

Wide-eyed, the Night Blossoms exchanged glances. *The princess?* one mouthed. The other nodded, and they both gathered their gowns up around themselves. Kneeling, they pressed their foreheads to the ground.

Utter silence. Kaiya opened and closed her mouth. Had she gone deaf? Her cheeks burned hot. Minister Hu barely covered himself with a woman's silk gown, exposing his rotund belly. Not like Kaiya had a clear view, since she kept her gaze averted. The smell...

"Where is Prin—the Blind Musician?" she said, this time louder and with all the righteous indignation she could muster. Never mind all the rules she was breaking.

"*Dian-xia.*" Minister Hu's voice, usually harsh, wobbled with what could only be worry. "The musician...the musician wanted to see the moonlight over the gardens."

Kaiya stared at his forehead. "Where are the guards? There were explicit orders that the Blind Musician stay here."

"Yes, well..." the minister licked his lips as sweat gathered on his brow. Then, his eyebrows clashed together. "You are supposed to be dining with the Crown Princess. Why are you here?"

Both of them were in compromising positions, and now it was a battle of wills. One Kaiya refused to lose. She turned to the Night Blossoms. "Where is the Blind Musician?"

One looked up at the minister, then back. Her lips trembled. "*Dian-xia*, the musician bribed the minister."

Lips trembling, Minister Hu plopped to his knees and slammed his forehead to the Ayuri wool rug. "Forgive me, *Dian-xia*. Please, please, do not tell the *Tianzi*."

Kaiya's jaw clenched. The ever-uptight Minister Hu, literally caught with his pants down, partaking of prostitutes meant for someone else *and* taking a bribe. "When will the Blind Musician return?"

"He said by dawn," the second Night Blossom said.

Kaiya twirled a lock of her hair, so unruly compared to the Night Blossoms' perfection. Where would Prince Hardeep have gone? Someplace with something more important than the realm's best food and a pair of beautiful women.

To think she'd almost shirked all sense of duty and would've tried to kiss him had he been here. "What are your names? What house do you come from?"

"Jasmine and Peony from the Jade Teahouse," one said.

"Be sure to tell your proprietress what happened tonight." Kaiya locked her glare on Minister Hu, whose head dropped again. "We will never speak of this again. And if I hear of any misfortune coming to the Jade Teahouse or its Night Blossoms, I will ensure that you are held responsible. Do you understand?"

"Yes, *Dian-xia*!" He knocked his head against the floor three more times.

"Now get back to what the *Tianzi* pays you for." Kaiya spun on her heel and left. She might have earned a life-long enemy in Minister Hu, but as long as she ensured Jasmine and Peony shared their story among their sisters, it would be leverage to use against him. She would send a handmaiden to the Jade Teahouse in the Floating World tomorrow to confirm everyone's wellbeing.

In the meantime, Prince Hardeep was gone, along with her impulse to escape marriage to Lord Tong. Her hand strayed to Tian's pebble.

What had she been thinking? The nation's stability depended on her sacrifice. She squeezed the pillow book, angry at herself for succumbing to its magic.

That's all this feeling was. Artistic magic printed in the lines and colors of illustrations. Not the true love described in old ballads.

Now, she had to protect the guards and secretary from punishment. With extra spring in her step, she hurried back through the alleys with much less care than on her way.

Until the same sound as before whispered on the night's breeze.

Footsteps? Breathing? It was almost a mingling of the two. The interloper who'd spoken, perhaps. She tracked it to its source, but saw nothing. Shrugging off her suspicions, she continued to the central plaza.

Dozens of soldiers, all armed for battle, marched toward the palace entrance in exacting ranks. It was strange, for this late hour, but thankfully nobody looked in her direction. The steps to the Hall of Supreme Harmony and imperial archives stood empty. There was no activity at the Hall of Pure Melody, at least not on the outside. Had her sleeping retinue been discovered, surely there would be quite the commotion there.

What a mistake. Father had said never to use magic as a crutch. She frowned at the pillow book, which she'd planned to give Prince Hardeep in hopes that it would spark his affection for her.

That wasn't true love. No, if someone were to love her, it shouldn't be because of some magic cut into the lines of a woodblock print. And how selfish it would've been to steal a kiss, then leave Hardeep pining for her. Guilt wrenched her insides.

She ran as quietly as she could. Up the steps. Through the double doors. On the other side, she blew out a breath and listened. In the central chamber, at least one of the three men snored. Other than that, no other human sounds carried through the halls. For now, at least, her most recent ill-advised escapade had gone unnoticed.

Kaiya returned to the central chamber, where Secretary Hong, Meiling, and the two imperial guards slept. She walked across the floor and bent down over one of the guards. "Wake up."

He stretched his arms out and yawned, but then rolled over back into sleep. At his side, the other snored.

Reaching out to both of them, she shook their shoulders. The second just grunted.

Sighing, she thought back to the book of musical magic. Had it told how to reverse a magically induced sleep? Kaiya mentally listed what she remembered: Inducing sleep. Evoking rage. Arousing lust. Stirring fear. But nothing on how to rouse someone from sleep.

Walking back to the guards, she pondered the problem. In order to put them to sleep in the first place, they had to already be tired. Her, too. The song, like a child's lullaby, had gone from a moderate pace to quieter and slow.

At least now her energy had returned. Meanwhile, these four had already benefited from half an hour of sleep. Maybe reversing the song would work, by starting slow and soft and increasing the tempo. Like her masters' duet, where each part interacted with the other. It was worth a try.

First, she shook them some more, in hopes that it would bring them to the edge of consciousness. She squatted low, feet flat and toes gripping the floor. The men's breaths, though light, rose and fell in near synchronicity.

She hummed, setting the beat to one's inhalations. Slow at first; then she increased the tempo.

The first guard responded, his chest rising in faster clips. The second and Meiling soon joined him. Secretary Hong, however, remained the same, like a bass beat; stubborn, fighting against her own song. She hummed louder, switching her focus to Hong's heart.

He squirmed a little, but still showed no other sign of waking. It wasn't working. Perhaps…she considered the storage room. A musical instrument should help magnify the effect. She started to the door.

Out in the corridor, boots clopped. Someone must have heard her song. This would not end well for her trusted servants.

She dashed out of the performance hall and slid the door shut behind her. Turning, she searched for the source of the footsteps.

Cousin Kai-Long—Lord Peng. He held a light bauble lamp in one hand, while a helmet was tucked under the other arm. Instead of court robes, he wore lamellar armor. "*Dian-xia*, I thought I would find you here. Or at Prince Hardeep's pavilion."

Her cheeks flushed hot. She fixated on the floor. How predictable she'd become. If he knew that she'd planned to kiss Hardeep…

"Come with me." He placed his hands on the sides of her shoulders and looked her up and down, very much like a tailor measuring her for a new dress. He pulled the hood of her cloak over her head.

She shook her head. The guards, Secretary Hong, and Meiling would all face punishment.

"There's no time to spare."

She searched his eyes. "What's happening?"

"I'm not supposed to tell you."

They were keeping secrets from her? "Tell me," she said. "That is my command."

He lowered his voice, as if the walls had ears. "Your wedding procession."

"What?" How was that even possible?

"I am leading it. We are headed to Wailian Castle tonight. Lord Tong wants to marry you tomorrow, before your brother's wedding."

So her marriage was going to happen, sooner than later. Much sooner. And they weren't even going to tell her. Maybe this was Minister Hu's revenge. Kaiya's heart sank. "I...I will get ready."

He shook his head. "You're not going. They are risking a decoy instead. Now, let's get you back to your room before anyone else starts looking for you."

"What? A decoy?"

"It is a trick, to get us into Wailian Castle and capture Lord Tong."

Kaiya's head spun. "He won't let that many armed men in, if any."

"Prince Hardeep asked to join us. His Paladin fighting skills make him better than twenty men. "

So that's where Hardeep had gone. But why? Had he made a deal with Father? Still, one man, worth twenty or even a hundred, could not fight against a garrison of thousands. Loyal men might all die, and the realm would fall into turmoil. "Take me with you. If your plan does not work, I will offer myself in exchange for your lives."

Or use the budding power of her voice to sing Lord Tong to surrender. Some things were better left unsaid, especially if they might not be reliable.

Kai-Long shook his head. "I can't endanger you. Now, hurry back to the residence. I have to go now, my staff is assembling." He turned and headed back toward the entrance before she could stop him.

Kaiya looked from the doors leading out, then to the doors leading into the performance hall. Two paths lay ahead: one kept her safe but threatened the realm; the other could end the rebellion, perhaps at the cost of her dreams.

There was no choice, really. She'd made her decision earlier in the day, when she sacrificed her hopes before all the hereditary lords. The difference was that now, another option lay ahead. She'd sung men to sleep. Maybe that's all it would take to subdue Lord Tong.

CHAPTER 38
Easier to be a Soldier
than a General

Kaiya's heart beat with a resolute calm, drowning out all other sounds in her ears. Squaring her shoulders, she strode toward the doors out of the Hall of Pure Melody. Surely, Yang-Di, smiling upon her in Heaven, would provide a means of mingling with the procession. *Her* wedding procession, to which she wasn't even invited.

She peeked out. Right in front of her on the Hall's steps, Cousin Kai-Long's command staff assembled. He, himself, stood at the bottom of the stairs, addressing them from left to right. She pulled back before his gaze swept over her, but he paused. Had he seen her?

Apparently not. He continued with his speech. She let out the breath she held and peeked out again. Surplus equipment was stacked right by the door. Weapons, armor. A set of lamellar armor and a T-slot helm, likely for a messenger boy, appeared to be her size and lay just within reach.

And how strange it was for a leader to stand at the bottom of the steps, instead of the top, leaving his men with their backs to her.

It couldn't be a coincidence. Heaven had sent her a sign. This was the right thing to do.

When the men cheered at Kai-Long's words, she grabbed the armor and dragged it in. It was lighter than it appeared; she'd have no problem lifting it over her head and shrugging it on. First, though, she had to consider her own clothes. The inner gown hung lower than the armor, and the silk was too strong to tear.

Slinking back to the performance hall, she bent over and relieved one of the guards of his dagger. His *dao* would complete the disguise, but she thought the better of it. Like the silver ring that marked his station as an imperial guard, the sword represented his honor.

After gauging the length of the armor on her, she cut the bottom of her inner gown. The long sleeves of her outer gown became her leggings, bound with strips shorn from its hem. She shrugged on the armored tunic, and everything more or less looked right.

Removing her hairpins, she let her hair drop to the middle of her back. Much too long. She started to cut it, as well, but paused. Untamable as it was, her hair was the only feminine thing about her. Instead, she tied it back in a pony tail, like a man. For once, it obeyed. How easy men had it.

She glanced out again. The command staff marched toward the front of the plaza, where a hundred soldiers stood in orderly ranks. A contingent of imperial guards joined in, flanking her decoy and an unfamiliar handmaiden as they marched to her palanquin.

Up on the steps in front of her, young soldiers collected the gear and supplies. One of them, a boy who might have been her twin in his armor, reached for the helm she'd planned to take. She stepped out and grabbed it.

His eyes widened. "You're not allowed in there!" The simple marks on his armor, so different from the elaborate symbols on the imperial guards, did not suggest a high rank.

She donned the helmet, which strained her poor neck muscles. "I thought…" Too high-pitched! She cleared her throat and lowered her voice, as if singing a bass song. "I thought I heard someone in there."

"Well, hurry up." He pointed at a bundle of short spears.

Hugging them in her arms, she followed the boy to a line of horse-drawn carts, laden with weapons and bandages. Several grooms held the reins of messenger swifthorses. One of her palace physicians, Fang Weiyong, gave instructions to medics.

Keeping her head low to avoid his eyes, she dared a glance at the palanquin, some hundred paces away. The decoy resembled her, or at least an idealized version of her…of course! It was undoubtedly the work of the magic bauble Kai-Long had used the night before to help her escape. In all likelihood, the best warrior held it now, and would use it to get close to Lord Tong.

Who could it be? An imperial guard, perhaps. Not one of hers, since Chen Xin, Ma Jun, Zhao Yue, Li Wei, and Xu Zhan were all gathered around the palanquin. Maybe it was Prince Hardeep, with his Paladin skills? It made sense, given what Kai-Long had said about Hardeep offering to help.

But for what reason? Why would he risk himself when his own country needed him? Kaiya's chest squeezed.

Then she shuddered as the decoy ducked into the palanquin. Better him than her! Even as heavy and languid as her limbs felt, it was far better to march all night than to ride in the suffocating confines of a glorified coffin.

"Soldiers of Cathay!" Cousin Kai-Long's voice carried across the courtyard. He made for a dashing figure, sitting astride a white imperial stallion. The low murmurs guttered. "Tonight, we will march along the north highway. All night, double time."

Kaiya's legs buckled at the thought, and the lightweight armor and helm now might have been a dwarven anvil. Maybe the palanquin wasn't such a bad thing. Using a Dragon Song to vanquish Lord Tong required energy; energy she wouldn't have after a long night marching.

Kai-Long pointed north. "Our goal is to reach the Great Wall gate by dawn, then the outside of Wailian Castle by breakfast. We will rest for a short while to eat while we coordinate with General Lu's Army of the North, and gather information about the traitor's defenses. That might be your only rest before you are called on to storm an impregnable fortress."

Mutters broke out, sharing Kaiya's sentiment. This was a fool's errand, an engagement that would only work if the decoy succeeded. Even more reason to try *her* way.

Holding up a hand, Kai-Long's voice rose to a crescendo. "This may very well be the most difficult operation you will ever take part in. However, I know you. The best soldiers Cathay has seen in centuries are up to the task. Let us teach the rebel Tong Baxian the punishment for violating the Mandate of Heaven!"

The soldiers erupted into cheers, but Kaiya cringed. If pretty words were enough to convince a man to throw his life away, there didn't need to be many orators to instigate wars. For now, she'd keep her head low, lest someone recognize her and end her first, and in all likelihood last, military campaign.

Horns blared, and the gatehouse opened. Kai-Long took the lead, followed by mounted senior staff, then the imperial guards surrounding her palanquin. The ranks of soldiers narrowed to six men abreast and filed out, their broadswords clanging and spears pounding. A light breeze caught the blue imperial banners.

The unit she'd joined, with the supply wagons and medics, followed on the order of a mounted officer. Luckily, years of dancing allowed her to imitate their body language and marching. As long as she made it past the gatehouse and all the familiar palace staff and guards, there would be little chance of anyone recognizing her.

"You!" a familiar male voice barked.

Kaiya turned, only to have the helmet slip and block her vision. She adjusted it and looked.

Just a dozen paces away, Minister Hu jabbed a finger at a clearly drowsy Secretary Hong, flanked by the two guards she'd sung to sleep. "It is your fault she is missing. If any harm comes to her, the *Tianzi* will have your head."

Heavens, this was a mistake. Perhaps she could force Minister Hu's silence by threatening to reveal his indiscretions with the Night Blossoms. However, it would have to wait until a successful return from Wailian Castle. And success wasn't guaranteed.

What a dilemma. Four people might face severe punishment if she didn't intervene; but then, her singing Lord Tong into submission might be the only way to keep the realm from sundering.

Shaking the uncertainties out of her head, she lifted her chin and marched. Through the plaza, into the gatehouse. On the other side, yet more soldiers assembled, joining the procession. By the time they reached the capital's north gates, they'd grown to nearly a thousand strong.

Thank the heavens Kaiya had gotten her second wind. What made her think it was enough to make it to the Great Wall, let alone Wailian County? She set her eyes forward, concentrating on the rapid rhythm of boots.

Boots! In her haste, she hadn't thought of that. She wore silk slippers. Perhaps no one had noticed in the dark, but at dawn…and that was assuming she didn't wear the soles through or give her poor feet blisters.

"What's your name?" she asked the young man from before.

"Su. Yours?"

"Wang." The truth was easy enough to remember.

The column of soldiers turned north to the gatehouse and the bridge beyond, but her supply unit continued west. She leaned over to Su. "Won't we travel with them?"

He laughed. "Where did they find you? They are marching too fast for the wagons to keep up for long. We'll take river barges to Honggang and meet up with the army. That Lord Peng is a genius."

Kaiya's chest swelled with pride. Cousin Kai-Long was already proving resourceful on a military operation. And they'd take a boat. At least that would save her feet; maybe even give her a chance to rest. Unless the river barges foundered and capsized in the dark…

Her unit arrived at Songyuan Quays, where the Jade River emerged from Sun-Moon Lake. At this late hour, light bauble lamps posted along the warehouses illuminated the wooden docks. Several river barges had already disembarked, while soldiers worked at loading others. With Little Su's prodding, Kaiya joined in the

435

effort, hoping not to embarrass herself as she moved the heaviest loads she could.

Which were about half the size of the others. With a shake of his head, Little Su helped her. Within half an hour, her unit boarded a barge. A drummer set the rhythm for the rowers, and combined with the spring melt current, they set off at a brisk pace.

For the first time in what seemed like forever, Kaiya had a chance to rest her feet. Back against a crate, she sat cross-legged. It was thoroughly unladylike, but it kept her slippered feet out of sight. Before long, they passed her wedding procession. At the head, she ducked, just in case Kai-Long or the imperial guards recognized her through the helm's T-slot.

After a while, the Iridescent Moon reached full. She sucked in a breath at its beauty. Usually in bed before midnight, she rarely saw the physical embodiment of the God of Magic in its full glory. Depending on the outcome of this battle, she might never see it again. Never see Hardeep again, if he didn't survive. Her chest squeezed, foreboding thoughts bouncing in her head.

"Wake up!"

Kaiya's eyes fluttered open. Little Su came into focus as he shook her shoulder. The boats were docking and unloading at a river town. An officer on horseback bearing the red wolf emblem of Cousin Kai-Long's Nanling Province oversaw the loading of twelve new horse-drawn carts. It was amazing to think Kai-Long had devised such a complex plan and coordinated the logistics in such a short time.

"Where are we?" She asked.

"Honggang." Su passed her half a pork bun. "Two-thirds of the way to the Great Wall."

And right on the border of Hongzhou, one of the rebellious counties. She'd visited it last year, and there appeared to be more docks now. Hills rose up not far past the town, and beyond, the dark outline of the mountains demarked the starry sky.

Once they'd loaded the supplies, they resumed their march. She gripped her spear haft so tightly, her knuckles turned white. Without the bulk of the expeditionary force, it was up to her unit of thirty exceedingly young men to defend against rebels and bandits. And the weapon in her hands...she could reasonably not kill herself using a straight sword and dagger, but a spear was another story.

Two hours, marching uphill at night. At least the paved highway made it a little easier. Windows lit up in the villages and towns along the road, but they didn't encounter any resistance.

Only at Chengfu Township, in a dale next to the Great Wall's gate, did she feel safer. Home to the gatehouse's imperial garrison, they would gain some reinforcements as they crossed into Wailian County.

Or would they? Their unit's commander refused an armed escort. "This is all part of Lord Peng's plan," he said. "The garrison needs to defend this town, since it effectively cuts the rebellion in two. In any case, the rest of the procession is just an hour behind."

It meant travelling through the hotbed of rebellion, though Kaiya didn't want to draw undue attention to herself by speaking up about the danger. Instead, they continued through the gatehouse to the other side of the wall.

As they descended through a mountain pass, a rubble-strewn path on the left led upward to what looked to be fortifications.

"Is that Wailian Castle?" she asked Su.

He shook his head. "No, that was Cloud Castle."

Cloud Castle… "That's where the last Yu Emperor held out against my… the Founder."

"Yes. The *Tianzi* razed it eight years ago, after another rebel lord defied him."

Another rebel? How had she never heard of this? Probably because she was a girl. Stifling dark thoughts, she continued marching until the pass opened up.

She scanned the darkened land below. To think that not long ago, this region had belonged to the Nothori Kingdom of Rotuvi. The trip down the mountain took less effort than the ascent. Still, Kaiya's entire body ached from the continuous strain. Thankfully, she would never have to walk such a long distance again in her life.

As they descended, the Great Wall and mountains blocked the view of the Iridescent Moon behind them. Without it, she lost sense of how much time passed. Up ahead, the black of night began giving way to the inky blue before dawn.

The commanding officer called a halt at a bluff overlooking the next town. He pointed at it. "Wailian Township supports Wailian Castle, with barracks for many of Lord Tong's soldiers. We will wait here until the rest of the army arrives."

Kaiya squinted. In the low light, it was hard to make out the size of the town, but beyond it, the green-tiled roofs of Wailian Castle's central tower sparkled in the first rays of morning. A single bridge traversed a ravine, which yawned between the town and castle battlements.

What had General Lu said? *A ravine surrounds the castle on three sides, and a sheer cliff drops away on the other side.* The rustling of water indicated a river running through the ravine. It was impossible to take by force, which meant Kai-Long's plan hinged on her decoy eliminating Lord Tong.

And somewhere, hidden in the roar of the river, was the clopping of horse hooves. Hundreds, rumbling like thunder in the distance, but getting closer.

Tugging on Su's sleeve, Kaiya pointed in the direction of the approaching horses. "Do you hear that?"

He stared at her, brows furrowed. "Hear what?"

"Horses!" she called out to the commander. "Horses!"

The commander met her gaze and scoffed. "I don't hear anything. It's…"

Some of the other boys' ears perked up. Others shuffled uncomfortably. Now, even the commander looked.

Cresting the path were dozens of mounted soldiers, all bearing the green banners of Lord Tong. The boys around her started backing away from the carts. Kaiya's heart pounded faster than the horses' hooves.

The commander lowered his hand. "Steady, boys. Don't flee. We are still flying Wailian's banners. Let me talk to them."

The Wailian cavalry surged up and surrounded them, training bows on the outnumbered boys. Their leader pointed a broadsword toward the supplies. "Surrender. Put your weapons and armor in the wagons."

How did the enemy know they were with the imperial army? Kai-Long's logistics had failed. They should have just waited for him instead of going ahead alone. Kaiya joined her trembling unit members in looking up to the commander. Surely, he would order surrender.

"Do as he says," the commander said.

Kaiya let out her breath. At least for now, they would live. Except that beneath her armor was the silk inner gown she'd butchered. One by one, the boys placed their swords and spears inside the nearest carts and started removing their armor.

Her hands trembled as she surrendered her own weapons. She was a prisoner of war, and that fate sent a chill up her spine. They'd find out she was a girl, and no one would recognize her as the princess.

Revealing her true identity would spare her gang rape, and get her an audience with Lord Tong, where she could try the magic of her voice. No, she was too

440

exhausted for that, and even if they believed her, it would end all chances of her decoy getting close to Lord Tong.

"You, too." One of the Wailian soldiers prodded her in the back with the butt of a spear.

She stumbled forward, with Su grabbing her arm for support. Brushing him away, she removed the helm. She shook out her hair, lifted her chin, and faced the leader. "Sir, I am the daughter of *Tai-Ming* Lord Zheng Han." Never mind that Tian didn't have a sister, these rank and file soldiers wouldn't know that. She lifted the armor to expose the fine silk underneath. "He will pay handsomely for my return."

"I knew something was off," Su said, eyes wide.

The leader's expression hardened. "Take off your armor and put it in the cart."

She crossed her arms and shook her head. With the gown shredded and the mismatched leggings, she'd look ridiculous.

"Or shall I have my men confirm your identity the hard way?"

Several of the soldiers closed in. Little Su backed closer, arms outstretched in protection. Her limbs froze and refused to obey. With fingers stiff, she worked the armor off. Around her, the men laughed. Heat flared in her cheeks, even as the cold bit her exposed, armor-chaffed shoulders.

The leader unpinned his cloak and tossed it to her. "Now march. Not a word."

Their own commander looked over the defenseless boys and nodded. "March." His voice sounded wrong.

Something heavy settled in Kaiya's gut. His tone didn't gutter in defeat. And Heavens, they were providing supplies for the rebellion! Still, her comrades obeyed without question. What choice did they have?

At the point of rebel spears, they trudged through Wailian Town, which now roused with dawn. Men with picks and shovels walked in queues, humming in unison. Kaiya listened for the marching song's spirit, in hopes it would invigorate her.

It didn't work. She was a lone girl surrounded by many men, none who knew her true identity.

CHAPTER 39
Failing to Plan,
Planning to Fail

The sound of defeated boys trudging over the highway pavestones rang in Kaiya's ears, so different from their confident march just earlier in the morning. Their supplies seized, taken prisoner by a rebel lord, exhausted from the long night…and who knew if they'd survive the day?

She shuddered as she walked through the town. Who knew how long her maidenhood would survive?

Right before the bridge, the enemy leader called for a halt. "Leave the equipment here. Follow me." He rode ahead. The bridge was wide enough for five of them to walk abreast.

Their own officer raised an eyebrow at the leader. Kaiya's stomach knotted. Her instincts were right; he'd betrayed them. He dismounted and beckoned. "Come."

Something sounded wrong, a tension in his voice. The rigidity of the rebels. Kaiya looked among her fellow young soldiers. Eyes down, shoulders slumped, it didn't appear that any of them shared her

443

suspicions as they plodded across the bridge. Up ahead, the castle gates opened, and a several armed men marched out.

Halfway onto the bridge, their commander turned around. "Sorry, boys."

From his saddle, the enemy leader twisted around, unslung his bow, notched an arrow, and shot. It lodged deep into their commander's back.

The commander choked on blood, his voice coming out in wheezes. "What about the deal?"

"The lord said to kill the entire unit, including you." He raised a hand and made a fist.

From the town side of the bridge, bowstrings twanged. Kaiya glanced back. The cavalry were loosing arrows. Screaming, several of the boys scrambled forward and trampled over each other. Maybe in their panic, they didn't see that up ahead, soldiers were advancing with spears.

Her heart rapped hard in her chest. This was it. An ignoble ending to her noble intentions. All these poor boys, most no older than her, slaughtered on Lord Tong's command. The bridge vibrated with their frantic steps.

Hear the waves and allow them to lend you their strength. The memory of Lord Xu's lesson sounded in her mind, almost as if he spoke to her now. Tired as she was, she could borrow the sounds of chaos and the vibration of the bridge.

She gripped the stone with her toes through the tattered slippers. Her blisters protested, lending an edge to her voice. "Stop!"

The boys froze in place. The ambushers ahead halted in the charge. The rain of arrows stopped.

Kaiya gaped. It had worked—on the first try, no less. Still, her energy guttered, buckling her knees and sending her panting for breath. Once they came to their senses, the murder would resume, and she didn't have the energy to reprise the feat.

Shaking the fatigue out, she reached up and grasped the side of the bridge for support. Once she gained her feet, she squared her shoulders and strode toward the leader. Her hand found Tian's pebble.

She summoned a tone of command, speaking as she would to a palace servant. "I am Princess Wang Kaiya, here to meet my betrothed, Lord Tong Baxian." She gestured to the cowering boys. "These are my honor guard. An attack on them is an attack on me."

The leader favored her through slitted eyes. She'd just betrayed Kai-Long and the decoy, and there was no guarantee Lord Tong would spare any of them, let alone believe her in the first place.

The sound of drums in the distance drew Kaiya's attention from the enemy leader on the bridge to the road behind her.

A man on horseback, flying Lord Tong's green, cantered through the city. "Princess Kaiya's procession is coming, maybe half an hour away."

The enemy leader turned back and frowned at her, then beckoned the prisoners. "Hands on your head. Come on, hurry. Help your wounded comrades if they need it."

Kaiya evaluated her unit. A few lay unmoving on the bridge or sprawled over the edge, and those at the back of the line appeared to have suffered varying degrees of arrow wounds. Still, most seemed uninjured. Many bowed their heads to her as they passed.

She searched for Su, the boy who'd travelled with her, helped her pick up the slack when her energy flagged. There he was, his arm hanging from another young man who helped him limp along. An arrow protruded from his back. Kaiya pushed her way through the others and took his other arm.

He looked up at her through drooping eyes. "Are you really Princess Kaiya?"

Despite his labored breaths, his tone sounded…hopeful. She nodded.

"Then it is my honor to die for you." He started to drop to a knee in salute.

She clasped his hand. "You aren't going to die." Not like she could tell, and blood flecked his lips.

The boy on the other side of him met her eyes and shook his head. "You saved us all."

Not all. Now that many of her adopted unit had been taken to the castle, she could see arrows protruding from some of the bodies. Doctor Wu had taught enough about anatomy for Kaiya to recognize at least two of the boys would not draw another breath. Her stomach churned, and it was all she could do to force down the vomit. Even now, Lord Tong's men were throwing their remains off the bridge. Others, like Su, might not survive.

With much of his weight on her shoulders, she trudged over the bridge. At the gatehouse, she risked a glance back. No sign of the imperial banners, even though the drumbeats grew louder.

On the other side of the gatehouse, she walked out into another bare yard, surrounded by high, crenelated walls. If an invading army somehow made it over the bridge, they would be trapped at low ground, easy targets from all sides. Just like she and her comrades were now. The men atop the walls trained repeating crossbows on them.

The gates ahead were open as soldiers escorted the prisoners and pulled the stolen supply wagons through. If they were to be slaughtered here, the gates would be closed to bar escape. Passing through the second gatehouse, the commander led them not to the next part of the castle, but down into rough-hewn tunnels.

The air grew chill and stale, and Kaiya's skin crawled as the walls pressed in around her. "What is this place?"

One of the boys ran a hand over a column. "I would guess these were mines."

Kaiya shuddered. If Wailian had that much firepowder, and if it were stored down here, one accident could cause the supposedly impregnable castle to implode. And she'd be buried under it all, unable to breathe...

447

Sweat gathered on her neck as her hands trembled. She turned to their nearest captor. "I am Princess Kaiya. These men need medical attention. And I demand to speak with Lord Tong."

He shoved her in the back. "Keep moving. Someone will confirm your identity soon enough."

Thankfully, after a few more steps, the corridor opened into a large chamber. Kaiya took a deep breath and wiped the sweat from her brow.

The injured lay on blankets while healers tended to their wounds. One of the boys screamed as they pulled an arrow out of him. Kaiya's chest ached at the pitiful moans. Still, she knelt by Su and held his hand.

Someone grabbed her shoulder in a heavy grip and spun her around. A larger boy from the regiment glared at her. "If I'm going to die, I'm not going to die a virgin."

Kaiya's mind blanked.

Several other hands seized the boy and pulled him back as he struggled.

"You ingrate," said another one of the boys. "She saved our lives."

A spear butt crashed into the offender's head, sending him to the ground. One of the enemies raised the spear again. "Stay quiet. Nobody touch her until we learn her identity. If she's no one important, you can have her. After we're done, that is."

Kaiya clenched and unclenched her sweaty hands. Surely, someone would be able to identify her.

Some of the boys, led by Su's friend, formed up around her.

"Don't worry," he said. "We won't let them do anything to you."

The reassurance wasn't enough to slow Kaiya's thumping heart, though the sentiment was kind. If she were in a position of real importance, beyond just a political tool, she'd reward him and the others who defended her.

For now, though, she'd have to wait. If her captors had bothered to tell Lord Tong, the decoy might fare worse than she.

Tian hadn't ridden a horse since childhood, and would never tease Jie again about how she looked after riding. Not the way his buttocks felt. Unable to enter the capital because of his banishment, he'd stolen an imperial stallion from a messenger waystation and followed the old dirt road along the Jade River at a trot. When his mount tired, he swapped it out for a farmer's draft horse who was none too keen about being ridden.

Eventually, he'd broken into an estate, appropriated a lady's riding horse, and made his way to Honggang. However, the beast refused to cross the river, so Tian had to leave it behind and swim himself.

The river town had been particularly busy at night, and he found out Princess Kaiya's wedding procession, thankfully minus Princess Kaiya, had passed through hours before. He'd followed, jogging uphill, sneaking through the town of Chengfu, and finally scaling the Great Wall with cat claws and coming down on the other side by dawn.

The ruins of Cloud Castle on the cliffs high above had brought back memories from when he was a fresh clan initate, and had taken part in the operation to capture the fortress.

He'd only afforded it a quick reminisce before continuing. Now he was bent over, hands on his knees, heaving for breath, on a bluff overlooking Wailian Castle. Along the outskirts of the town, four thousand twenty-three enemy soldiers formed up in lines.

The imperial procession of a thousand and seven crowded the highway through the town, all the way up to the bridge. From their vantage point, they had no way of knowing that an army just under four times their size was ready to envelop them.

The castle gates opened and soldiers flying green flags emerged. At the head of the imperial procession, the leader dismounted from his white stallion, his body language looking familiar. Eight porters lowered the palanquin. Jie was supposedly inside, unaware a new rival Water Snake Black Fist clan was defending the castle.

He had to warn them, even if it meant fighting through both the enemy and an imperial procession that had no idea who he was. He thought back to the poor horse he'd left behind, the one he'd promised himself to track down and return if he survived.

Survival didn't seem likely. Not without a plan, not without knowledge of the castle's layout or defenses. Certainly not with enemy Black Fist agents who knew Black Lotus tactics.

If Jie had known how relaxing a palanquin ride was, she'd have signed up to be a princess sooner. The fast pace and mild bouncing had rocked her to into a deep slumber, the most relaxing sleep she'd enjoyed in quite a while.

Now, though, someone rapped on the palanquin's sliding window, jarring her awake. "*Dianxia.*" Chen Xin used the honorific, even though the real princess' five imperial guards had probably guessed she was a decoy. "We have arrived."

Jie propped herself up and opened the window. Indeed, Chen Xin's mug blocked her view. She gestured him out of the way and leaned close to get a better view.

Cannons pointed from Wailian Castle's battlements, trained on this very spot before a bridge. In all likelihood, a bombardment would exact heavy causalities on troops waiting to cross through the bottleneck.

She turned to Chen Xin and used the *Mockingbird's Deception* to imitate the princess' voice. "What is the status of General Lu's armies?"

His eyes rounded for a split second before he shook his head. "They are on the other side of the castle, held in place by an army from Rotuvi camped near our fortifications. General Lu is sending reserves, but the best they can do is attack the castle's rear, up the cliffs."

Jie sucked on her lower lip, but switched to the princess' hair twirling. Without General Lu's armies in support, this battle hinged entirely on her getting close to Lord Tong and forcing him to surrender. The window glided shut from the outside.

"I think it is the real princess," Chen Xin whispered, incredulous. "It was her voice."

"It was that magic marble." The roll of Zhao Yue's eyes carried in his tone.

"Jie, then?" Li Wei said.

Apparently, not everyone was apprised of the plan, though the imperial guards were smart enough to figure it out. Or maybe that was giving them too much credit. They were, after all, swordsmen and not alchemists.

She took stock of her weapons. In addition to several sharp hairpins, a garrote wound into her hair and pressed the magic bauble to her scalp. A knife was hidden in her sleeve; a vial of male-targeted toxin in her sash. And under the cushion, she'd stashed a Black Fist straight sword and several throwing stars and spikes , in the unlikely event they allowed the palanquin into the castle.

Outside, someone in robes approached and dropped to a knee. When he spoke, it sounded like cloth dragging across a washboard. "Lord Peng, greetings. I am Steward Qiu. We are honored to receive Princess Kaiya to Wailian Castle. Will she alight and come in?"

Sliding the window open, Jie cleared her throat and copied the princess' voice. "It is not for the common folk to lay eyes on the princess."

The open window provided the view of a middle-aged man with a porcine nose in green robes. His irises shifted back and forth, and his voice cracked like dried mud. "Very well. Lord Tong would be honored. Allow me to receive the swords of Lord Peng and the imperial guard for safekeeping."

Safekeeping, indeed. She put a hand out of the window and beckoned Pig Nose Qiu. "The laws of the empire require an imperial princess be protected by five imperial guards at all times." Pig Nose might not know for sure, but it would keep the princess' personal guards happy.

Qiu chewed on the inside of his cheek, looking more like a cow than a pig. "Even still, courtesy demands I protect their swords for them."

Lord Peng's voice cut through the debate. "Very well, five guards, as well as me and my aide. You may protect our weapons."

Aide? Jie contorted to see whom Lord Peng indicated, but Pig Nose Qiu's flat, round face blocked her view. "And my handmaiden," she added. Feng Mi, while young, could easily handle a few men as long as they didn't fight like Black Fists.

"Men," Lord Peng said, his voice carrying back to the soldiers. "I leave you in the capable hands of General Feng until I send word."

"Yes, *Dajiang*!" the men shouted in unison.

The palanquin lifted and started forward onto the bridge. Jie closed her eyes and listened for the number of distinct footsteps. Lord Peng, his inordinately heavy aide, the five imperial guards, Feng Mi, Pig Nose, and two enemy soldiers.

And hundreds, if not thousands of soldiers in the castle itself. Maybe, just maybe they could take the gatehouse with the eight of them, or sixteen if the palanquin bearers were of any use. But then the rest of their procession would have to charge across the narrow bridge under a hail of arrows, musket fire, and cannon balls.

Hopefully, Lord Peng would have enough sense not to try. No, the fate of this mission rested on her ability to neutralize Lord Tong himself. As the Founder said, cut off the head, and surely, the demon would die.

The sunlight dimmed as they passed into the gatehouse.

Doors slammed shut in the front and back. All went dark, so dark even Jie's elven vision did not take over. Lord Peng cursed, while daggers rasped from sheaths. Hidden among the commotion, several men with large lung capacities high in the rafters whispered

454

in barely intelligible Arkothi. One word stood out though.

Black Fist.

Jie reached for her sword.

Glass shattered inside of the palanquin and outside. A musky scent percolated in the tight confines. Deer antler velvet, used in Black Lotus toxins to target females. Jie covered her nose.

Still, too late. With that one whiff, her head would begin to spin any second now.

The shouts of men, echoing so loudly just seconds before, subsided.

All went black.

CHAPTER 40
Unmistaken Identities

Jie's head and shoulders ached as slippered feet brushing across wood floors nudged her out of sleep.

That muted musk smell lingered on her...someone must have used a Black Fist contact toxin, and of course, it would blot out some of her memories. What had she been doing?

Right, going to Wailian Castle to capture Lord Tong. They'd been ambushed, but beyond that...

Feigning unconsciousness, she took stock of her situation. A rope made from smooth fibers bound her wrists above her head. She was completely naked, her hair askew. Her captors must've suspended her from something above, but in their foolishness, they let her toes touch the hardwood floors. A fountain rustled somewhere behind her; she would have never heard the footsteps over the gurgling water if they hadn't been so close.

She opened one eye a fraction. Torture devices of all types lay neatly arranged on a bloodwood table in front of her. Chains and ropes hung from the ceiling. A sturdy blockwood saltire cross with manacles rested against a wall in front of her. Whoever her captors were, they'd soon learn that no amount of pain would get her to reveal sensitive information.

Wait. She studied the table. The flaying blade and hot poker made sense, but since when did torturers use feathered whips and paddles? This was no torture chamber. It was some deviant's playroom. What Feng Mi had said about Lord Tong's Floating World habits left little doubt as to the identity of said deviant.

How had she gotten here? She searched her scrambled memory. They'd crossed the bridge, entered the gatehouse, and then…

Nothing. Curse every god and goddess in the Heavens! Whatever had happened, they must have failed. And now…

A whip cracked into her back, sending a wave of pain through her. She bit her lip and tensed up. The sick turtle egg wouldn't hear her scream—wait, she was supposed to be Princess Kaiya. She faked a whimper. Maybe it wasn't entirely fake.

A man came around to her front, whip slapping in his palm. Black hair streaked with white framed a mask that covered his entire face. A paunch poked out from his green robes. "Welcome to Wailian Castle, Princess Kaiya. Since this is how you will spend most of your time here, I felt you should get acquainted with your matrimonial duties."

Blinking away sham tears, Jie looked up at him. At least for now, he believed the ruse. "As you command, Lord Tong."

"Good girl. Now tell me, why did the *Tianzi* send a bride with an escort of a thousand men? If I didn't know any better, I would think my father-in-law-to-be planned to attack."

"Please, My Lord, we aren't married yet. Please cover me." She teetered back, exposing only her side. Baiting him. Once he came close…

"Answer me first." He drew the whip across her belly.

Yelping at the searing pain, she shook her head. "I don't know much of military matters, *Jue-ye*, but my father said I would need protection as I travelled through Fengshan Province." Tell him what he wanted to hear, address him with a title reserved for *Tai-Ming*, and maybe he'd believe the *Tianzi* had incorporated the new province and promoted Tong. If he let his guard down, he might come within leg's reach. Her muscles tensed, not from the pain, but in anticipation.

"And why did we find so many weapons on you and in your palanquin?" He stepped forward and ran a finger up the inside of her thigh.

Grabbing the rope, Jie jumped and pulled herself skyward, then twisted behind Lord Tong. She wrapped her right leg around his neck and hooked the left knee around her right ankle. Arching back, she took advantage of the new slack in the rope and pushed his head forward in the modified leg choke. He clawed at her shins, gasping for air.

Four, three, two, one. He went limp. When he crumpled to the ground, Jie lowered herself, feet firmly on his unconscious form. Reaching with a leg, she seized a flaying blade between her toes. Thank the Heavens—or rather, Black Lotus training—for flexibility.

A rope dart zipped in from behind her. It wrapped around her ankle and yanked the blade loose before she could cut through her bindings. She contorted to find a large Cathayi boy holding the other end of the line.

Behind her, clapping carried over the fountain's bubbling. "Very good," said a gravelly voice...

That voice, where had she heard it before? The palanquin stopping in front of the bridge and Pig Nose Qiu flashed in her memory. She twisted again to see the man from the bridge with the round, flat face. "The real Lord Tong, I presume?"

He grinned and nodded with a haughty bow. "*Not* Princess Kaiya, I presume?" He gestured to the unconscious man. "I was not about to risk myself, not when my informants told me about a decoy."

So he knew about the decoy. And he had an informant. Still, maybe the pretense might work. Chin down, she shook her head.

"Don't insult my intelligence. Look." In his hand, the magic bauble dangled from her garrote. "I wouldn't imagine Princess Kaiya to have so many scars. Really, it looks like you belong in this room."

Though she wasn't prone to shyness, his leer made Jie want to cover herself.

He laughed. "And the tapered ears. Yes, I know you are Jie, once the most promising Floret in the

459

Floating World. I'd already been banned from most of the Houses, but of course my old friends Lords Shi and Yang spoke longingly of you. Of course, their inability to control their lust is why they fell to your clan while I still live."

What? Had he been secretly behind the conspiracy eight years ago? And how did he know about the clan? "How—"

He held up a finger and tsked. "I have long known about the Black Lotus' involvement in the Floating World, and that you were one of them."

"Kill her, Your Lordship," said the boy in heavily accented Cathayi. "She is too dangerous to leave alive."

Lord Tong waved him off. "I will hold my own counsel on this, Bovyan."

Bovyan? The brutish ruling race of the Teleri Empire? It would make sense, given what the altivorc in the palace had said about an agreement between Lord Tong and the Teleri.

Still, this boy looked too small, and his features were undeniably Cathayi. The Bovyan race, the cursed descendants of the Arkothi Sun God's mortal son, usually grew even larger, easily a head above the average human male, with fair skin. Tong must be mistaken.

"So, let me guess the *Tianzi's* plan." Lord Tong steeped his hands beneath his chin. "After I refused to go to Huajing, he sent you here to kill me. He'd then send his armies into this castle. No, you don't have to answer."

Jie sucked on her lower lip. What could she say? At each turn, Lord Tong was a step ahead of the *Tianzi's* plans.

He twirled the magic bauble on the cord. "Thanks to this, I know the girl we captured earlier really is Princess Kaiya."

It couldn't be true. She'd last seen Princess Kaiya in the alleys of Sun-Moon Palace, while learning to imitate her voice. Far away, in the capital. "You lie."

"Not as much as you. She's not as pretty as this makes her look. I'm quite disappointed."

So it was true. Jie hung her head. In everything, she had failed. She'd almost be happy for Tian to see her failure, if that meant being able to see him again.

He gestured to the Bovyan. "Keep an eye on her. Make sure nothing is in reach." He pointed to the wood cross. "I want her to have a good view of the real princess when I take her. Then, I'll brand her to show her father—if he survives the attack on the prince's wedding"

Cradling Su's head in her lap, Kaiya hummed a lullaby while trying to ignore his labored, dying breaths.

Time dragged between each shorter inhalation. Tears welled in her eyes. She should have never come with the wedding procession, should have just stayed in the safe confines of Sun-Moon Palace. Dear Kai-Wu would be getting married tonight, and she'd miss it.

And for what? She was stuck in an old mine, with at least one boy who wanted to take her virginity, and apparently no chance of singing Lord Tong into surrender. How foolish she'd been, to think she would ever be more than a political tool.

She reached down and clasped Su's hand. His cold fingers stung hers, and she almost pulled back. His lips were pallid. She shook him. "Wake up, Su. Wake up."

His friend shook his head. A tear slid down his cheek and plopped onto the rough-hewn floors.

Kaiya's chest tightened, and her shoulders heaved. No, she couldn't cry. Not when all these boys saw her as an imperial princess. Sniffling, she straightened her spine and squared her shoulders.

The metal door swung open. She turned to see. To berate whatever guard came in, for letting a boy die. Her heart leapt into her throat.

Chen Xin, Zhao Yue, Li Wei, Ma Jun, and Xu Zhan spilled in, their faces bruised and their blue robes torn in places, their magic breastplates taken. Oh Heavens, if they were prisoners, it meant that the decoy—Hardeep—had failed.

She gently laid Su's head on the ground and stood. "Guards."

Their eyes widened in unison. It would have been funny if not for the grave circumstances. Immediately, they sank their knee, fist to the ground. "*Dian-xia*," they shouted.

"It's true!" one boy said.

"She *is* the princess." Another could barely speak.

"She saved us."

The boys dropped to their knees and pressed their foreheads to the ground.

She certainly didn't feel like a princess. Wearing just a ripped-up inner gown, her shins exposed when she took off the shorn sleeves of her outer gown. "Rise. You knew me as Wang, and so it shall be now." She turned to Chen Xin. "What happened?"

"*Dian-xia*," he said. "Why are you here?"

Why indeed. The truth would make her look even more stupid than she felt. She shook her head. "It doesn't matter. Tell me, what happened?"

He sighed. "Lord Tong knew our plan. He separated us from the rest of the procession, and then ambushed us in the gatehouse."

"And Hardeep?"

Chen Xin cocked his head. "The foreign prince?"

She nodded. "Wasn't he my decoy?"

"No," he said, shaking his head. "It was...it was...Deputy Yan's daughter."

Now it was *her* turn to stare at *him* incredulously. "That strange minister?"

463

Chen Xin nodded. "She helped us track you down the night you went missing."

A reminder of yet another stupid choice. She swept her gaze over the guards. "And Kai-Long—I mean, Lord Peng?"

They exchanged glances and shrugged.

Ma Jun said, "We were fighting with our knives, in the dark. It was almost as if our opponents could see, even when we couldn't. When they subdued us and opened the doors, Lord Peng, his aide, and—"

The door creaked open again.

Two enemy soldiers thrust a man dressed in the colors of Kai-Long's Nanling Province in. He stumbled face-first into the ground. The imperial guards flipped him over.

"The aide." Xu Zhan pointed to the markings on the man's collar and then looked up at her.

Kaiya nudged the guards to the side and studied the unmoving man's face. Bronze, not golden-toned like the Cathayi; a high-bridged nose.

No, it couldn't be.

Heavens…Prince Hardeep. She patted her hands over him, checking for injuries. He had no visible wounds, but he didn't look to be breathing. She leaned over and pressed her ear to his heart.

Nothing. Her own heart might have stopped. No, they wouldn't have brought him here if he were dead. She closed her eyes.

Something pulsated. Slow, resolute, like waves pounding against a sea wall.

She let out a long sigh and looked up at her men. "How did you not recognize him as the Ankiran Prince?"

The guards exchanged shrugs. Li Wei said, "He wore a helmet the whole time, and never left Lord Peng's side."

And now, not even his Paladin skills could save him from the trap. This was her fault, too. Doubting her progress in musical magic, Hardeep had likely made a deal with Father. Join in the attack on Wailian Castle in return for Cathay helping to repel the Madurans. Despondent, she hummed again, imitating the lute song he'd taught her.

He blinked several times and focused on her. "Princess Kaiya! What are you doing here?"

Heat flushed in her cheeks. Looking around, hoping no one spoke Ayuri, she said, "I had hoped to use the lessons you taught me. I wanted to sing Lord Tong into submission. I don't think he'll see me. I'm so sorry."

His hair swept through the dirt as he shook his head. "There is nothing to apologize for. When Lord Peng told me of his plan, I volunteered to help, to vanquish Lord Tong so that you would not have to marry him. I came for you."

She'd been wrong. He hadn't made a deal. Tears threatened to blur her vision. Oh, to be able to thank him with the only thing she could give. Cradling his head, she leaned in, eyes closed, lips parted. Who cared if her men saw? Her first kiss, maybe her only kiss, would belong to him. None of the guards moved to intervene.

The door groaned open again. His head snapped in the direction of the sound, just before their lips met.

No! Kaiya looked up to see who'd interrupted them now.

Eight soldiers, including the leader who'd captured them, stood by the doors.

"Princess Kaiya," the leader said. "Lord Tong will see you now."

One of the soldiers stepped in and seized her arm.

The imperial guards leaped to their feet, ready to intervene, even without weapons. Throwing their lives away, for her. The boys, too, all pushed forward.

Kaiya raised a hand. "Stand down. I will meet with Lord Tong."

Her guards hesitated, yet their every muscle twitched.

Hardeep staggered up. He stomped a foot on the ground. "Stop." His voice echoed in the cavern, the vibration shaking in Kaiya's core.

Around her, everyone froze in place.

He looked from guard to guard, then to the boys. "There is no need for anyone to die. Trust your princess."

He had spoken in Ayuri, but the imperial guards and the boys all shrank back. The tension in their postures melted.

Kaiya exchanged a smile with Prince Hardeep. "Thank you. I will end this war now." She walked out of the prison surrounded by traitors. If only she felt as confident as she let on.

They marched her out of the tunnels, and she gulped the fresh air. No matter what happened, at least it would happen above ground. Through the yard, they headed to the five-story main keep. After passing through yet another gatehouse, they arrived in the inner bailey. Servants opened the double doors.

The nightingale floorboards chirped under her tattered slippers. The sound was meant to deter spies, but right now gave her comfort. It was also a rhythm that she might be able to borrow. Another set of double doors slid open, revealing an audience chamber.

Two men guided her into the room, where she was greeted by the scrutiny of several important-looking warriors. At their head sat a middle-aged man with a round face and flat nose. A flabby paunch poked out from under his green robes. Failing to sing him into surrender would mean enduring him, acting out the pictures of the pillow book. Her shudder was interrupted when he reached down and placed a musical instrument on his lap.

The Dragon Scale Lute.

His goons must've recovered it while Hardeep was trying to protect her.

A grin formed on his lips. When he spoke, it sounded like rocks rattling in a sack. "Do you like it?"

Her eyes must have betrayed her.

"Of course you do, since you stole it." He looked past her. "Isn't that right, Little Li?"

Kaiya followed his eyes.

Wringing his delicate hands, Chamberlain Li met her gaze before averting his eyes to the floor. With his powdered face, he was as pretty as he'd been back in Huajing. "Yes, *Jue-ye*."

Lord Tong grinned. "Ever since receiving the instrument that could repel Avarax, I've tried many different types of strings and searched for a true Dragon Singer to play it."

Kaiya lifted her chin. "I'll never play it for you."

His gravelly laugh sent a shudder down her spine. "Foolish girl. You can't. Only a Dragon Singer. Which I happen to have." He nodded toward Chamberlain Li.

Just as she had feared. Was that why he'd been practicing with a lute that night? Kaiya gawked.

The uncertainty on Li's face shifted as he tightened his lips and straightened. He made a tentative bow.

"Taught by the elf lord Xu, no less." Lord Tong sighed as he patted the Dragon Scale Lute. "Yet it seems I rushed him here for nothing. The lute's magic is gone."

Kaiya's head spun, even as her chest ached. Chamberlain Li was a Dragon Singer? Taught by Lord Xu? All her dreams of proving her worth by reviving the dead art melted. Lord Tong had brought the Lute here, probably to use on the imperial troops, but now it

468

seemed she'd used the last bit of its magic in the Temple of Heaven.

With a feral grin, Lord Tong gestured toward a cushion in front of him. "Now, *Dian-xia*, sit."

Brushing her shredded inner dress to her shins—well, the hem didn't reach that far anymore—she knelt. "Lord Tong—"

"Master. You may call me Master."

His men chuckled. Heat flared in her cheeks. Not like they were even married yet. She opened her mouth to protest.

"We will be wed at midday, before your brother's wedding. I will marry into the Wang family and invest my ancestral tablet into your family temple."

In less than two hours. Why so urgent? And why would a powerful lord wish to forsake his ancestors and take on his wife's name? She raised an eyebrow.

"You are wondering about the immediacy, wondering why. Before your brother speaks his vows before Heaven, my allies will slaughter him, the Crown Prince, the *Tianzi*, your paternal uncle and his sons. The old Lord Peng and his heir are dead, and the current Lord Peng is in my custody. All heirs to the Jade Throne will be dead, leaving only you, a girl, with imperial blood."

Kaiya's head spun. How could this even be possible?

He grinned "You will obey me. Otherwise, your men will die. The imperial expeditionary army is trapped,

469

and functioning Dragon Scale Lute or not, we will crush them."

Her blood ran cold. Not because of his threat, but because his finger rested on one of the lute strings.

Her shoulders froze; her heart hurt so badly it must have stopped. If he strummed...

He did. The finger flicked across the string.

The sound came out flat, lifeless, even duller than a regular musical instrument. How could that be? When she'd played, its song had radiated out in eerie desolation and sent warriors into a panic. Now, it merely vibrated, perhaps only loud enough for her keen ears to pick up.

It was true, its magic had been depleted.

He grinned so the edge of his lips nearly touched the flabby crinkles in the corner of his eyes.

Straightening her spine, tilting her chin, she locked gazes with him. The lute string still buzzed, lending her strength she didn't have on her own. Like the interplay of her music teachers' duet, she'd merge the lute's frequency with Lord Tong's heartbeat.

Rooted to the ground, your spine aligned, let your heart impel your voice. Listening for Lord Tong's pulse, she rose and gripped her feet to the floor. Where was his pulse? In this room, with poor acoustics, it hid among the other sounds. Still, she had to try, had to guess. She hummed to the frequency of the lute string.

His fingers quivered. His men rocked on their feet. It was working! The rebellion, put down by a girl! Chamberlain Li stared at her, wide eyed.

Her vitality guttered. Her already depleted spirit wavered, unable to sustain the hum. It began to crack.

Then her energy failed. Her knees buckled, and she dropped to the floor.

Lord Tong straightened. He lifted his chin to one of the soldiers. "Start the attack. Crush the imperials." He then turned to her. "Let me show you where you will be spending most of our married life."

CHAPTER 41
Explosive

While an attacking army had little chance of scaling the ravine walls to the castle walls, a single Black Fist could do so with ease. At least, that's what Tian had thought at first. Exhausted from a whole night of riding, swimming, climbing, and jogging, he found the task more daunting once he started.

He'd chosen a sparsely patrolled west side of the castle, now shadowed in the early morning. Still, if anyone actually spotted him on the descent, he'd make for any easy target. Hand under hand, foot after foot, his fingers and toes ached. He glanced back at the castle several times, freezing at any flash of color on the battlements.

At the bottom, sixty-two feet below, he rested next to the churning rapids of a hundred-twenty-three-foot river. Boulders stuck out in places, but they lay too far apart to jump. Dark as twilight at the ravine's bottom, he had no sense of the depth while slogging across. Halfway through, the frigid waters only came to his waist.

Then his foot slipped on a slime-covered stone and he went under. The swirling current swept him at least a dozen feet before he clung on to a shrub growing between some rocks.

Gasping for air, freezing from the chill waters, he floundered across and heaved himself onto a cold boulder. Once he caught his breath, he stripped off his wet clothes and moved around to generate warmth. If an enemy arrow or freefall didn't claim him, hypothermia might.

As he waited to regain a semblance of energy, he looked up at the daunting task ahead. The castle side of the ravine rose higher than the other, and then there was the climb up the walls to the battlements.

He shook his arms and legs to limber them up before starting the treacherous ascent. His muscles screamed for every foothold and handgrip. His body seemed to weigh more than usual, demanding more of his knees, shoulders, and elbows as he struggled to find purchase on the ravine wall.

It was seventy-two feet to the top of the cliff, another twenty to the top of the castle's outer walls. With no signs of patrols, he slunk over the side and pressed up against the inside parapet. Supposedly, the half-sized Madaeri in the Eldaeri northeast thought of his last twelve grueling hours as *fun*. If he ever met one, he'd tell them just how insane they were.

Tian turned around and peeked over the parapet. From this vantage point, it appeared as if the entire complex was divided into three walled-off sections, with watchtowers at the intersections of the walls. The sole entrance stood at the center of the south wall, with a gatehouse leading into an outer bailey. In times of peace, the soldiers might drill there. Today, however, it was a deathtrap. The imperial army, or at least those who survived the charge across the bridge, would take fire from all sides before having to file through the second gatehouse.

In the northeast corner, protected in the inner bailey, stood the main keep. Green-tiled roofs demarked its five levels. Jie's palanquin had entered an hour and a half earlier, so by now, she had either neutralized Lord Tong or been captured.

Or killed.

His gut twisted. No, Jie didn't die easily.

Just below him was the main ward, stretching the length and breadth of the outer walls. Twenty-seven wooden buildings of varying sizes would provide cover while he searched for Jie. The banging of metal from one of the twelve stone structures suggested at least one smithy. Despite being six and a half times as large as the rest of the castle, this section was nearly abandoned at the moment.

He was about to climb down, when a squad of men in lamellar armor ran across the yard to meet another now coming out of a nearby wooden building. Tian ducked down below the parapet and listened.

"The girl who escaped is still unaccounted for," one solider said.

Jie, no doubt. If anyone could escape an ambush—

"Find her! She can't be more than ten," said another.

Too young to be Jie. The handmaiden, then. Which meant she was a Black Lotus member. Likely an initiate and not a full adept. If she were too young and inexperienced, she would be frightened and forget her training. But since they hadn't found her yet, she had probably found a way to blend in.

A good idea for himself, and the easiest way to hide in plain sight. And to keep warm. When the voices faded and the footsteps trailed away, he shimmied down the wall, jumping the last ten feet to save time. Landing lightly on his feet, he dashed to the closest building. He peered into an open window.

Sixteen cots lined both the east and west walls. At the fifth one from the right, a young man struggled with his lamellar tunic. A broadsword lay on his bedding. Tian leaped through the window, rolled across the floor, and landed on his feet just behind the hapless man. All without a sound. A very easy kill, which would save time looking for armor.

Hold the dragonfly with care. Princess Kaiya's voice prodded him from where she stood safely in Sun-Moon Castle, forty-seven miles away and four thousand, twenty-three days in the past. Instead of breaking the soldier's neck, Tian stepped through the young man's knee and wrapped an arm around his throat.

The soldier struggled, hands flailing, but then fell limp. In linking motions, Tian shimmied the tunic off the man and lowered him onto the bed. He then shrugged the armor on, tightened the buckles, and retrieved a T-slot helmet and the broadsword. Not his preferred weapon, but it would have to do.

Now to find the Black Lotus girl. If she'd tried to infiltrate the castle, she would probably take the guise of a servant. Right now, those girls would be in the kitchens rolling rice balls or cutting strips for bandages. Leaving the barracks, he headed to the closest stone building.

Sure enough, inside, several women and girls gathered around a table, laughing and chatting as they pressed balls of rice in their hands. None of them seemed familiar. He made his way toward the castle, poking his head into kitchens and barracks.

Halfway to the inner bailey, he spotted a girl kneeling by a stone-lined circle, working a winch. A well, in all likelihood, though unless there was a cistern, the well must have gone at least seventy-two feet to reach the aquifers. Tian marched at an angle to get a look at her face. She kept her head down, and even turned in such a way that revealed less of her face as he passed. She was either shy, or...

Tian came up behind her and placed a hand on her shoulder. He'd started to tap a code when she seized his arm and twisted. He reeled toward the opening and would have careened down the well had he not had the sense to hook the edge with a foot and catch the winch with his free hand.

Still, she had superior leverage. She'd be able to send him over with a simple sweep of her leg.

"Black Water," he said. Hopefully, even in the heat of the moment, she'd recognize one of the many code words that allowed Black Lotus members to identify each other in disguise.

Her pressure relented. "Who are you?"

"Zheng Tian."

"Oh!" Eyes wide like cups, she helped him up.

Armor jangled from behind them, enough sound for two men. "What is going on there?" a gruff male voice called.

Tian spun and pressed a fist into his hand. "I tripped. Thank the Heavens. She saved me."

The taller of the two soldiers waved. "Well, get your water and hurry to your post. Lord Tong will order the attack soon."

Soon. Tian's guts knotted as he watched the two soldiers march toward the outer bailey. He turned to the cute girl. She looked familiar. Right, she'd come to the temple three thousand, one hundred and thirty-seven days ago, after he and Jie had rescued her from the Trench... Feng Mi was her name, and he'd taught her the *Ghost Echo* technique. "What happened?"

"Lord Tong knew we were coming. Clan traitors helped ambush us in the first gatehouse, but I escaped."

"I don't think they're traitors. No, they're a new clan. Now what about Jie?"

Feng Mi shook her head. "They attacked her first, and she never even moved. From where I hid, I saw them take her, unconscious, into the main keep."

From where he'd watched on the bluff, he knew there had been at least seven more soldiers, plus the eight porters with Jie. "What about the others?"

"The imperial guards couldn't fight in the dark. Lord Peng surrendered and was escorted to the inner bailey. His aide escaped. He told me to find the princess, but I haven't seen him since."

"Which way…wait, the princess?"

Feng Mi shrugged. "I suppose he meant Jie. As for the guards, I overheard Lord Tong's men saying they were taken into the caves below."

Tian tapped his chin. "Where is the entrance to the caves?"

She pointed to the sluice gutters on the roofs. "I think they feed into the underground cisterns, and there might be an access point from this well." She leaned over and called into the hole.

Indeed, the echo sounded like there might be a side passage at the bottom. Still, "They took the guards in through the well?"

She shook her head. "There's an entrance near the second gatehouse, but it is guarded."

"The prisoners need water, too." He grinned.

"They were looking for me." Her shoulders slumped.

He patted her on the back. "You escaped. You gathered information. Now there are two of us. Come, let's find the—"

A horn sounded in a sequence of blares, two long, one short.

Tian tracked it to its source. The main keep. He looked to Feng Mi. "What was that?"

She frowned. "I haven't learned their signals yet."

A cannon boomed from the front walls. More blasts followed, eight in total. Then musket fire crackled. Muted yells and screams carried from Wailian Town.

He met her eyes. "Lord Tong has started the attack. We need to hurry, or the entire imperial procession will be destroyed."

Together, they jogged toward the outer bailey. At the rear gatehouse, she pointed to another stone-lined hole, this one wide enough for eight men to enter abreast. The two guards with swords and spears stepped aside to allow them to enter. After sixteen steps, the rough-hewn passage descended at a sixteen-and-a-quarter-degree incline, with columns supporting the cave every fifteen feet. The walls rocked with each cannon volley. Hopefully, the tunnels wouldn't cave in, at least not until they got out.

A hundred and forty-two paces in, they came to a metal door with a guard outside. He held a spear in one hand, while a broadsword and dagger hung on either side of his waist. In the narrow tunnel, it would be easy to get inside the arc of the spear. Still, there might be an easier way.

Rehearsing the line in his head, Tian pressed a fist into his palm. "Lord's orders. We are bringing water to the prisoners now. Before the fighting gets too intense."

The guard unlocked the door. It groaned open as he pushed it.

"Come on. Make sure the prisoners don't attack." Tian drew his sword and gestured for the guard to enter with him.

Inside, several expectant faces looked up, including a familiar imperial guard: Chen Xin, the one who'd played a minor role in Tian's banishment. Who knew if he'd recognize Tian eight years later?

No time to consider such a trivial matter. Yanking the enemy soldier's helmet off, Tian smashed the sword pommel into the back of his head. When he collapsed to the floor, Tian took his own helmet off. "Lord Tong has our troops surrounded. We need to neutralize the cannons. And open the gates." Not like five guards, one barely-conscious foreigner, eight porters, and twenty-seven boys, all unarmed, stood a chance.

Chen Xin raised a hand. "Our duty is to the princess."

Tian gawked at him. Surely, he knew Jie'd been a decoy.

"The real princess," Chen Xin hissed. "She's here. Not like you care about her."

Turtle's egg! Tian glared at him. Still, Princess Kaiya was *here*. His childhood friend, the girl who promised to marry him. His shoulders tensed. "You will never make it to the main keep."

"At least we can try," another of the guards said.

Tian pointed at Feng Mi. "She is the most equipped to try."

A particularly testy guard with flat knuckles growled. "Give me your sword."

Leave it to an imperial guard to think he was a better swordsman. It wasn't a fight worth contesting. Tian passed it over and pointed to the soldier he'd knocked out. "There's another sword, spear, and dagger—"

Two of the guards, one with a triangular head and the other with a scar on his chin, wrestled over the sword. Chen Xin glared at them, then let out an exasperated sigh and turned back to Tian.

"—plus two guards at the entrance to the tunnel. Feng Mi and I will take care of them and bring their weapons."

Chen Xin favored him with a tight expression. "You have three minutes. If we don't hear from you, we'll do it our way."

Such a desire to get themselves killed. Tian rolled his eyes. Beckoning Feng Mi, he said, "Approach in silence. I'll take the one on the right, you, the left. You have weapons?"

She nodded. Given her size, she'd have to use lethal force to neutralize her target. Who knew if her target had a family who would miss him?

Cannon bursts, musket shots, and repeater clicks volleyed in succession, all growing louder the closer they came to the mouth of the tunnel. Behind the two guards, he motioned for her to stop. Beyond them, soldiers ran into the gatehouse, carrying crossbow bolt bundles and rolling kegs of firepowder. None looked in their direction. Just before the next cannon volley, he jabbed a finger forward. He leaped behind his man, yanked off his helmet, and hook-punched him in the temple. For good measure, he continued with an elbow to the other side of the head. His victim collapsed, just as Feng Mi's did, blood spurting from his neck.

Taking ahold of both men's arms, Tian dragged them back into tunnel. Unsurprisingly, Chen Xin and the imperial guards were approaching the entrance.

Tian raked a gaze over them. "I told you to wait."

"I gave you three minutes." Chen Xin bent over and retrieved one of the swords.

Tian ground his teeth. "Most of Lord Tong's men are on the walls. Repeaters and muskets. Get in close. Their weapons lose their advantage."

Flat Knuckles grunted. "We are going to rescue the princess."

Tian's own knuckles must be white. He loosened a fist to point at the outer walls. "Loyal men are dying."

"You are right, but our first duty is to the princess." The youngest-looking guard pressed a fist into his hand.

Curse their sense of duty. Reversing the roles Tian had planned meant he'd storm the walls and fail; while the imperial guards would attack the main keep, and likely not make it past the gatehouse. There were two wild cards. "Feng Mi, go with the imperial guards. Find Jie— Wait." The only way he stood a chance of surviving the wall alone was to become a remorseless killer with singular focus and no fear. In short, "*The Tiger's Eye*. Use it on me."

Eyes shifting from the already-running imperial guards back to him, Feng Mi's face blanched. "I...I am not good at it."

"You have to try." He stared at her hands.

With a sigh, her scowl hardened. She arranged her fingers in a web and then twisted them into a loop and hook. "Your mission is to take the wall."

Tian waited for a second. The technique's effect did not wash over him. Still, Feng Mi didn't know that. He flashed a hand signal, which she'd hopefully mistake for success.

With a smile, Feng Mi spun and took off after the imperial guards.

He turned and beckoned the twenty-three able-bodied young imperial soldiers, with two spears and three daggers among them. Wait. "Where is Lord Peng's aide?"

One of the boys thumbed back the way they'd come. "He couldn't move. He's with our own wounded."

Tian scanned the yard, where the imperial guards decimated the enemy soldiers carrying supplies. He pointed. "Scavenge a weapon. Follow me into the gatehouse. Once you are all inside, close the door. Don't let Lord Tong's men through. Now go."

He raced toward the gatehouse. The armed boys followed close behind. As long as they stayed in the gatehouse, they could cut off one of the supply lines and keep themselves relatively safe.

At the entrance, three men raced out. Stepping inside the arc of the first's swing, Tian seized his attacker's arm and twisted him into the chop of the second. Snatching the first's sword, he ducked under the hack of the third while slashing through his knee tendons. As he rose, he stabbed into the face of the second. He swept up a second sword and charged into the gatehouse.

Sunlight from the doors on the second level silhouetted soldiers now coming down stone steps. Tian engaged; bobbing, cutting, and sidestepping as he worked his way up. One, four, six enemies lay dead or incapacitated by the time he reached the second level. He yelled to the boys, "Hold the gatehouse."

On the top of the walls, he scanned the outer bailey. At the center, stone-filled glass jars surrounded three kegs, one open, exposing a black powder. A firepowder trap. It would rain glass shards and stones onto an invader as they tried to file through the second gatehouse bottleneck. Somewhere, there was a way to ignite the open barrel.

He looked up to the outer wall, about three hundred feet long, from where the castle defenders coordinated the deadly barrage on the imperial army. He poked his head back into the gatehouse, to find four of the boys right there. "Stay here. Don't come out. You'll get yourselves killed. And open the inside gate… Wait." He pulled the closest one out and pointed at the firepowder trap. "Roll the barrels to the inside gate of the first gatehouse. Put those glass jars between the barrels and the gate. Then find a way to light it. From a distance."

The boy ogled him. "But…"

"Just do it. For your comrades stuck outside the castle." Without waiting for an answer, Tian sprinted around the inner walls to the outer parapet. If he had been tired earlier, he was now functioning on nervous energy alone.

He emerged at the rear of the lines and attacked with broadswords in either hand. The first nine men with muskets and crossbows never had a chance; they either fell fumbling with their swords, or without knowing what hit them. Others took close shots at him, near enough for him to knock their muskets or crossbows off-line so the projectiles would hit their own men. Still, it was a sea of enemies. His two swords meant nothing, and his second wind began to wane.

He dared a glance over the outer walls. Imperial soldiers crowded the bridge below, caught between the defenders on the battlements and the ranks of enemies in the town, closing in around them. It was hopeless.

Then several of the boys joined in, following the path he'd blazed, their own swords and spears flashing. A cannon fired, and it was all he could do to get out of its way as it recoiled back on its two wheels. A musket barrel swept toward his head and he ducked, nearly ramming into the soldier cleaning the cannon muzzle, but coming to a pause with a crossbow in his face. He dropped to the floor just as the string twanged, and hacked at the wielder's legs. The musketman behind him grunted.

When he popped back up, they were loading the cannon. The gunner held a torch, ready to light the fuse once his crew of two pushed the artillery into position. Thwarting the cannon team meant protecting a dozen imperial soldiers in the town. Tian slashed at the pair, dropping them. Spinning out of the way of a barrage of bolts, he finished his twist beside the gunner. They stared at each other for a split second before Tian cut through him with both blades.

The cannon... Tian dropped his left sword and caught the torch as it slipped from the gunner's hand. He beckoned the boys. "Help me turn it!"

The gun balanced over the wheels, making it easy to rotate. Two of the boys pushed the barrel while Tian shoved the breech in the opposite direction. It now pointed along the battlements. Enemy soldiers screamed, gesticulated, and gawked.

"Clear!" Tian swept his sword back and forth, gesturing the boys to the side. He lit the fuse right near the barrel.

The muzzle flashed, sending a ball into the crowd. The cannon recoiled, grazing Tian and knocking him down. His head slammed into the parapet. The world spun. A dozen men charged into him—or was it just one?

An explosion below rocked the front walls, sending his attacker—only one—lurching into him.

Jie's ears twitched as the walls of Lord Tong's playroom shook with each cannon volley. Between the booms and the staccato of musket fire, it sounded like there were eight cannons and over a hundred muskets. More importantly, she was underground, albeit close to the surface.

There was nothing saving the imperial army from total annihilation, unless she could find a way out. She fiddled with her bindings again. Getting out of the rope would be easy, except—

"Stay still," the Bovyan said.

Except him. He'd clung to the shadows, and besides the rope dart, there was no telling what other weapons and tools he had at his disposal on top of his Black Fist skills.

Maybe the cursed Bovyan race's lustful streak could be used against him. Conjuring her most alluring pout, she twisted to the source of his voice; or maybe not, if he'd used a *Ghost Echo* to throw it. With little slack to work with in the rope, she widened her stance, arched her back, and exposed her rear.

He gulped, revealing his position to be just where she'd thought. If he got close enough…

A knife rasped out of its scabbard and he stepped into view. "I warned Lord Tong you were too dangerous to leave alive."

CHAPTER 42
Songs of Despair

Hands still bound above her, and with only her toes on the floor of Lord Tong's playroom, Jie had only seconds before the Bovyan gutted her.

Grabbing the rope, she sprung up into an inverted position and pulled herself hand over hand to the rafter. She hung there, upside down like a bat.

"Fool, you're still in my reach." He leaped after her, slashing toward her neck.

She flipped back down and pulled the rope into the path of his cut. His dagger shredded through the fibers, and she landed in a squat, one hand on the floor.

His snarl resembled the Black Lotus Temple dogs when they'd cornered a fox by the well. Get in his head and he'd make a mistake. She flashed him her most irrepressible smile and shrugged.

He growled and stabbed again, but she spun out of the way and snatched up the flaying blade from the table. With back and forth thrusts, she cut though the last of the bindings. Warmth rushed into her hands, sending tingles down her fingers.

She stuck her tongue out at him. "Can you defeat a naked girl with a shorter weapon?" Probably so, but she was probably twice his age and four times as experienced. "Though maybe your weapon isn't so long."

Dropping into an offensive stance, he twirled the dagger into an underhand grip. One on one, in these circumstances, she didn't stand a chance in a fair fight.

Which was why she wouldn't fight fair. With a *Mockingbird's Deception* to imitate Lord Tong, she used a *Ghost Echo* to throw her voice to the room's entrance behind her. "Bovyan! Look out behind you!"

He spun.

She darted in and slashed the tendons of his dagger hand. His fingers slackened and the weapon slipped from his grasp. She caught it in her other hand. As he gawped at his useless limb, she plunged the dagger into his gut and raked it through his intestines. With the other hand, she drove the flaying blade up under his ribcage.

Blood spurted from his liver. Gasping, crumpling to the floor, he tried to keep his insides from spilling out. He bowed his head. "It is my honor to be defeated by a better foe."

Enemy or not, he didn't deserve to suffer. Tian had always said as much. Darting in, she slashed his carotids with the flaying blade. Then she spun and ran. Behind her, his body thudded to the floor and his wheezes stopped.

The corridors appeared otherwise abandoned, though perishable food supplies lay in crates. She listened for the cannons, felt for breezes on her bare skin. The floors felt rough and cold beneath her feet. Then, something piquant caught her nose. Firepowder. Sniffing, she followed the scent through a few twists and turns. At last, she came to a room with dozens and dozens of barrels.

To think this escapade had started with Tian's suspicions. Here was the proof. Proof she was about to destroy, so as to turn the tide of what had to be a hopeless battle.

Who knew how much damage a firepowder explosion could do underground? Maybe Tian. By now, he probably would've calculated the volume of the cave and tunnel space, counted the kegs and estimated their combined blast pressure.

Definitely not her skillset. She cracked a few of them open with punches and kicks. With several back-and-forth rocks, she managed to heave one onto its side. Luckily, it didn't ignite and blow her to tiny bits.

Following the breeze and sniffing for the fresh air, she rolled it down the corridor. The farther away she got from the arsenal and the closer to an exit, the better chance she'd have of surviving her plan.

Then, the last of the barrel's firepowder spilled out. Kneeling, she struck her blade against the stone floor in a shower of sparks.

The cannons boomed and musket fire crackled in the distance as Kaiya pressed her palms to the floor and tried to push herself up. With supreme effort, she brought a hip under herself. Trying to channel magic into her voice had left her limbs languid, her core as flaccid as egg custard, and her head muddled like heavy fog.

And she'd failed.

Now, loyal men died at the castle gates because of her vanity, her belief that she could sing Lord Tong into submission. Instead, he devoured her with his eyes, his pig face contorted into a feral expression reminiscent of a wild boar about to feast on truffles.

His cushion hissed as he rose from the gaudy chair and set the Dragon Scale Lute onto the seat. He knelt down beside her. "What's wrong, my slave? No magic on your lips?"

She gawked at him. How did he know?

He placed two fingers under her chin and lifted it. "Of course Little Li and my spy both told me about your efforts."

Spy...no wonder he knew about the music. About the trap.

"I am just glad you didn't give yourself to that foreigner. I will be your first. Your only." He withdrew his hand. "Now, kneel before me. Show me you have at least a remote semblance of grace."

No. No matter her shortcomings, she still had her dignity. She glared up at him.

He clucked his tongue. "My, my, you do have some spirit, after all. I will have to break you of that. Now kneel, and maybe, just maybe if you do so fast enough, I'll spare the foreigner."

Kaiya's chest scrunched. She brought her knees up under her.

"Avert your gaze. You will not make eye contact with your master."

All the better to hide the tear forming in her eye.

"Now, kowtow before me."

She shook her head. An imperial princess could only show such complete submission to the *Tianzi* himself.

"Hurry, and I will call off the attack. Think of the lives you will save."

What choice was there? He held all the leverage. She pressed her forehead to the floor, completely defeated by this vile traitor. To think he'd use marriage to establish a legitimate claim to the Jade Throne. Tears trickled down her cheeks and plopped onto the floor.

He snapped his fingers and one of his men shuffled over, then waddled back. Kneeling over, the closeness of his large body muffled the sounds around him. His breath tickled her ear. "I am your master now." Something cold and smooth wrapped around her neck. It tugged and twisted at her nape.

A collar?

"You belong to me." He stood and laughed; a taunting chortle, reducing her to something small and insignificant. How mortifying.

But maybe there was a chance. Head still to the ground, Kaiya eased open the fingers of her tightly balled fist, forced her tired legs to relax. Every nerve fiber tingled. Ready to spring.

"Now," he said. "Your decoy is an exotic little treat. A true beauty compared to you. You will watch me do to her what I will do to you. Come."

His feet treaded past her.

He was making it easy! She leaped forward towards his chair.

"Foolish girl," he said. The collar around her neck wrenched her to a stop. He gave it a tug and she stumbled backward onto the floor. "Apparently you aren't so compliant after all. Captain Zhu, go to the dungeons and cut out the foreigner's right eye."

No! What had she done? Tearing at the collar, she scuttled back from him, toward the Lute. The soldier marched toward the doors.

An explosion rumbled from somewhere not far in the distance, rattling the walls.

Lord Tong yanked the leash again, forcing her to her feet and nearly twisting her fingers. With another jerk, she staggered toward him.

A second blast swelled out from near the front of the main keep, underground. The floors quavered and rocked. Lord Tong slipped, and she bowled into him.

494

They tumbled to the floor, with her landing on top of him. Rafters above cracked and splintered.

Ears ringing, she set a hand down to the floor to push herself back up, but found his dagger instead. Pulling it from its sheath, she cut the hand that held the leash.

He grunted and let go, and she snatched up the frayed end and backed up. The soldiers closed in around her. She spun and ran the last four steps to the chair. Her hands wrapped around the Dragon Scale Lute, which, like before, seemed to throb with heat. She placed her fingers over its strings. Perhaps she could coax the last of its energy out.

Lord Tong lumbered to his feet. "Go ahead. It is a useless piece of junk. I regret wasting the resources to bring it here. If you even try it, I'll have your foreigner tortured before your eyes."

Her hand froze. What if it didn't work? Hardeep would suffer even more.

No, Lord Tong couldn't be trusted to keep his word. Chamberlain Li huddled in the corner, a look of horror on his face as he stared at the instrument.

She strummed out a few notes. Just as when Lord Tong had plucked it earlier, only a barely audible sound came out.

He shrugged. "I told you so."

In the corner, Li's posture relaxed as he blew out a breath.

"Now," Lord Tong said, "I will have to deliver on my promise. Guards, go stop Captain Zhu, so my bitch can watch her lover lose an eye. Then his fingers, one by one. Then his skin. I'll have the tanners turn his brown flesh into a suit of armor for her."

Her stomach roiled. Her failure was complete, and Hardeep would die an agonizing death because of it. To think she'd resented her fate as a political tool; now she was a rebel's pet, his means for gaining power. This was the most dismal moment of her life.

Her eyes strayed to the dagger, blurry through her tears, which she'd left in the chair. One last choice. Die here, and Lord Tong would have no reason to harm Hardeep. He'd lose his tool for gaining the throne. All it would take is a stab to the—

Let your heart impel your voice. The words of the book sounded suspiciously like Hardeep's voice in her head.

Of course, Lord Tong had plucked the string while gloating. When she had used the Dragon Scale Lute before, it had been under times of duress or fear. Guilt-ridden for strong-arming Chamberlain Li. Scared of assassins. Worried about trespassing in the Temple of Heaven.

And now, resolved to end her life. His attention on the knife, Lord Tong took a step toward her.

She thrummed out a chord. The bass strings keened like a beast led to slaughter. The treble notes wailed like a mother mourning her dead baby.

Lord Tong's next step faltered. The fingers of his hand, outreached to do something horrible to her, slackened. Then, his rounded eyes squinted. Maybe it wouldn't work. He didn't care for music, beyond its potential power.

Unlike her, who reveled in music and had received a lesson from the mysterious Lord Xu. *It is not the strength of the pluck that matters, but the intensity of your emotion,* the elf had said. *Only the power of your intent can compel the sound beyond its physical limitations.*

Gripping the floor with her toes, straightening her spine, Kaiya grasped her sense of hopelessness and despair and plucked out the few bars Hardeep had taught her. Beneath her fingers, the Lute emitted a chorus of screams, like horrified children fleeing Avarax's fiery breath.

Lord Tong stilled, his lips quivering. His breath rasped through his thick nose. Li cowered behind him, but his expression also betrayed an emotion she recognized too well in herself: disappointment in one's self.

Her next chords moaned like a man trapped beneath a collapsed building as Avarax descended. Stuck, unable to flee. Only able to watch.

Covering his ears, Lord Tong stumbled. His quavering men backed away. Then, they clawed at one another to reach the entrance first. Li disappeared with them.

She continued the song, with the change in pitch now moaning like souls rising from their graves on Ghost Day.

The power of the world coalesced through her, and again, her belly felt like hundreds of thousands of worms writhing over each other. Her energy flagged. The room spun around her, fading at the edges and closing into blackness.

CHAPTER 43
Sunset Over Wailian

Face to the sky, Jie's chest heaved as she took in deep breaths. She'd barely cleared the tunnel before the underground stores of firepowder exploded. With the rumbling fires giving chase, her bare feet scraping on the rough ground, a leap and forward roll saved her from the column of fire that belched from the hole. A few other bursts of flame spat out from other tunnel openings. Anyone in the caves would be incinerated.

Then, the eerie music had radiated from the main keep, like the collective wails of prisoners led to execution. Jie's heart rattled in her chest, and every nerve fiber screamed for her to flee. It felt just like the horrendous song from the Temple of Heaven two nights before.

Cannons and muskets fell silent, and even the yells of bloodlust quieted. She sat up and scanned the outer walls. Many of Lord Tong's men lay cowering on the battlements, even after the desolate music came to an abrupt end.

The main keep creaked and groaned. Jie sat up and twisted to see. The inner bailey's western walls now lay in rubble. The same side of the keep gaped open, with flames licking the interior walls. Men ran out, yelling and screaming.

Her bare skin prickled in the cool breeze and she stood up.

"To me, soldiers of Cathay!" Lord Peng's voice cracked at first, and then settled into a tone of command. He marched out of the second gatehouse, broadsword pointed forward. How gallant he looked at the head of a small but growing band of imperial troops.

More yells drew her attention. Lord Tong, unmistakable with his pig nose, wandered out of the main keep. His pale face and distant stare might have belonged to a ghost. His shaking men groveled at his feet, but when he didn't respond, they pulled at his sleeves and begged him to take command.

At the inner bailey gatehouse, Salt-and-Pepper Chen Xin, Fox-Faced Zhao Yue, Lefty Li Wei, Boy-Faced Ma Jun, and Flat-Knuckle Xu Zhan were dispatching the handful of Tong's soldiers who kept a semblance of resistance. The imperial guards' fighting was deadly and efficient, beautiful to watch. Little Feng Mi slunk behind them, her hands trembling too much to be of use.

Out of disguise and with such distinct features, Jie's identity would be compromised. She hurried over to mingle with the people who already knew her. Feng Mi's eyes widened, and she bent over to retrieve a cloak from a fallen man. She draped it over Jie's shoulders.

"Thank you." Jie pulled the hood over her head.

Feng Mi pointed. "Look."

Lord Peng's gait grew more resolute with each stride, his commanding presence rallying his men. They charged toward Lord Tong's soldiers, who dropped to their knees and placed their hands on their heads. Lord Tong himself just stood, staring blankly past his captors.

Lord Peng pushed past friend and foe alike. He took Lord Tong's hair and yanked it back. "For betraying the *Tianzi*, your punishment is death." He raised his sword.

Jie surged toward them, nearly tripping on the long cloak. "Wait! We need to find out his co-conspirators."

Too late. Lord Peng's sword chopped into Tong's neck, sending blood spraying. The body slumped to the ground.

The last holdouts fighting the imperial guards lowered their weapons. The imperial guards did, too. Perhaps it was better this way, to end hostilities as quickly as possible.

Peng beckoned to one of the soldiers. "Remove Tong's head, mount it on a spear, and parade it before his men. That will ensure their quick surrender."

The man pressed a fist into a palm. "As you command, *Jue-ye*."

Lord Peng gestured toward other imperial soldiers. "Form up and disarm Lord Tong's men. Spare the rank and file, but his senior retainers must be immediately executed to discourage future treason. Do not allow them any last words."

Chen Xin marched over, his comrades behind him. He gestured toward the burning castle. "Lord Peng, please spare some men to help us search for the princess."

Jie followed Lord Peng's gaze to the fires. "So Princess Kaiya joined the procession after all?"

Feng-Mi nodded. Lord Tong had been telling the truth about Princess Kaiya, and now she was likely trapped inside.

Shaking his head, Lord Peng put a hand on Chen Xin's shoulder. "No one could survive that. I cannot spare men on a futile mission. I do not command you, but I highly suggest you do not throw your life away."

Jie looked back at the fortress. Flames blazed on the outer walls. It would soon become a conflagration. Lord Peng was right. She turned to Feng Mi. "Why didn't you sneak in earlier instead of slinking behind the imperial guards?"

The girl stared at the ground. "I wanted to, with Zheng Tian, but the imperial—"

What? Jie put both hands on Feng Mi's shoulders, not caring if the cloak blew open. "Tian is here?"

Feng Mi nodded and pointed toward the outer walls. "The imperial guards insisted on saving the princess and left Tian to attack the outer defenses."

If that fool got himself killed, trying to take the walls all by himself... Jie tightened the cloak around her and dashed toward the outer bailey.

Punctuated by sharp twangs and a loud crack, timbers splintered, and walls groaned in a song just as doleful as the one Kaiya had played on the Lute. Her body rocked to its rhythm.

No, someone was shaking her.

"Wake up!" The voice filled her.

Energy trickled into her limbs. Her eyes fluttered open. Blue irises encroached on her visual field, for the third time in as many days. Hardeep's soot-covered expression melted from concern to relief.

She bolted up into a sitting position. "Where are we?"

"Thank Surya." Hardeep smiled at her. His cape was gone, and his was armor singed. "We have to get out of here. The castle is burning."

No wonder it was so hot. With his help, she scrambled to her feet. "What about the Dragon Scale Lute?"

"Ruined." He pointed at the smashed resonator. The strings sprawled unwound in a tangled mess. Even the scale soundboard lay shattered from the center out, looking much like a spider web. "Ruined beyond repair."

She cast a last glance at the cinnabar-red scale, the instrument of a rebellion's undoing. Was a shard missing? "We should take what's left of the scale."

"No." He shook his head. "Leave it buried beneath the rubble. Now come."

She searched his eyes. Perhaps he was right. Better to leave it here, forgotten, lest it fall into the hands of someone with less-than-noble motives. She took the hand he extended.

Limping along, he guided her through the smoke-filled halls. The soot in her lungs forced out ragged coughs. Flames leaped from side passages. Burning beams crashed in their path. Each time, Hardeep with his Paladin skills pulled her out of harm's way. Still, her energy wavered.

"Up ahead!" He pointed to where the castle's entire outer wall had collapsed.

Behind them, more columns and beams cracked and fell. They didn't have much time.

Eyes dry and aching, throat singed, her energy guttered. She could never pick her way through this rubble. Her vision faded and her wobbling knees gave out. She would just hold him back. "Go…on. Save yourself."

He swept her up into his arms and staggered through the debris.

Pain shot through Tian's ribs as he pushed an unconscious man off of him. Limbs protesting, he sat up and looked.

Lord Tong's soldiers all knelt with hands on their heads. Seventeen of the boys under his charge stood among them, weapons at the ready. A path of bodies started from the intersecting walls of the outer bailey and ended at him. All these men whose lives he had taken, just because of some lord's greed and ambition. Imperial soldiers, some just boys, dead as well.

And for what? The realm was weaker for all the precious lives wasted.

"Tian!" Jie's voice rang from somewhere on the walls.

He turned to see the half-elf, clasping a cloak—and apparently, all she wore was a cloak—running among the bodies and kneeling men. Little Feng Mi trailed behind her.

Ignoring the searing pain in his ribs, Tian groaned to his feet.

Jie shot into him, wrapping her arms around him, and igniting a new surge of agony through him. "You fool. What did you think you were doing, attacking a wall by yourself?"

"I had help." Grimacing, he unwound her arms. He'd have to check to see if she'd picked his pockets later. "Uh. The boys are staring. You ought to find some clothes."

She stepped back and pouted. Behind her, Feng Mi giggled.

A loud crash drew his attention to the main keep. Flames wrapped around it like a torch head, consuming it. If anyone were still in there, they'd be ashes by evening.

He sucked in a sharp breath. The princess had been taken there. He looked at Feng Mi. "Did you find Princess Kaiya?"

Casting her gaze down, she shook her head in slow arcs.

Oh no. His first love. Once a dear friend, though they hadn't communicated in three thousand, one hundred and forty-seven days. A pit sank in his gut and his shoulders slumped.

Jie squeezed his hand.

"Look!" One of the boys pointed toward the main keep.

Tian spun.

A man emerged from the west side of the main keep, carrying…

Tian squinted. In the man's arms, he cradled a girl in a tattered dress.

Jie blew out a sigh. "Thank the Heavens. The princess. She is moving."

If only his vision were as sharp as a half-elf's! His hand tightened around Jie's. "Are you sure?"

She nodded. "No mistaking that acne-riddled face."

The man set the princess down. Her gangly legs wobbled. Had she always been so skinny? Tian had always remembered her as being graceful and beautiful as the weeping *danhua* tree in Sun-Moon Castle. He started toward the closest steps down.

Jie tugged. "No, you must not compromise your identity."

Tian's chest squeezed. Jie was right. After all this time, Princess Kaiya was a throwing star's heave away and she might never know he was there. Just like Jie and Feng Mi, his name would never appear in the histories of the Battle of Wailian Castle. Not that it mattered.

"Come," he said. "Let's go home."

CHAPTER 44
Enemies Far and Near

Peng Kai-Long stood atop the tallest watchtower, watching the sun set over the mineral-rich hills between Walian County and the Nothori Kingdom of Rotuvi. The foreigners had withdrawn their troops from the border, their deal with Lord Tong now moot.

Still, Cathay was weak. No lord would have dared rebel against the throne just a decade ago. Foreign nations wouldn't have presumed to meddle in Cathay's affairs. The *Tianzi*, so shrewd and decisive in his earlier years, had grown soft. The two princes would never command respect. It was up to Kai-Long to lead Cathay back to greatness.

And Heaven must have smiled upon him for everything to work out the way it had. That, and Kai-Long's own ability to gauge the shift in winds. He looked down at the Cathayi chessboard, the pieces positioned where he'd last left off with his mysterious opponent. His new advisor, no less, who was late.

"Right cannon moves right three," a male voice came from the ceiling.

Kai-Long's soul must have jumped out of his body. He searched for the source.

The Water Snake clansman kicking his legs from the rafters appeared to be of middle age, his eyes so sunken his head might be mistaken for a skull. "Greetings, Lord Peng."

Kai-Long studied the spy. "We meet at last."

The man shook his head. When he spoke, it sounded like the voice of a particular serving girl in Sun-Moon Castle. "We've met. The night Miss Yi helped you smuggle Princess Kaiya out of the protection of the palace. That was me. I drugged her and took her place."

Kai-Long nodded in slow bobs. Yi was an expert liar, which is why he'd chosen her. It turned out, it hadn't been her at all. Still... "You made a mistake, leaving the illusion bauble where it could be found."

"Who said it was a mistake?" The clansman's shrugged and turned to the chess board. "This is the first time I have actually seen the board."

Boastful snake. Kai-Long was just two moves from finally winning. He shifted the piece over to where the man indicated, and then moved his own elephant up and over. "It has been interesting playing this game by messenger." Which had also been their means of coordinating through coded letters.

The man nodded. "Your strategy has been unpredictable."

"The Founder wrote that a good leader must ride in the winds like a kite."

The man grinned, his gaunt face now looking like the symbol of the Pirate Queen. "As did Lord Tong.

Still, he failed. Games, unlike life, are played with rules."

Kai-Long scoffed. "Real life is about preparation." He should know. He kept every heir to the Dragon Throne ahead of him sterile through a simple toxin. With spies in the right place, he'd known about Lord Tong's plan for years, and used his company, Victorious Trading, to stockpile firepowder for when Tong made his move.

The man yawned. "And you certainly prepared. Would you have really helped Lord Tong?"

Kai-Long looked around, making sure no one was within earshot. "He kept up his end of the bargain by having my father and brother killed. Had the *Tianzi* sent the bulk of his armies here, as we had hoped, then I would have joined Lord Liang and led my own armies to attack the imperial rear, trapping them between the Great Wall and here. Just as I promised." Actually, he had planned to occupy the capital with the help of Lord Tong's allies in the South, but some things were better left secret, at least until this advisor earned unquestionable trust.

"And yet, you betrayed Tong. Why?"

"Once his allies abandoned the attack on Prince Kai-Wu's wedding, he had already lost." Fool that he was for keeping the princess' decoy alive, even after Kai-Long's warning. "He would have revealed all the conspirators."

The man shook his head. "No, earlier. Why push for marriage to Princess Kaiya instead of the original plan for encouraging a siege of Wailian Castle?"

Because it was a last-ditch effort to get her killed. "I didn't expect her to suggest marriage, for the *Tianzi* to approve it, or for her to show her worth." Though really, she was like a rat, surviving where she shouldn't have. First, on the night he'd smuggled her out of the castle into an ambush, where it could have been pinned on the Madurans targeting Prince Hardeep; and then when he told Tong to wipe out the supply brigade that he'd lured her into joining.

"I see. Well, as promised, the Water Snake Clan is at your service, though we must lay low until the Black Lotus clan forgets about us."

Kai-Long grinned. He was one of the privileged few to know that Black Fists were more than just imaginary child snatchers. Furthermore, beside the *Tianzi* himself, he was now the only lord to have some under his employ. "We will maintain contact through our normal channels."

"As you command, *Jue-ye*."

"What shall I call you?"

"My former comrades in the Black Lotus knew me as the Surgeon." The man melted into the shadows, but then his voice came from the general on the chessboard. "Chariot moves left three. Checkmate."

511

Flanked by an aide, Haros Bovyanthas marched toward his office in the Assembly Hall of Telesite to wait for the election's results. Because of his birth to a virgin, his promotion to First Consul of the Teleri Empire was a foregone conclusion. After all, the Keepers of the Shrine of Geros all believed the prophecies proclaiming that he would be the one to end the first of the three Bovyan curses.

He chuckled to himself. The prophecies hadn't kept his rivals in the Directori from assigning him to the inconsequential duty of administering relations with the kingdoms of the northwest. Until now, it didn't matter. Let them bumble over the futile invasion of Eldaeri lands. Brute force alone would not prevail, and that was all the Bovyans knew.

Except him. As a youth, he'd read the Cathayi Founder's work, *The Art of War*. Wang Xinchang was a warrior genius, even if his descendants were nothing more than petty merchant princes. Incorporating his strategies, Haros had used his position to cultivate relationships and turn his spheres of influence into profitable income streams and new tactical tools. How ironic that all of these would be turned against Cathay when the time was right.

Warriors all thumped their chests in salute as he passed. His steward opened his door and Haros walked in.

And gawked.

Sitting in *his* chair was the Altivorc King himself, with feet kicked up on *his* desk. Bedecked in a dapper uniform and crowned with a silver circlet, the King of the Orcs held a message addressed to Haros in his filthy paws.

"How did you get in here?" Haros jabbed a finger at the King.

The King lowered the missive and bared his fangs in a patronizing smile. "Now, now, Haros, there's no need to be rude."

Frowning, Haros turned back to the aide outside the door. "How did he get in here?"

The steward's mouth hung agape. So unsightly for a Bovyan. "I...I don't know. The door was closed from the time you visited the Shrine and the Conclave."

"I come, I go." Shrugging, the King flicked the paper over. "It looks like you have bigger problems than pest control, though."

Amazingly, the message flew in a straight line. Haros snatched it out of the air and skimmed it. He then looked back at the Altivorc King. "Everything proceeds as planned."

The Altivorc King lowered his feet and leaned forward on the table. "Lord Tong is dead. Without him, you can't influence Cathay."

Apparently, the thousand-year-old King wasn't as all-knowing as the legends proclaimed. Haros laughed. "Lord Tong would have never succeeded. My agreement with him was all a ploy to plant my operative in their country. Cathay will not be taken with the sword alone. It will take eight years to undermine them from within."

"How old are you now? Thirty?" The Altivorc King counted off on his fingers. "If the curse remains in place, you'll die in three years."

Haros crumpled up the message. "You were the one who identified my mother. You must know I will be the one to end the curse."

Boots clopped to a stop at the entrance. Haros turned to see the messenger, dressed in the robes of the Keepers of the Shrine of Geros.

He pounded a fist to his chest. "Your Eminence, congratulations. You have been elected First Consul."

Haros turned back to gloat. "You see—"

The Altivorc King was gone, the chair empty as if no one had been there.

With a snort, Haros turned back to the courier. "When is the Eye-plucking ceremony?"

"Tonight. Once you will receive the Eye of Solaris and Pin of Geros, you will formally take the name, Geros Bovyan, XLIII."

Haros dismissed the man with a wave of his hand, then covered his right eye. All the previous First Consuls claimed they could see through the Eye of Solaris. Then again, men were liars.

He lowered his hand. Losing an eye was worth the chance to become the greatest Bovyan since their progenitor, the mortal son of Solaris. He smoothed out the message and read it again.

Perhaps this Peng Kai-Long, who had captured the impregnable Wailian Castle, would prove to be a more worthy adversary than Cathay's emperor. Haros would have to tell his spy to keep close eye on this upstart lord.

In the meantime, while Haros plot to undermine Cathay simmered, it was time to turn his attention to the Eldaeri Kingdoms. His spy there had already gotten into Tarkothi Prince Aryn's good graces, and seeded discord between Tarkoth and Serikoth. Haros would succeed where his political adversaries had failed.

Humming *Whims of Fate* as he untangled the imperial stallion's mane, sixteen-year old Li Bin considered the strange twists and turns his life had made. Born to his town's most famous musician, who'd once entertained the *Tianzi*, he would've never expected to become Lord Tong's chamberlain and pillow boy. Now he'd managed to join the army, by mingling with the injured imperial troops in the aftermath of Wailian Castle. He'd since been reassigned as a groom in Sun-Moon Palace.

"*Dian-xia.*" The pretty face of Lady Lin Ziqiu peeked around the horse and flashed a radiant smile. "Oh, Li Bin, it's you."

Li Bin swallowed hard and looked down at his feet. A niece of the *Tianzi*, Lin Ziqiu was beautiful, even in riding clothes. Indeed, with the exception of Princess Kaiya, every imperial family member and close relative was good-looking.

He bowed and stammered, "My Lady."

"Have you seen Princess Kaiya? I am supposed to go riding with her." She extended a hand.

"No, my Lady." Li Bin shook his head. He proffered the reins.

"Thank you." Her hands felt surprisingly rough and calloused for a noblewoman's.

He hazarded a glance up to find her studying him. Lines creased her brow. He jerked his head down.

"If you see Princess Kaiya, please tell her I am at the cavalry field."

"Yes, my Lady," Li Bin lied. He was good at it.

Good enough to trick Lord Tong into believing he had the skill to play the Dragon Scale Lute—which was why he'd happily acquiesced when Princess Kaiya had demanded it that night. He might be a talented musician, but he was no Dragon Singer. He'd known when the elf had given up teaching him.

"You know, you have a beautiful voice." Ziqiu giggled. As she led the horse out, he held a low bow.

Then his gut clenched.

Princess Kaiya would arrive any moment to get her horse. If she were alone, he might be able to take vengeance. For her role in the death of Lord Tong. For realizing *his* dreams of reviving Dragon Songs.

But no, a complement of imperial guards always accompanied her. And, even without all the makeup Lord Tong had insisted he wear, she might recognize him through the dirt on his face.

It would be better to hide now, and bide his time for a better chance.

EPILOGUE
Diverging Paths

Jie found Tian in the corner of her eye as they walked along the docks of Jiangkou Harbor. Two weeks had passed since the Battle of Wailian Castle and the foiled attack on Prince Kai-Wu's wedding. Plots uncovered by Tian and her, respectively. While Lord Peng received the accolades for his improbable victory, in Black Lotus fashion, she and Tian headed to receive their rewards.

"Here's my steed." Jie jerked her head at the Tarkothi ship *Indomitable*, where sailors prepared for departure. It was far easier to watch them work than to make eye contact with him. Her heart might have been a rock in her chest, if a rock weighed more than a dwarven anvil.

Tian turned and looked up at the hulking black ship. "Make sure Prince Aryn keeps his hands off of you."

She grinned. "What if I want to put my hands on him?"

Tian's expression betrayed neither concern nor jealousy. "As long as it doesn't cloud your objectivity."

Was that it? Jie sucked on her bottom lip before letting it go with a pop.

Tian's face hardened. "I should be going with you."

While she might appreciate the sentiment, "As the Founder said, *Never send a man to do a woman's job*."

"Did he say that?" He cocked his head.

Jie giggled. "No, that's *my* proverb. Will you miss me?"

"I will always miss my little sister. Just be careful. You are going into a foreign land and you barely speak the language."

Jie's chest squeezed. Still the little sister. "I will have at least a month immersed with the Eldaeri sailors. I'm sure my Arkothi will be fine by the end." If *fine* meant laden with chauvinism and curse words.

His eyes and mouth made perfect circles. Perhaps he was thinking the same thing. The surprise melted and he started turning toward his own berth on the *Wild Orchid*.

She tugged at Tian's official robes to take out some of the wrinkles. "You need to make a good first impression, Junior Clerk Zheng. See you in a few years."

While she was off tracking the Water Snake Clan to its source in Arkothi lands, what kind of man would he grow into? And when they met again after those few years, her body still wouldn't have matured into a woman's.

Tian cast a surreptitious glance back at Jie as she headed up the dock to the *Indomitable*. She was just a girl, all alone with a bunch of sailors. Then, she'd go on a lonely, deep reconnaissance mission into Serikoth and the Teleri Empire itself.

Perhaps they were chasing their tails. In the end, Master Yan had only been able to uncover two *Yu-Ming* lords conspiring in the failed attack on Prince Kai-Wu's wedding, and none of the foreigners Jie suspected even attended: the altivorcs had wandered into restricted areas of the palace and been expelled the night before the wedding. No Golden Scorpion ever surfaced. With Lord Tong dead, they hadn't been able to confirm any of the alliances he'd established, either foreign or domestic.

The only reliable leads were the large boys of the Water Snake Clan, who Lord Tong had referred to as Bovyan. Never mind that the ruling race of the Teleri Empire were huge and fair-skinned. Still, the Teleri's vassals in Rotuvi had threatened the imperial army in the North, preventing General Lu from helping in the siege of Wailian Castle. It couldn't be just a coincidence.

Which was why Tian was now headed for a new position as a trade official in the Kingdom of Iksuvi. In reality, he would serve as head of information in the

Northori Northwest, as a reward for his uncovering of Lord Tong's plot.

Farther than ever from Princess Kaiya.

Kaiya listened to the songbirds warbling outside the Hall of Bountiful Harvests, her hands trembling. This was where her unlikely adventure had begun when she first greeted Prince Hardeep.

Here too, it would end. Father had allowed one last meeting with Prince Hardeep, a reward for her role in subduing the North and for his in saving her.

Servants opened the doors. Chen Xin and Ma Jun snapped into a salute.

Secretary Hong bowed and extended a hand inviting her to enter. "The *Tianzi* will allow you to meet Prince Hardeep alone."

Alone. She smoothed out her court gown. If only she had a mirror. She'd spent hours preening, in hopes of giving Prince Hardeep a perfect last memory of her. Taking a deep breath, she stepped over the high threshold.

Prince Hardeep pressed his palms together and bowed his head. Dressed in a ceremonial *kurta*, he looked so handsome. So perfect. It was hard to imagine that just two weeks before, as he carried her out of the burning castle, his face had been covered in soot. Even then, his hair never seemed out of place. He looked up and smiled at her.

Her heart fluttered. How could she have ever suspected he might be a Maduran Golden Scorpion, using foul magic to influence her? In retrospect, her own insecurities had planted seeds of doubts over his noble intentions, when all he'd done was encourage her to act on her morals.

"Princess Kaiya, thank you for seeing me off."

He made it sound so...trivial. A simple parting, after everything they'd been through. She bowed her head. "It is my honor to do so. I am sorry I could not do anything for your homeland. The treaty with Madura remains in place for one more year, and the remains of the Dragon Scale Lute are buried beneath Wailian Castle." Not that Father would allow her to go to Ankira, anyway.

He shook his head. "It doesn't matter. You have given me something more precious. Hope."

Tears threatened to ruin her make-up.

"Will you sing for me? As a memory of our meeting."

An audacious request under normal circumstances, but there was nothing normal about the two of them. He had guided her to the power of Dragon Songs, made her find her purpose beyond political marriage. She cast a glance out of the Hall, where her guards and Secretary Hong stood. Who cared what they thought? She owed Hardeep this courtesy. "I've put words to your lute song."

His eyebrow lifted and his lips quirked into a smile. She'd spent the last two weeks composing the lyrics. Toes gripping the floor, spine straight, she let her spirit guide her song about an uncertain girl who'd found purpose beyond the circumstances of her birth. Jubilation coursed through her, sending each nerve tingling. Even if he wouldn't understand the words, he would feel her intent.

"So much emotion," he intoned.

She drew inspiration from his voice, pouring her soul into words. With each note, her spirit floated higher until it reached a crescendo. His irises sparkled back at her. No matter what anyone else thought, she felt truly beautiful in his eyes. Finishing her song, she looked up at him through her lashes.

In three quick steps, he stood before her and clasped her hands. Warmth surged through her. He leaned in, breath hot on her neck.

"Thank you, Princess Kaiya. Your voice, just like the legendary Yanyan's, could enchant the dragon Avarax. I may return home empty-handed, but my heart is full." He withdrew, his lips tracing across her neck. Electricity coursed through her, every nerve on edge.

He turned toward the door.

No! He was leaving. It was too soon.

"Wait." She loosened several dwarf-forged platinum pins binding her voluminous hair, sending unruly locks tumbling down to her waist. Fiddling with an errant tendril, she proffered the jewels, each worth a soldier's annual pay. Hopefully, he wouldn't be insulted.

523

"Prince Hardeep, please accept these as my personal apology for not being able to help you."

He plucked the simplest hairpin, her favorite. The brush of his finger across her palm sent a jolt of excitement up her spine. He pressed the jewel to his breast. "I will keep this one as a bittersweet souvenir of you and your voice."

Kaiya started to speak, but no words came out.

Lips trembling upward, Hardeep unpinned from his shirt a shard of cinnabar, shaped into the likeness of Ankira's nine-pointed lotus. He pressed the trinket in her palm and closed her hand around it. His large, strong hands wrapped around hers. "Please accept this as a symbol of our meeting. When you gaze at it, remember that no matter how far away I am, I will be thinking of you."

Warm like his smile, the lotus jewel buzzed, sending pleasant pulsations through her.

He turned and left. When he reached the door, he bent his head with a sidelong glance at her. "Once you have grown in your music, I am sure you will come to me." Without waiting for a response, he marched out of the hall.

Was it her pulse or the lotus jewel vibrating so rapidly? Kaiya reached back toward a column to steady herself. Yes, when she was ready, she would go to him.

Flip the page for a short chapter that bridges Book 1 and 2.

PRELUDE TO
Orchestra of Treacheries

Holding the music in her head, Kaiya arched back under the sweep of her *jian* straightsword and lifted her leg into a kick with the point of her toe. The blade passed within a hairbreadth of her cheek as she transitioned the movement into a precise stab. She held the nearly inverted pose, grateful for not nicking her now-pretty face with the complicated technique. Until today, she'd held back on the *Dance of Swords* for fear of marring her now smooth skin with a self-inflicted scar.

It'd taken a year of drinking bitter herbal medicines to finally quell her rebellious complexion. Vanquishing thoughts of Prince Hardeep had proved more difficult. Since then, the *Tianzi* had arranged a dozen introductions to self-absorbed sons of first rank *Tai-Ming* and second rank *Yu-Ming* lords.

None could compare to Prince Hardeep's charm. Those three days, a year past, still twisted her stomach into cartwheels when she thought about them.

Which was too often.

Kaiya tried to cope with unfulfilled love by immersing herself in dance and music. At times, it worked. At other times, she would stare at his lotus jewel for hours on end. After all, why did she practice, except for the secret hope of Hardeep returning?

Applause from the doors interrupted her concentration. With a *jian* in either hand, Kaiya pirouetted into a cross-legged low stance to avoid tumbling into an embarrassing heap. Her gaze fell on her sisters-in-law Xiulan and Yanli, whose floral outer gowns trailed across the gleaming wood of the training-hall floors. Several handmaidens followed them.

Crown Princess Xiulan's dark eyes danced with mirth, reminiscent of the whimsical gardenia motif of her pink outer gown. "Kaiya, you're hiding here to avoid a second meeting with Lord Chen."

Kaiya shuddered at the thought of the *Yu-Ming* heir from Jiangzhou Province, the latest in a long line of rejected suitors. "Young Lord Chen may be handsome, but he's as dumb as a rock. And he wouldn't stop looking at my chest." As if there was much to see.

Yanli sighed. The gold pine branch design of her green robes suited her usually subtle pragmatism. Today, her tone bordered on irritability. "Don't be so picky. Some counties of Jiangzhou grow restless, and your marriage to one of their *Yu-Ming* would go far in reasserting imperial authority there."

Kaiya twirled to her feet, flipping the pair of swords together. The lightweight *jian*, considered the marriage of elegance and practicality, at first seemed like the perfect metaphor for her purpose in this world. Yet even if she could choreograph the exact movements of the blades, her own life was more like a cherry blossom petal, carried on the whim of fickle political winds. "Is that why you married my brother? So your father could proclaim allegiance to mine?"

She held the swords out. The imperial guard Zhao Yue, up to now as motionless as a statue, strode forward. Bowing, he received them in two hands and shuffled backward to his unassuming place by the door.

Yanli opened her mouth, but Xiulan cast a furtive glance, silencing her. The Crown Princess smiled. "Oh, Kaiya... Yanli's situation was different. How could the *Tianzi* deny such a torrid mutual love?"

How could he deny *her* love for Hardeep? And *torrid*? Sappy would be a more accurate description of Kai-Wu and Yanli. At any other time of the month, Yanli would've waxed poetic about it.

Today, she pursed her lips. "It was just as much a reward for our province's longstanding loyalty." Her eyes bored into Kaiya's, pushing her point. "Yes, our love was enabled by the unprecedented leeway your father allows his children. But that indulgence has left you unmarried at seventeen! Please, stop being selfish and think about his poor health. It would ease his mind to know the imperial bloodline was secure."

Xiulan looked down at the ground.

Kaiya sighed. With the White Moon Renyue's passage toward new, her sisters-in-law's normally cheerful demeanors turned first to nervous anticipation

527

and then invariable melancholy. Xiulan had been married for three years, Yanli for one, and neither had conceived.

That left her, a girl with skinny hips and no husband, to conceive a son and ensure the continuation of Wang family rule.

Yanli's eyes narrowed as they followed Kaiya's hand straying to the lotus jewel inside her sash. "You're still pining over Prince Hardeep, aren't you?"

Kaiya's cheeks burned. Telling Yanli about the prince had been a mistake. "No," she lied. She was older and wiser now. Of course the foreign prince had tried to manipulate a naïve girl. Maybe even used his Paladin powers.

Oh, but his smooth voice, those blue eyes… She mentally chastised her younger self for venturing into the present.

Shaking her head with a knowing smile, Yanli took Kaiya's hand. "Kaiya, even if Ankira weren't occupied and its royal family scattered in exile, their prince would never be a match for you. Don't let an idealized memory set the standard for a suitor."

Kaiya nodded. It was true. He was a foreigner, after all. She would forget about him. This time, the thousandth time, it would work.

Xiulan took her other hand. "Yanli is right. Your brother and I were arranged to marry, and yet we fell deeply in love. It's not impossible."

Yanli gave her hand a gentle tug. "Come. Lord Chen is waiting."

"Like this?" Kaiya freed a hand and waved at her plain robe and unmade-up face. Her appearance was more suited for, well, someone practicing a dance.

Yanli's eyes sparkled mischievously. Her dear sister-in-law was still there, buried under the disappointment of another failed cycle. "It will send Lord Chen a message, won't it?"

Kaiya rolled her eyes. "I did say he was as dumb as a rock, right?"

They shared a giggle before straightening their postures into epitomes of imperial dignity. It had been so hard in the years preceding that fateful encounter with Hardeep, so easy just a year later.

With Xiulan in the lead and trailed by imperial guards and handmaidens, they glided through the alleys toward the Phoenix Garden. A year after Xiulan had shown Kaiya the pillow book, she still hadn't made use of it.

At the edge of the garden, they paused. In the pagoda where they'd dined the night before the fall of Wailian Castle, the handsome Young Lord Chen was talking to another man whose posture looked familiar. He made a gesture, and Young Lord Chen bowed…and left? Without so much as acknowledging he'd seen her.

Kaiya exchanged glances with Xiulan, whose brows furrowed. With Young Lord Chen's departure, there wasn't much point—

The other man turned around and met her gaze. Cousin Kai-Long! It had been almost a year since they'd last met. He'd returned to his home province of Nanling, and apparently had instituted land and trade reforms.

Kaiya nodded toward Xiulan and Yanli. "I am going to greet Lord Peng. Perhaps we can have tea later?"

"An hour, in the *Danhua* Garden." Xiulan smiled, and then she and Yanli, along with the bulk of the imperial guards and handmaidens, shuffled out of the garden in a flash of color.

Watching them leave, Kaiya glided over the arching footbridge to the pagoda. Chen Xin, Zhao Yue, and Han Meiling kept a respectful distance.

"*Dian-xia*." Kai-Long bowed his head, addressing her formally. Even though he was an elder cousin, her position as a princess from the direct ruling line ranked her above him.

Kaiya smiled at him. "Cousin, you do not need to stand on formality."

"As you command, Kaiya." He grinned back.

They'd repeated the same exchange, almost verbatim, for years now. She covered a laugh. "What brings you to the capital?"

"I am here brief to the *Tianzi* on my progress in governing Nanling Province. It has been wildly successful." Kai-Long's smile faded. "Unfortunately, I am also reporting on the latest incursions from Madura. Since our trade agreement expired, they have sent even more of their Golden Scorpions across the Great Wall to steal firepowder."

A note of sadness laced his voice. He still suspected the Golden Scorpions of assassinating his father, even if Lord Tong had taken credit for it. She placed a sympathetic hand on his arm.

He nodded at the gesture, smiling wryly. "Madura's greedy ambitions will turn our way before long. I am going to beseech the *Tianzi* to finance the Ankiran resistance, which has fallen into disarray since Prince Hardeep was gravely injured."

The prince! Blood rushed from her head and she stretched a hand out onto the balustrade to keep from falling. Hadn't she just banished the prince from her heart? Yet mention of his name alone nearly caused her to faint. "Will the prince survive?"

He nodded. "Yes, he escaped to Vyara City. He is under the care of the Ayuri Paladins."

Kaiya covered her mouth to bury her shocked exhalation. She quickly lifted her chin and composed her expression into one of distant concern.

Her cousin drew in close, reaching into the fold of his robe. He pressed something into her hand and whispered in the secret royal language, a tongue which none of her retinue would understand. "A message for you, from the prince. He recently initiated contact with me to ask for my province's aid."

She kept herself from looking at her trembling hand and fought the urge to unwrap the tightly folded parchment. Not in front of prying eyes. Did he remember her after all this time? If so, did he feel the way she hoped he did?

531

As he left the garden for his audience with the *Tianzi*, Peng Kai-Long kept his face composed to hide his delight. From watching Princess Kaiya's reactions to the simple mention of a name, he confirmed what he'd suspected from her rejection of so many eligible young lords: Prince Hardeep still held sway over her heart, even if they hadn't spoken or corresponded a year.

Before stepping into the castle, he stole one last glance over his shoulder to see the princess. So poised moments before, now reduced to a pathetic ball of female emotion. This was why women weren't fit to rule. Governed by their feelings, they lacked objectivity.

And were easily manipulated.

Walking through the castle halls, Kai-Long congratulated himself for his quick thinking. After his spies had told him of her second meeting with Young Lord Chen, he'd moved swiftly. He gave her the forged letter in hopes it would shatter any budding romance between her and the handsome young man. Her trembling hands told him it had worked.

With a scholar of Ayuri poetry and a master of written magic in his pay, Kai-Long could pass on as many letters as it would take to keep the princess yearning for a foreign prince—one who must've forgotten her after all this time.

Perhaps he might even offer to smuggle a message for her. It would help him control the princess further. Through her, perhaps even influence the *Tianzi* himself. More importantly, it would keep her unmarried.

Servant girls knelt and slid open doors. New ripples in his plan occurred to him. Sun-Moon Palace had many eyes and ears. If word leaked that the princess was corresponding with the exiled Prince of Ankira, the Madurans would have a motive to intervene. When the Madurans acted, they rarely did so with restraint. At least, that was what the Cathayi Court believed, thanks to the rumors he spread.

The nation's beloved princess, murdered by agents of the rogue Kingdom of Madura.

He liked the idea of it, even if making it happen would require careful planning. It would extinguish one source of potential heirs to the Dragon Throne, and stir up enough outrage for Cathay to take punitive action. He would just have to wait and see how well he could control her, and then decide whether she was worth more to him dead or alive.

Orchestra of Treacheries, Book 2 of the Dragon Songs Saga, available now.

If you wish to follow Jie's adventures in chronological order, **Masters of Deception** takes place between **Songs of Insurrection** and **Orchestra of Treacheries**.

Sign-up for my newsletter and receive a free copy of **Prelude to Insurrection**, a short story about Jie.

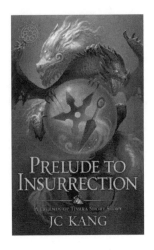

Celestial Bodies

White Moon: Known as Renyue in Cathay, and represents the God of the Seas. Its orbital period is thirty days.

Iridescent Moon: Known in Cathay as Caiyue, it is the manifestation of the God of Magic. It appeared at the end of the war between elves and orcs. It never moves from its spot in the sky. Its orbital period is one day, and can be used to keep time.

Blue Moon: Known in Cathay as Guanyin's Eye, it is the manifestation of the Goddess of Fertility. Its phases go from wide open to winking.

Tivar's Star: A red star, a manifestation of the God of Conquest. During the Year of the Second Sun, it approached the world, causing the Blue Moon to go dim.

Time

As measured by the phases of the Iridescent Moon:
Full = Midnight
1st Waning Gibbons = 1:00 AM
2nd Waning Gibbons =2:00 AM
Mid-Waning Gibbons = 3:00 AM
4th Waning Gibbons = 4:00 AM
5th Waning Gibbons = 5:00 AM
Waning Half = 6:00 AM
1st Waning Crescent = 7:00 AM
2nd Waning Crescent = 8:00 AM
Mid-Waning Crescent = 9:00 AM
4th Waning Crescent = 10:00 AM
5th Waning Crescent = 11: 00 AM
New = Noon
1st Waxing Crescent = 1:00 PM
2nd Waxing Crescent = 2:00 PM
Mid-Waxing Crescent = 3:00 PM
4th Waxing Crescent = 4:00 PM
5th Waxing Crescent = 5:00 PM
Waxing Half = 6:00 PM
1st Waxing Gibbons = 7:00 PM
2nd Waxing Gibbons =8:00 PM
Mid-Waxing Gibbons = 9:00 PM
4th Waxing Gibbons = 10:00 PM
5th Waxing Gibbons = 11:00 PM

Provinces of Cathay

Province	Ruling Family	Resources
Dongmen	Zheng	grain, stone, guns
Fenggu	Han	timber, rice, grain
Huayuan	Wang	livestock, rice, wheat, lumber, firepowder, guns
Jiangzhou	Liu	timber, wheat, silk
Linshan	Lin	wheat, millet, timber, porcelain
Nanling	Peng	livestock, steel, stone, gems, crossbows
Ximen	Zhao	fishing, rice
Yutou	Liang	fishing, rice, iron, copper, fish paste
Zhenjing	Wu	ships, rice, fish

Human Ethnicities

Aksumi: Dark-skinned with dark eyes and coarse hair. On Earth, they would be considered North Africans. They can use Sorcery.

Ayuri: Bronze-toned skin with dark hair and eyes. On Earth, they would be considered South Asians. They can use Martial Magic.

Arkothi: Olive-skinned with blond to dark hair and light-colored eyes. On Earth, they would be considered Eastern Mediteraneans. They can use Rune magic.

Bovyan: The descendants of the Sun God's begotten son, they are cursed to be all male and live only to thirty-three years of age. They are much taller and larger than the average human. Their other physical characteristics are determined by their mother's race. They have no magical ability.

Cathayi (Hua): Honey-toned skin with dark hair and eyes. High-set cheekbones and almond-shaped eyes. On Earth, they would be considered East Asians. They can use Artistic Magic.

Eldaeri: Olive-skinned with brown hair. With features and small frames, they are shorter in stature than the average human. In a previous age, they fled the orc domination of the continent and mingled with elves. They have no magical ability.

Estomari: Olive-skinned with varying eye and hair color. They are famous for their fine arts. On Earth, they would be considered Western Mediterraneans. They can use Divining Magic.

Kanin: Ruddy-skinned with dark hair. On Earth, they would be considered Native Americans. They can use Shamanic Magic.

Levanthi: Dark-bronze skin and dark hair. On Earth, they would be considered Persians. They can use Divine Magic.

Nothori: fair-skinned and fair-haired. On Earth, they would be considered Northern Europeans. They can use Empathic Magic.

Acknowledgements

First, I would like to thank my wife and family for the patience they have afforded me as I pursued my childhood dream of fiction writing.

A shout-out goes out to my old Dungeons and Dragons crew: Jon, Chris, Chris, Paul, Conrad, and Julian, for helping to shape the first iteration of Tivara twenty-five years ago. Huge thanks to Brent who contributed so much backstory to the new literary version.

A gigantic thanks to my sister Laura for her spectacular job with the maps.

Thanks to the readers and writers on Wattpad for their encouragement and feedback.

Infinite gratitude to writers over at critiquecircle.com who motivated and helped me along the way. Jason, for patiently providing countless ideas. Kelly, for amazing input, character development and all the other advice. Victoria, for showing me how to layer scenes. Andy, for unparalleled wordsmithing. Ernie, for teaching me the fundamentals of fiction writing. Lindy for her sharp eye. Taylor for the numerous suggestions. Laurel, Joyce, Tracy, Traci, Larissa, Alicia, Kathyrn, and Ardyth for beta reading; and all the others who critiqued.

Finally, a huge thanks to all my readers for the encouragement you've given me. The Sisterhood of Tivara knows who they are.

Special Thanks

This special edition of Songs of Insurrection was only made possible by many generous pledges and donations.

From Patreon, I would like to especially acknowledge Elena Daymon and Samantha Mikals. I'm humbled by your support; as well as Dianeme Weidner, Spring Yang, Nicholas Klotz, Scott Engel, Mary Luu, Dexter Bradley, and Lindsay Shurtliff.

From Kickstarter, many thanks to Dyrk Ashton, Wraithmarked Creative, Zach Sallese, Dian, Ben Nichols, Rich Chang, Henrik Sörensen, Dan & Robert Zangari, Philip Tucker, Steven Hall, Jan Drake, Michał Kabza, Cody Allen, John Idlor, Kathy Jones, Nic Guinasso, Doug Williamson, Susan Voss, J. Zachary Pike, KE Sizemore, yesterspectre, Bobby McDonald, Andrew Barton, Michael Tabacchi, Emmanuel MAHE, Nicholas Liffert, A.Y. Chao, Artgor, Michael Mattson, Alexander Darwin, Krystal Xu, Caroline Atkins, Angela Engelbert, Shawna Dees, Nicolas Lobotsky, Justin Gross, Joey Hendrickson, Sarah Polk, Lawrence Wight, Eddie, Graham Dauncey, Jennifer, Virginia McClain, Christian Holt, Christopher Kranz, Leanne Yong, Kanyon Marie Kiernan, Scott Engel, Ivor Lee, Dan K, Mike Filliter, Ryan Kirk, James Yu, JC Cannon, Michelle Rapoza. Craig A. Price Jr., John Jutoy, Derek Freeman, Gerald P. McDaniel, Mat Meillier, A. Hakes, Helena Jones, Ashley, Charlie Gipson, Lapiswolf, PurpleSteamDragon, Laura E Custodio, Megan Mackie, Ashli Tingle, Stacy

Shuda, Anna Lee, Don Quaintance, Anne Kinney, Jessica Stone, Stanley, Derek Alan Siddoway, Ting Bentley, Ernesto, Gary Phillips, Dianeme Weidner, Timandra Whitecastle, Paul Cassimus, Paul, Walt Mussell, JohnYu, Chris, and Andre.

About the Author

JC Kang's unhealthy obsession with fantasy and sci-fi began at an early age when his brother Romain introduced him to the *Chronicles of Narnia*, *The Hobbit*, *Star Trek*, and *Star Wars*. As an adult, JC combines his geek roots with his professional experiences as a Chinese Medicine doctor, martial arts instructor, and technical writer to pen multicultural epic fantasy stories.

Made in the USA
Columbia, SC
14 February 2021